RIVER OTTER

By

Mark Wildyr

Herndon, VA

Published in the United States by STARbooks Press, PO Box 711612, Herndon, VA 20171. Printed in the United States

Cover Design by Emma Aldous: www.arthousepublishing.co.uk

Herndon, VA

Contents

PROLOGUE

White Stone Hill, Dakota Territory, September 5, 1863

The sun rising over the smoldering village promised a hot day. The sky was clear blue and cloudless, except for the cumulus of black buzzards circling expectantly overhead. Smoke from blazing lodges rode the wind, burning eyes and carrying the acrid smell of gunpowder and the stench of death across the prairie to the coulees and the short, wooded hills where the Dakota warriors had taken refuge. The very air tasted bitter to the tongue. They were tired; their horses, spent. Even the earth beneath their moccasins seemed exhausted.

On the run from the Star Chief Sibley since the battle at Big Mound two moons past, they had stood to fight him again at Dead Buffalo Lake. Now for the span of two suns, they had done battle with another Star Chief called Sully, a relentless warrior who spent his time drawing pictures with pigments soaked in water when he wasn't killing tribesmen.

Today would bring no respite. The blue coats and their thunder guns were still there, hovering like the feathered bone pickers circling overhead. The white army had inflicted a terrible toll on the Dakota. Warriors were accustomed to staring into the face of death, but how could even the bravest stand against big guns that shredded men and horses with bursts of fire and thunder?

Inkpaduta, whom the Americans called Red Cap, a dour, pox-scarred war chief, had led them through these many days of slaughter, fighting with a ferocity born of a deep, implacable hatred of whites. He had a wily mind, vicious fangs, and terrible claws, but Sully had numbers, firepower, and tenacity.

The shelling began again with the booming of cannon and the ear-splitting eruption of hot shells. The fusillade was not so effective now that they had the protection of the gullies and the hills, but Sully would soon be on the move. Their ranks decimated, the Indians withdrew, abandoning food and provisions and leaving their women, children, and wounded to the mercies of the Americans. All was lost now, but at least some of them would live to do battle another day.

1

CHAPTER 1

Teacher's Mead, Dakota Territory, Spring 1864

A whistle drew me outside where a child's voice from atop the hollow hill behind the house directed my gaze south. Less than half a mile away, six mounted warriors rode west between the Mead and the near shore of the bloated Yanube River. They were too far away to identify, but they did not have the look of Sioux.

Cuthan joined me on the porch. "I guess we know why the blue coat went flying by here. Do you think they're renegades, Otter?"

An hour earlier, a trooper had passed on the south side of the river, riding hard for Ft. Yanube.

"If they are renegades, they've thrown away the advantage of surprise, but we'd best get everyone inside."

I looked toward the near field where seven-year-old Alexander stood in the middle of the freshly turned rows. A hand shaded his eyes as he stared at the riders. He caught his father's wave, dropped the bag of corn seed he was holding, and started for the house. John, younger by two years, shot around the corner of the porch, eyes agog. He'd given us the warning from the hill.

"Do you see them, Pa? Do you see them?"

"We see them, Son," Cuthan said. "It took sharp eyes to spot those riders in the tree line. You did well."

Glowing from this praise, the boy self-consciously snatched off his hat and slapped it against his leg to free it of dust, as he'd seen his father do a thousand times.

The warriors had halted and were talking among themselves. After a moment, they headed in our direction at a slow, cautious pace. Each cradled a long gun in his arms.

Cuthan's wife, Mary, stepped out onto the porch. "What's happening?"

"Get back inside," I said sharply. Those warriors should see a family of natives, not a yellow-headed American woman. "Where are the girls?"

"They're in the house. Oh!" she gasped as she caught sight of the warriors.

"Go inside with your mother," Cuthan said to the two boys. "Let's join them, Otter."

"I want to talk to those men."

"We can talk through the door."

"I want to know what's happening. The best way is to go out and talk like men." I said.

"I'll get our rifles."

"I'll go alone and unarmed. If anything happens, send Mary and the children through the secret tunnel into the hollow hill. You stay in the house. Fight them off if you have to."

"I'm not going to let you ..."

"Think of your wife and fry and do as I say. I'll be all right."

I walked to the barn, trying to appear unhurried. White Patch, anxious for exercise, danced in anticipation as I threw a halter over his long nose. I didn't bother to saddle the pinto. I would have preferred to greet the strangers in my breechclout, but Mary considered them uncivilized, so I refrained from wearing mine around the Mead. I stripped my white man's shirt over my head and dropped it in the dirt. Getting rid of the garment made me look more like who I was.

By the time I left the farmyard, the riders had almost reached the line of trees bordering the old game trail running in front of the place. When I got within a hundred paces of the leading horseman, I gave the open-handed salute. He returned the gesture as we pulled up facing one another.

"*Hah-ue.*" I spoke the Lakota greeting even though I could see these were foreign Indians, Southern Plains from the looks of them. Four wore their hair in a *pay-shah* — a roach. One was in braids, and the sixth wore a turban of some sort. "I am River Otter."

"I don't speak Sioux," the leader said in passable English.

I repeated my name in the American language.

"I have heard of you. The Last Yanube, they say."

"Almost, although the man who farms this land has the same blood I do. What can we do for you?"

He squared his impressive shoulders. "I am Big Scar. My men and I are Cherokee."

"You are a long way from Cherokee country, and you do not have the look of a wandering star-gazer."

They broke into laughter and chattered among themselves for a moment.

"Do you fly the Stars and Bars or the Stars and Stripes?" Scar asked.

"Neither. We are peaceful tribesmen who want no part of the war. We are content to let the whites kill one another while we mind our own business."

4

The Cherokee leader was a striking, reddish-hued man with a meaty nose and a purple scar across his right cheek. He wore his hair in a stiff roach and was dressed in fringed buckskin trousers, a leather vest, and a bone breastplate. He pursed his heavy lips. "A warrior should choose a side and fight for it." Lifting a bare arm, he indicated his companions. "Join us and raise the hatchet against the people who killed your village."

"Those people are dead now, and I had a hand in seeing some of them to that end. I have no quarrel with the others."

"Are there tribesmen in the area who will join us?"

I motioned over my shoulder. "My adopted son, Cuthan, and I are the last bloods in the hundred fifty mile stretch between Ft. Ramson and Ft. Yanube, although occasional travelers come through the territory going from where they have been to where they are headed. You seem to ride with some purpose in mind. Was it you who frightened the army man who went flying past earlier?"

The men laughed again. "You are right. He was running away from us. We intend to stop him before he reaches the fort up the river."

"Then I apologize for detaining you."

"No need. The way the blue coat was flogging his horse, he'll ride the animal to death and have to walk the rest of his journey."

"Why do the Cherokee come all the way up here to frighten our whites? Don't you have enough of your own?"

"Aye, more than enough. But we are part of a big Confederate army come to take this country away from your whites and give it to ours. We are the Native Detachment of McComber's Battalion."

I kept my Indian face in place. McComber's Battalion meant nothing to me. "There is a Confederate army behind you?"

"The main detachment is at Ft. Ramson."

"Have they taken the fort?"

"They are doing battle for it as we speak. We are to catch the outrider and stop him from bringing reinforcements."

My heart lurched. I felt as if the blood drained from my face and puddled in my moccasins. The American's rebellion had reached out to touch us.

"I see no singing wires," Scar said. "Does that mean they have no telegraph at Yanube?"

"Nay, it does not reach that far." I saw no harm in answering honestly, since I perceived this as a test of something he already knew.

5

"Good. Who is with you in the stone house? I see two rifle barrels sticking from gun ports. If I didn't know better, I'd say this was Ft. Yanube. It is built like a blockhouse.

"That describes Teacher's Mead. The stone house was built back when there were hostile tribes in the area."

"And the rifles pointing at us?"

"One is in the hands of Cuthan Strobaw, the son of Cut Hand, last chief of the Yanube. The other is held by his wife."

"Tell them it would not be wise to be so unfriendly when next we meet." He waved his companions toward the river before turning back to me. "The farm to your east. Is that owned by bloods, too?"

"That is the home of some foreign settlers. They, too, take no sides in this war. They came across the ocean to farm in peace."

The man nodded. "The river is angry. Is there a walk-across?"

"Our snowmelt is just ending, so you've come when the waters are at their highest. The best walk is thirty paces to the right of the big cottonwood you see yonder. Even it is dangerous this time of year. I would not risk it."

Scar had to get his men to the other side in order to catch up with the dispatch rider, and my last remark was a subtle challenge. He fixed his eyes on me for a long moment, although I was unable to discern if it was rudeness or merely his adoption of the American habit of staring. Then he wheeled and caught up with his companions as they rode for the river at a leisurely pace.

I returned to the house and related all I had learned to Cuthan and Mary. Alexander, as was his nature, remained quiet and solemn. John and his younger sister, Rachel Ann, danced around demanding to know if there was going to be a battle. Little Hannah was only two, but she joined in what she considered a game.

We watched from the porch as the six Cherokee Confederates urged their reluctant ponies into the rushing current. They were halfway across the Yanube when the last man in line cried out as his horse lost its footing. The brave in front of him twisted around to see the cause of alarm, and his pony, too, dumped him into the angry waters. The others laughed and jeered until Scar sent them downstream to catch their companions. I was sorry to see both horses wade ashore, apparently without injury. The incident had cost them nothing but a dunking and a delay.

"Cuthan, go put a saddle on Patch and find my shirt. I dropped it in the dirt before going out to meet the invaders. Mary, fix a travel bag with jerky. You might want to let your father know what's happening. The Cherokee asked about his farm. See if you can persuade him and your brothers to come back here."

"You're going to warn James?" Major James Morrow was the commandant at Ft. Yanube.

I nodded. "The Cherokee was right. That blue coat will ride his horse into the ground before he reaches the fort."

While they went about accomplishing the chores I'd given them, I loaded my Henry repeating rifle and put spare cartridges in another bag. When I was ready, I accepted the supplies Mary had fixed and went outside. Cuthan had the pinto saddled with a bedroll tied behind the cantle.

"You understand this creates danger for you, don't you?" I shrugged into the shirt he handed me.

"Aye. If the Cherokee learn of your ride, they may try to take revenge on the Mead."

"Even so, it is something I must do."

"This I know. How long do you figure it will take you to reach the fort?"

Patch can trot most of the way if I rest him often enough. I should cover the fifty miles in four American hours."

Cuthan glanced at the sky. "It will be dark by the time you arrive."

"That is good, I think. It will give me some cover."

Patch caught my sense of urgency and was eager to race, but I reined him in. Distance was the aim, not speed. My main problem was figuring out where the Reb Irregulars were. Scar had not demonstrated any anxiety after crossing the river. When I last saw him, he and his companions had been traveling at a walk. I veered slightly north to keep the thin screen of trees lining the river between the Cherokee party and me.

CHAPTER 2

An hour later, I spotted the Confederate warriors riding abreast, still at an easy pace. Although I could not hear because of the roar of the rushing river, they appeared to be laughing and talking as if unconcerned by their deadly mission. Were they roostered on white man's liquor? I put a ridge between us and allowed Patch his head. He broke into a gallop that would put me well ahead of them. Once I was out of sight, I slowed to a canter and moved closer to the riverbank. I didn't want to miss the trooper if his horse failed him.

I spotted his dead mount on the far shore after another hour, but there was no sign of the rider. I was beginning to wonder if Scar and his men had somehow passed me and caught up with the messenger when I saw him staggering along in the twilight no less than five miles from Yanube City and safety. There was no walk-across at that point, so I was forced to put Patch into a gallop to reach the bridge spanning the river at the outskirts of town. Once on the south bank, I headed east again. With any luck, I would reach the trooper before the Cherokee came upon him.

As soon as I approached him, he reached for his handgun. He had lost his carbine, which was likely pinned beneath his dead mount. Exhausted and uncertain on his feet, he was too slow. I brushed past him and tugged the reins, causing Patch's rump to send him tumbling in the dirt. I was off the horse and had a knee in his back before he had a chance to recover.

"Listen to me. I am Otter from Teacher's Mead. The Cherokee are on your trail. They've found your dead horse by now and will be coming to run you down. I am going to get up now. Do you understand I mean you no harm?"

He nodded mutely and scrambled to his feet when I rose. He backed away from me, wild-eyed. He was young and probably inexperienced. I mounted and offered him a hand up. After a moment's hesitation, he accepted. I pulled him aboard and wheeled Patch, making for the fort.

The dispatch rider got us an audience with the commandant much faster than I would have been able to do. James tried to hide his surprise at seeing me, but that was quickly wiped away as the young trooper came to attention and reported that Col. Wallston was under attack at Ft. Ramson by the Rebels and requested relief. I then added what I knew.

9

"McComber's Battalion," James said to his adjutant, a lieutenant I did not know. "That's a mounted infantry unit out of Arkansas, I believe. What the devil do they want with Ft. Ramson?"

The lieutenant shook his head.

When James looked at me again, I saw he longed for a private moment, but there was no time. "Thank you, Otter, for your aid. This man owes you his life."

I nodded acknowledgement with a solemn face while my heart lifted at what I had read in his look.

Within minutes, the post came alive. Although night had fallen, James sent a message to Yanube City's mayor advising him of the situation. After furnishing me with a fresh mount and making arrangements to house Patch until I could return, he turned out the fort, leaving only a single troop to guard the post and the town.

James had less than a full battalion under his command. Many of his units had been ordered back east and the remaining ones were seldom up to strength. The two troops on the move should have represented about two hundred cavalrymen. I doubted they would reach half that number.

I took my leave of James and crossed to the north side of the river over the bridge, trailing two signalmen and two troopers to provide protection for them behind me. James and the rest of his column intended to proceed up the main road on the south side of the Yanube. I pushed my party hard, and we were soon ahead of the battalion. They were some distance behind us by the time we skirted the hills sheltering the Mead. Shortly before dawn, I hailed the house lest Cuthan think he was under attack.

I quickly explained the situation to him and to Mary's father, Hans Jacobsen. Her brothers, Jacob and Christian, had not yet arrived. They were leading the Jacobsen's livestock to the Mead in case their farm was attacked. Then I led the four blue coats up the easternmost of the three hillocks behind the house.

The wig-wag signalmen chose a bald spot big enough for them to work. I watched in the growing, rose-tinted dawn as they unfurled signal flags and set up their equipment. My curiosity was immediately aroused, but all they had time to tell me was the flags signaled the numerals one through five in pre-arranged groups. A signalman on the receiving end then converted the wags into letters. It was a clever way of communicating over long distances. I had heard some of the southwestern tribes did the same thing with mirrors and bits of metal to reflect the sun.

As the light grew stronger, we could make out the battalion moving on the other side of the river. The officers rested their men on the plains directly south of the Mead. The forced march would have taken a toll, particularly on the animals. They needed time to recover. I feared James would attempt the dangerous river crossing, but he elected to communicate with us by means of signal flags.

When Cuthan joined us on the hill, he told me they had seen no sign of the Cherokee since the foreign Indians crossed the river yesterday. No doubt the warriors had made haste toward Ft. Ramson upon discovering their target had eluded them. I had no idea if there had been eyes on me when I picked up the dispatch rider. If so, we could expect retribution.

Cuthan went back down the hill as Jacob and Christian herded their horses and cow into the yard. After the men drove the livestock into the Mead's large barn, Cuthan appeared indecisive for a moment before walking to his fields in an attempt to make at least some part of this day appear normal.

I remained on the hill to keep watch with the signalmen and their guards. Across the river, the column had settled down to a meal before resuming its march. Two Absaroka − or Crow − scouts struck out eastward. They did not get far. One of the signalmen let out a shout and pointed downriver to a column of men approaching from the east. This was no party of Indian irregulars; it was a military unit in force directly in the path of the Union battalion.

Immediately, the two signalmen conferred to compose a message. I watched, fascinated, as one of them grabbed a pole holding a four-foot black flag with a white square in the center and began waving it continuously back and forth. When he had the attention of the signalmen across the river, he undertook a series of movements that began at the vertical and ended in the same position. It was a laborious procedure, but much less time consuming than sending messages back and forth by horseback.

"He's alerting the Major there's troops approaching," a corporal named Nelson explained.

I pointed to the tree line on this side of the river. "Then he ought to also tell him the Cherokee Irregulars are already here." I turned and called down to Cuthan, who was tilling the near field with Alexander leading the plow horse. John and Rachel Ann followed along behind to break up excessively large clots.

"Get everyone inside. The Cherokee are back, and they have soldiers with them."

"What about you?"

"I'm going to stay with the signalmen. An extra rifle might come in handy. You protect the family."

"How close are they?"

"Five minutes."

He immediately took the horse to the barn and locked the building behind him before herding the children toward the house. Hearing little John demand a rifle to shoot the renegades made me smile. The child's Indian name was War Eagle, our way of calling a golden eagle. With his thick black mop laced with strands of his mother's yellow hair and his onyx eyes studied with gold flecks and his bold, fearless manner, the boy was well named. In the old days, those traits would have given him powerful medicine.

Christian, a tall, good-looking *zjee-zjee* near Mary's age, labored up the hill. A moment later, his older brother, Jacob, joined us. They would help out on the hill while Cuthan and Hans held the house.

The Cherokee went to ground the moment they spied us atop the hill. Despite the approach of the enemy, the signalmen — or at least the one doing the wig-wagging — needed to stand in clear sight of his own men across the river, which put him at risk from enemy fire. But no gunshots came, even though there were furtive movements in the trees below us from time to time.

What would I do if I were Scar? I'd bring up the Confederate soldiers accompanying me and mount a diversionary assault straight up the hill while my warriors and I crept up on the defenders from another front. I looked around. The center hill topped this one by approximately twice my five-nine height. If Scar gained control of that point, he could gun us all down.

"Corporal Nelson, the hill behind us is higher than we are. I've met the Cherokee leading those warriors down there. He is a fighting man. He'll creep up the back side of these hills and take that ground."

"And we'll be like ducks without feathers on a smooth pond."

"Aptly said. I'm going over there."

"Take Miles with you. The three of us and your friends will stay and fend off the attack from the Rebs below." He waved at another man, this one with some years on him. He wore no stripes on his arm, but I saw faint outlines where two had once rested. He'd gotten into a bit of trouble, probably recently.

I collected my soldier and navigated the small depression between the two adjoining hillocks. It was obvious Miles had seen action before; he immediately selected a good position and settled down to wait. I wasted breath telling him what he already knew, but it was important we both saw the situation the same way.

Half an hour went by, and there was still no assault. The soldiers would wait until Scar had time to get into position. I glanced across the Yanube River where James was getting the reduced battalion into a defensive skirmish line, using the rushing river to anchor his left flank. The wig-wag signalman from the battalion was busy with his flag. It was an oddly graceful dance for something so serious.

"Hey, Miles," the corporal yelled. "Scouts say the Rebs ain't got no cannon with them, so all we gotta do is hold off the ground troops."

"That's a blessing," the man lying prone nearby remarked sourly.

Still nothing happened, except the approaching Confederates straightened ranks and began marching to the beat of a drum. I'd anticipated a sea of gray, the color of their uniforms, but most seemed to be in work clothes with a few martial touches such as campaign hats or sashes. The officers appeared to be the only ones in full military dress. The column wheeled about and marched south, so that their lines faced the Union soldiers. Shouted orders were barely discernible at this distance, but the troops dismounted and turned their mounts over to others who led them to the rear, eight horses to one tender.

"Shit," Miles said. "They ain't cavalry. They's mounted infantry." He spat a wad of tobacco and swiped his mouth with a sleeve. "That's all right, we ain't much more'n that. Only the officers carry sabers in our outfit."

"Seems to me a six-shooter's reach is longer than a saber's blade." I said.

"'That's the truth, and a carbine's longer than a handgun. And we tote them both."

"What do you judge their strength to be?"

"Near to our own. If they come all the way from Ramson, their boys is tireder than ours."

Our attention had been diverted to the plains south of us. "Well, that battle's theirs," I said. "Ours is up here. Keep an eye out. Those Cherokee are close."

"You can bet on that."

Just then, a figure rose up to the left of Miles. I jerked up my rifle and pulled off a shot, catching the warrior in the throat as he raced to bring his tomahawk down on the soldier's head. I immediately threw myself to the side and twisted around. A second man popped up from behind the hill and loosed an arrow. It passed through the space I had occupied a moment before. I got off a second shot but wasn't sure if I hit the man.

I heard sustained firing from the eastern peak. The signalmen were under attack. That must have been a sign to the Rebs. Fighting broke out on the plains beyond the river.

I rolled to my right and reached the cover of a fallen tree, putting my back to the south. The warriors would have climbed the north side of the hollow hill. I couldn't see Miles, but he was still with me because I heard the bark of his carbine. With the element of surprise lost, the Cherokee opened up with their firearms. Miles kept up a steady stream of curses as he returned fire.

I spied two warriors running at him from the west and shouted a warning. I took out the one in the lead. Miles brought down the second man. Where were Scar and his other red Rebs? The hair on the nape of my neck rose. I whirled to find the Cherokee leader rushing up the slope at me. Abandoning his rifle to fight in the old way, he had worked his way around the hill until he was behind me. With no time to bring my Henry to bear. I dropped it and twisted away. His hatchet lodged in the log I'd used for cover. I rolled into his legs. He went down.

Quick as a snake, he struck my jaw with his elbow, sending my senses flying. Instinctively, I brought my knee up into his groin and kicked him over my head. He must have been in agony, but he got to his feet and faced me, knife in hand. Snarling, he came for me.

He was bigger than I was and faster. I saw no profit in hand-to-hand combat. I feigned a lunge at his legs.

He drew back, expecting me to drop and roll into him again. Instead, I threw myself at the log where my rifle lay abandoned. He caught his balance and leapt at me, knife raised.

I made it to the log, but again I had no time to bring to get off a shot. Instead, I swung the barrel against his head with all the force I could muster. The scar from which he took his name split apart, and blood flowed like a river. He stood transfixed for a moment. Then he shook his head.

As I took aim at his broad chest, a man raced from the forest to aid his companion. I swung around and shot him through the belly. When I turned back to Scar, he was gone. Vanished. I glanced at Miles to ask if he'd seen the Cherokee leave and found a renegade standing over him, pulling a long blade out of his back. I shot that one through the head.

Corporal Nelson and his group still had a battle on their hands, but I wanted Scar. To my mind, he was more devious and dangerous than all the rest. He would not forget or forgive my betrayal and the slaying of his companions. My head was finally clearing, so I got to my feet and began tracking him.

He had fallen when I brought my rifle to bear, probably to evade my shot. I found where he had lost his purchase and rolled part way down the hollow hill. After about twenty feet, he'd struck a sapling and saved himself from sliding farther. From there, the blood trail circled around to the west where he gained the cover of the forest on the backside of the hill.

As I pursued the wounded Cherokee, a bullet slapped into the earth beside me. I ducked and turned to see three Confederate soldiers in the Mead's yard. Two rifle shots from the house dropped one rebel where he stood and struck another in his leg. The third one hightailed it out of there. Cuthan and Hans were effectively guarding our flank.

I returned to tracking the Cherokee. Spatters of blood made the task easy, even after the man reached the forest. When the blood trail dried up abruptly, my skin crawled. A trap!

The noise he made launching from a tree behind me gave me time to throw myself backwards. He overshot me, but his left foot caught my right shoulder, throwing me hard against the bole of a pine. I lost my grip on the Henry. We both reached the weapon at the same time.

Scar grasped the stock and swung the rifle up in a vicious arc. I evaded the blow and barreled into him, throwing him against a tree trunk and separating him from my rifle. He was hurt, but I didn't wait to find out how badly. I lunged again, this time with my knife in hand. The blade bit deep. He cried out and rolled away, wrenching the hilt from my hand.

I watched in amazement as he plucked the blade out of his side and pushed himself upright. I lost a precious second gaping at him before scrambling for the rifle. He tried to brush it aside, but my shot tore through the wound I'd made with my knife. He staggered and then came at me again. This time, I shot him through the heart.

As I lay recovering from my exertions, distant gunfire brought me back to the present. A battle was still raging out there. Using the rifle stock as a prop, I levered myself to my feet and made my way to the top of the hollow hill.

The situation there was in hand; the fighting had ended on this side of the river. Corporal Nelson bent over one of the signalmen, who lay sprawled in the dirt. Christian was examining Jacob's bloody shoulder. The younger brother laughed and rumpled his hair. The wound wasn't serious.

I hailed Nelson, who yelled that the Major had sent a squad across the river walk, and they were now chasing the Rebs back downstream. I glanced to the far shore and found the battle had progressed perhaps half a mile to the east.

As weary as I was, I crossed the small valley between the two hills and joined the Jacobsen brothers and the soldiers. The surviving signalman was waving his flag earnestly in that odd wig-wag ballet.

Corporal Nelson took a deep breath. "We whipped them, uh ..."

"Otter. I'm Otter. These men are Jacob and Christian Jacobsen, our neighbors."

"Howdy, gents. Appreciate your help. We whipped them, Otter. The Rebels are in retreat. About all they can do now is fight a rear guard action to slow the Major in relieving Ft. Ramson."

"You mean they'll battle for the next hundred miles?"

"Off and on. We outfought this bunch pretty bad, so they'll just try to turn a two-day forced march into a four-day fight, but they don't have much pluck left. How about the Irregulars?"

"All I saw were six, and there are six dead Cherokee on the hill over there. Miles didn't make it. One of them knifed him in the back."

Nelson shook his head. "He was a mean bastard but a good soldier." The corporal's eyes came back into focus as he looked at me. "The Major sent a signal saying we done a good job. Guess we did, too. He's sending a detail up this side of the river from the fort. They'll keep a signal post here for the time being. The others will guard them and get rid of the bodies. Clean up your hill some, I guess. Oh, and he said to tell you they're bringing your horse."

"Thank you. James ... uh, the Major said something back at the post. He said he didn't know why the Confederates would want Ft. Ramson."

"Me, neither. It's got no strategic value to the Reb cause. Unless they just want to tie some troopers down while they go off and do

16

something sneaky somewhere else. I'm sure Ft. Ramson telegraphed for help, so there'll be reinforcements coming from other places, too."

"Unless they cut the lines before they attacked," Christian said.

CHAPTER 3

At the beginning of the Month of June Cherries, James closed down the signal station on the eastern hill at Teacher's Mead. I was proud of him. He had not only successfully relieved Ft. Ramson, but he had also chased the Rebels out of the territory. The battle on the south bank of the Yanube River had been his first command against an opposing organized military unit. Of course, many would argue the tribesmen — particularly the Sioux — were equal to any cavalry in the world, and he had done battle with them many times.

Two months after the attempted invasion, I was only just beginning to realize how lucky we had been. No one had suffered a loss — beyond a drop of two of blood when Jacob had put his shoulder too close to a passing bullet. There was no damage to any of the farm structures, and more amazingly, neither the Rebs nor the Cherokee had taken time to burn the Jacobsen farm.

With the disappearance of the last *wah-shee-chue* from the farm — who happened to the surviving wig-wag signalman from the day of the fight — Cuthan's family finally settled back into a familiar routine after all of the excitement. Thus, I deemed the time right for my departure to help build a farm with James. To delay longer would put me at risk of having to winter in nothing more substantial than a buffalo skin tipi. I had often done that in the past, but too many years spent in a comfortable house had weakened my will in that direction.

I leaned against the fence of the Mead's little cemetery and let my eyes roam over the headstones: Billy Strobaw, the Teacher and the famous Red Win-tay, who had been first mentor and then mate for most of my life; Cut Hand, the last chief of the Yanube; Lone Eagle and Butterfly. They were powerful forces from the past anchoring me to the Mead. I turned and looked at the stone house Billy and Cut Hand had built. Dog Fox and I were the only ones who survived to enjoy the fruits of their labor. Dog Fox, who now bore the name Cuthan Strobaw, and his children were all the family I had left. These were the elements clutching at my heart and holding me close to this place. All that was or had been precious to me was here.

Yet, other things argued for my leaving. Cuthan's title to the Mead under the terms of Billy's will had only recently been upheld by territorial authorities, thanks to his conjuring trick of turning Cut Hand's son, Dog Fox, into William Cuthan Strobaw, the natural son of his Yanube wife, Butterfly, and himself. The fraudulent documents supporting this claim had all survived scrutiny, but it was Cuthan's marriage to Mary Jacobsen that held the fabrication together.

The decision had been a narrow run thing and fanned resentment because some whites felt Indians should not be allowed to hold land. Because the Mead was a desirable property situated on the river between Ft. Ramson and Ft. Yanube, the animus against bloods ran especially deep. I was a full-blooded Yanube, so it was possible I represented a danger to Cuthan, or at least served as a provocation to the Americans.

Then there was the other matter. In the fall of '62, James and I had stood at this very spot as we mourned the loss of a loved one.

"Otter, I am tired," he had said. "Before long, I am resigning my commission, war be damned, and retiring to some acreage north of the fort. I don't suppose you would come with me?"

I had agreed without fully comprehending the nature of the invitation. James certainly knew of my liaison with Billy; indeed, he had enjoyed his own for a brief time, but his expectations of me were left unstated. I was in a state of indecision over those prospects, an unusual condition for me. I usually knew my mind in such matters. I had been with no one since Billy's death, and James was a handsome man and a comfortable companion. Intimacy with him was not distasteful to contemplate. Then fate intervened to confirm the soundness of my reasoning. Mary's handsome brother, Christian, rode into the yard on his way to Yanube City, and I took advantage of his travels to send a note to James advising of my impending arrival at the farm site.

# # # # #

The following morning, I hitched my mare to the traces of a buckboard piled high with personal belongings and tied Patch's reins to the wagon bed. I do not do farewells gracefully, especially with a heart rent in two. As painful as it was to leave Cuthan, the loss of the children was almost unbearable. Their energy and curiosity and enthusiasm were what kept me young. Of this I was absolutely convinced. Their tears at my desertion almost undid my resolve. I hugged each of them, kissed their mother's cheek, and shook hands with their father before taking my seat on the wagon.

Steeling my will, I reined the mare down the wagon trail on the high side of the river toward a plot of land seven miles north of Ft. Yanube.

Two years after we had made our agreement, I was finally going to meet my commitment to James.

Less than an hour into my journey, a party of horsemen passing on the far side of the river prompted me to take cover in a thin copse of trees lining the north bank. Uncertain if I had been observed, I jumped from the buckboard and freed Patch's reins, just in case.

Those men had the look of militia, as vicious and unpredictable as the *mah-doh-dah-gah*, the big bear of the north. The riders could be out on patrol or simply looking for trouble, and there was often little difference between the two. The war back east had virtually denuded the countryside of military dragoons — they were now calling themselves cavalry — and ceded virtual control of the territory to this gang of killers.

I remained in hiding as the riders grew small in the distance. If they continued in their present direction, they would pass the Mead. Could they be headed there? If so that boded ill.

As the distant riders passed from view, my sense of unease increased. I unhitched the draft animal from the buckboard and hobbled her near a small rill in a hollow somewhat distant from the wagon. She would have both grass and water until my return.

Without a thought for abandoning my worldly belongings, I headed east back down the wagon track, chugging White Patch, named for the bit of white circling his left eye, into an easy lope the pinto could maintain for hours, despite the summer sun. A scraggly line of trees on the north bank of the Yanube provided some relief from the heat.

I paused to allow my mount to blow at a small rivulet that had once marked the divide between the hunting grounds of the Yanube and our enemies, the Pipe Stem Draw People. They were all gone now — my Yanube kinsmen annihilated in a cowardly ambush, and the Pipe Stem moved west to the Laramie country with our mutual cousins, the Sioux.

Pulling Patch's muzzle from the stream before he bloated, I set off down the track again, this time at a brisk pace. The militia riders had too great a lead to for me to overcome, but I wanted to be near enough to the Mead to provide aid if it was needed.

A third of a league shy of the farm, I found where the party had forded the river and headed straight north. There was little but empty country in that direction, but the militia often patrolled such terrain. On the other hand, if they had circled and approached the Mead from behind, they intended the worst kind of mischief. I followed their trail

21

until I found where two horsemen had left the group and rode straight for the hollow hill visible in the distance.

There was no sign of the main party on the northern horizon, but the countryside was deceptive. It often appeared to be a flat piece of earth when in truth, it was cut with washes and unexpected draws called ha-has. The militia could be miles ahead of me or merely yards. The two men who had ridden for the farm's guardian hills were of more immediate concern. I turned Patch east and rode in their tracks.

The pony snorted as we discovered one mount tethered at the base of the hills. I found the second a little farther to the east. The men had separated; one climbed the highest mound, the hollow hill, while the other scaled the eastern hummock.

I tied my pony's reins to a tree a hundred feet back down the trail where he would not be noticed and scrambled up the more heavily forested western hill. I reached the top of the stubby hillock and spotted a man still struggling up the hollow hill. He had not advantaged any of the game trails and was having a problem with the ascent. The second man was not visible.

Turning to look down upon the Mead, I saw Cuthan and his two sons at work in the fields. They made as calm and pastoral a scene as any described in the books I had read. Yet mayhem was about to visit them unless I put a stop to it.

When the rifleman reached the top of the hollow hill, I stood where Cuthan could see me and fired a warning shot to alert him to trouble. Then I ducked as the bushwhacker sent a careless bullet my way before racing back down the hill. He stumbled and fell, but scrambled to his feet and kept going.

Considering Cuthan warned, I took off after the fleeing man, uneasy over not knowing where the second militiaman was. I burst out of the trees onto the plains as a horse tore through the underbrush and bore down on me. The rider brought up his rifle, but I had the advantage of solid ground beneath me. I shot him from the saddle.

The second man had also reached his mount and angled off to the north to avoid me. Although well out of range, he emptied his six-gun in my direction. As he came abreast of me, I got off a shot but only managed to wing him. He almost lost his seat, recovered, and disappeared into a gully.

I ran to the lip of the draw, but the curve of the ditch hid him from sight. My inclination was to give chase, but I was in a conundrum. If I left the corpse at Cuthan's back door, the Americans would use that as an excuse to drive him off his land. Yet, I would suffer the consequences if the wounded man had recognized me.

I talked my way to the dead man's mount grazing not far away and hoisted the corpse aboard the nervous animal, not an easy task for a man of my middling size, but I got it done. Then I used a stone to scratch a message in sign language in the sand to warn Cuthan of the attempt on his life. He was a thorough and cautious man; he would investigate and discover my message. Then he would erase any trace of what had happened here. Even if he failed to find it, the scratches in the earth would be meaningless to others. Satisfied I had done all I could, I made for the trail north of the river toward my buckboard, leading the roan bearing the corpse along behind me.

Those men had clearly come to kill Cuthan. I had prevented that, but by allowing one of them to escape, had I compounded the danger to us? I doubted the wounded man had gotten a good look at me, and my pinto had been tethered at some remove from the kill site. There was little likelihood he knew no more than some Indian had fired on him. I did not believe he would claim Cuthan was the man, since the militiaman would have to explain why the two of them were on the hill behind the house, thereby opening himself up to questions he would not want to answer.

I picked up my pace. I needed to get the dead man far away from the Mead and make discovery of his body as difficult as possible. When I reached the rill where I'd watered Patch earlier, I discovered the injured horseman had joined the wagon trail and paused at the stream to treat his injury. All of this could be plainly read in blood in the grass, scraps of his shirt ripped into bandages, and drying urine where he had relieved his bladder before moving on.

As I drew near the copse of trees where my wagon was hidden, I saw he had approached the buckboard, circling it at least once before attempting to paw through my belongings. Had he searched for medicine in aid of his injury or for something to identify the wagon's owner? He likely reasoned the driver was the man who had shot him and his companion.

He was apparently in some distress from his wound, as he had accomplished little beyond disturbing my heavy buffalo hide tipi skirts and leaving traces of blood on them. Yet, before riding on toward Yanube City, he'd taken the time to mark the buckboard with two unobtrusive notch marks on a corner so it could be identified.

Apparently, he was weakened by his wound but cogent enough to reason things through.

I spent a precious few minutes scanning the landscape for any sign of an ambush, examining each fold in the earth, the movement of every leafy twig in the almost breathless air. A barking wolf — what the whites called a coyote — was the only creature I saw moving on the flat expanse of dry plains stretching south from the Yanube to the distant, blue-hued humps of the Little Island Mountains. It was from there Cut Hand had first led Billy Strobaw to the People of the Yanube some thirty-two snows past.

Reassured by a messenger bird — a gray-plumed mourning dove — playing among the cottonwood branches, I set about undoing the trap laid for me. I found the draft mare munching grass at the bottom of the ha-ha exactly where I had hobbled her and hooked the animal — made skittish by the smell of blood — into the harness.

The Yanube River was as familiar as the backs of my hands, so I drove to a deep spot in the normally broad, shallow river. Working rapidly, I hacked off the bloody skirts of my *ah-kah-pay*, my tipi skins, filled them with rocks, and bound the body of the militiaman into the hides. I felt no stirring of regret as I cast the dead bushwhacker into the river.

After loading my goods onto two pony drags made from lodge poles and my remaining buffalo skins, I worried the wagon into the current and watched it sink out of sight. I was satisfied the low flow of the river next winter would be sufficient to hide both body and buckboard, but I had to count on the weight of the wagon to keep the corpse from washing away during the spring flood tide.

I turned north off the wagon road for a quarter of a mile, dismounted, and walked back to the road to obscure any trace of my passing. I also erased the wagon tracks a distance on my back trail to a go down to the river so they would not betray where I'd disposed of the buckboard. Then I made false marks as if the wagon had crossed the water.

Finally convinced it would take a keen eye to expose my misdirection, I released the dead man's pony to go where it would and made my way back to Patch and the mare. Then, keeping a keen eye out for the militia patrol, I crosscut the prairie toward the land James had bought.

CHAPTER 4

I had no trouble finding James's property, even in the dark. He had left a marker of stones to denote the exact center of the 160 acres he'd claimed on Turtle Crick, a fair-sized tributary to the Yanube. The cairn rested in a small, lush meadow with a hillock to the north crowned by pines and oaks. Cottonwoods hugged the banks of the stream. This sheltered place would make a comfortable home.

Far removed from the familiarity of Teacher's Mead, I sat alone before a small fire gnawing a rabbit bone and harboring doubts. In truth, my heart was not fully at peace with this thing. I had loved Billy from the moment I laid eyes on him, no matter that I had only ten years at the time. It was only after Cut Hand and Lone Eagle and Butterfly had their time with Billy, that he had accepted my physical love. From that point onward, I was content with life — as was he.

I liked James. Admired him. He was a handsome man capable of stirring a list. Yet my blood did not sing at the thought of him. Was I examining shadows that did not exist? He had been a steadfast friend to Billy and the Yanube over the years. He had come on his own hook — against the express orders of his superior — to bring word of the massacre of virtually the entire Yanube *tiospaye* by a troop of cavalry under the command of a cowardly Indian hater named Smith. I sighed and determined to do my best for James, whatever that entailed.

I was tired. It had been a long, demanding day. The shooting of a man took its toll on any caring, feeling human being, and I considered myself to be of a sympathetic nature. I picketed the horses on opposite sides of camp to double the chances of detecting unwelcome visitors. Patch was trained to give warning of predators. The mare was a shadow jumper.

I settled on the coarse blankets of my bedroll and breathed a silent song to the Great Mystery. The spread of the heavens — shot through with glittering stars, both noble and mean — made a vast dome of the black sky. I studied the Seven Persons, which Billy had called the Big Dipper. A faint breeze cooled my face and carried the comforting rustle of swaying boughs gently to my ear. The heavy fragrance of pines on the hummock — so different from the scant perfume of cottonwoods along the crick bank — laid the sharp taste of resin on my tongue, or so it seemed. I stilled my doubts, calmed my breathing, and closed my eyes to slip away into sleep.

# # # # #

I came awake at Patch's first snicker. Dawn had not broken, but the night hinted at the coming light. I silently rolled out of my blankets and regained my feet. A horseman moved quietly through the darkness, pausing at the pinto's side.

"Otter?" The call out was soft.

"Here, James. I did not expect you so early, or I would have had something ready to break our fast."

Leathers creaked as James dismounted and tethered his big army horse to Patch's picket line. "I brought jerky and hardtack, but coffee would be welcome if you have any among your stores."

I pulled out a bag and a battered old pot while James lit the dead campfire. We worked in silence and ate beside the low flames without speaking. Finally, he put down his mug. The tin clinked against stone.

"I was happy when Christian brought word you were on your way. I can only be gone from the fort for the day, so I needed an early start. We have considerable planning to do." He paused. "Does this thing we are contemplating sit well with you, Joseph Otter?"

I paused to show I was giving the question the thought it deserved. "It does. I have cogitated long and hard and decided it is good. Even though I'm not sure what is expected of me."

He chose to evade my inferred question. "Will you not miss your home at the Mead?"

"Aye. Sometimes it will touch me with sadness, but it is something I have to do. First, I need to tell you about yesterday."

He did not speak as I related all that had taken place, withholding only the hiding spot of the body and the buckboard so James could honestly deny such knowledge should he need to. "Is there no end to this war?" I finished.

He understood I meant the War Between the States that had pulled so many soldiers away from the territory. "Not in the foreseeable future. We thought it would be a short-lived thing, yet no one can see the end of it. The rebels got the upper hand early, but I believe things have turned around now.

"The Union's leadership hasn't matched the ability of the Confederate generals, but late last year, one of ours, a fellow named Ulysses S. Grant, whipped the southerners at Chattanooga. That split the Confederacy and gave the North control of the Mississippi river. It also got Grant promoted to commanding general of all the Union armies."

James paused before confessing he wasn't certain Grant was equal to Lee's capabilities. "But with the superior manpower and industrial capacity of the North behind him, I think he'll get the job done. The Union will survive, but the fighting's not yet over."

"What of your Virginia plantation? Your family? Have they disavowed you for remaining true to your oath?"

"I suspect my name is anathema to them, but I've had no direct news. I can only pray I will be able to provide my family some protection when this is finally done."

I ran a hand over my eyes. "So it is likely to be some time before your unit is up to strength. That means the militia have all the time they need to send out their *oh-zue-yea*."

James laughed. "They'd be shocked to hear themselves called a war party."

"Is that not what they are? They were contemplating murder yesterday."

"That describes them pretty accurately. I can rein in most of their excesses, but as yesterday's events prove, I cannot contain them all."

"Would you like to take to bed until the sun comes up?" My words asked more than was obvious.

"Yes, I believe I would. If you will join me in my rest."

That told me all I needed to know.

James rose and slipped suspenders over his shoulders before stripping away his tunic and boots. When he was settled on the blankets, I lay beside him, sensing his tenseness.

"Otter, you need not do this if it is against your nature."

"You know my nature. I mated with Billy for twenty-two years."

"Were there others?"

"Nay. I have lain with no one else, neither man nor woman. Just Billy."

"You loved him." It was not a question. "I know you don't love me, so ..."

"I like you James. A great deal. I admire and respect you. That is fertile soil. Maybe love can grow."

"I hope so. But this must be done with your eyes open. Billy taught me the Indian philosophy of the Circle of Life. He explained how men fit naturally in that circle and commanded respect for who they were. The white man believes differently."

I nodded into the darkness. "Yes, he explained that in your culture a man must fit the mold society casts for him. There is little room for departure. The standards are strict, and your people reject anyone who cannot be forced into that mold."

"So people like me are considered deviants. Sodomists. Apostates." His voice held a note of sadness. "They will apply those strictures to you, as well. If we undertake this liaison, we must be extremely careful."

"This I already know."

"I understand that, but I have to make sure you are aware it can be deadly. If we were to be found out, it could kill us."

"Does that discourage you?" I asked.

"No, but I cannot accept the risk on your behalf."

"I am who I am. I do what I do. I live according to my own tenets. I do not purposely harm other men. I do not steal or rob. I am true to my faith as I see it. It does not breech that faith to split the blanket with you if that is what you wish."

"Not wish," James said in a scratchy voice. "Need. Desperately."

"Then here I am." I placed a palm on his broad chest and smiled into the darkness. "Do you remember when you and Captain Jamieson came to the Mead with your dragoons? The captain went north to scout out the Sioux. You went to the Pipe Stem Draw People."

"I recall."

"When you returned that night, Lone Eagle and I watched from the secret tunnel in the bathing room while Billy thrummed you."

"Is that so? Uh, what did you think?"

"Lone Eagle thought it was fun to watch. To me, it was painful."

"Because you loved Billy."

"Aye, but I was just a child then, and he did not look at me in that way."

"Then you know what he did for me."

"Now, that is what I will do for you."

"If it is not too much to ask."

Strange that this commander of men, this seasoned soldier who had been through the mud should be as shy about what he pursued as any youthful swain courting his desires. I slipped out of the flannel shirt I'd donned against the night's cool air and released the drawstring to my breechclout.

Then I lay waiting as James removed the rest of his clothing. His fair skin made a grayish blur in the predawn night. Many of my blood thought this paleness unattractive, repulsive even. I did not find it so, no more than a white river stone resting beneath the water beside red and black and brown pebbles was off-putting. It was the nature of the thing.

A moment later, James lay beside me with his head on my chest. Sensing hesitation, I placed a hand to his cheek. "It is all right. I have a need, too."

He clutched my hand. "Is that true or a ruse to ease my mind?"

"It is true. I confess to a Cupid's cramp at this moment."

"Then we must relieve it."

He placed moist lips to my nipple and suckled like a child. It rose beneath his ministrations and sent a shiver down my back. I was pleased this was happening in the dark of night; glad I could pretend it was Billy beside me on the blankets. I experienced no guilt at the thought. I knew James would hold onto the same specter. In time, we would both release Billy to resume his journey. Would that ghostly trek be to the white man's Heaven, or to the Western Land of the Yanube where his loved ones waited? Was it possible they were the same destination?

James moved to my belly and groin. He took my flaccid member into his mouth, and it reacted, easing my mind over whether this would prove to be barking at a knot, or if I had the will to complete the act. It had been three years since I last lay with Billy, so my flesh hardened, demanding physical release despite the hesitancy of my mind.

As he bent over me, his head rose and fell in the darkness. My cock strained upward, swelling until I feared it would burst. His hand fluttered across my belly, my chest. He found my sac and gently kneaded my stones. Familiar sensations overtook me, carrying me back until it was another who was sucking at my groin. Abruptly, I returned to the present. This was James drawing me to climax. Some of the intensity went out of the thing, yet the rush of my body, the gush of my seed, and the contractions of my orgasm seized me in a violent grip. I forced his head down on me as I ground myself against him. A groan escaped me. I relaxed my headlock and caressed his blond locks, shot with a scattering of gray.

He came up off me. "Was I adequate?"

"More than adequate. Did you not feel the earth tremble?"

He chuckled. "No, I merely felt your belly muscles quivering." He laid his head on my chest. "I know you imagined it was Billy, but that's all right."

"Perhaps a ghost stood at the edges of both our minds, but it was clear to me James Carleton Morrow was taking care of my needs. In time that image will fade, and no one will stand between us. That is important to remember. For both of us, I think."

"I don't mind sharing you with Billy." He cleared his throat. "But I am glad you feel this will work."

"I will show you how much I believe it will work."

"Now? So soon after ..."

I interrupted him. "It has been a long time for me, as well. I am ready again."

James cupped my rising staff. "Then I am anxious for it."

I crawled between his legs and positioned myself. Without speaking, I grasped James's ankles and placed them on my shoulders. My throbbing cock searched his flesh until it found an orifice, and I pressed forward. He opened to me. I slipped effortlessly into that deep, dark channel.

He groaned. "Oh, Otter, it has been so long. Fuck me."

I started slowly, teasing him with timid thrusts. Then I withdrew and eased back in until my groin was hard against his buns. I wiggled my hips, changing the position of the cock buried in him. Then I jabbed hard, penetrating deeper. After minutes of play, I began a steady, controlled thrusting, intent on finding a rhythm pleasing to us both. After a while, I altered the cadence, changing the game. I lunged hard and deep, drawing groans from him. I leaned over until my lips toyed around the fringes of his mouth, promising a kiss and then moving elsewhere.

I reared up on my knees and stabbed again, viciously, violently, steadily. I grasped my lover's throbbing cock and ran my hands over his naked body.

"Oh, yes, Otter. Like that! Like that."

I clasped his head between my hands and concentrated on finishing the thing. I fucked while James flayed himself.

He came with a great whoop, spurting semen on both of us. I was right behind him. My contractions drew great shudders from me and sent my seed pouring into him. Finally, I fell forward and pressed my lips against his. Our climaxes passed as we kissed.

Finally, I spoke. "If we must be so secret about this thing, I hope they did not hear your shouts at the fort."

James chuckled as I pulled out of him. "Forgive me, but it has been so long. That time you spoke of — when you and Lone Eagle watched us. That was the last time for me."

I lay at his side and caught the faint odor of tobacco and some sort of ointment he used after shaving. I knew not what he detected from me. I'd had no opportunity to bathe following my exertions yesterday.

I touched his cheek. "You are a handsome man. Many should have wanted you. Both men and women."

"Ah, there's the problem. I have no interest in women. Oh, I enjoy their company. Pay them court in a harmless way. To cover my real desires, I suppose. Yet, I have no carnal need for them. As for men? Well, it would be to my ruin to be caught with one of them. So I deny myself. Did Billy not tell you my history?"

I shook my head in the easing darkness. "Nay. He never revealed the secrets of others, but of course, I read his journal and know your father caught you with his serving boy and sent you off to school.

"Where my roommate and his friends promptly raped me." He sighed aloud. "When I was appointed to the Point, I resolved to hold myself chaste to avoid any other such incidents. I remained that way until Billy came to Yanube City after he divorced Cut Hand over that woman, Morning Mist. Was that her name?"

"Yes. It was the hardest thing either of them had ever done, but Billy's faith would not allow him to share Cut Hand with another, and Cut's responsibilities to the *tiospaye* required he live among them with a wife and children."

I rose and walked naked to the crick with a water bag, returning to cleanse us both with the frigid water. James suffered my touch with a gasp before speaking.

"I treasure being cleaned up and tended like this."

"I believe this thing will work, James, so long as you allow me to release Billy's image slowly."

"I will allow you time, but I must warn you again. We have to take great care."

"When others are around, I will be your servant. The hired hand who tends your crops and looks after your household."

"You are not my servant."

"Yes, I am. And you must treat me in that manner when others are around."

"Then I ask your forgiveness in advance."

"You have it. Now, it is growing light and your servant must prepare you a proper meal."

"There is no one around, so we will do it together."

31

I paused before rising. "We have already done something Billy and I did not do until his last year."

"What is that?"

"We star-slept with nothing between us and the heavens."

"That we did, and I am grateful for it. I have bivouacked with a thousand men, but never before in such intimacy. Still, in the future, it will be safer to have something to cover our heads."

"I will set up my tipi until we have more substantial protection."

# # # # #

We spent the day planning our merestead. We positioned the house in our minds and decided upon constructing the outhouse first. Winter was apt be upon us before the place was finished, so it was important to shelter our animals against the cold and the wolves. We would make it a tight, comfortable building and sleep in the hayloft until our home was completed.

We paced out the acreage for our first planting, but the turf in this country was tough, so we recognized we could handle little more than a small field at first. When I mentioned that one of Mr. Deere's steel plows would cut a good bit off our timetable, James confided he had already ordered one. He had also arranged for the delivery of a considerable amount of lumber. That pleased me because the trees sheltering the property would be spared from cutting. I preferred a sturdy stone house such as the one at the Mead, but there was little river rock available along Turtle Crick.

That afternoon, James gave me a signed piece of paper saying Joseph Otter, a hired hand, had legal access to his property. He was embarrassed such a device was necessary as protection against what he proclaimed as "unknown circumstances." I understood him to mean the local militia. Just before he departed for the fort, James shyly asked me to flank him again. He wanted to do it in the daylight so he could watch me work over him.

After I scouted the area to make certain no one was skulking about, we stripped and lay on our blankets. I was proud of the admiring stare I drew from James. Those blue eyes never left my face as I made a powerful entry of his body, inspiring confidence that ere long his gaze would turn into one of love. Alas, if only it were that simple for me. Nonetheless, I took a great deal of pleasure in the act and in observing the man beneath me.

It was easy to see the handsome, tin soldier right out of the Point James had been when he first came riding into the Mead at the head of his troops. His muscles — now, as then — were taut and strong. He was a military man, and that was not an easy life, yet one that kept him fit. His features were fair, although years in the scorching sun had bleached the hair from golden wheat to cut hay and laid a hard cast to the skin around his eyes. The man writhing beneath me was truly desirable.

"Oh, Otter," he gasped. "If you only knew how often I've needed you in the years since we … ahhh … first spoke of this."

"Now we have all the time we need."

My breath came in gasps as my time approached. I broke the rhythm to avoid a climax. I was determined to give him all I could, but before long the tipping point was near. I beat him with my hips, making sharp slapping noises, punctuated by his grunts.

Judging the time right, I grasped his large, pale cock and began pumping urgently. He came with a loud groan almost instantly. His seed was pearly white, with a sheen I had once seen in a gemstone called opal. Fascinated, I watched it pool on his chest in the line of pale hair running down his belly. Then I closed my eyes as orgasm struck. I raised his legs until I was almost sitting atop him and pumped furiously, releasing my sperm and shuddering through a climax.

Eventually, I fell over on my back, breathing heavily. "It was good."

"Aye. Very good. Thank you, Otter."

This time, it was the master who hauled water to wash his servant.

CHAPTER 5

The next morning saw my days of leisure firmly behind me. The work ahead was daunting, but I chose to settle on one task at a time rather than be overwhelmed by the whole. Dressed only in a *chay-ghnah-kay*, a breechclout, I slipped on my moccasins and began my first task. My tipi turned into a poor imitation of the real thing because of the bloody skirts I'd had to cut away. Although it opened to the east, the First Direction, little else about the lodge was traditional. It resembled a poor summer tent more than a proud Yanube dwelling.

That done, I turned to the building of an *oh-ee-hay-yea-dee-pee*, or what James called a necessary. He would expect one, and in truth, I had become accustomed to the white man's way of eliminating the body's wastes. I was not yet absolutely convinced defecating in a smelly, enclosed place was healthful, but it was certainly convenient, especially during the long winter months.

I studied the trees and bushes beside Turtle Crick and determined from the bend of the blackberry bushes and scrub oak that gusts tended to blow in from the west, whereas the taller pines tended to lean to the south. Fortuitous, because that dictated downwind was also downstream. Satisfied with my choice of locations I began the arduous process of excavating a pit armed with only a long-handled shovel for digging and a tomahawk for chopping. This proved to be a difficult and time-consuming task that ate away the morning.

Next, I constructed a brush shelter over the hole, which would have to suffice until there was lumber for a proper structure. Ready for a rest, I made a mid-afternoon meal of the jerky and hardtack leftover from yesterday, saving the pemmican in my haversack for the evening.

After eating, I marked the four corners of the barn with stakes and took to the shovel again to level the ground. I decided the outhouse would also open to the east, away from the prevailing winds. I worked steadily, skimming layers of earth away until the sun began its downward trek. By then, I was satisfied the floor to the future structure was sufficiently level.

I was preparing to find a pool in the crick deep enough to soak away the dirt and sweat when Patch whinnied. The pony stood gazing off to the south with his ears rotated forward. The mare beside him lifted her head and looked in the same direction. Four horsemen about a quarter of a mile distant were making straight for me. I stood beside the rude shelter, my repeating rifle near at hand, as the riders splashed across the crick and rode up. The leader — or at least the spokesman — was a hard-bitten man about my own age who wore fringed buckskin and a battered campaign hat. I believed him to be an ex-dragoon who'd been kicked from the service, although I might have been wrong. He showed no recognition of me. His companions seemed made of the same leather.

"Who're you?" The man leaned forward over his saddle horn, a long-barreled Walker Colt Forty-four short gun held carelessly in his left hand. "You speak American, boy?"

"Yes, I speak English." I instantly regretted my choice of words. Revealing I was better educated than this bully wasn't smart. "My name is Joseph Otter." I would have given the full name Billy conferred upon me years ago — Joseph Strobaw Otter — but I wanted no connection to the Mead as these men were likely looking for my notched buckboard and bloody tipi skins.

"What're you doing here?"

"I live here. Maybe this will explain it." I rummaged around in a sack and offered James's note. Deciding I couldn't assume the man was literate, I explained the letter's contents. Then, unable to hold my wayward tongue, I added, "Who're you fellas?"

The spokesman glanced at the paper and handed it back. "We're members of the Upper Yanube River Militia, authorized by the territorial governor to keep peace in this country. These are duly sworn members of my unit. Was you here yesterday?"

I stowed the letter back in the bag. "Met the Major here yesterday and got my orders from him. He told me where to lay out the barn and how he wanted the farmhouse set." I pointed with my chin. "Got the ground leveled for the outhouse."

The leader motioned to his men who peeled off and rode around the small meadow. Two went over to inspect the horses hobbled near the stream. The other one began a sweep of the place, probably looking for the buckboard.

"How about the day before that?" The leader was a thin-chested man with an unhealthy look about him.

"Got here in the morning and set up camp. Scouted the area some so I'd know a little bit about it when the Major showed up."

"You've got a lot of gear." The man indicated my packs. "How'd you tote it?"

I nodded to the spare lodge poles lying near the crippled tipi. "Made a couple of pony drags, you know, travois."

"Where'd you come from, Joseph? That's your name, right?"

I grunted and allowed my shoulders to slump like a man overcome by his travels. "A long ways off. Clear from the Laramie country."

"You Sioux?"

"No sir, but kin. I was born around here. Yanube. When we got wiped out, I went west with a few other survivors. Got homesick and came back. Heard the Major was looking for a man who knew a little about farming. Lucky for me, I guess."

"Ain't that woman's work?"

I waved a hand in front of my face. "Used to be. There's not no game to speak of no more, so I can't go hunting. No Indians around to fight. So I guess that leaves woman's work or an empty belly. Besides, things ain't like they used to be."

"True enough. How come you run around nekked? You ain't no praying Indian in that getup."

"Hallelujah, praise the Lord Jesus!" I held my hands up, palms outward. "Yes, sir. Joseph Otter got himself saved. That's how I come by the name Joseph. These are my working clothes. I got trousers and shirts in my packs."

The militiaman looked as if he thought he was being flummoxed, but let it go when his men came back one by one and shook their heads.

"You seen anybody else around?"

"Just Major Morrow."

"No other red bellies?"

"None around, I don't guess."

"Wrong. They's a teepee pitched no more'n a mile north of here."

"Haven't been north of that hill over there." I might as well play their game. "They tame Indians?" I couldn't bring myself to say "Injuns."

"Who knows? We on our way to check them out. You see any strangers around, you come to Yanube City and report it to the magistrate. Hostiles ambushed some of our men. Killed and scalped one of them, and we aim to catch them and string them up. You hear me?"

"I hear you."

Without another word, the man spurred his horse, brushing me aside. I recovered my balance and watched them ride over the hill. Scalped? When I dumped the jasper in the river his crown was firmly attached to his head.

I grabbed my Henry and followed them on foot. Once over the hill, the forest played out quickly, and the land opened up into a broad prairie. The four horsemen were cutting through the grass heading northwest toward another small patch of woods. That was probably where the other tipi was situated. I stayed in the trees until well west of them and then cut across the savanna, making directly for the pine-covered knoll.

As I crossed a dry wash, I stopped short. *Seen-day-ghlah*, an aggressive little prairie rattler, lay coiled in the sun atop a flat rock. His vibrating tail warned me to keep my distance. I gave him a wide berth and went on my way.

I heard raucous voices before I reached the edge of the small clearing where a traditional buffalo skin tipi stood. The four men were bracing a woman and two youngsters, presumably her sons. My inclination was to step forward and interfere, but I decided to be prudent. The element of surprise might tip the balance should things become violent.

The scene grew ugly but stopped short of the point where I felt obligated to meddle. The militiamen walked their horses through the camp, trampling supplies and upsetting cooking pots and utensils, rendering some of them useless. The older boy, a youth of about eighteen summers, tried to object, but when two of the men drew down on him, he kept his wits and froze. The other lad, somewhere around six, remained calm, despite the deep anger shaking his thin frame.

Things would get out of hand soon if I didn't do something. Slowly, I edged back toward the gully. The snake had given me an idea. It was still taking the sun on its rock, so I removed my loincloth and threw it over the reptile. I had trouble keeping it from slithering away, but managed to grasp the edges of the garment and contain the creature within the apron. The serpent writhed and rattled so fiercely I was afraid I wouldn't be able to hang onto it as I made my way back to the glade.

By the time I reached the tree line, one of the men was approaching on foot, head down as he presumably searched the ground for wagon tracks. When he was close enough, I slung my loincloth like a clumsy slingshot and released one side. The flying rattler landed against the man's thigh as I slipped back behind a tree. I heard a hoarse, frightened cry and then the roar of a handgun. It took the stricken man three shots to hit the scaly creature.

Naked and vulnerable, I stood stock still as the others rushed to aid their companion. They were so close I stood in danger of discovery, but I didn't move a muscle. The militiamen had lost interest in everything except giving aid to the snake-bitten man. After doing what they could for him, they mounted up and rode south in the direction of Yanube City. As soon as they were out of sight, I fastened my loincloth in place and stepped into the open.

With a surprised gasp, the woman placed herself between her two sons and me. The older one abruptly pushed her aside and stepped forward. His fearful ferocity eased as I gave the open-handed salute.

"*Hah-ue*. I am Otter."

"I see you River Otter." The woman stepped up, speaking in my own tongue. "Is it really you?"

I took a closer look. "And I see you … Dew Drop?"

"Yes, it's me," Spotted Hawk's niece said. The old man had been the *tiospaye's* shaman for as long as I could remember until he crossed the Great Divide and took the Western Road. This woman's brother, Badger, had succeeded him. I thought they had all fallen in the massacre. Indeed, I had seen a host of them with my own eyes, but there were too many to calculate who might have escaped the slaughter.

"I did not know you survived." I said.

"Barely. I was with Badger's family when the blue coats cut us down. I grabbed my son and fell on top of him. I shut my eyes and waited for their bullets to kill us, but they walked on by. After they left, there were a few of us still alive. I saw Morning Mist and Dog Fox. We wanted to go south to the winter campgrounds to join the other bands gathering there, but she insisted on taking another direction. I never saw her again."

"She made her way to the Mead, and later to Stone Knife's camp. He took her in."

"I heard that you and Teacher buried them. All of them."

I nodded. "Yes. It was a day I will never forget."

Dew Drop shuddered. "It was horrible. I can hardly speak of it yet."

"Where did you go after the disaster?"

"To the Cheyenne. And then to the Dakota." She indicated the younger boy. "There I found favor with a fine Teton warrior who was Little Bear's father." The shine in her eyes clouded. "He fell at Cabin Crick down in Indian Territory fighting those colored soldiers with the Cherokee colonel, Stand Watie."

She drew the youth forward. "This is Standing Rock. He is Yanube. His father was Strong Bow."

I offered a shake, and the youth gripped my forearm. "Aye, I remember your father. We used to play and hunt together." I released the boy's arm and turned to Dew Drop. "I am sorry you have lost two husbands. Life is hard."

"That is the truth. What are you doing here? Was that snakebite your doing?"

I smiled and told her of the visit by the militiamen, and my fear they were up to mischief. I said they were seeking the owner of a buckboard without revealing I was that man.

It did not take long to learn the family was in distress. There was little game in these parts, and they were subsisting on fish Standing Rock was able to catch in the shallow stream and rabbits he killed with his bow.

I made a snap decision and addressed the older boy. "Do you hold with the Old Way?"

The youth looked politely over my shoulder as he answered. "Why do you ask?"

"Because I want to know if you are a man who takes care of his responsibilities, or if you are the kind who stands on a mountain of pride while his mother and brother starve. Will you work to fill their bellies?"

Rock's chest puffed up. "I am a man."

"Good. Then you will listen to what I have to say. Do you speak English?"

The youth switched tongues. "I speak American, if that is what you mean?"

"I work for the Yellow-Leaf Chief of the American fort on the Yanube. I am to build his house and his barn and plant his crops. I can use some help."

The youth's eyes bulged. "You want me to do that kind of work? *Woh-zjue-pee?*"

"I'll be a farmer," Little Bear spoke up. "I'll be a good farmer, too."

"You speak English, too. Good. How about you, Dew Drop?"

She looked blank for a moment before shaking her head. Too bad. Although I suspected she understood more than she let on. Billy's influence had reached most of the band, and he had made sure the younger children spoke at least the basic elements of the white man's language.

Rock showed some mettle when we got into the spirit of the thing, bargaining hard over the price of his labor — even though I suspected he didn't fully comprehend what that toil would be. We spoke of stores and supplies, not money, and eventually came to terms. I wasn't certain James would approve this bargain, but I had enough silver coins with me to stand the cost on my own if that proved to be the case.

Rock and Little Bear accompanied me to my camp where I gave them half of my supplies. As they left, I told the older boy to be here soon after sunrise the next morning. Rock grunted, although I wasn't certain if it was in agreement or acknowledgment.

After they departed, I stripped and soaked away the sweat and dirt of the day's labor in the crick, even though it was the shank of the afternoon. Afterward, as I ate sparingly of my remaining pemmican, I wondered how nettlesome the militia was going to be. The whole lot of them seemed to be slippery, and I was beginning to suspect they did not hold James's gold oak leaf in much awe.

CHAPTER 6

Standing Rock did not make it by dawn the next day, but he wasn't as late as I had feared. He was a naturally industrious young man, but homebuilding was woman's work, and even though what we were constructing was no simple tipi, some of his attitude leaked out at times. I ignored it and set him to work leveling the plane where I intended to build the house.

At midday, Dew Drop and Little Bear showed up. She had prepared a meal from the stores I sent her the previous afternoon. While my new helper and I labored moving dirt and rock, Dew Drop set about remaking my miserable hovel into a proper tipi. By the end of the day, I was satisfied with what had been accomplished.

Before nightfall, the woman and the younger boy set out for their own lodge, but Rock elected to remain behind, claiming he could get a little more sleep if he stayed the night. As we sat around the fire pit in the center of my now commodious tipi, Rock made himself comfortable.

"Aren't you going to tell me grandfather tales?" A bit of insolence showed through the words.

"Those are best told in winter."

"Then tell me some win-tay tales. You lived with the one they called the Red Win-tay, didn't you? They say he was *zjee-zjee*."

I examined the youth obliquely. "Yes, he had yellow hair."

"On all his *dahn-chahn*?"

"Aye, on all his body. But what business is that of yours? Are you thinking of becoming a two-face?"

"No, I'd never be one, but I've been thinking of taking one."

"Hah. You don't even have a proper wife yet."

"You didn't either."

"How do you know these things?"

"I don't remember anything from back then, but I've heard talk about you. They say you were his win-tay before you made him yours. Maybe I'll try it out with you. See how I like it."

I hid a smile, yet I couldn't help teasing the boy. "So you're growing hard for me?"

"No, but it's moving around in my loincloth."

I made a disparaging sound through my lips. "At your age, it moves around for anything." I waved a hand. "You can borrow my mare.

She's on a picket line over there." Rock frowned as if he were insulted, so I lightened the mood. "Is that where your name comes from? Standing Rock."

The boy flashed a broad smile. "No, but it ought to be, because that's what it does. Do you want to see it?"

"No, thank you. I prefer modesty in my hired hands."

The point struck home. Rock's frown returned, but he dropped the subject, asking instead what tomorrow would bring.

"We will finish leveling the place where the house will sit. Then I will clean up and go into Yanube City for supplies. You will get some of your wages then."

"I will go with you." Rock's announcement reminded me of Lone Eagle back when he still had his childhood name of Little Eagle. Both possessed the arrogance of untested warriors.

"So you will. You will help pack the supplies. You can ride the mare."

"Rather have the gelding with the white patch on his eye."

"That one is accustomed to my legs astride his back."

# # # # #

The planned house would not be as roomy as the barn, but the grade at the site was steeper, so there was a great deal more earth to move. I was pleased to see the nature of the soil beneath the sod. It was loamy and held enough sand for healthy farming. If the field to the west James and I had plotted was of similar content, the farm should prosper.

Turtle Crick was said to be a perennial stream. Although I did not know how low it ran in the wintertime, the high water mark showed that like the Yanube, it grew swollen during the spring runoff. Since the property sat on a bench on the north shore of the crick, we would need a bridge so James could travel back and forth during the high water season. That would have to wait, although there was a book on building such spans in Billy's library I'd brought from the Mead.

We quit work at high sun to munch on antelope jerky Dew Drop and Little Bear had brought. I preferred buffalo strips, but the big beasts were scarce these days. Besides, there was no one to organize a proper hunt. After Dew Drop and the boy went back to their own lodge, Rock and I bathed in the crick. The fetching youth displayed a yard that was halfway erect, but my developing relationship with James precluded what would undoubtedly have been a rousing and delightful romp. Rock didn't seem particularly disappointed when the display of his manhood was ignored. We set out for Yanube City shortly after bathing.

Rock kept a vigilant eye on our back trail during the trek, a good and necessary habit these days, but the trip of just over two leagues across flat prairie cut by occasional ha-has was uneventful.

Yanube City had grown considerably since I'd been here last. That would have been in '61 shortly before Billy died. The fort, which had been contained within a tall wooden stockade, now sat at the northern edge of town without a palisade in sight. The post's buildings, all single-storied except for the headquarters, were drawn up in rows, almost as if in parade formation.

The older portions of the thirty-year-old military post were log and sod structures. The newer ones appeared to be hand-sawn lumber painted a gray color. It was a sandy, dusty place, but the groundskeeper had coaxed a growth of green grass directly in front of the headquarters. A row of sickly elms around the edges of the grass field battled the elements for survival — with the eventual outcome still in doubt. The scarcity of uniformed soldiers was quite noticeable.

I halted at the guard post on the southern end of the fort and handed over a note to the corporal on duty, explaining it was a message for Major Morrow seeking an audience. I was dressed in civilized trousers and shirt, but Rock wore nothing but moccasins and loincloth, earning curious and sometimes hostile stares. Nonetheless, the sentry waved over a private and sent him to the headquarters with the missive. We waited in the sun until the messenger returned to escort us forward.

James received us in his office on the second floor of the headquarters building. I noted it was considerably larger than the cramped quarters occupied by the former commandant, Major Jamieson, who had proven to be a false friend when one of his underlings, a brigand named Captain Smith, ambushed the Yanube on their way to winter quarters.

"Otter." James rose and offered an American handshake. "I didn't expect you."

"Major." I took his hand briefly and then stepped aside to wave Rock forward. The youth came grudgingly. Was this his first close encounter with a soldier? "I have taken the liberty of hiring this man and his family to help with the building of the farm. His name is Standing Rock. His mother, Dew Drop, cooks for us, and his younger brother, Little Bear, helps where he can. I came to introduce him and get your approval."

"Well, young man, I'm glad to meet you. I approve of Otter's choice and expect you to obey him while you are in my employ."

There was an awkward moment when James offered a handshake. After a notable hesitation, Rock finally grasped James's forearm in the Indian fashion.

"Are you a good worker, Standing Rock? Damnation, Otter, we've got to do something about that name. That's a mouthful."

"He answers to Rock."

"We need something more Christian. Uh, you know what I mean. Like Billy did for you, Joseph." James paused to think. "There was an upstanding family named Brandt down the valley from our plantation. That's a fine, strong name. I think we'll enter him on the rolls as Brandt. How does Lucas sound for a first name?"

Although it was evident Rock comprehended what was going on, he stood mute, so I accepted for him. Then we settled on Matthew Brandt for Little Bear. Dew Drop became Helen on the spot. James was seeking to convey what little protection he could to the family, although none of the recipients of his largess would understand. Besides, it would be a meager shield because the family was clearly native.

We spent a few minutes sketching out a rough plan for the house and discussing the nature of the lumber scheduled for delivery within the week. When I was certain I understood the concept James had in mind, Rock and I took our leave.

Our next stop was to see Timothy Bowers. The last time I had seen the blacksmith's forge, it had been at the edge of town. Now homes and small shops surrounded the enterprise. I asked the smith to fashion some cooking utensils and vats for holding water. Timothy, who went by Timo, had a long history with the Mead. During the winter of '34, a cooper by the name of Benjamin Bowers and his family wintered over at the Mead after an ill-fated late start for Ft. Yanube. They had battled a heavy snowstorm and endured a violent encounter with the Sioux, both of which they barely escaped with their lives.

The sight of Cut Hand, a pure quill Indian, had sent ten-year-old Timothy and his little sister, Beth, into a panic. Cut spent the long winter months of the family's enforced stay at the Mead, trying to ease the children's fears. Timo had become slavishly devoted to Cut Hand, and retained the pet name his idol had given him to this day.

Our business done there, I took Rock deeper into town toward Brown's Mercantile. Caleb Brown had owned the only trading post in the little village sprouting up around Ft. Yanube called Yawktown at its inception. Later, wiser heads prevailed, and that unfortunate name had been abandoned in favor of Yanube City. For some years, Billy had grubstaked Caleb in the beaver pelt trade with J. J. Astor's American Fur Trading Company. Brown, and others like him, had been of immense help in fending off challenges to Billy's will.

As we approached the large two-storied brick building occupying an entire block on a street now called Main Avenue, a man exited the store and came to a complete halt, almost blocking our way on the boardwalk. He was a stranger, a thin man with stooped shoulders dressed entirely in black. He reminded me a Black Crow, a name the Canadian Cree gave Jesuit friars who came among them.

As we grew nearer, he lifted his head and the impression of a carrion bird was heightened. He had small round eyes that gleamed as if from an inner light. His nose was so long and hooked, it almost drooped over his bloodless lips. I had thought him old, but as we approached, it was evident he was a man of no more than thirty snows. He had little color to his skin and none to his attire save black.

"Sinful!" he spat in a stentorian voice that took me by surprise. Thunder like that should have come from a big man. "Cover your flesh, young man! Do not flout your nakedness before Christian folk."

I pushed Rock ahead of me and brushed past the unmoving man. I halfway expected him to turn and follow us, but when I glanced around, he was standing as if planted, still glaring at us through predator's eyes.

I noted a change as we entered the store. Our presence drew frosty stares. A stocky man with smooth features and bristly iron gray hair moved forward to intercept us with words belying his attitude.

"May I help you?"

"Yes, please. I need to see Mr. Brown."

"I am Mr. Brown. What do you want?" The pseudo-servile manner disappeared.

"I'm speaking of Mr. Caleb Brown."

"I'm Abel Brown, Mr. Caleb's nephew. He's not ..."

"What's going on here?" a voice demanded.

At first, I did not recognize Caleb. His once sturdy frame was so shrunken and bent he had to throw back his head in order to see where he was going.

"Ah, Otter, my friend." His physique may have shriveled, but he still retained his spirit.

"You know this ..."

"Know him? He's one of this store's oldest patrons. For years, I've been trying to get him to buy on tick, but he's strictly a cash customer. He's to be accorded the greatest respect and service. Am I understood, Abel?"

"But they're ..."

"Am I understood?" Caleb managed to stand straighter.

Yes, Uncle Caleb." Again, the words did not match the demeanor.

The merchant waved his nephew away and took my hand in an American handshake. "I apologize for my nephew. He's an import from St. Jo, and doesn't yet fully understand our ways." His small eyes twinkled. "And who is this likely young fellow? Your son?"

"No, he comes from the Laramie country, although he was born near here."

Caleb took my meaning. "Ah, one of the survivors."

I nodded. "He bears the name Lucas Brandt, although he prefers his birth name, Standing Rock."

"Well, Standing Rock, it is nice to meet you." The old man held out his hand and left it hanging there until Rock clasped it in his own. Caleb turned back to me. "And how may I serve you this afternoon?"

I explained we had been hired by Major Morrow to help construct and maintain his farm and outlined the items we required. The old gentleman remained by our side as I selected my wares. Caleb saw to the totaling of the bill, the sacking of the goods, and their loading aboard our two horses. Some of those designated for the latter duties, appeared resentful since neither Rock nor I offered assistance.

As he accepted payment in bank notes and some of my silver, Caleb spoke in a low voice. "I'm afraid things are changing, old friend. As you can see, my health is declining. I have done my best to sow an attitude of proper servitude in my brother's son, but alas, I'm afraid it has fallen on fallow ground. One of these days, I'll no longer be able to come to the store, and ... well, I'm afraid attitudes may change even more."

James would have to handle the trading once the old man was gone.

Caleb cleared his throat. "I am never one to turn away custom, but there is a general goods shop and a modest hardware establishment side-by-side over on Grand Avenue. That is two streets over. Their selections are less ample, but as they are struggling to build their businesses, I doubt they would turn away patrons. Nor will we," he hastened to add, "as long as I am able to attend to affairs."

"I understand, Caleb, and I appreciate the advice. Perhaps you can clear up something for me. As we entered the store we encountered a strange man who took offense to Rock's dress."

"A black raven of a man?"

"Yes, you could say that, although I might be tempted to claim he more resembled a vulture."

Caleb laughed. "Indeed, that might be more apt. I suspect you are speaking of the Reverend Jeremiah Berglund. He is a recent arrival in our fair city. He's attempting to build a church on the south side of town. The City on the Hill, I believe he calls it, although there's nary a city nor a hill in sight. It's an unaffiliated congregation, I understand. Our world is changing," he said. "And not always for the better."

I thanked him and left with Rock in tow. A glance at the boy's expression revealed he had followed all of the conversation. He was a sharp one, this young man.

Next we went to the gun shop where a second generation of management had already succeeded the original. Thomas Hawkes had sold me many a weapon over the years, yet his son, William, only grudgingly accepted my silver for an early model repeating rifle and some shells. Rock went wide-eyed when I turned them over to him.

"Try not to shoot yourself, any of your family, or me," I said to the eager young man. "This is for hunting game."

We next stopped at the livery stable where I saw a mustang gelding with the look of speed about him. When I asked Rock's opinion, the youth hopped the fence to the corral and examined the animal more closely. After walking around and feeling the flanks and shoulders of the edgy, short-legged plains horse, Rock delivered his opinion.

"Good *mak-k-ue* and *shnee-zjay*." He referred to the mount's chest and withers. Ankles might be a little slender." He waved a hand in the mustang's face. The animal shied but did not panic. He examined the pony's teeth. "A good horse."

"I agree. Come on."

We entered the stable and began the bargaining process. My opening bid was countered with another. I did not know the owner, a man named Patrick Pauley. I had often slept in the stable on Billy's trips to town because Indians were not permitted in the inn, but at the time another man ran the place.

In the midst of our haggling, Rock spoke up unexpectedly. "Don't buy a dead *tatanka*, Grandfather. He's too small to be of much use on a farm."

"A dead what?" Pauley asked, his eyes skittering back and forth between Rock and me.

"Buffalo." I was amused. The boy was a trader, but then what Indian wasn't? "That is true, but he might be of some use to us." I played my young friend's game.

The liveryman's face turned red. "This ain't no plow animal. Nor a trace horse, neither. He's good riding stock. Comes from down Texas way, so he's had some training hazing livestock."

"Looks more like a Comanche travois horse than a cattle hazer." I pursed my lips and adopted a doubtful scowl. "Hmmm. Then he'll be no good to us."

Pauley spat out of the side of his mouth. Tobacco collected in a shiny, chocolate colored pool in the dirt. "Good riding horse."

"Then give me a decent riding horse price."

"I ain't taking no pelts or blankets. Good hard chink is all I take."

"I am not offering pelts or blankets. Silver."

"All right, I'll go down to ten dollars, but that's my bottom."

"I'll go five, and that's my top."

"Ain't no way."

Rock surprised me again. "I'll go seven-fifty. If that's not good enough, we'll find one somewhere else." He turned to me. "I hear there's still some wild horses down around the Little Islands. I can catch us one for less than that."

The liveryman shot another brown wad onto the ground. "All right. I'm getting robbed, but seven-fifty it is."

"Done." I paid over some of my own silver and accepted a piece of paper allowing me to obfuscate the existing brand on the animal and replace it with one of my choosing."

I bought some leather for the pony while Rock tossed a rope halter on the gelding and led him out of the corral. As we prepared to leave the livery stable, I asked what he was going to name the pony.

"Me? You want me to name him?"

"Why not, he's yours if you do a good job working at the farm until the winter snows come."

Rock's spine straightened as he struggled to hide a huge grin. "Then I will have to ride him until he tells me what his name is." He saddled the mustang and vaulted aboard, reins in one hand and his new rifle in the other. He turned the gelding and started for the farm, leaving the trace mare and me to trail along behind with our purchases.

# # # # #

Dew Drop was waiting at the farm to serve the evening meal. Little Bear had already devoured his portion. The Americans view us as stolid, undemonstrative people, but the woman grew as excited as a child over the variety of bait we packed from town. She seemed particularly pleased with the airtights — food sealed in metal cans. As soon as we had eaten, I gathered everyone around the campfire and informed them of their new names. Dew Drop and Little Bear readily accepted the pseudonyms, but Standing Rock vented his spleen.

"Why do I have to go around calling myself Lucas?"

"You saw the attitude of the people we met today. The old ones like Mr. Brown who understand our history with this land are dying off. Those replacing them have no idea of it."

Rock switched to Yanube. "Why do I care? This is our land, anyway. Why don't they just go back where they came from?"

I answered in the same tongue. "That battle has been fought and lost. They are here, and they will remain here. They will continue to come until they cover the countryside like ants. That is why this farm is so important. Major Morrow understands us. His home will be a sanctuary for you."

"We should just leave and go someplace where there are no white men."

"And where is that? The Americans are all around us. The Canadians are to the north, and the Mexicans to the south. There is nowhere left to go."

"Maybe the Canadians or the Mexicans will treat us better."

I changed to English and deliberately addressed him by his new name. "Lucas, you will learn that despite the customs and languages dividing men, we are all basically the same. You have no use for the Americans, and the Americans have no use for you. Why should Canadians and Mexicans be any different? You are not one of them, so you will be an outsider. At least here we are outsiders in our own country. Perhaps that lessens the pain a bit."

"Or makes it harder when we see how they change everything. They have no right to do that."

"True. But that is something man does merely by appearing on the horizon. Cut Hand and Billy did exactly that when they built Teacher's Mead. The Sioux did it. Everyone does it. The strong push out the weak, and the weak must learn when to push back and when to be patient. Otherwise, they will perish."

Rock sneered. "You are calling us weak. You think I have to be Lucas Brandt because I'm weak?"

"We *are* weaker than the white man. In numbers and in weapons and in the way he sets down his roots and remains in one place. That way, he lays claim to the land, and so does his neighbor and his neighbor's neighbor, until it is all taken. Listen and believe what I say. When dealing with the Americans, you are Lucas Brandt. To others, you are Standing Rock, a man of the Yanube."

"The Yanube don't even exist anymore. They've all become Dakota ... Teton." Rock's tone turned bitter.

"I am Yanube. You mother is Yanube. You are Yanube. More importantly, we are who we are. How does it harm her to be known as Helen Brandt to those strangers over there in the white man's town? If it makes dealing with them easier, why should you care?"

Little Bear spoke up. "I don't care. I'll be Matthew Brandt. I like that name."

Rock rounded on his little brother. "What's the matter with you? Don't you have any pride?"

"I have pride. I'm a *real* Teton. My father was a Dakota warrior. Those people can call me anything they want, but I know who I am. Calling me Matthew won't change anything."

CHAPTER 7

The lumber arrived, and I went to work teaching Standing Rock how to use planes and hammers and saws. The lad was bright and caught on quickly, even if he pretended to be reluctant about his work. It was a false face. It was obvious he had taken a liking to carpentry.

Although he was as well put together as any young man his age, he was not overtly handsome ... merely pleasant looking. The comely one in Dew Drop's family was the younger boy, even though his beauty was not yet truly formed. Nonetheless, Rock had a trait that stirred the blood and made it easy to form a list for him. For one thing, he possessed a worthy rod — as he clearly revealed whenever we cleaned up in the crick after a day's work.

His presence was so powerful that I was tempted to have congress with him and relieve his curiosity about win-tays. I had not played that role since the day of the massacre of my people almost fourteen snows past. On that fateful day, Billy and I had wordlessly reversed our relationship so thereafter I was the husband. Even now, I could not explain the change that came over us, but it worked well for the remainder of our time together.

Nonetheless, I was sorely tempted to accept this fetching young man's touch, but under the old laws of the *tiospaye*, I was married to James. Of course, under the old customs, I could have taken more than one mate. Yet, I kept my hands and thoughts to myself.

The unrequited interest in young Standing Rock provided an advantage. Whenever James found time to visit the farm, he benefited from prolonged thrummings that were both more urgent and more energetic. I knew he wondered at the relationship between Rock and me, but he didn't ask. Had he done so, I would have been totally honest about my thoughts and my forbearance.

I suspected Rock had figured out my arrangement with James because I always sent him away when the Major arrived. The boy had probably hung around a time or two, lurking in the thin forest while we made love inside the tipi. Ah well, that was no more than Lone Eagle and I had done in years past. Perhaps the spice of hidden eyes and ears spurred me to superior performance.

I turned away from such thoughts and glanced to where Little Bear struggled with a siding board twice his size. He dropped the piece of wood to the ground, grasped one end, and dragged it over to his brother. The boy was surprisingly helpful for such a small fry. He had a sharper eye for a level plane than either of us and would tackle a hammer and nail with zest — if ineffectually.

Before I planned to raise the outer walls, I sent Bear to the Mead aboard Patch. It was a long trip for one so young, but the boy was vigilant and careful. I gave instructions to travel cross-country and avoid the road for a distance before turning south to follow the river. Three days later, the lad returned with Cuthan's entire family to help us lift our framework into place. The families meshed well together. Dew Drop and Mary got busy preparing a meal for when we broke to take sustenance. Although there were eleven years between them, Rock and Alexander got along well, and Bear and John took to one another immediately.

The Sioux child was fascinated by John's unusual yellow-speckled *hee* — hair. The effect could be both attracting and off-putting, but it was certainly demanding of attention. The boy stood out in a crowd. The earthly traits of his Indian father had battled with those of his Scandinavian mother with the outcome not totally resolved in either's favor.

Dew Drop and her family got their first practical experience with their new handles. Mary insisted on addressing them as Helen and Lucas and Matthew. Dew Drop and Bear readily responded, but Rock often ignored his civilized label until faced squarely. He learned the Strobaw children's earth names, and made a point of using them. To Rock, Alex immediately became Red Sun, and John answered to War Eagle that day more than ever before in his entire life. Rock called Rachel, Snow Drift, and Hannah, Silver Moon. His boldness did not extend to Cuthan, whom he addressed as Mr. Strobaw.

Once the framework of the barn was lifted into place, Cuthan and Alex helped Lucas and me start hammering the siding in place. The younger boys' task was to haul buffalo grass hewn from the prairie and mud dug from the crick to the site. Then they helped the women mix a tabby and pack it between the inner and outer walls for insulation. The barn began to look like a proper outhouse rather quickly after that. I decided to construct a gambrel roof as I'd seen in some of Billy's books — one with two different angles joined at a hip. This allowed for the storage of more hay in the loft than in a barn with a simple steeped roof.

The Jacobsens were tending the Mead's animals in the family's absence, so Cuthan planned on over-nighting. When we halted work that afternoon, I designated my customary upstream pool on the crick as the women's and girls' bathing place. We males used a smaller, shallower spot around the bend. Cuthan and I soaked away the day's dirt and aches in a spot a little removed from where the buff boys cavorted in the water. Watching shards of the setting sun catch in John's strange mop struck me as a fitting end to the workday.

"I don't remember Dew Drop's family from the old days. Did you know them?" Cuthan asked.

I nodded. "The husband better than Dew Drop." I explained her history and the loss of two husbands, the latter while fighting under a Confederate Cherokee officer at war with the Yankees.

"Stand Watie?" he asked.

"You've heard of him?"

"I fear he's the cause of some of the resentment against us."

I shook my head. "How can that be? Most of the rebel officers are white men, yet they pick a blood chieftain to fear?"

"There's great resentment of the white southern officers, too. But they seem to reserve a special fear for a red man in command of others."

"It's only one more layer of bigotry, I suppose."

He nodded at Lucas and Matthew. "What do you intend to do with them? Do you have an interest in the woman?"

"Not the kind of interest you mean."

Cuthan shifted in the water. A stray beam of sunlight reflected off his broad, rose-bronze chest. Although he was an extremely handsome man of not yet thirty English years, I had never lusted after his flesh. He was Cut Hand's issue by blood, but I had considered him Billy's son for so long that I looked upon him as my own.

"You are a strange one, Otter." He gave an indulgent smile. "When I was a youth and learned of the life you and Billy lived among us, everything seemed natural and normal. Even the fact my father took Billy as a wife in the old days did not startle me." He gazed straight into my eyes like a white man. "Now, it seems less natural."

"That is the influence of your wife and her family. To them, what Billy and Cut Hand had between them and what Billy and I shared was sinful. Bestial. It does not seem that way to me."

"I could never consider you sinful or evil. I know you for the good man you are." He did not ask after my relationship with James. He likely had no need to do so. Again, he indicated Dew Drop's sons. "If you need to, you can send them to the Mead. They'll be safer there. This is too close to Yanube City."

"I am hoping James's station as commanding officer will offset the danger of proximity."

"Perhaps. But if it gets to be too close a thing, send them. Mary can use Helen's help around the place, and I can certainly use another pair of adult hands." Cuthan considered Rock splashing water like a gleeful child. "Well, almost adult hands."

"He does grown-up labor, but he has to be coddled sometimes. He has the old division of labor mentality. Tell me, has the militia come around looking for their missing companion's corpse?"

"Nay. Although the day after you left me the warning, I believe someone was skulking around. But I never caught clear sight of anyone."

"As was clearly demonstrated, they can watch from the hills behind the house and you will never know until it's too late. Those men were bent on killing you, Cuthan."

"I know. Mary's father gave us two of his hounds, but they keep running back to familiar ground. We're slowly bonding them to us, and before long, they'll be good guardians. In the meantime, the boys or I climb the hills regularly to scout out the countryside. When the hounds decide the Mead is home, I'll feel better about the children going up there with the dogs."

"There is something you should know." I told him the wounded man had marked my wagon, forcing me to get rid of it. I also spoke of the four militiamen who showed up to nose around and later harass Dew Drop and her family.

"Did the scalawag die of his snakebite?"

"Likely not, else James would have heard of it and told me. But they were looking for the buckboard and the body of their accomplice."

"This puts another face on the thing. I think we should change our plans and start back to the Mead."

"I agree. Perhaps you should leave now."

He scanned the sky. "No, we're tired. We'll start back tomorrow morning after we get the rafters in place. We can push hard and make it home by nightfall."

"Leave early on the morrow. Rock and I can handle the rafters."

"You can, but it will be done more quickly if I help. We won't tarry long. We started to bring a wagon because of the girls, but decided it would be faster to go horseback and cut across the prairie. I'm glad we made that decision."

The boys weren't done playing when we got out of the crick and dressed, so we left them to their antics. Mary and Dew Drop were not only clean and properly clothed, but had seen to their coifs, as well. Mary's golden tresses were pulled back and restrained by a blue bow. Dew Drop's black hair fell in braids on either side of her broad face. They kept Rachel Ann and Hannah busy so they wouldn't sneak off to peek at the naked boys in the crick. Eventually, the women announced our supper was ready.

When darkness fell, the ladies, both big and small, took over the tipi while the men and boys bedded down under the stars. The night was calm and peaceful, broken only by distant yips and howls of coyotes and an occasional giggle from one of the boys when little Hannah made noises like gravel falling upon stone. The child had snored almost from birth.

I rose with the dawn, and Cuthan was immediately at my side, ready to commence work. We dragged Rock out of his blankets and put up with his grumbling as we tackled the rafters. They were already sawn, so it was a matter of hoisting the frames and nailing them in place. The work went quickly.

We were almost finished securing the last one in place when Rock straightened to full height atop the structure and pointed with pursed lips.

"Somebody's coming."

Six horsemen approached from the south.

"Militia," I said.

"Let's get on solid ground," Cuthan suggested.

We scrambled down and rounded up the women and children. For lack of a better place, I herded them into the barn. Then Cuthan and I went outside to await the arrival of the riders. Rock joined us with his rifle in hand.

"Put it away," I ordered.

The riders splashed across the crick at a gallop. Had I made a mistake?

CHAPTER 8

The same snaky ruffian who'd led the militiamen the last time pulled to a halt just short of where we stood. The lout had an emaciated look about him. The other riders formed a rank behind him. I scanned the group seeking the man who had been snake bit but didn't spot him.

"Thought this was Major Morrow's place. Looks more like a Injun village to me. He know y'all's camping out on his property?" The rider tugged the reins, making his mount dance.

"Why don't we ride over to the fort and ask him?" I said calmly. I took note of the good-looking chestnut with a splayed right front hoof the man was riding.

"Don't smart mouth me, boy. I asked you a question."

"And I answered you, Mr. ... Mr. ..."

"It's Major. Major Hiram Hardcastle. You'd do well to remember that, boy."

A southerner. Definitely a southerner. He had the look of a lunger who was too mean to just lie down and die. I judged him to be frothy because his lungs wouldn't allow him honorable service in the war. So he took out his frustration and fear on anyone he perceived as weak.

"Major Morrow has approved hiring Lucas Brandt as my helper." I indicated the youth on my left, "His mother, Helen, is our cook. His brother, Matthew, helps as he can."

Hardcastle gave us a fishy look. "And who might this other'n be?"

"I'm Cuthan Strobaw." His voice was strong but not aggressive.

Hardcastle turned his head to spear him with a look. "From over at Teacher's Mead?"

Cuthan nodded and called Mary and the others out of the barn. "This is my family."

"What're you doing over here?" Hardcastle was beginning to add two and two and might just stumble onto four.

"Joseph Otter put out the word he needed help with a barn raising, so we responded."

Mary moved to her husband's side. "My father and brothers are keeping an eye on the Mead while we're away. I believe you might know them."

"I know old Hans Jacobsen and his brood." Hardcastle spat in the dirt. "And I know all about you, too. Good-looking woman who went squaw on us. With the breed son of an old pederast, at that."

I laid a restraining hand on Cuthan's arm.

Mary fought her own battle. "A woman who saw a good man who would take care of her and raise a fine family. As for that old man you speak of so disparagingly, he left a legacy the likes of you will never be able to match. What's this all about, anyway?"

"Well, Missy, it's about a murdering redskin who thinks he can get away with killing a white man. The governor of this here territory deputized me and these boys to keep the law in this part of the country. That's what we aim to do. If your man done the killing, we'll get him. If this one done it," he jabbed a thumb at me, "we'll find him out, too. If the kid here done it, I'll make a haversack outta his hide. Y'all can count on that. Now where's your wagon?"

"What wagon?" Cuthan asked.

"The one you come over here in."

"We came horseback. Any wagons we have are at the Mead."

"Y'all brought them kids horseback?"

"Every step of the way."

Cuthan was beginning to go stiff-legged, so it was time to put an end to this before tempers got out of hand. I stepped forward.

"Major, I'd appreciate it if you'd stop by the fort on your return to Yanube City and let Major Morrow know the barn is almost raised. That will save me a trip to town."

"I ain't your messenger boy. I got better things for my time." Hardcastle wheeled his mount. "Come on, men, we got more patrolling to do."

As the riders pounded out of the little glen, almost collapsing the tipi in their haste, I noted a slight man dressed in black on a blue roan mare with one white stocking. The Reverend Jeremiah Berglund. Why would a man of God ride with the militia?

"Cuthan, I think you and your family ought to start for home."

"I agree. The militia headed back toward town, so they'll take the road. I'll bet a box of cartridges they'll end up at the Mead. If we cross-cut, we can beat them there."

"Leave the children if you want, and we'll bring them later."

"I'm going with pa," Alex said.

"Me, too," John piped up.

Cuthan and his family were packed and mounted within minutes. I put a hand on his pony to halt him. "You know he's figured things out, don't you?"

He nodded. "He's knows you were the man with the buckboard. Or at least suspects it."

"If I were you, I'd leave the barn unlocked so they can search for a marked wagon all they want."

"Good idea. I think I'll send John straight to Hans and his sons. They might want to drop by for a quick visit."

I grunted agreement. "We'd go with you, but that would be a provocation."

Cuthan grinned. "Be a provocation? Otter, sometimes you sound like a professor. You had too much exposure to Billy and his Moorehouse College education."

"He drummed it into you, too. Send Alex with word if anything goes wrong."

As Cuthan set off for the Mead at a good pace, I was proud of him. He had kept a cool head in a potentially dangerous situation. I glanced at the agitated youth at my side. This one wasn't so contained. It was a wonder he hadn't exploded and set the whole thing ablaze.

"Why do we have to take that from those skunks?" Rock snarled.

"Don't talk skunks down like that. They are honorable animals. But to answer your question, there were half a dozen of them, all spoiling for a fight. We had women and children here. Were you ready to see them slaughtered just because of your pride?"

"If a man doesn't have pride, he's not a man. You called me by that name. You called me Lucas. Like I can't be proud of who I am."

"Rock — nay, *Lucas* — a man should be proud of who he is and what he stands for. That doesn't mean he always has to drape it around his shoulders like a *shee-nah*, a blanket. There's good pride, and there's foolish pride. Learn the difference."

The youth drew himself up. "Pride is pride. If you don't show it, you don't have it. And don't call me that name."

He turned and stomped away, leaving me to shake my head. The boy vaulted aboard his horse and dug his heels into the pony's flanks. Thankfully, he headed north.

"I fear for him." Dew Drop's voice at my elbow startled me.

"Like the rest of us, he is caught in a time when life as we lived it is ending, yet we can't quite see the life that will come."

"What will happen to us, Otter?"

"We will survive. Most of us. Some won't, but most of us will. It's a narrow, rocky trail that lies in front of us."

61

"You have to stop calling me Dew Drop. I want to be Helen now. And I will call you Joseph."

"No, I am Otter. I've learned how to deal with them. If I tried to change now, it would call more attention than it distracted. Besides, I've reached an age where it doesn't matter. You will be Helen and Little Bear will be Matthew, but if you think that is all it takes to save you, then ..."

"No, but it is a start."

# # # # #

Lucas came back within the hour, rage still smoldering in his dark eyes. I expected a rebellion when I addressed him by his American name, but he merely tucked his head and picked up a hammer. Without a word, he set to work completing the outhouse.

Sullen hostility hung in the air for the next two days, and we spoke little while working on the barn and awaiting news from the Mead. None came until James arrived for his next visit. One of the Jacobsen brothers had come to town for supplies and told him Hardcastle and his bunch showed up and searched the Mead thoroughly. Hans and his sons had arrived hard on their heels, so trouble was averted.

James looked over the nearly completed barn. "Things are coming along quickly. I trust Lucas is a big help."

"He's labor worth his hire. Of course, Cuthan helped a lot, too. I expect we'll move into the loft in a couple of days and live there until the house is built."

"I worry about you out here alone. Why don't you suspend work on the farm and move to town where I can give you more protection."

Thoughts of the Black Crow building his nest of hate in that town sent shivers down my back. Why would such a man give me fright?

"No, here is where I belong. The winds sweeping this country have shifted, and I have to cope with them as they are, not as they were."

He didn't insist, and I knew why. The nature of our relationship stood in greater jeopardy of exposure if we lived among the town folk. Besides, I wouldn't have been happy there.

James studied me with his bright blue eyes. "I need you, Otter. I cannot express how much. I find myself thinking of you — sometimes when other matters should be occupying my mind. I'll be addressing the troops, and suddenly an image of you will intrude."

"I think of you often, as well."

He gave a wan smile. "Not so vividly, I imagine. But I am pleased at the way things are working out between us. Now if this damned war will just end so I can resign my commission and work here beside you."

"Is there any sign of the ending?"

"It's back and forth. I think Grant's going to prove his mettle in the end. Since he took over in March, he and the President have devised what looks to be the first organized strategic operation of the war. In May, he engaged Lee in what they're calling the Battle of the Wilderness in Spottsylvania County, Virginia. It was bloody but indecisive.

"Grant broke off and moved south to get between Lee's army and Richmond. They fought another battle at Spottsylvania Courthouse to a standstill, but it cost both sides huge casualties. It's clear to me this is a war of attrition, one the North can better afford than the South. Grant's not fighting for territory. He's fighting to destroy Lee's army."

"A war of attrition can take a long time."

He nodded. "Yes. While I can see the ending, I cannot see the end."

When James had showed up, Helen quickly served a meal, cleaned up after us, and departed, taking Matthew with her. Lucas was nowhere to be seen, but his pony was still tethered beside Patch and the mare, so he was around somewhere. While taking another look at where we intended to do our first planting, we spotted him on the bank by the bathing pool drying off with an old shirt. His red-brown skin glowed in the afternoon light. As usual, his large rod was half-erect.

James flushed and glanced at me. Now was the time to speak of it, so I stopped him with a hand on his arm. "I have not touched him, nor permitted him to touch me."

"Permitted him?"

"He showed some feeble interest in win-tays, but I am content with what I have."

"I am pleased you feel that way. In the same breath, I have to admit the sight of him inflames me."

"He will be gone soon, and we'll bank that fire. Although, I must warn you, I think he's hung around and listened to us in the dark a couple of times."

James laughed. "Then let's christen the loft tonight. But Otter, please see if you can't get that young man into a proper pair of trousers."

A few minutes later, Lucas followed his family to their lodge. James and I climbed into the loft and spread our blankets. He had lost his shyness at disrobing in front of me. In fact, I believe he appreciated my admiring glance. He sprawled on the bedding and watched as I, also naked, doused the lantern and moved to his side.

"I am always amazed at the feel of your skin," James said. "It has a wonderful texture."

I snorted. "It seems to me I can begin to feel the years on it."

"Would that the years had been so kind to me."

"How can you say that? You are handsome, striking in both feature and form. You are a desirable man."

"Show me how desirable."

"Lie on your stomach. Tonight, I want to feel my entire body touching yours."

I spread the firm mounds of his *ue-zay*. A moment later, I savored the delicious sensation of sliding into the man beneath me.

"Love me tonight, Otter. Love me long and gentle."

I spread myself atop him and stretched my arms over his, slowly thrusting in and out, languidly loving James.

He sighed contentedly. "I live for this moment. I dream about it in my lonely quarters at the post. Sometimes … ah, that was good … sometimes I get the urge to desert my troops and come to you."

"I'm ready whenever you come. Having these few moments with you allows me to live the rest of my life."

"That's it. That's precisely it. I would shrivel and die if I could not feel you inside me. Oh, fuck me, man. Give it to me now. Hard."

I propped myself up on my arms and grew more energetic. My thighs slapped his butt, making audible love noises. James groaned and began rising to meet me as I lunged faster, more urgently.

"Oh, Otter! My beautiful Otter."

His spasming muscles let me know he had come. Moments later, my own explosion sent ripples of pleasure up and down my body. The sound of labored breathing replaced the slap of flesh against flesh. After a few moments, I rolled over and relaxed against the freshly laundered blanket smelling of soap. It was scratchy to my skin. James did not smoke to excess, but he had a light air of tobacco about him. The faint musk of sated sex hung in the air.

"We forgot to bring water," he said.

"Nay. There's a bucket in the corner."

I rose and brought water and rags to cleanse us and then collapsed beside him. Things were silent for a few moments.

"Tell, me," James said into the darkness. "Does Billy still haunt our couplings?"

"No. He's ceded the ground to the living. He approves, you know."

"I think he probably does."

"I know so. When he knew he was dying, he told me as much in that way he had of imparting things so you believe his ideas were your own."

"Then I am pleased."

We grew quiet again, and in time James slept. I covered his nakedness with a blanket and lay back to consider the day. I didn't get very far before sleep overtook me.

# # # # #

Thanks to Cuthan's help and Lucas's strong back, the barn was completed well ahead of schedule. During the building process, I had learned Lucas possessed a lively intellect and quick wit. He often plied me with questions about why we were doing this or that, making me wonder how he would take to tutoring. Before the massacre, Billy and I had taught Cuthan and his family — indeed all of the *tiospaye's* youngsters — pounding every fact, concept, and philosophy possible into those little heads.

I wagered Cuthan and I were better educated than most men in the territory. In fact, Billy and I had also tutored Hans Jacobsen's children before there were schools in the area. As he had the other day, Cuthan often teased that I sounded more like a college professor than a savage in a flap and moccasins. Watching the bronzed, nearly naked Lucas at work nearby, I resolved to broach the subject of learning this evening after work.

I moved my things into the loft of the barn to take up residence there until the house was finished. Before dismantling the tipi and storing it away, I offered Helen the use of the shelter. She declined, preferring her own lodge in the glen north of the farm. That was likely because we never knew when James would show up on one of his visits. After she served a rabbit and corn stew for the evening meal, she took Matthew and returned home.

As we lay soaking in the pool, Lucas making his usual display of hard muscles and semi-rampant organ, I attempted to broach the subject of tutoring, but it went awry when I used the wrong approach.

"Lucas ..."

"Don't call me that. At least while nobody's around."

"Yes, I will call you that. All the time. You have to become Lucas to me so you can become Lucas to everyone else."

65

"I'm not Lucas. I'm Standing Rock. That's my name. That's who I am. And I'm proud of that."

I sighed. To reach this young man's mind without destroying his spirit would not be an easy thing. "Do you remember when those militiamen rode into the glade the other day?"

"Of course."

"They wanted to kill you. They wanted to kill all of us. Simply because we're in their way. We're like boulders in the cornfield to them. Better to dig us up and cast us away, than plow around us. But their law — as imperfect as it is — puts a halter on their wants. So they have to find an excuse that will be acceptable to their society before they can murder us."

"We ought to kill them. All of them," Lucas muttered.

"And in that, you are the mirror of the white man — a red man who wants to kill whites because he doesn't understand them. It's been tried, Lucas. It didn't work. There will be lots of killing ahead of us, killing on both sides. I can feel it coming."

"Good! I want to be there when it starts. I want to *start* it."

"It will start when the time is right. No one man will start it. No one incident will bring on the bloodshed. Things far bigger than you or me will set it off."

"If I can't start it, I want to at least be a part of it."

"Then you have to survive until that time arrives. You can best do that by becoming Lucas. Accept the name and get into a pair of the white man's trousers. Hunker down and don't attract attention. You can take pride in your heritage without being an obvious thorn in the eye of the whites. Some of them, believe it or not, are decent men and women."

"Like Major Morrow?"

"Yes, like James, and like Cuthan's wife."

"She's pretty in a kind of washed-out way. Like bleached buffalo hide."

"She's a good woman. Do these things make sense to you?"

"I guess."

"So you will become Lucas, at least to the whites, and do whatever else you need to?"

"No britches."

"I have a pair of fringed buckskin pants. You can start with that."

"That wouldn't be too bad."

I smiled on the inside. That had gone better than I'd expected.

"You're doing it to him, aren't you?"

My eyebrows climbed. "That is no more your affair than you flogging your own staff is mine."

"Hah! I don't get as noisy as you two when I do it."

"Stop being a child and grow up."

He pointed to the tip of his penis jutting up out of the water. "I am being a man about it."

"Go take care of it on your own." I got out of the pool before my staff betrayed me. I didn't linger, but I suspect Lucas proceeded to take care of his need. The thought of it almost drove me back to the crick.

That evening, I lit a couple of lamps in the loft and pulled out some of my books. Lucas showed no interest in looking at the letters making up words but could not hide his curiosity about the passages I read aloud. At least, it was a start.

# # # # #

As we worked on the house, I was determined to bring ready water into the building — just as Billy had done at the Mead. I hired Timo Bowers to fashion a digging auger suitable for tunneling a well. When we reached the water table, which was not deep this near the crick, the blacksmith forged pipes and a water-lifting pump.

By the time we'd laid a foundation of native rock to the house and cemented it with a mortar of clay and small stones, I was able to set the hand pump directly into the cooking room floor. Now water would be available without the need for hauling. As with the outhouse, I built the dwelling with inner and outer walls insulated with a mixture of buffalo grass and mud to provide protection against the bitter winters.

The roof had a steep pitch so most of the snow would slide off and the rest would shed its weight quickly as it melted. I built the house with wide eaves so dripping water would not invade the interior. I was pleased at the way James exclaimed in approval each time he visited the farm to inspect the progress.

As happy as I was with the way the house was coming along, I was nearly elated by the way Lucas adjusted. The youth's curiosity led him to learn quickly, not only becoming adept at handling tools and utensils, but also drawing him into the books. I made a point of creating rough sketches of the house, noting dimensions along the edges. As I had hoped, Lucas asked about them. Without his realizing it, I soon had him studying the English alphabet and learning the American numbering system.

Matthew, even more inquisitive than his brother, soon demanded to be included. Once again, I was teaching. It was a source of great pleasure and an honorable thing to do.

Lucas had named his mount Whispering Wind and outlined his own right hand on the opposing flank of the animal in red paint made of natural elements. This was his way of branding the pony. He found endless excuses for riding; any chore beyond the boundaries of the glen was pursued horseback. The youth often cajoled me into races across the plains. Lucas grew inordinately peeved when he lost and unduly jubilant when he won.

Anytime I begged off, Matthew took up the challenge. I smiled to watch the child stick like a tar baby to Patch's back. The pinto was faster than the mustang, but Whisper had greater lungpower. On the short course, little Matthew would win; on longer races, his big brother usually came home first. Lucas recognized this early and demanded a longer track.

I often considered my good fortune in finding this Indian family to help with my work and fill my idle hours; nonetheless, I missed Cuthan and his brood. This was the excitement of new friends while the other represented old, familiar roots producing new branches.

As the days passed and the farmhouse came close to completion, I began to hope the white man resting beneath the buckboard at the bottom of the Yanube had been forgotten. Early on, had it not been for the warrant of James's protection, I was convinced the militiamen would have come for me even with no proof of my involvement. Yet, each day without an invasion by armed horsemen or word of another assault on the Mead gave me heart.

# # # # #

One day, as Matthew and I tied pony drags on Patch and the mare for what I hoped would be the last of the prairie grass needed for insulating the house, Lucas took Helen back to her lodge to collect some things for the evening meal. She planned to bring a few more of her belongings back with her. Under the pressure of my urging, she had agreed to move to the farm. The event was proceeding slowly as she was accomplishing it by dribs and drabs.

Matthew and I mounted and waved goodbye, crossing the crick to the south as Helen and Lucas headed in the opposite direction to her camp.

It was near high sun when Matthew straightened and looked off to the east, shading his eyes with one hand and holding a small crescent-shaped scythe in the other. I followed his gaze and saw a group of horsemen on the horizon, heading north.

"Militia," the boy hissed.

"Looks like it. Let's keep an eye out for them in case they return this way."

"There's nothing up that way, is there?" he asked.

"Major Morrow told me there was a group of Sioux camped out on Trickling Water Crick."

"Where's that?"

I pointed with my chin. "About ten miles that way."

"Let's go warn them the militia's on the way."

"They have too great a lead on us. Maybe they're just patrolling."

"I don't like them." Matthew returned to his work.

Perhaps half an hourglass later, both pony drags were well filled. As we were preparing to go back to the house, a distant, frightening sound reached my ear.

"Was that a gunshot?" Matthew asked.

I cocked my head. When the shot was repeated several times, I snatched my knife from its sheath and cut the ropes holding the drag poles to Patch. I leapt aboard the pony and shouted for Matthew to go to the barn and stay there. The pinto splashed through the crick and pounded over the hill. I cut straight across the savannah for Helen's tipi. All was quiet except for the thunder of Patch's hooves and the pony's labored grunts.

I rode recklessly into the small clearing. Helen's camp was a jumble. The tipi was overturned onto the cook fire. A bare leg stuck out from beneath the smoldering skirts. With only a quick look to make sure the assassins were no longer about, I slipped off the pinto and rushed to throw the buffalo skins from the fire. Helen lay with bloody gash in her neck. She had also been shot in the stomach. I made sure she was dead before going in search of Lucas.

I found him splayed across a ledge of rock. His naked torso was mangled and painted red with blood. He wore the fringed buckskin trousers I had given him. One moccasin had come off when two bullets struck his chest and drove him back over the ledge.

I whirled as a high-pitched wail shattered the grove. Matthew fell across his mother and sobbed uncontrollably for long minutes before lifting his head. "My brother! Where's my brother?"

"Over here."

I caught the boy and hugged him tightly as he tried to race to Lucas. "Let it be, son. He's gone, too."

CHAPTER 9

A blazing sun sucked moisture from every living thing it touched. The air in my nostrils was as hot as the rage in my breast. Two innocents lay dead, slaughtered like prey by brutish hunters, trophies never to be displayed but secretly shared with kindred killers.

After securing the bodies wrapped in buffalo hide to pony drags, I lashed one travois to Patch and another to the mare while Matthew sat on the ground hugging himself, a forlorn figure. I judged him still in shock.

"Son, get out of those white man's *uen-zoh-ghee* and put on your breechclout. Today you will be Little Bear."

The boy stared at me blankly.

I touched his arm. "You will dress as a Teton warrior in honor of those who were your mother and your brother. We both will. Today, I will be River Otter."

He looked up at me through unnaturally large eyes. "Can we lay them away now?"

"No, we are going to take them to the fort so all will know what happened."

Bear's spine stiffened. "I'll take Rock's ... uh, his rifle and shoot them. I'll kill them all!"

My shoulders slumped. How could I make this child see his own survival was at stake? "We will ask the white man to do that for us."

"He won't. Why would he?"

"Not all are *doh-kah*, our enemy. Some are honorable. Some are bad. Just like there are good and bad men among our blood."

"I don't believe it!" the boy shouted in dialect. "They're all bad."

"Go do as I say."

Bear stripped off the white man's trousers I had bought for him and left them in the dirt. Naked, he strode to the spot where the tipi had stood and searched among the wreckage. Moments later, with his loincloth in place, he picked up the rifle his brother had been holding when he fell.

I shook my head. "We will leave the *mah-zah-wah-kahn* at the farm. We will not go armed into the white man's town. We will not invite him to slaughter us, as well."

The child's lips compressed into a thin line, but he nodded. We mounted and returned to the farm. As we came into the farmyard, we found Whisper standing before the barn door. The pony must have fled the sounds of the slaughter and returned to the place he knew best. For a moment, joy overcame the misery hounding Bear's features. Without a word, he jumped off the mare and went to the mustang.

I left him speaking softly to the animal in Dakota as I took our weapons to the loft and changed out of my white man's clothing. When I returned, Bear mounted his brother's pony and led the mare by the reins as we started to town. Neither of us spoke a word on the long, sad ride.

The sentry outside the fort's entrance fingered his rifle nervously as two Indians in loincloths and moccasins, approached with two drags carrying what were obviously bodies covered by buffalo skins. Without pausing, we rode straight for the headquarters building.

"Halt! Hold on. You can't go in there."

Another soldier started for us, but as he made a grab for my reins, a sergeant stepped out of the administration building and called him back. Then the Three-Stripe stood waiting on the portico.

"Tell the Major that River Otter and Little Bear are here."

The man eyed the shrouded forms resting on the two travois and nodded. "I'll do that. You wait right here."

He turned and strode into the building. Moments later, James rushed out.

"Otter, what ..."

"Major Morrow," I said stiffly. "I want to report two murders."

"Is it ..."

"A Yanube warrior and his mother were shot down like dogs in their peaceful camp by members of the militia."

James cursed and turned to the sergeant standing at his back. "Take the bodies to the medical unit. I want the sawbones to examine them." He lifted his gaze to me. "It's something I have to do, Otter. He may have to testify as to what happened to them."

I grunted and lifted a hand in the face of Bear's half-uttered objections.

James turned and bellowed for his adjutant, "You and the boy come inside. The men will take care of your mounts."

When we were seated in his office with a young lieutenant named Rodgers hovering at his side, James listened to my explanation of what had happened. He asked a few well-chosen questions and then instructed Rodgers to mount a patrol. After the man left to carry out his orders, James asked if I had anything else to tell him.

"It was the militia. We saw them pass well to our east."

"Do you think they saw you?"

"I'm sure of it. They were at quite a distance, and I believe they mistook Bear for his brother. They turned and headed for the camp in the glade after they passed out of our line of sight. We heard the shots and went to investigate."

James glanced at the silent boy by my side. "He saw them like that?"

I nodded. "When I saw there was nothing I could do for either of them, I took a look around. The tracks told the story. The raiders were led by the man with the splayfooted chestnut."

"Hardcastle. Can you identify any of the others?"

"No. Just the Major. They rode into the camp expecting easy pickings. Instead of Little Bear, they found his older brother there. He tried to protect his mother and died for his efforts." My voice turned bitter. "In trousers, by the way. I tried to keep them alive by turning them into Lucas and Helen, but they died because of who they really were."

I paused to glance at the child sitting beside me, not certain how he would take my next words. "Tomorrow, I will take Little Bear to the Mead. He'll be safer with Cuthan than with me."

The boy said nothing. Perhaps he hadn't even heard me.

"You should remain there, too. I'm not certain how much protection I can provide for you now."

"I will take him to the Mead, but I will come home. The house is almost finished, and that will make things safer."

"Why?" James asked. "Why would they attack a lone woman and what they thought was a small child?"

I shrugged. "Perhaps it was pure hatred or just for sport. She was an Indian woman. They were white men. She was convenient and of no consequence."

"You think they went there to rape her?" James looked as if he wished he could take his words back, but again, Little Bear failed to react.

"I think they went there to kill them as a provocation to me. Rape would have been merely a diversion."

"Why provoke you?"

"They know I killed their assassin at the Mead, but they can't prove it."

"If they were after you, why not just wait until you came to find out what happened and finish you then?"

"Because they haven't worked up the courage to take you on directly. After all, I'm your hired hand. But if this slaughter had goaded me into attacking them, they would have the excuse they needed. They were counting on me doing something rash."

"I take it they were gone by the time you and Matthew arrived."

That brought a reaction. "Don't call me that. I'm not Matthew."

I ignored the lad's outburst. "They had already ridden off to the west, keeping the hill between us. I followed their trail to where they entered Turtle Crick, but it was a poor effort to throw me off their track. I easily found where they came out downstream. Then they headed straight back to Yanube City. They couldn't afford to waste too much time because at least one of them was wounded. There was blood on the trail."

"I'll ask around for an injured man."

The lieutenant knocked and entered to inform his Major the patrol was ready and waiting. When we went outside to mount up, Little Bear came alive.

"Where are my brother and mother?"

"The fort's doctor is looking after them for us," I said. "I want you to stay with them until we come back."

"I'm going with you to find those men."

"The Major is going to see the ambush spot for himself. We'll not go hunting the killers this day."

Confusion clouded his face. "What about my mother and brother? We have to take care of them. It has to be done right."

I glanced at James, who was already aboard his large cavalry horse. "It is the family's responsibility to bury its kin. Normally, the bodies would be mounted on scaffolds until the bones are clean before burying."

"Not such a good idea nowadays. Let the boy come along. It will do him good to see we're making an effort. No matter how futile." James wheeled his charger, leading the patrol north. A sergeant gave orders to the squad, and the column fell in behind him. Bear and I brought up the rear. How many of the curious eyes following our passage through the outskirts of town belonged to the killers?

James halted the troop just short of the tree line sheltering the camp and beckoned the sergeant and me forward. Bear came along uninvited. When the four of us entered the clearing, I immediately spotted fresh prints but held my tongue other than to read the story told by the signs. After the sergeant went to dismount the men for a

Mark Wildyr

thorough search of the area, I pointed out a heavy splash of blood on a bush. Some of the troopers found a second pool.

"Looks like the boy got two of them," James said.

"Good. Two will be harder to explain than one."

"Sir," the sergeant yelled. "There's something over here."

My stomach lurched. He'd found the tracks I'd noticed. Someone had been here since Bear and I left for the fort. There were fresh hoof and moccasin prints around the overturned tipi.

"Another party was here. Four ponies." The sergeant pointed to the northeast. "They came in here and went out in the same direction." Unfortunately, the Three-Stripe was a trailer who could read sign.

James examined the markings in the earth and led me apart from the others. "This complicates things."

I nodded. Now the murdering militiamen had an opportunity to claim others had done the killings. The fresh horse prints were barefoot, so the riders were probably the Sioux camped out on Trickling Water. They must have been nearby and came to check the situation for themselves after Matthew and I rode for the fort.

"I can swear those tracks weren't there when I left this place."

"Your word's good enough for me, but ..."

"But it wouldn't count for much in a white man's court."

"Worse, it gives the killers a chance to explain the wounded men. They'll claim they got in a firefight with hostiles, and those tracks make the story plausible."

"The militiamen don't know about them."

"No, but a sergeant and a squad of nine troopers do. It won't take long for the story to spread all over town."

"So they'll get away with murder."

"I'll investigate the killings, but I don't hold out much hope. Let's bide our time. They'll trip up sooner or later."

Bile rose in my throat, almost choking me. My eyesight went blurry at the edges. James's scowl told me he shared my frustration.

The sergeant and half his contingent went northeast, tracking the unknown party, while I led James and his remaining men over the trail the militia had taken. When we arrived back at the fort, James dismissed his men and went straight to the medical building. All that remained of the boy's family lay on adjoining tables covered by white sheets.

"What can you tell us?" James said to a captain with a medical corps insignia on his uniform.

75

"Gunshot wounds, both of them. But the woman appears to have some bruises, and there's a knife wound to the throat. I'd say someone manhandled her first. Then the young man probably showed up, and all hell broke loose."

James turned back the sheet and looked into Lucas's dead face. "How do you know they didn't kill the boy and then manhandle the mother?"

I felt rather than saw Little Bear move into a far corner of the room.

The doctor rubbed his chin before answering. "Because they'd have had their way with her if that was how it happened."

"So she wasn't molested."

"No. They got interrupted, I'd say. At least, the young man spared her that ordeal. Even if it cost him his life."

"Major, may we have the bodies?" I inclined my head. "It's important to Bear that his family gets proper treatment."

The doctor nodded, so James led us back to his office where I provided all the information I knew about the family for the military's records. It was a ploy to get the boy out of the way while the soldiers bound his family into shrouds and carried them to the pony drags. As soon as we were informed they were secured to our mounts, we took our leave.

We traveled half the distance to the farm in silence before Bear spoke. "It was bad, wasn't it? I mean, the other men coming."

"Yes. It gives the murderers a chance to claim the Sioux were there first. They can say they tried to stop the murders but were too late."

"We know that's not true. We saw the militia's tracks. The others weren't there."

"True, but the killers will dispute our words."

"And they'll believe the white men, won't they?"

I was silent for a distance. "Let me ask you a question. If a white boy and a boy of the blood came to you and said they saw a bird, but one claimed it was a hawk while the other said it was an eagle, who would you believe?"

"My own blood."

"Why?"

"Because he would know one bird from the other."

"Is that the true reason?"

Bear looked baffled. "What other reason could there be?"

"Think on it. The people of the blood have been here always. Even so, the white men have been here long enough to learn a hawk from an eagle. Many of their children were born here and have lived their lifetime in this country."

"So you think I would believe the one over the other because he was one of us?"

"Just so. And in this matter, there are only two of us to claim the one thing while there will be many of them to claim the other."

"So my brother and my mother will never be avenged."

"I believe these men — or at least the bad ones among them — will get their punishment. They will be slain or found out and disgraced. It may not be you or me or the Major who gets this done. But a brigand is a brigand and will live and die as a brigand. Does that make sense to you?"

The boy nodded. "But it doesn't help much."

"Ah, but it does. It does not purge the *sah-pah yah-zah*, the black ache, from a man's heart, but it lets him keep his sanity."

CHAPTER 10

The fetching young Yanube warrior who had provided me with help and companionship did not get a traditional burial atop a scaffold exposed to the hot sun. I had trouble convincing Little Bear someone, perhaps his brother's murderers, would tear it down and desecrate the corpse. When the boy eventually saw the wisdom of consigning his family to a grave, he spent half a day laboring alongside me to hack a hole in the hard, unforgiving earth in the very glen where they had died.

We placed food and water and all of their possessions in the grave to sustain them on the journey to the West. Little Bear kept only his brother's rifle and Whisper. I suspected he was silently vowing to run down the killers with the horse and slay them with the weapon. I prayed time would purge the thirst for vengeance from him.

We sang prayers to the All Powerful to protect the two souls on their journey and begged a great welcome when they arrived. Then we shoveled dirt into the pit and walked the horses over the spot to obfuscate the gravesite.

With the burial over, we returned to the farm where we stripped and bathed in the pool near the farmhouse, a sort of cleansing ceremony for both of us. Bear was not his usual yammering magpie self as we allowed the water to soak away the contamination of death. A sweat lodge would have been better, but I hadn't gotten around to building one yet.

"Why do they hate us?" he finally asked.

"Why do we hate them?"

"Because they kill us."

"Ask one of the *wah-shee-chue* that question, and you will get the same answer. There is a long history of red men and white men killing one another. Sometimes one side is at fault, and sometimes the other. There is right and wrong on both sides, but that is not a whole answer, Matthew."

"I don't want to be Matthew anymore."

"You *must* be Matthew, now more than ever. Tomorrow you will put on your white man's trousers and cover your shoulders with a shirt."

"I won't do it." His words were not sharp, merely determined.

"I will not force you. In time, you will see I am right."

"What do you mean, that wasn't a whole answer?"

"There is more to it than that."

I talked until *Wi* dropped to the western horizon and *Han* heralded the approaching night, explaining the cultural divide between our peoples, and how that spread fear and mistrust. I described the difference in the way we viewed the land — the one seeking to acquire it and bar others from it; the other believing it belonged to all and seeing no value in claiming a specific plot to call home forever. I stated my belief that each had something to recommend it.

As Billy had preached to my people those many years ago, so I now spoke to Little Bear. The red man's time was ending. The Europeans would come until they covered the plains like locusts and sucked the very marrow from the land. We were seeing Billy's vision come to pass. *Tatanka*, the great woolly beast that gave us sustenance, would disappear, and the tribes would be shunted into some unfamiliar place. Or slaughtered if they refused to go.

How much of this the child comprehended, I did not know. But I would approach this thing as Billy had done — repeat it until the ears that refused to hear opened to the truth. It was not a heroic tale I spun, but one that would doubtless prove to be accurate.

That night, Matthew threw his blankets close by my side in the hayloft. The boy had trouble letting go of his conscious self. Eventually, his shallow breathing and occasional whimpers told me the sleep that came was but a modicum less tortuous than awareness had been. Despite my words to the child, I nursed my own rage throughout the night.

# # # # #

We rose early the next morning, and after breaking the night's fast, I dressed in white man's clothes, including a black, flat-brimmed felt hat many tame Indians wore. I cajoled Matthew into pants and shirt. I wanted to wash away the painted outline of Lucas's hand on Whisper's flank, but Matthew objected so strenuously, I relented. Then we set out for Teacher's Mead, cutting cross-country rather than taking the road.

We left well before the sun reached its strength, but the trip was more than fifty miles, so we went steadily, walking the horses but resting them often. As I was not certain how long I would be gone, I brought the mare along, fitting her with a pony-drag to haul the carcass of an antelope I'd shot. Occasionally, Matthew or I would ride the mare to spell the other mounts.

Cuthan's new hounds raised a ruckus with deep braying and sharp barks when we approached the hills of Teacher's Mead late that afternoon. They came at us on a dead run, spooking the horses and causing Matthew to reach for his rifle. I stayed his hand and halted the ponies to await the dogs' arrival.

The big animals, one black and the other brown, both with long floppy ears and madly whipping tails that rendered false their threatening snarls, danced and drooled around us. The dogs snuffled the antelope on the travois and almost panicked the mare. John rode out to call them off, shouting a gleeful welcome as he came. The boy was hatless, and his gold speckled black mane sparkled in the western sun.

"Otter! Matthew! What are you doing here? Where are Lucas and Helen?"

When neither of us answered, John's grin died, and a glimmer of fear lit his clever black eyes. He grew solemn. We rode the rest of the way in silence.

Cuthan and Alex walked in from the field to greet us in the yard. Mary was still wiping her hands on an apron as she stepped out onto the porch with the girls. Mouth-watering aromas spilled from the house.

Their cheerful greetings fell away when I explained what had happened. Mary immediately took charge of settling Matthew into the household. As the family had grown, Cuthan converted the western portion of the house into bedrooms for the children. This newest addition to the family would room with John, who was elated. Matthew was less so.

After servings of smoked fish — bass instead of the herring Mary preferred — and *frikadoller* — pork and beef meat balls with radish, cucumber, and tomato slices — she dished up another Danish dish, *koldskäl*, a dessert made from buttermilk, lemon, vanilla, eggs, and sugar. I am not a man to overeat, but knowing I was about to return to meals of my own making, I tucked away more than my share. Fortunately, Mary took pleasure in others appreciating her efforts.

When the meal was over, we adults sat around the kitchen table bringing one another up to date on affairs. The Mead had seen no more trouble, but Cuthan was a careful man. Although he relied upon the hounds to warn of approaching strangers, he regularly sent one of the older children up the hill to scout the horizon as well.

We talked into the night, concluding the attempt on him was to drive the family off the Mead because of its strategic placement between Ft.

Ramson and Ft. Yanube. The Jacobsen property abutted Cuthan on the sunrise side.

Like many young men, Cuthan was secure in the belief of his own immortality and was more concerned that I was the target in the militia's sights. He expressed distress the protection afforded by Major Morrow seemed to be weakening. Yet he voiced hope it might provide some cover.

"It did nothing for Lucas and Helen. They paid a terrible price for the bastards' hostility to me."

"Dew Drop was such a gentle woman," Mary said with a sigh.

Cuthan and I exchanged glances. Strange that Mary, who always called the other woman by her American appellation, had spoken her true name. No Indian would utter that name for at least a year after a person's death, lest the shade be lured back to the familiar world it had recently left. I had only referred to the two as Lucas and Helen, names unlikely to recall their ghosts. Perhaps there was more of the Old Way left in me than I thought. Billy would have scolded me good-naturedly.

Cuthan cleared his throat and picked up the conversation. "Their lives may have ended in the same manner had they never met you."

I dropped my head, knowing his eyes — black, gold-sharded orbs that were mirrors of John's and Cut Hand's — were studying me closely. "That does not lift the guilt riding my shoulders."

"Nay, I expect not. These are hard times."

"And likely to get harder. Caleb Brown gently warned my custom would be unwelcome in the store when his nephew takes over management. I felt hostile stares as I moved through the town."

"Even when there were entire bands of us in the area, we weren't treated like that."

"A lot of history has gone by since that time. Because of the fierce war in the east, the settlers fear there are not enough soldiers to protect them. So they turn to less savory characters for their safety. That gives the no-goods power, and power is not a good fit with some people."

"That's crazy. The soldiers James has in his command probably outnumber all of the bloods in this area. They ... we are no threat to anyone. There are no tribes, no bands. Just a few stragglers or people who've settled and adopted their ways."

"Fear is not always rational."

We talked the matter to death without resolving anything other than pledging to remain vigilant. Then we retired. All of the children were already asleep except for Matthew. He'd struggled to stay awake in order to sleep with me in the little cabin near the barn where I'd lived after Billy died.

# # # # #

I felt as if my heart were hung over the moon as I rode the north side of the river toward Yanube City. My chest cavity was hollow, empty of organs and muscles and nerves. I had difficulty drawing breath. The air around me had no texture, no strength to lend my lungs. As Patch and I led the mare westward, my eyes failed to feast on the majestic beauty of the flat countryside and the silver wiggle of the river rushing to dash itself to death against some distant ocean.

All I cared for in this world was at my back, fading farther and farther into the distance. Save James, of course. But I was no longer certain James was enough. Although never a father, I had always had family around. James was a liaison, an intimate comrade, but was he family? Perhaps someday — but not yet. We did not share enough history.

I wondered if Hardcastle had a family. Was he home at this moment surrounded by loving children, taking pleasure in their company, in teaching them life lessons and survival techniques? Or was he holed up somewhere like a reptile, alone and plotting to take his unhappiness out on those weaker than he was? My heart returned to my chest with an ache as I imagined it so.

My mind was so numbed I was taken by surprise when a horseman moved out of the tree line and blocked my way. At that moment, I recognized life held little value for me even though I quickly perceived the meeting did not represent danger.

"*Hah-ue.*" The man blocking my way was a solid individual in breechclout and moccasins with the look of a Sioux. A white hawk feather dangled from the crown of his braided locks. Like most of his lineage, he had strong features. Good features.

"*Hah-ue.* I know you … I think."

"And I know you, River Otter. My father spoke of you and the Red Win-tay often."

"You are Dull Lance, old Chief Stone Knife's son. The Red Win-tay traveled to Ft. Ramson once and talked you out of the army's jailhouse."

"Just so. Me and two of my companions."

"Stone Knife took his band to the Laramie country a long time ago. What are you doing here?"

"My father crossed the Great Divide and walks the Western Road. The *tiospaye* disbanded and was absorbed into other fires."

"What of the one called Morning Mist?"

"Ah, that witch. She married one of our warriors, but she was such trouble, they left the band and went elsewhere. I heard she died a few years later. Probably from a flint heart."

So Cuthan's estranged mother was dead. My first impulse was to turn back to give him the news, but that was merely an excuse, one that would bring a fresh rending of the soul when I departed again.

"Things are not good in the Laramie country," Dull Lance said. "My men and I came to visit our old grounds, hoping we would find a better life here."

"I doubt it. The country is filling up with Americans. Right now, they are staying close to the river, but sooner or later they will fill the land south to the Little Islands and then drift north. The soldiers are no longer patrolling the territory. Now it is the militia, and some of them have a hatred for people of the blood."

Dull Lance told of nearly running afoul of such patrols a time or two. He confirmed he and his three companions had investigated the sound of gunshots and come upon Helen's camp the day of the murders. They left the area quickly but had stood their ground like men when a group of soldiers led by a Three-Stripe had caught up with them. They answered questions and then went on their way.

"What will you do now?" I asked.

"We are camped out on the Trickling Water and will stay there until we decide. Some argue to go back to our families. Some want to bring our families here."

I resisted the urge to offer advice. It had not been asked. I merely grunted to acknowledge his words.

The Sioux turned the talk back to the murders. "We saw the militia earlier that day before they circled around to the pine glen."

"Was the leader a thin man astride a chestnut?"

"Aye. An unhealthy rogue with a mean look about him."

"You were close enough to see that?"

"We were hidden in a draw. They never saw us, but we could have reached out and counted coup on them."

"Was there another man who looked like a black crow with them? He would have been on a mare with one white stocking."

"I did not see such a man."

"Do you know what they did?"

"The signs said at least two died. Someone else was shot. Since your tracks and those of the little one were freshest, we guessed the woman and the young man were killed. We thought you should know what we know."

"Thank you for the information. Where are your men now?"

The Sioux motioned over his shoulder. "In the trees keeping watch."

"Good. Be careful, my friend."

"Take your own advice, Otter. You were surprised when I came out of the trees."

"True. I am glad it was you who woke me from my trance and not Hardcastle."

"The man on the chestnut?"

I nodded. "He is a man full of hate."

Dull Lance smiled grimly. "He is not the only one." He wheeled his horse and slipped through the trees. Moments later, I heard the band ride north.

My mind held onto the image of the handsome man longer than was normal. I do not usually dote on the looks of other males. Was my unrequited yen for young Lucas still too fresh, or was I drawn to the man because he lived the life I unconsciously longed for? I had lived peacefully among white men since I was ten-summers-old. Perhaps my heart yearned to throb with a warrior's pulse.

#

I headed straight for the blacksmith shop in Yanube City. Timo Bowers was well-regarded in town, and would likely know what was going on with Hardcastle and his clique of Indian haters. He gave me a huge grin as I entered his forge.

"Otter, good to see you." The smith frowned suddenly. "I heard what happened. I am sorry about that young man and his mother."

Relieved Timo had introduced the subject, I accepted his American handshake and asked what he knew of the affair.

"Just what everyone knows. The militia came upon the lodge unexpectedly and the boy panicked, shooting one of the men. They killed the youth in defense of themselves, and when the woman came at them with a hatchet, they had to shoot her, too. She opened a gash in Charlie Vass's thigh that might still cost him his leg."

"And the other one? The one Lucas shot?"

"Lucas. So that was the lad's name. He was a likely looking youngster. Too bad he panicked at the sight of the riders. Well, that was a man named Heston Hines. A ne'er do well who took to riding with the militia last year. He won't be much of a loss to the community."

"He died?"

"Yep. Toted him home stone dead. Shot right through the head."

I steadied my voice. "Have things like this been happening lately? There aren't enough tribesmen around these parts to cause problems, are there?"

"More'n you might think. There's a band of Sioux camping out on Trickling Water Crick less'n twenty miles from here. Due north of your place, I'd say. Keep a close eye out for them."

"Have they done mischief?"

"Not that I heard. A bunch of the militia was riding out to check on them the day the accident happened."

"Accident?"

"You know, Lucas getting panicked and killing Heston Hines."

"But nobody else has been attacked or killed?"

"No, but Joshua Millhorn's been missing for months now. He was riding with Hardcastle's group on patrol when they got in a skirmish with some renegades. He got separated from the others, and nobody's heard from him since. Another man riding with them that day was wounded pretty bad. Hardcastle thinks it was the same Sioux. The ones hanging out on the Trickling Water."

Convinced I now had all of the information Timo possessed, I ordered a few hooks and hangs for the cooking fireplace at the farm and then headed straight to the fort. James was in his office.

"That matches up with what I've learned," he said after I filled him in. "How much do you trust Bowers? Do you think he's part of it?"

I shook my head. "Timo had too strong a bond to Cut Hand to get mixed up in this kind of stuff."

James hesitated. "Otter, if you go looking for vengeance, I won't be able to help you."

"I wouldn't expect you to. Isn't there any way to rein these people in? I fear another attempt on Cuthan's life."

"They're legally authorized by the governor and work hand-in-hand with Julius Gadsby, the local magistrate. That short, fat Englishman's the real power in this town. Charlie Allberg is a joke of a mayor. If the militia goes too far over the line, I can step in. But they have to be caught *doing* something. It's not enough that we simply know they are. We have to prove it."

A frightened look came over him. "Be careful. If anything happened to you, I don't think I could stand it. My time with you and Billy are the only decent days I can count in my life."

"Nonsense. You have a good life. You're healthy and respected. You have the responsibility for this fort and all these soldiers. Many would gladly trade places with you."

"Yes, those who don't know the fear and loneliness I've endured. Fear I'd be found out as a sodomite and lonely for someone to share it with."

My voice grew husky. "When are you coming to the farm again?"

"Not until week's end. I can manage an overnight stay then."

"Good. My staff is looking forward to it."

"We'd better talk about horses or the weather or highbinders like Hardcastle. Much more of this, and you'll have to flay me atop this desk."

"Then I'd best be off."

# # # # #

No people of the blood lived in Yanube City, but I knew one who helped out at the livery stable. Bent Nose was a Dakota who came from Minnesota when the '62 Sioux Outbreak over food rations had been put down. The government had executed thirty-eight native men over that mess in the largest mass hanging in American history. The very next year, the Sioux were expelled from Minnesota into Nebraska and the Dakota country.

Bent Nose had found his way to Yanube city and begged work off of Patrick Pauley at the livery stable. Pauley had no use for Indians, but Bent Nose was so good with horses, the livery owner gave him the name of Ezekiel and let him sleep in the stable. The bigot didn't even seem to mind when everyone conferred "Pauley" on the old Indian to complete his civilized name.

I waited until no one was around to slip into the livery stable. Bent Nose was hanging some tack gear on one wall when I called his name. He refused to look at me.

"You was that Red Win-tay's man, wasn't you."

I grimaced. While the Lakota had a long history of respect for Two-Faces, the Dakota were more apt to look upon them with disdain. "That's right. He was best friends with the Major in charge of the soldiers at the fort. Now I work the farm for that same army man." Figuring that established a pecking order, I repeated my statement. "I need some information."

"What kind? I don't never go nowhere but here and to my camp outside of town."

"You hear things, and I want to know what you hear. I want to know about this militia chief called Hardcastle."

The Sioux's face closed up. "Don't know nothing about that man and don't want to, neither. He's a bad one. A skunk trying to wear a wolf's skin." Bent Nose was thin and stooped, probably close onto sixty, but I could see sinew beneath the flesh.

"And you're a warrior trying to hide under a flunkey's skin. Don't play false with me. Tell me what you know about him."

"Enough to stay out of his way."

"What does Pauley say about him? Men talk when they're together, and you hear them."

"He's a killer. Killed your family up north of that farm you work on."

"How do you know?"

"I was here when they come back with a wounded man. Had a bad cut on his thigh."

That would have been the Vass fellow Timo had mentioned. "Did they call the medical man for him?"

"No. Pauley bandaged him up here in the stable. From the way they talked, another man got killed."

"Is Pauley one of them? One of the militia?"

"Uh-huh. A chief of some kind." Bent Nose's dusky face was in shadow, but his bright eyes caught the light on occasion and glistened. He moved like a grounded bird, in little jerky motions.

"Who else was with them that day?"

"Man from the big general goods store. Brown I think his name is."

"Must be the nephew. Who else?"

"The gunsmith."

"William Hawkes? Anybody else?"

"Naw. More'n that rode up, but they went on their way, and I didn't see them."

I thought over what he'd told me and then asked if anything like it had happened a few weeks back. Bent Nose told me a group of men had met in the livery. A man had been wounded then, too. They had talked about another who was killed.

"How come you wanting to know things like that?" the old man asked. But I didn't think he really wanted an answer.

CHAPTER 11

I went to make certain everything was all right at the farm and to leave the mare in the barn before riding straight back to town. Bent Nose put Patch in the corral with Pauley's sale horses and reluctantly allowed me to nap in the hayloft. Sometime after dark, he woke me when he came up to claim his own bed. After thanking him for his help, I slipped out of the stable and made my way afoot down the dark streets toward the center of town. Bent Nose hadn't known where Hardcastle lived or if he had a family, but he'd heard the militia chief liked to frequent the Swinging Door Saloon and the Rainbow House.

Yanube City had only a few gas-fed street lamps, so it was relatively easy to remain unnoticed as I made my way to the corner of Brown's Mercantile directly opposite the Swinging Door Saloon. The store was closed and dark, so I settled back into the recessed alcove of one of the two entryways fronting on Main Avenue and prepared for a long wait.

Sooner than expected, Hardcastle and two men came stomping down the opposite side of the street. They likely had dinner at the Rainbow House and were ready for some hard drinking and gambling at the saloon.

I was a successful hunter because I stalked my prey carefully, learning its habits, fears, and desires before going in for the kill: sly Coyote; nervous Deer; curious Antelope. Yet, I could not long lurk in doorways and alleys to gain knowledge of Hardcastle without attracting attention. Most of the town was quiet, but traffic between the Rainbow House and a couple of drinking establishments at either end of Main was relatively brisk and exclusively male.

Hardcastle surprised me by exiting the saloon less than an hour later, alone this time. He paused to light what appeared to be a thin cigar with a Lucifer stick before stalking south on Main. I followed, staying in the shadows on the other side of the street. Once we passed from the gas-lit area, shadowing him became easier. A *hanwi pay-chah*, a new moon failed to appreciably cut the darkness.

We had no sooner left the commercial area than Hardcastle angled across the street, the same side I was on. The buildings — now residences — were farther apart and provided less cover. I advantaged bushes and shrubbery whenever possible.

Suddenly, he disappeared around the corner of a building. I crept to the edge of the alleyway and peered through the darkness. There was no sign of movement. Was this a trap? Then I smelled urine and made out Hardcastle pissing in the dark. I glanced up at the building. The sign across the façade almost caused me to laugh aloud. The militia major was peeing on the Rev. Berglund's City on the Hill. Hardcastle grunted as he shook himself off.

A moment later, he came out onto the street again, still buttoning his trousers. He passed no more than three feet from where I crouched. It would have been easy to take him, so why had I hesitated? Where was my rage over Lucas and Helen? I had killed before. Some men deserved to die, and this was one of them.

Hardcastle set off to the south again, moving a little faster now. Uncertain of my own intentions, I followed more discretely. Finally, the militiaman cut across a yard and headed for a house. The hair on my neck rose when someone hailed him from the darkness.

"That you, Brown?" Hardcastle called out.

A figure rose from a chair on the deeply shadowed veranda. I detoured out of their line of view and pressed against the side of the house. Although the men were standing close together and talking in low voices, I could make out what they were saying. The second man spoke in the Midwest tones of Abel Brown, Caleb's nephew.

"Gadsby wants the problem out at Teacher's Mead taken care of. Now."

"What put a burr up his ass?" Hardcastle's voice grated on my eardrums. "We got time. Need to let the killing of them two Injuns settle down."

"We don't have time. Gadsby got word the stage line's definitely going through. A company honcho is on his way from St. Louis to pick out the way stations. The Mead's a natural. Gadsby wants the problem settled before the agent arrives. When everybody else finds out what's going on, burning out those Indian squatters would be too obvious."

"Hell, they ain't squatters. That redskin's got title. Got upheld in court despite all his Honor could do."

"As far as I'm concerned, they're squatters. They should've been removed and sent to that Half-Breed Tract up on the Mississippi. That's the only place they ought to be able to hold land."

"Then spend some of your uncle's money and take care of the problem that way."

"Forget it. We don't have time now."

Hardcastle's laugh sounded like a rasp drawn across hard rock. "Besides, you tried it already and didn't it get done. Hell, it was your uncle who put a stop to it."

"That's water over the dam. So when are you going to handle the Mead?"

"We're planning on a patrol tomorrow sometime."

"Do it then."

"What do I use for an excuse? If they hole up in that blockhouse, it's gonna take cannons to get them out of there. Can't burn them out, the place is made out of rock. We'll have to shoot our way in. How we going to explain our casualties?"

"Get some dynamite."

"That's an idea. Y'all oughta have some in that store of yours. Or the gunsmith. We can stand on that hill behind the place and just roll it right down on top of them."

"Good. Then you can claim they were storing weapons and explosives and planning an insurrection."

"Yeah, planning a rising right under our noses ... until we found out and put a stop to it. That'll spin a good tale. All right, we'll do it tomorrow. I'll gather the men, and we'll head out in a couple of hours. I want to get there early. Y'all bring the dynamite."

"You can have someone pick it up at ..."

"That ain't gonna happen, Abel. Y'all's coming with us."

"Don't be ridiculous. I can't afford to be ..."

"Be what? Be seen with the likes of me? Is that why we meet on my front porch in the dead of night? So nobody'll see y'all cavorting with the militia. Hell, man, y'all holds the rank of captain in the damned thing."

"That's just honorary."

"No, it ain't. Y'all got a commission. Y'all might be rich and Gadsby's chief flunky, but I'm still your commanding officer. I'm ordering y'all out on that patrol tomorrow."

I eased away as the two men continued to argue. I had to get to James. Was he abed yet? If so, a sentry would be loath to awaken him. I crossed over a block to the west of Main Avenue to avoid meeting Brown should he go that way.

After picking up Patch at the livery corral without rousing anyone, I rode for the fort about a quarter of a mile to the northwest. Once there, a sentry challenged me and wasted fifteen minutes arguing. My claim of a disaster at the Major's farm finally convinced him to summon the

Corporal of the Guard, who went to the Duty Officer, who finally roused James.

As I faced my slightly tousled lover alone in his private quarters, I understood why I hadn't knifed Hardcastle. It would have devastated James to know I had killed a man who needed killing and yet have to bring me to justice. I experienced a flicker in my guts that left me wondering if it was a birth pain. The birth of true feelings for this man? When I finished telling him what I had heard, he rose and paced the room.

"So that's why the Mead's so important. The southern route of the overland stage was discontinued in 1861 because of the unrest. But the northern route is still in operation. I've heard rumors Wells Fargo was planning on coming to Yanube City, but I had no idea a decision had already been made. The Mead's fifty miles east of here. That makes it an ideal way station."

"Why is a way station such a big thing?"

"Because it's a steady stream of revenue. The Mead is also the perfect site for a town. Those bastards want to get their hands on Cuthan's property and build their own town." James stopped pacing. "The question is, what do I do about it? I could go to the magistrate, but he's in on it. He'll just deny everything."

"At least, he will abort the raid if he knows you're onto them."

"This morning's raid maybe, but they'd just plan it for another time. We need to catch them in the act, and this is the time to do it. Lieutenant!" he bellowed.

The fresh-faced young lieutenant opened the door. "Sir?"

"I want a patrol mounted now. No bugles. No fuss. As few lights as possible. I don't want the townspeople to know about it. One platoon. Fully armed. Provisions for two days. I suggest the Second Platoon of F Company. Lt. Mills is a capable man."

"Yes, sir."

"Get my mount ready. I'm accompanying them. Notify Captain Ricks he'll be in command in my absence."

"Yes, sir!"

Within the hour, the Second Platoon of F Company moved quietly out of the fort and turned north. James gave the east road a wide birth so no sign of our passing would alert the militiamen. When I found an easy game trail, James ordered the troop into a canter. Riding steadily, but without pushing the horses, we would reach the Mead in about six hours. The men and animals settled in for a long trek. By the light of the weak moon, the seemingly endless plains stretched out before us.

A nighthawk suddenly swooped low over my head, startling me and sending shivers down my spine. This was an omen bird. Night-loving creatures created fear among the superstitious. I did not count myself among them; nonetheless, I wondered what sort of warning the bird portended? And for whom?

About five in the morning, James and I broke away from the column as it passed well north of the hollow hill. Lt. Mills planned to circle around behind the Mead and rest the troop on the Yanube to the east. James and I headed straight for the farmhouse. Alerted by the hounds, Cuthan was waiting for us on the porch with a long gun cradled in his arms.

"James, Otter? What are you doing here?"

"You've got trouble coming down the road," James said. "Probably not more'n a couple of hours behind us."

We explained the situation and went into a huddle while Alex, John, and Matthew scampered up the three hills behind the Mead to keep an eye out for raiders. Then Cuthan put the dogs in the barn out of harm's way. Mary and the girls got busy fixing everyone something to eat. While this was going on, James posted some of his men on the eastern ridge looking down on the house. He concealed the rest of the troop in the thin forest between the front of the house and the river, a sparkling ribbon a mile to the south. Then everyone settled down to wait.

# # # # #

It was close onto seven-thirty when Matthew alerted us to riders approaching from the west. Cuthan called the boys off the hills and sent the two younger ones inside. James and I argued against it, but Cuthan went into the nearest field while Alex started mending tack gear on the porch.

"They'll know something's up if no one is working this time of day," Cuthan had insisted. "Give me fair warning when to take cover."

James and I scaled the west hill and found a spot where we wouldn't be easily seen when the raiders climbed the back of the hollow hill with their dynamite. A group of about ten riders halted a mile from the Mead for a consultation. After a few minutes, six of them rode directly for the house. They obviously planned to pin everyone inside while the other four men climbed the hollow hill with the dynamite. I spotted a familiar splayfooted chestnut with the group coming straight for the house. There was no blue roan gelding with a white stocking among them.

At my shrill chirp, Cuthan straightened his back, put aside his hoe, and started for the porch at a normal walk. He collected Alex, and they had almost made it through the door of the house before a bullet struck the stone wall not two feet from Cuthan's head. They darted inside just as six hooded riders thundered into the clearing, firing wildly.

I held my breath, wondering if the troopers would obey orders not to open up until James blew his whistle or unless they were discovered and fired upon. The shutters were already drawn on the house windows, so those inside were in little danger provided they stayed low. Cuthan would see to that.

The six men rode back and forth in the yard firing handguns and raising a fearful racket but doing little damage. Within minutes after the assault began, we saw the other four raiders lugging a heavy keg up the back side of the hollow hill. The bastards wanted to make sure they had enough powder to bring the roof down. By the time they reached the crest, my finger was itchy.

"Are you going to do it, or am I?" I muttered in a low voice.

"I am. I don't want you involved. After all, they're militia."

"No, they're not. They're hooded killers. Don't give them a warning. Three of them will turn their guns on us and the other one will throw the powder down on the roof."

We heard the boom of a rifle. Cuthan was firing back. The four men on the hill crouched over the keg. One struck a Lucifer. Another held the fuse at the ready. In a moment, sparks flew as it caught fire.

James's whistle rang clear and sharp over the furious melee below. The raiders on the crest paused in confusion for a second. Then the man holding the keg of powder struggled to fling it down on the roof. James shot him through the torso. He dropped the dynamite as he fell. The other three raced down the hill, the keg rolling right behind them and gaining ground.

I didn't wait to see the outcome, I whirled and took a bead on the rider of the chestnut, who had turned to flee as soon as the troopers stepped from cover and fired rifles into the air. Hardcastle didn't even reach the tree line before my Henry barked. The bullet punched the murderous thug from his saddle. Apparently the nighthawk had been looking for him.

A huge explosion shook the ground, almost throwing me from my feet. I turned to see three raiders thrown aside by the blast of their own dynamite.

The remaining militiamen surrendered to the cavalry troopers except for one. A horseman who had remained in the shadow of the trees bolted the field without firing a shot.

James whistled for a sergeant's attention and sent him and two troopers after the disappearing rider. The man had too big a lead for them to catch him, but they'd track him back to his hidey-hole.

The soldiers collected the survivors, three injured and three unharmed. They all smelled of alcohol and fear. They piled Hardcastle and the other two dead raiders beside the survivors, and one by one, James unmasked them.

Abel Brown wasn't among the group. No surprise. He'd doubtless been the man who was desperately seeking to outrun the sergeant and his two troopers. I knew none of the other men except for one. Yanube City was going to need a new gunsmith. William Hawkes was among the dead.

CHAPTER 12

The raid on Teacher's Mead had been thwarted, but the after-clap brought mixed results. James's troopers tracked Abel Brown straight to his home. But the merchant denied everything, so Magistrate Gadsby refused to take action. Even the soldiers' testimony was not enough to move him. It made no matter that Gadsby was involved in the scheme, himself. The territorial governor supported his local man, and went even further, confirming Brown as the new head of the local militia. The rapscallion had bought himself a promotion to major for the price of a keg of black powder. The raiders captured by the soldiers were fined, sent home, and forgotten. The dead were quickly buried in near secrecy.

So far as I know, Hiram Hardcastle's name was never again uttered in Yanube City. It was as if the white culture adopted the natives' name avoidance custom. No one wanted the ex-militia leader's *wah-nah gee*, his ghost, hanging around.

On the other hand, the plan to bring the stage to Yanube City was made public, which had the effect of exposing more attacks on Teacher's Mead for what they would be — naked greed. That provided a bit of cover for Cuthan and his family.

A half-hearted attempt was made to censure James, but when Lt. Mills and members of the Second Platoon of F Company related what they had witnessed, that effort withered away. Consequently, the protection James extended to me held greater potency because he had demonstrated a willingness to stand up to the excesses of the militia.

Although I kept a wary eye out, no one bothered me. Or perhaps I had it roundabout. No one bothered me because I kept a wary eye out. I came to understand Abel Brown was not a naturally industrious man and led very few militia patrols in the territory. He was more disposed to send others, and those men often found a good spot to catnap the day away before returning to report everything as peaceful. A slothful way to collect a day's pay, but infinitely better for me and other Indians than Hardcastle's method of conducting business.

Summer faded into fall with the appearance of the Comanche Moon. I labored alone — except for the occasional help James provided on his infrequent visits — and managed to complete the house before the bitter winter fell upon the countryside. To preserve as much of the forest as possible, I had limited harvesting wood for fuel to fallen trees and the remnants of sawn lumber used in the construction of the barn and farmhouse.

I'd bought a wagonload of peat brought down from Canada by a half-demented trader. One of Billy's books proclaimed it as a material high in carbon content that burned slowly at low temperatures. The fuel did not create roaring fires, but it lasted a long time, and a little dry wood tossed atop it provided extra heat when it was needed.

The small mound behind the farmhouse did not provide the same protection as the taller hollow hill at the Mead, but it was sufficient to blunt the blue northers that would soon blow in. The town's glazier had not yet finished the glass panes for the windows, so despite all of my caulking, the house was still drafty. I laid in stores and made pemmican and jerky to augment my diet over the winter, so I was prepared for the coming weather.

I had much of Billy's library with me to provide diversion during the dreary daylight hours and a snug bed for the nighttime darkness. Patch and the mare were comfortable in the barn with enough fodder in the loft to sustain them until spring. I was as content as any man preparing for prolonged isolation from human contact could be.

The first snow, which was not really a full-throated storm, brought wolves howling down from the north. The lonely cry of the beasts took me back to my first winter at the Mead with Billy. He and Cut Hand had divorced, and Billy's short marriage to Lone Eagle had ended as well, terminated by the young warrior's need to propagate his line. Then came Billy's time with Cut Hand's sister, Butterfly. My resentment of that union died when a serpent struck her while she was heavily pregnant.

That year, I had finally mustered the temerity to insist on remaining at the Mead with Billy instead of traveling south to winter quarters with the band. He had objected, but his heart wasn't in the protest. I grew erect remembering the night I had shocked him by crawling into his bed. But it had been good, and we remained together for over twenty years. The wolves had howled that winter, too, but I'd had my beloved for companionship and comfort.

I was preparing to take to my blankets the night the first weather moved in when I heard someone in the yard. Surprised to find James dismounting from his horse, I rushed outside and helped prepare a stall in the barn for the big animal. Then we lugged the heavy packs he had brought into the house and closed the door against the chill.

"Snow's not too bad yet," he said. "I'll have to head back tomorrow, but I needed you one more time before the winter keeps us apart. Let me thaw out from the ride a little, and then I want you to thrum me within an inch of my life."

"I will do my best."

"That is always enough." James looked around and nodded approvingly. "You've done a good job on the house." He indicated the canvas-bound packs we'd brought inside. "I have the panes of glass the glazier threw for the windows."

"I'll install them tomorrow. The fireplace won't require as much fuel once they're in place."

James warmed his hands before the fire. "Have you had any more trouble?"

"Nay. Everything's quiet. And you?"

"I'll likely not get another promotion before resigning my commission, but that's not important."

"What is the news of the war?"

James stared into the dancing flames. "It continues to go back and forth, but I believe Grant's strategy is working. Admiral Farragut sealed Mobile Bay, one of the rebel's last ports. Atlanta fell on the second of September, and President Lincoln was reelected earlier this month."

I knew James was stalling, but I waited him out. Finally, he turned around to face me.

"There's been another massacre. I don't know if it will stir up the tribes or if it will finally break them."

"What happened?"

"A Colorado Militia Colonel named John Chivington attacked a camp of Cheyenne and Arapahoe at Sand Crick, a place where the Indians had permission to camp, by the way. Most of the men were out hunting, but Chivington attacked even though Chief Black Kettle was flying the American flag over his lodge. Word is they wiped out somewhere between 200 and 400 non-combatants: women and children and old men. And Chivington's a Methodist minister, for God's sake."

So Jeremiah Berglund wasn't the only man of God who rode with killers. My stomach fell away as another such murderous raid leapt to mind. "Wiping out the Yanube at Hampton's Homestead wasn't the first disaster, and slaughtering Cheyenne and Arapaho women and children at Sand Crick won't be the last."

"I'm afraid this news, when it becomes widely known, may embolden our own militia. Abel Brown's been a passive commander since he took over. Got the bejesus scared out of him at Teacher's Mead, I suspect. Caleb was outraged over the whole affair and threw him out of the business."

"Good for the old man," I said.

"Chivington's move may put some bone in Abel's spine."

"We'll have to be more careful. At least, the winter will give us a respite."

"It's outrageous that none of the Mead's raiders ever faced justice. And worse, Gadsby still sits in his chair." James walked over to me. "Make me forget all of this madness."

I pulled down his suspenders and stripped him of his uniform. Then, for the first time, I lowered my head to his groin and drew the rising staff into my mouth. The image of a Sioux warrior named Dull Lance, teased my mind briefly.

"Otter," James sounded shocked. "Oh, Otter."

Dismissing my momentary distraction, I pushed him down onto the bed, removed my clothing, and knelt over him. We kissed deeply before I left a wet track with my tongue down his torso. I traced the thin line of blond hair from navel to bush, tugged at the pale yellow curls, and once again slipped my mouth over his engorged cock.

"You don't know how much I love you." His voice choked up. "I don't have the ability to describe how deeply I feel for you. I ... oh ... I think of you all the time." He wrapped his legs around my waist and began moving his hips, throwing himself forward each time I went down on him. Soon, he let out a throaty gasp and shuddered through an orgasm.

I stayed with him until it was past. As I came up to study the handsome man beneath me, I made a decision, a commitment. "After all this time, I can honestly say I love you."

"I wondered if I would ever hear those words. And if they'd be sincere when they came. After what you just did for me, I believe they are true."

"I came to it slowly, but I have arrived. Now if the world will leave us alone, we can go about making one another content."

"This war. This terrible, miserable war! Won't it ever end?"

I rested my head on his broad chest. "It will end when its time comes."

#####

During my long association with Americans, I had fallen into the habit of marking the high holiday of Christmas. I admired and revered the Christ of the Holy Bible as a true and Godly man whose teachings were worthy of study. I even accepted the tales of miracles and the wonderment of His Resurrection. Many native tribes ascribed to myths that abound with supernatural beings dying and reappearing again. Did not our dead walk the Western Road? To walk, a man must have form, and to have form after death was resurrection or something akin to it.

Soon thereafter, the Moon of Middle Winter gave way to the Moon of Hard Winter — or as the Americans termed it, December passed into January — and in my solitary estate, I observed the dawn of the first day of the year called 1865 by the whites. This was said to be an auspicious day, one that set the tone for the New Year. Would it see the end of the war back east? I prayed so.

I donned snowshoes I'd made earlier that winter and ventured outside into a world that was white from horizon to horizon. The irony of this did not escape me. Upon careful examination, the snow held shades of blue and yellow and even green where it crested in thin, wind-driven waves. It was as if nature mimicked the Caucasian race — white but with an amazing range of hues.

I no longer needed steps to access my porch; the snow had risen to the level of the veranda. I forked fodder for Patch and the mare and mucked out the place to the extent possible, given the freezing temperature outside. It was important that the animals had a clean and snug accommodation, such as I enjoyed.

After discovering the long burning potential of peat, I had rigged a rude stove that kept the inside of the commodious barn above the freezing point. Even so, every morning I broke a skim of ice on the animals' water tubs. This morning, I threw a rope halter on Patch and climbed aboard his bare back to give him a little exercise. The pony seemed to enjoy fighting snow banks to reach the crick. His breath was labored within the first hundred yards beyond the stream, so I turned back. The return was easier since the pony followed his own path through the snow.

Once I had exercised both animals, I brushed their damp coats until they were dry, speaking to them as if they were cognizant human beings. I had just finished lamenting the duration of the war, when I sensed movement behind me. I whirled with knife in hand to find a tall, blanket clad figure swaying in the doorway.

101

CHAPTER 13

"I see you, River Otter."

I peered at the indistinct, backlit figure. "Dull Lance?"

"Aye." The warrior gave a shaky openhanded salute and moved into the building.

"I am surprised to see you. I thought you and your band had returned home, or at least moved to a winter camp to the south."

"Would that we had." His breath sounded labored.

"Are you in trouble?"

"Aye. My men are all dead, along with the two women who came to join us."

"Come into the house where it is warmer and tell me what happened."

Dull Lance staggered as he turned, but I resisted the impulse to lend a hand. This was a proud Sioux warrior in the prime of life who would not appreciate unwanted assistance. I judged him only about two or three years older than my forty-three snows.

Once inside, I seated the near-frozen man at the table in my eating room and built up the blaze in the fireplace. Only then did Lance open the blanket to reveal a bloody wound to his side. I forgot my reservations and leapt to my feet.

"You're hurt."

"Bullet. Passed through. I will survive."

"Likely the bullet, but perhaps not the infection. Will you permit me to treat you?"

When he nodded assent, I retrieved Billy's Pandora's box, a parfleche filled with medicines and herbs. I spread rags as blotters against the blood, put him on the bed, and stripped his shirt away. Although the inside of the cabin was growing warn, he still shivered. The bullet had gone completely through his side without striking any vital organs, although Lance would probably piss blood for a while.

I cleansed the wound with warm water, washed away the dirt, and stuffed it with a powder made from comfrey, yarrow, and goldenseal. These would aid in closing the wound, controlling bleeding, and possibly inhibiting infection. Then I smeared the entry and exit points with honey to seal against infection. After that, I bound the injury tightly and covered his shivering frame.

"That's the best I can do. The doctor in town can probably help more."

"No. No American doctor."

"The binding must be changed daily or your injury will get infected. Might already be infected. You need a proper medical man."

He dismissed the idea with some feeble teasing. "If I felt better, I might try it with a win-tay."

His words were meaningless; he was in no shape to act on them. Nonetheless, it struck such a chord that I responded to his banter sharply. "If you felt better, I might have to get my skinning knife. I have not been a win-tay for a long time. Besides, you're a Dakota. They don't countenance that kind of thing."

Lance shrugged the blanket from his torso. His aureoles were dark, almost black. His flesh was dusky and firm. He gave a weak smile. "Perhaps I've lived around the Lakota too long."

"Stop talking nonsense and tell me what happened. How did you come by this injury?"

"My men and I — there were four of us plus two of our wives — found a cave up on Trickling Water and decided to winter there. Bears do it, so why not Sioux?" He laughed, bringing a grunt of pain. "We spent the fall stocking it with firewood and hauling in stores. It was not bad."

"What put an end to it?"

"Militia. We were out hunting. Afoot. Each went his own way. The hunting was hard this deep into the winter, so this was the best way to do it. I went upstream toward the badlands, but long before I got there, I heard gunshots and thought my companions had made kills and were celebrating or signaling. There was no cause for alarm because the white men were all bundled up and sitting in their houses staying warm."

There was bitterness in his tone. "I had no rackets for walking in the snow, so I was slow to return. The gunfire had stopped before I arrived. But I was wrong. I was careless and blundered into a bunch of militia. One of them saw me and got off a shot. It caught me in the side and knocked me over. They came for me, but I still had my rifle. I killed one of them, and the others ran off."

I shook my head. "Why would they be patrolling this time of year?"

"They must have trailed one of my men. He managed to make it to the town south of here and stole a calf. But that was several suns ago."

Someone, perhaps the farmer who lost the calf must have followed the thief's tracks far enough to guess it was the Sioux camped on the Trickling water who took his animal. The militia waited for a snowsquall to pass before riding out for an ambush.

Lance had struggled to his feet after being shot and staggered to the cavern. He found the women dead, killed with their cooking pots in hand. The other men had come running — just as he had — and were slain as they arrived. He must have been the only one to raise a rifle to the killers. When one of their own had been hit, the raiders didn't bother to look for Lance. They merely took all of the horses, leaving him to die alone on the frozen prairie.

"Can you identify any of them?"

"Nay. All white men look alike to me save those who've been scalped."

"Bald, you mean?"

"Aye, the hairless-headed men."

"Well, you're safe for the moment. I have some stew at the back of the stove. You must eat some fat to replace the blood you lost."

"This is the Yellow Leaf Officer's house?"

"Yes, but don't let that concern you. He won't be back here for two moons or more."

"Won't he lead a column to track me and make sure I'm dead?"

"No. The army doesn't murder innocents." Even as I voiced the thought, I remembered the slaughter of my people by a renegade captain of Dragoons. "Not under this commander, anyway. The major is a decent man. You can remain here until you regain your health."

"In his house? Won't that cause you trouble?"

"Not even if he should find you here."

"This is not like any army man I know. I will sleep in your barn."

"It is warmer and more comfortable in the house. Besides, I'll need to change your bandages regularly."

I fixed a bed of blankets in a corner of the kitchen near the cooking stove Timo had made for me before winter set in. Although it was yet morning, Lance's ordeal had left him weak and exhausted. After eating a tin of stew, he took to the pallet. His slumber was fitful, no doubt troubled by thoughts of his slain companions. Satisfied he was truly asleep, I left the house.

The sun turned the glistening landscape into a blinding blur, but did little else except put a hard crust atop the snow. I daubed soot from the outhouse stove above and beneath my eyes as protection against the glare and led my pony outside.

"White Patch, my friend." I draped the pinto's back with a large blanket and strapped on a white man's saddle. "We have a way to go. So show me your pluck." I barred the outhouse door before circling the hill and turning north.

Even though the snowfall was not yet as deep as it would likely get before the spring thaw, it was a miracle Dull Lance had reached the farm. I guided the pinto through the meandering, unsteady tracks the wounded man had left, both to make it easier on the pony and to obscure Lance's trail. Whenever I occasioned upon traces of blood, I obliterated them.

It was well into the afternoon before Patch covered the ten miles to Trickling Water, but that did not worry me unduly. The return would be easier as the trail was already broken.

I put my knife hilt through the ice and allowed Patch to take water and blow. Mountains of clouds the color of my rifle barrel were building over the western horizon and would soon obscure the sun. Noises on the other bank brought my mind back to the task at hand. The wolves were working on the bodies sprawled at the entrance to the cavern. Three rifle shots in the air finally frightened the stubborn, starving brutes into a short retreat. The *shuen-man-nee-due-dhan-kah* was a medicine animal, and I would not kill one unless Patch or I was threatened.

With one eye on the lurking animals lest they attempt to get to the pinto, I took a quick look around. The story was clearly laid out in the tracks. The militiamen had come from the southeast, apparently on the trail of one of the women. After killing the two females, they slaughtered the Sioux warriors as each rushed back to the cave. I dragged the mutilated bodies as deep into the cave as possible. There was no protection available for the corpses beyond collapsing the snow overhang to seal the entrance. Perhaps it would be sufficient to prevent the odor of rotting flesh from reaching hungry predators still hovering nearby, but I doubted it. I sang some of the old prayers beseeching the All Powerful to protect these men and women as they traveled the Western Road.

Satisfied I had done all I could, I retrieved Dull Lance's rifle where he had dropped it and headed back to the farmhouse. As Patch struggled over the trail he had broken earlier, I wondered if the effort was worth the cost. I owed the Sioux nothing, yet they were cousins of the blood as well as fierce and mighty warriors. They deserved my respect. As a more practical matter, nothing was now left to show a wounded man had made his way to the farm. That alone was worth the effort.

When I finally reached home, I spent an hour rubbing down Patch, allowing him to drink from the water tub and giving him extra rations. When I went inside, Lance still slept. I dried and oiled his rifle before leaning it against a corner wall. Then I got out of my wet clothes to wash away the sweat and dirt of my labors. Finished, I turned to find him watching from his blankets.

"You are a handsome man, Otter."

"Hah, I might believe you had some interest if you weren't a Dakota." I covered my nakedness with a blanket before he saw I was reacting to him.

"Maybe there's some Lakota blood running through my veins."

I was beginning to think he was serious and not merely toying with me. If so, this would be either a contentious winter or an interesting one. I thought of my declaration to James and decided to put an end to it.

"If you keep this up, you will sleep in the barn. I told you, I have not been a win-tay for many, many snows."

The question in his eyes remained unspoken, so I gave no answer. To reveal my relationship with James might pose a danger, although I wasn't exactly sure how. A Lakota wouldn't give it a cross thought, but a Dakota? There was no need to cede Dull Lance an advantage, however slight. I distracted the man by retrieving his rifle and handing it to him.

Lance's face lit up as he accepted the weapon. "You went to Trickling Water?"

"Aye. Those-who-were-there required some dignity. I put them in the cave and collapsed the snow over them. It is scant protection, yet it was all I could do for your people."

"I am in your debt forever."

"Then there was the other matter. Your trail that once led straight to my door doesn't exist any longer. I rode through it both coming and going. There is nothing to link you to the farm."

"They will see your tracks."

"Perhaps, but I am not a stranger with a wound in his side. Do not worry. I can handle myself." I slipped on a pair of trousers and pulled a shirt over my head. "There was a storm moving in from the west as I returned home. We'll have no visitors for quite a spell."

# # # # #

I had not set in stores with an extra hungry mouth in mind, so I cut back on my rations in order that Lance could feast on fat and regain his strength. He was no fonder of being shut in than I was. As quickly as he was able, he accompanied me outside to care for the animals. That suited me perfectly; he was less dangerous outside the cabin than inside.

I needed to deal with this growing list for the warrior before it got out of hand. I could not hide my occasional erections forever. Before disaster overtook me, I stumbled upon two ways of dealing with my rising lust. Each time I felt moved by his presence, I called up an image of James. The trust and loyalty my mate accorded me proved sufficient for me to retain control over my baser instincts.

I also encouraged him to talk about growing up in his father's *tiospaye* and his life as a warrior. I was astounded at the nostalgia − and yes, envy − his word pictures engendered. News of the Yanube survivors who had taken refuge in Stone Knife's camp brought me closer to my childhood. I tried not to take pleasure in the dislike Morning Mist had engendered in her adopted home. After all, had she not been so spiteful, Billy might not have divorced Cut Hand, and I wouldn't have had two decades with my beloved. Even so, I was human enough to take satisfaction in learning she was hateful to all, not just to Billy. It was hard to reconcile the pleasant-natured Dog Fox − Cuthan − with so vile a dam. Yet, anytime a sense of being cheated out of my heritage rose up, I recalled my years with Cut Hand and Billy and Lone Eagle … and James. Was that not a life rich enough for any man?

Dull Lance recovered from his injury rapidly. He broke open the scab protecting the healing wound more than once during his attempts to help with chores, but he did not seem to suffer from the events. Whether due to my ministrations or his natural resistance, he was successful in holding infection at bay.

The regular routine of changing the bandages necessitated intimacies between us, and more than once, I was compelled to hide my flesh's response when touching his naked skin. I was not always successful; nonetheless, Lance's efforts to pursue closer contact remained half-hearted and playful, although consistent.

I had been dreading spending the long winter months alone, so a kinship − quite apart from lust − quickly built between us. One evening as we spoke in the dark of the warm cabin, Lance revealed more of his history than he had perhaps intended. He spoke of riding with Inkpaduta.

"I thought you were in the Laramie country."

"I was. But after Stone Knife's *tiospaye* dispersed, I wandered."

That was not surprising. By nature, the Sioux were nomadic. I wondered why Dull Lance had not assumed the responsibility of holding his father's band together, but decided against pursuing the question. Instead I asked about Red Cap. "What sort of man is he?"

"Hard. He lives hard. He hates hard. And he fights hard."

"Some consider him little more than an outlaw leading a band of thieves."

Dull Lance shrugged. "That is what he thought of all the whites he ever encountered. One man's outlaw is another man's hero. He is a man with scars — both on the outside and the inside. The white man's spotted pox scarred his face as a child, but he survived the disease. After his father was killed, his brother became chief of the band. During the Hard Winter, they were starving and begging for food."

The Hard Winter was the winter of 1856-57.

Dull Lance told how a drunken whiskey dealer had murdered Red Cap's family and displayed his slain brother's head on a stake. His people were not treaty Indians, so there was no annuity for them. When a member of his band shot a dog that had bitten one of the People, the whites took away their guns and left them no way to hunt. After that, Inkpaduta began harassing the settlements.

From what I had heard, Red Cap's search for vengeance had started long before that. But let Dull Lance have his truth as he would. It made no matter now.

The Sioux paused, remembering. "Big Mound was not so bad. People were talking peace when one of the braves killed a medical man, and the battle began. The soldiers chased us away, but there was not much loss of life. A Star Chief called Sibley came after us. We fought again at Dead Buffalo Lake. That one was worse. We retreated again, but it still wasn't too bad.

"White Stone Hill was where another Star Chief named Sully whipped us. He killed half of us with his rifles and big thunder guns. We lost everything, but some of us got away. Many of the women and children were taken. My wife and son were among them. I never saw them again. I don't know if they are dead or alive."

I now understood the source of Dull Lance's anxiety over the whites. I had once stood at the same juncture until I learned to discern the culpable from the innocent. He had not yet taken that difficult step.

# # # # #

Every time I picked up a book, Lance watched me closely. When he asked if it was hard to understand the white man's scratches on paper, I offered to teach him to read and write. He refused until the ennui became so great he was accepting of any diversion. Lance was not a slothful man by nature.

I found a sheltered spot where I could dig out some crick sand. When it was dried sufficiently, I carefully printed the English alphabet on a scrap of ledger paper, and handed Lance a square of wood covered with sand. As I had done when I was a child, Lance practiced writing the letters with his finger in the sand until he was adept at the exercise. Then I taught him to sound out the letters and combine them into words.

It was good to be teaching again, even if my student was older and not as eager to learn as Cuthan and his children had been. Or Lucas and Matthew.

As Lance grew stronger, I took advantage of a few clear, calm days to set about a major chore well before the Goose Moon foretold a thaw. I had carefully measured Turtle Crick's high water marks and knew the brook would be impassable during the spring runoff. Conversely, the crick would never be at a lower run than during the frozen months. It was a perfect time to begin construction of a bridge. Lance and I studied the situation and checked pictures and descriptions of spans in one of my books before sacrificing some timber on the backside of the hill behind the house.

Although they were not large trees — so far as girth went — the task required the aid of both Patch and the mare to drag them through the deep snow to streamside. We almost froze — both feet and hands — while sinking the pilings, but we accomplished the task before another storm drove us back inside the house.

In fits and starts, we worked on the bridge whenever cabin fever drove us outside. In the height of winter, wolves began hovering close to the cabin, maddened by the smell of the horses safely locked in the outhouse and the scent of two humans in the area. We took to carrying our weapons when venturing outside.

Advantaging a few good days sprinkled among the bad, we finished the bridge before the first Chinook blew fresh, warm air over the north hill, thawing the icicles hanging from the cabin's eaves. I reckoned James would make a visit soon, so I decided to go hunting for green meat.

There was little game in the area. It had been nearly hunted out some years ago, but sometimes the winter drove moose or elk or even deer down from the frozen Canadian territories. We slogged our way over the hill behind the house on snowshoes and kept to the thin line of trees that eventually led to the glade where Helen had set up her camp. The memory of the two buried there was so powerful I almost believed their ghosts haunted me — especially the shade of Lucas. I missed him acutely, and that brought thoughts of Matthew, safe some fifty miles to the east with Cuthan's family at the Mead.

Lance and I hunted together because of the danger from starving wolves. The animals were a problem as the winter stretched out its frigid touch. We encountered nothing except some of the carnivores for the first two days, but our patience was rewarded on the third. We surprised an antelope and brought it down with a single shot. As we made our way toward the fallen animal, three rangy, four-legged brutes raced from the trees on a line for the carcass. Lance shouted a warning and shuffled toward the antelope. The wolves reached it first and turned to protect their claim.

Firing over their heads failed to discourage the beasts, so Lance darted at them, swinging his gunstock as a club. The largest animal, the dominant male, evaded his blows and lunged. A bullet from my Henry pierced the wolf through the heart as he leapt. The beast crashed into Lance, bowling him over. The other two made a run for him, but my shots frightened them into retreating a distance. Yet, they smelled blood and weren't about to leave without a share of the spoils. We gave them their fallen comrade. We were not yet out of sight before the beasts began ripping their dead leader apart.

The trip back to the house took a physical toll on both of us. The added weight of the antelope's carcass drove our snowshoes deeper into the crusted snow. We were exhausted by the time the animal was gutted and hung in the barn to dry. I locked the outhouse securely in case the rest of the wolf pack followed the blood trail back to the farm. After we cleaned ourselves with water heated in metal pots, we settled down, me to my reading and Lance to laboring over the alphabet to compose simple words in English. We retired early that night.

The next day, we butchered the antelope and hung parts of the animal in a small, enclosed room in the barn used for cold storage of meats and vegetables. I had not yet figured out what to use during the warm months of the year. I wished for the cool cavern of the hollow hill behind Teacher's Mead, but there was no such natural accommodation available at this farm. I would likely need to dig a cellar, a task I did not relish. Simply digging the pan of the house and sinking my well had required extraordinary effort.

After finishing with the antelope carcass, we limbered up the two horses. The snow had long since been packed down in the exercise area, but Patch was frisky and seemed anxious to tackle the fresh powder that had fallen during the night. I urged him over the new bridge and out onto the plains. The mare was not so adventurous; Lance kept her near the south bank. Patch plowed through the drifts until he tired.

As we re-crossed the new bridge on the way to the barn, Dull Lance pulled the mare to a halt and shaded his eyes. "Soldiers are coming," he said. "I will leave."

CHAPTER 14

Dull Lance had good eyes. I could make out only a distant line of riders approaching from the south.

"Go to the barn and start rubbing down the horses. Stay out of sight and let me handle the soldiers. They're likely out on patrol and checking to see I'm all right."

We led the horses into the outhouse, and I had almost finished wiping down Patch before I heard the thump of hooves on the bridge. One horseman.

I nodded reassuringly to Lance, went outside, and was pleased to see James riding into the yard. His big cavalry mount blew steam through his nostrils after struggling through the snow. The rest of a squad-sized patrol had turned and was passing the farmhouse on the east.

"This is a surprise," I said.

"No more than the new bridge. I've been thinking about one, but decided to wait until my retirement. You've accomplished much."

Aware he had intimacy on his mind, I held up my hand. "I had help. We have a guest."

He frowned. "Who?"

"Dull Lance, one of the Sioux from up on Trickling Water. They were ambushed and wiped out by the militia at the beginning of snowfall. He was wounded but managed to get to the farm. I sheltered him here for the winter."

James turned and gave a loud whistle. The officer leading the troop through the snow pulled up and looked in our direction. James waved him forward.

"That is where they were headed," he said to me. "Major Brown reported an attack by hostiles with the loss of one man, but weather set in, and this was the earliest we could mount a patrol."

The lieutenant James had summoned was halfway to the bridge.

"I went up there," I said quickly. "It was as Dull Lance said." I described what I had found, saying it confirmed the Sioux's story. "Even though he was wounded, he managed to make his way to the farm, and I tended him."

"I'll have to take him back and have him tell his story."

My pulse raced. "Then you condemn him to death. The magistrate is in their bag. You know that."

"You are sure of your interpretation of what happened?"

"I read signs very well."

"I know you do. I've summoned Simmons back, so I'll have to tell him something."

"I'll tell him about my visit to the site without mentioning Dull Lance. He's Stone Knife's son, by the way."

A thin young lieutenant with old eyes rode over the bridge and saluted from horseback. "Yes, sir?"

"My man here has visited the site. He can direct you to the spot and tell you what he found."

"Do you want me to accompany the patrol?" I asked.

"No, that won't be necessary. This is Lt. Edmund Simmons. Just tell him what you told me."

I explained what I had found and what I'd done at the site. There had been enough snowfall so my trail would have been covered, but I gave precise directions so the lieutenant could locate the spot without difficulty.

"Where is he?" James asked after Simmons returned to his command.

"In the outhouse."

Dull Lance stood in the middle of the barn glaring belligerently when we entered. I would have sworn one eye flashed dangerously while the other held a look of confusion. After introducing the two men, I stepped aside while the Sioux told James his story.

"Well, Otter, you've put me in a fine basket," he said at length. "The civil law is after this fellow, and here he is on my farm."

"The civil law sent you to find him?"

"Nay, they mentioned no survivor. But they reported the incident, and we were obliged to look into it."

"Then no one knows Dull Lance lives."

"There will be an accounting of bodies when Lt. Simmons returns from patrol."

"When he reaches the cave, there will be nothing to give him a count of the camp. Only the militia and the number of horses can do that. The killers stole the horses, and I'll warrant they have said nothing about the number of people they slaughtered."

"I will leave this place," Dull Lance said.

"How far will you get?" I was unaccountably alarmed at the sudden prospect of his leaving. What did that mean? "The thaw is near to setting in, but there's apt to be more weather before it arrives. You'll die out there."

"I will die in the white man's prison or on his gallows. If I am to die, I want to do it in a place of my choosing."

"No," I said. "You will stay here until the weather turns. Then you may take the mare and be on your way."

"Does the blue coat agree?"

We both turned to James.

"This is a risky thing you are proposing."

"Aye, but you know what the militia will do. They are determined to kill every blood between Ft. Ramson and Ft. Yanube. When this war ends, they may no longer have a free hand in the matter, so they're determined to accomplish the task before that end comes."

For half a lifetime, James had dealt with the Yanube and the Pipe Stem People. Lance was a Sioux, and James had a less firm idea of their value system. "Dull Lance, Otter and I are going into the house," he said at length. "There are things we must discuss. You remain here."

Lance merely grunted.

The door had no sooner closed than James put a hand to my shoulder. "Damnation. I rode out because I had need of you, not to deal with some renegade."

"He is no renegade. And I have need of you, as well." That was true enough, with all the temptation Dull Lance had provided, my staff demanded attention. "He will remain in the barn, so let's take care of our need."

James slipped his suspenders over his shoulders. I watched him disrobe before stripping naked.

"I dream of you like this," he said. "Your dark skin glowing by the fire."

Impatient with words, I moved forward to clasp him by the biceps. I pulled him forward until our bellies met. My member pulsed against his hard stomach.

"I ache for you every night." There was a note of desperation in his voice as he enfolded me in his arms. He crushed his lips to mine.

I cupped a buttock in each hand and tongued one nipple and then the other. It took no more than that to inflame him. James pulled us over onto the bed.

"Make love to me, Otter."

Despite the urgency of my need, I took my time, straddling his hips and moving the palms of my hands over his pale chest and belly. Then he pulled me up until the tip of my staff rested on his lips. I pressed forward until my cock disappeared into his mouth. We remained still and silent for a moment before I began hunching. His hands went crazy, exploring every part of me they could reach. I hadn't intended to ejaculate in this manner, but I'd been tempted almost beyond endurance for months, and I misjudged. Before I could withdraw and cool off, my nerves sent waves of small explosions throughout my body. I groaned as I erupted. When it was over, I rested a moment before rolling over onto the bed.

"That was magnificent." James whispered as if afraid words would shatter his memory of the experience. "I'm always amazed at how powerful you are."

"It is you. You coax everything I have out of me."

"Not everything, I hope. I still need a good flanking."

"I've enough strength for that. After a brief rest, that is."

"Not too long, I hope. The patrol will be returning before long. I figure it will take them about three hours of travel time."

"The snow's still deep up there, and then they'll have to dig the bodies out of the cave."

"Well, then, you can take the devil's own time and give me one to remember you by, as it were."

"Are you returning to the fort with them?"

"Aye. I told the lieutenant I wanted to check on your welfare and the state of my property. I'll have to go back with them."

"And Dull Lance?"

"I suppose he can stay on."

"With that decision made, I think mayhap I'm up for a round. One for you to remember me by."

I turned James on his belly, marveling at the white marble of my lover's flesh where it was hidden from the sun. Rampant and ready, I parted his buns and made a long, slow entry. He groaned in pleasure. After teasing him a bit, I got down to serious business. It pleased me when I could drive the sperm out of him without aid of hands or pillows or any other artifice. James always thought that amazing.

"Good Lord ... uh, what are you doing to me?"

"Giving you something to remember me by."

"Oh, harder. Deeper. You're a magnificent savage." He groaned. "Yes ... yes! Now. I'm coming now."

His spasming sphincter drove me over the edge as well. My cum spurted into him as he squirmed through his own ejaculation. Then I lay spread across his back as we fought to regain breath.

"Damnation, Otter," he finally gasped. "You sure you haven't been flanking that fellow out there in the barn? Seems you've learned a thing or two since we did this last."

Once I would have taken offense, but he'd struck closer to home than was comfortable. Besides, I recognized this was something more than teasing. He sought reassurance.

"Nay, there were no Sioux tricks in there. That was pure Yanube."

James reached back and touched my cheek. "How did I ever find you?"

After we rested sufficiently, we cleaned up and returned to the barn. James was declaring himself satisfied with the state of our household and expressing specific pleasure over the new bridge as we entered the barn. He looked a bit startled when we found Lance standing against one wall, a blanket around his shoulders. I'm sure he had hoped Lance took off during our absence.

I kept up the patter. "We still need to construct a cooling room for hanging meats and the like during the warm months. I can think of no other method than digging a cellar."

"Should I hire some men from town to assist?"

I shook my head. "No, I'll find my own help. Perhaps Dull Lance will lend a hand."

"Otter tells me you were of considerable help in constructing the bridge. Are you willing to help with the cellar, as well?

Lance pushed off from the wall. "I'm no good at scratching in the earth, but I can help … in payment of your aid."

"Good," James said. "Then it's settled. You are to remain out of sight here at the farm. I want to hear the lieutenant's report before I make a firm decision, but Otter has never led me astray. I expect what Simmons finds will support your claim. If so, I see no need to reveal your presence to anyone. Once the ground thaws, you help Otter dig his cellar. That will square things up, and you can be on your way."

Once again, Lance grunted.

His studied nonchalance brought blood rushing to my face. "This man has just delivered your life back into your hands. Remember this and be grateful."

CHAPTER 15

Lt. Simmons returned from Trickling Water to report he found what I had described. He expressed no suspicion a member of the doomed encampment had escaped. Dull Lance was safe for the moment.

After James's departure, I remained nettled at Lance's demeanor. He seemed to nurture an underlying resentment. Perhaps it was his dislike of being under a white man's thumb. I suspected he had not yet accepted the fact that life had changed. Like many, he dreamed of a time when the white tide was rolled back and these broad plains were once again delivered over to their rightful owners. Sadly, that would never happen.

Or perhaps it was something else entirely. He was a Dakota, so his sometimes playful and sometimes serious advances to me may have awakened carnal desires he believed exposed a weakness in him. One that I might seek to advantage.

Whatever the cause, he slowly descended into surliness. To counteract this, I required more help from him around the house. Mucking out the barn and caring for the animals became a routine task for him. He readily accepted working with the horses — that was man's work — but did not comprehend the necessity for cleaning out the waste. That was not an unreasonable attitude for a man whose culture had lived clean and relatively disease free for centuries by merely picking up from one place and moving to another when the landscape became polluted. Mother Earth was infinitely more efficient at cleansing her own breast than was man.

As winter further lessened its grip, Lance took it upon himself to do the hunting and trapping along the crick. By then, the wolves had followed wild game farther south. When deep thaw finally arrived, he bowed his back over the shovel to help dig my cellar without complaint, although I occasionally saw rebellion lurking behind his dark, restless eyes.

We devoted our evenings to rest and study. In time, I managed to assign my unstated attraction to him to its proper place, and our friendship strengthened. After Lance finished puzzling over his English lessons each evening, we would talk. Perhaps spurred by things he was learning, he began exhibiting a curiosity about the white man's way, especially the manner in which townspeople went about their lives. He asked more and more pointed question about how Americans thought and about how the white power system worked.

"If Major Morrow is the army chief, does he not command the militia that raided our camp and slew my companions?"

"Nay. At one time, the army's rule was supreme. Before the Americans were so numerous, there was no civilian authority in the territory. As they started establishing towns, they brought their civil laws along with them. Think on it like this. Among the Sioux, there is a war chief and a peace chief. There are clans and soldier societies and shamans. No one is supreme. When your father was misco of your band, if he did not lead wisely, his people were free to join another fire. Families came and went among the various bands."

I explained how the civil authorities gained ascendancy as the population in the area grew more numerous. The military was now tasked primarily with protecting the settlers from the tribes and putting down armed insurrection.

"I do not understand. If it was your Major's responsibility to protect the whites, why did the militia come for us?"

"You have heard me speak of this big war back east? It has drained away the strength of the army out here, so a militia was formed to do much of what the army once did. But they do not have the order and discipline of the military and are nothing but brigands seeking to drive every blood from the territory."

"Yet they leave you alone."

"Only because I am the hired hand of the army chief. That provides me some measure of protection. It also helps that I know many of the round bellies in town, although most are growing old and passing authority to younger men. Men I do not know well."

"Who is the leader in town? This place they call Yanube City."

"There is a mayor, a misco, selected by the people who live there, but he is of little consequence. The real power — outside of the military — rests with a man they call a magistrate, a judge named Julius Gadsby. Amos Brown, who holds the rank of major, commands the militia. It does his bidding."

"So this Major Brown sent those people after us. Is he a big man worthy of the power he holds?"

"Not particularly. Neither by character nor stature. He stands little taller than I do, but he is thick-bodied. Not fat, but what the Americans call stocky. He has hair the color of a rain cloud, and it bristles like spruce needles. I suspect he is no bigger on the inside than he is on the outside."

Lance grimaced at my description and picked up the book he was attempting to read. I recognized he hid behind the act while he mulled over what he had learned and tried to reconcile it with more familiar tribal customs.

# # # # #

The excavation work was nearly completed by the time James came for his next visit. He arrived alone this time, his pony clopping hollowly over the bridge spanning the brimming stream. Lance immediately retreated to the outhouse.

James dismounted and watched him disappear into the barn. "How did it go with that one?"

"It went well. He has not only earned his keep but has also started learning to read."

"Hmmm, I wouldn't have suspected him of that ambition."

"Nor I. But I am always glad when someone wants to learn. How long am I to have you this time?"

"I can stay over until tomorrow. Then I must return. I see your cellar is about dug."

"I'll start lining and covering it after you leave. Until then, I'll husband my strength for other activities."

"I'll have a word with Dull Lance before we go inside."

I trailed him into the barn where Lance was haltering the mare.

"I see you, Major," the Sioux said.

"And I see you, Dull Lance. You've recovered from your injury, I see."

"Aye. I am now fit enough to dig in the earth for Otter's cellar."

"Excellent. Where are you off to?"

"The horses have not been exercised today. I'll give them a workout."

"I intend to remain overnight this trip."

"Then I will sleep in the loft tonight."

Lance mounted the mare and reined her out through the big double doors. As we watched him go, James spoke.

"How do you know he won't keep right on going?"

"No matter. I intend to give him the mare when he leaves, so I'll suffer no loss. Come, let's go inside so you can bring me up to date on the war. It has ended, I hope."

"Nay, although Grant's strategy is working. The rebels captured Ft. Steadman in Virginia, but it was a Pyrrhic victory. They lost 4,000 men killed or captured. We're closing in on Richmond, the Confederate capital. I believe this year will see the end of the rebellion."

Once inside, I handed James a cup of strong coffee, and we settled down for a talk. For the first time since his resignation had been refused, he was considering putting in his papers again. As we spoke, the future of the farm began to take firmer form in my mind. When Lance returned with the mare and took Patch over the bridge for his exercise, we moved to the bed.

He preferred to undress me, taking time to touch and caress each bit of flesh as it was revealed. By the time I lay naked on the bed, I was throbbing with desire and endeavoring to purge images of Dull Lance from my mind. James stripped and sat astride my hips. Then he rose and impaled himself. He moaned as he sank down upon my rampant staff.

"Ahh. I have missed this so much. Sometimes it is almost unbearable being so far away from you." Making a spring of his folded legs, he bounced up and down as if to the beat of an unheard drum.

I gripped his cock loosely in my hand and allowed the motion of his body to masturbate him. Our self-denial soon caught up with us, and his movements became more rapid, more urgent.

"Oh … dear Lord, how I love you. How did this perfect thing come to be?"

I drew him down to me. "Don't tempt fate with foolish questions. Kiss me."

I began bucking up into him, increasing the tension, heightening the passion. Our release came almost in unison as we kissed. During the height of it, I rolled over so that I was on top and thudded harshly into his quivering channel.

Spent, we lay side by side, seeking to regain normal breath. After a few moments, James slept. I rose, cleansed us both, and covered his sleeping form before dressing and going to the barn where Lance was rubbing down the pinto. I felt myself flushing as I imagined he knew what I had been doing. He surprised me by asking about the war.

"The Major believes it will end this year."

"In victory for the blue coats? And then what happens?"

"It will take some time for things to settle down, but they will need to do something with their soldiers. More of them will likely come out here."

"What of the militia?"

"They may stand down, although I do not know that to be the case. There has never been a war like this one. Not for the Americans, at any rate."

"Too bad. That means they will stop killing one another." He paused. "Where is the Gold Leaf Chief?"

"He's resting."

As Lance led Patch to his stall, his manner led me to suspect something was amiss. I sought to reassure him. "When the major goes back to the fort, we will finish the cellar, and you will have fulfilled your bargain. You will be free to go."

He did not acknowledge my words.

# # # # #

Dull Lance and I resumed work as soon as James departed the next morning. Lance cut some small trees on the back side of the hill and used the mare to snake them down to the house. We stripped the branches away and used the logs to brace the sides of the underground room. Within the span of three suns, we had completed that task. It required two additional days to cover the entire structure with a thick layer of sod. Our last task was to hang a door.

I was pleased with our efforts. Not only would the interior maintain a cool, even temperature, it would serve as a shelter when *Wakinyan* battled *Iya* across the prairie. That was a Siouan interpretation of what the Americans called a tornado. By this time, the snowmelt had flooded the crick so that the bridge was no longer a convenience; it was a necessity.

"What will you do?" I was in an uncertain state of mind as we cleaned up after the final day of work.

"Go back to my people."

"You have no thought of remaining in this territory?" Did my question betray a hope?

"Why? Are there other bloods here?"

"A few." I reconsidered my answer. "Very few. Cuthan — Dog Fox — lives at Teacher's Mead, and there is one of your blood who works at the livery stable. But there are few others."

"That must be the livery stable man's camp I've seen north of town."

"His name is Bent Nose, but the Americans call him Ezekiel Pauley."

"Do they give everyone a foreign name?"

"Just about everyone."

Dull Lance shook his head. "There is nothing around here for me. I will head back to the Laramie country."

My heart lurched at his words, but surely it was the angst brought about by the departure of a treasured friend. To cover my reaction, I blurted the first thing that came to mind. "Is there a new wife awaiting you back there?" In all the long winter nights, we had never discussed Lance's family beyond old Stone Knife and the wife and child he had lost at White Stone Hill.

He glanced over my shoulder. "Nay. She lies in the cave on Trickling Water."

I was surprised at how deeply this Sioux buried his true self. Suddenly, he was a stranger again. The companion who had shared the house with me was gone, leaving this enigma standing before me. I had been battling hard to keep from asking him to tarry until warmer weather. Now I was less certain that would be wise. As we stood beside Turtle Crick, I told him when he left on the morrow, to do so on the back of the mare. She would carry him home faster.

"She is a good animal. Why have you given her no name?"

I stared into the rushing water. "I never name any ponies except my war horse. Today, that means my riding horse. I can give you no reason other than that."

"It is enough because it is your custom. Now she will become Long Legs."

"A good name."

# # # # #

Early the next morning, I offered Lance clothing and stores since he had arrived with none of his own. There was little of mine that would fit his larger frame, but I had some of Cut Hand's clothing stored away, and those better matched his size. He chose to dress in the old-fashioned way for his journey: fringed leather leg sheathes, called chaps by some, that reached to his loincloth; calf-high moccasins; and a buckskin shirt, once fancy but now worn. Many of the beads and dyed porcupine quills had fallen away, and the fringes were torn or missing.

As I watched him mark twin slashes on his cheeks with soot mixed in grease, I felt an unexpected tug in my chest. Was that tremor for this warrior … or for the warrior's life I had long ago forsaken but still missed? Or did it merely illustrate how deep the cleavage was between us? I had not decided the issue as we partook of a medicine smoke and sang prayers in preparation for his departure. We used a cob pipe since the Yanube's fine calinite calumet, one of the band's few remaining treasures, rested in a medicine bundle hidden in the hollow hill at Teacher's Mead.

I watched Dull Lance ride out of the farmyard before the sun cleared the eastern horizon in the belief an important part of my life had been wrenched away. He skirted the hill behind the house to travel north. Later, he would turn to the west. The journey back to the Laramie country was a long one. Even as my heart struggled in my breast, I wished him well, despite his strange turn of character. And my own had changed, as well, I suppose. Heretofore content to remain committed to my life mate, only now did I realize the depth of the struggle I'd waged to keep from succumbing to the Sioux's powerful lure.

Although being alone did not usually bother me, Lance's departure left the cabin empty. Patch was already jumpy. He missed the company of the mare.

Tomorrow, I would take some of my silver pieces and purchase another animal to give him companionship. That was practical, as well. We needed a draft animal on the farm. Perhaps I would even take a small gold coin and see if I could begin to make this look like a real farm, one with a cow and chickens. That thought turned my mind to the prairie wolf. Those sly coyotes would snatch hens faster than I could buy them. Best rig up a means of defense against the beasts before donating a rooster and a brood of hens to them.

I spent the rest of the day transferring my available foodstuffs to the cellar, affixing a sturdy stock lock to the door, and then marking off the dimensions of the field I intended to plant when one of Mr. Deere's iron-bladed plows arrived. I resolved to check on its delivery tomorrow while I was in town.

I thought I knew every book in the library Billy had collected over the years, but I discovered an unread tome ascribed to Plato holding forth on Socratic logic and ethics. It was interesting enough to consume the evening.

# # # # #

As I made my way toward Yanube City the next morning, smoke off to the west caught my attention. Upon investigation, I discovered the smoldering remnants of a tipi. Bent Nose's camp. Tracks told of at least four shod horses milling around the place. Militia probably; however, the fact the horses wore shoes meant little. Many of the tribesmen now rode mounts with iron-covered hooves. A considerable amount of blood made me fear for old Bent Nose's state of health.

125

Changing my plans, I rode for the fort instead of the livery stable. I had to wait for a meeting to break up before seeing James to relate what I had seen.

He grimaced. "That's what the meeting was about. Bent Nose gunned down Amos Brown and Patrick Pauley. Killed both of them. He got away, but the militia rode after him and killed him in a shootout. His body's on display over on Main Avenue."

I looked out the window of the office. "Bent Nose did not shoot the man he worked for, much less Major Brown. He did not even own a gun."

"He got one somewhere. It happened right in Pauley's livery stable."

"Was there a witness to the shooting?"

"Several. Brown was sending the militia out on patrol and had gathered them at the stable."

"Did anyone actually see Bent Nose doing the shooting?"

"No, but the shots came through the window near where he was unloading feed from a wagon. Not only that, he ran away."

"He ran for his life. He knew he'd be the first one they accused." I paused before asking the next question. "Was anyone with him?"

"No, why?"

I sighed and examined the top of his desk as I spoke the suspicion that had been building in my mind. "Dull Lance left yesterday morning for the Laramie country. He'd been asking questions about the militia. He wanted to know who the leader was and what he looked like. He holds Brown responsible for the attack on his camp. One of the women killed there was his wife. I also told him Bent Nose worked at the livery."

"Damnation! I'm sorry, Otter, but I must report what you've told me to the civil authorities."

"I told you this knowing what you must do." The pain in my breast was almost physical.

"Excuse me, I have to send a messenger to the magistrate and mount a patrol to go look for Dull Lance. I'll not relate the fact you ... *we* harbored the renegade for the winter. I will merely state you saw him and came to report the sighting." He paused. "How do you know he won't betray us when he's caught?"

"You won't catch him. Not alive at any rate. Do you want me to go with the troopers?"

"That would be too much to ask. Thank you for the information. Why did you come to town, by the way?"

"To buy a replacement for the mare. I gave her to Dull Lance, as promised. I also wanted to check on the plow and perhaps buy a cow."

"The plow arrived yesterday. You can pick it up at the freight office." James hesitated. "Otter, be careful. The town believes an Indian assassinated two officers of the militia without provocation. They'll be edgy."

"I will buy a horse and a cow another day. Anyone at the livery is apt to be a bit touchy. But old man Petrov at the freight office has known me for years, so I will go pick up the plow."

"All right. I've ordered the seed you wanted at the feed store. You ought to be able to get that, as well. But be careful."

I left the fort and entered a town that had not even existed in my childhood. I had seen it take root and grow. Now the hostility around me pressed like green rawhide across my shoulders.

CHAPTER 16

Petrov, the freighter, did not regard me through unfriendly eyes; he simply did not look at me at all. Usually bluff and forthright, the burly Russian shifted his gaze restlessly. I had long ago grown accustomed to the American way of staring directly at a man, a trait once considered rude. Now I found the lack of direct scrutiny disturbing. He was *koh-kee-pay*, afraid of me.

Despite the coolness of the greeting, I was forced to tarry while I mulled over what to do with a plow too heavy and bulky to drape across Patch's back. As I cast around for poles to make a pony drag, Petrov admitted he had some extra animals and a buckboard he was willing to sell. The atmosphere thawed slightly as I bargained for the items. We reached a deal when he agreed to throw in harness for the wagon. I loaded my plow in the buckboard and headed to the feed store with two new horses: a sorrel that looked as if he might make a decent riding horse, and a good, solid black mare. The black, a plodder, drew the buckboard. I tied Patch and the sorrel to the rear of the wagon.

My reception was just as cool at the feed store. The heavy-bellied clerk stirred himself sufficiently — although reluctantly — to hand over the seed Major Morrow had ordered and accept payment in silver without comment.

On the way home, I reined in the black when I came across signs of a column of men. James's patrol, no doubt. The trail led north a distance, and then cut west to pass Bent Nose's ruined camp. From there, he would head northwest with the main body while sending scouts to his flanks to search for the spoor of a rider. The two scouts who usually accompanied his patrols were Absaroka from the Yellowstone country. They had a long history of conflict with the Sioux.

I urged the black forward, battling mixed emotions. I doubted the patrol would catch Dull Lance, and for that I was glad. But did not Bent Nose deserve justice? Had Lance involved the old Indian in his scheme or merely taken advantage of him to gain information and access?

I reached the farm without incident and rumbled over the bridge — the first wagon to do so. After dismounting, I examined the area around the house and barn carefully. Satisfied neither Dull Lance nor any other intruder had been around, I untied Patch and the sorrel from the rear of the buckboard, freed the black from her traces, and wiped down the animals before feeding them. I was pleased with my bargain. The horses seemed sound, and the wagon would come in handy around the farm.

My thoughts drifted back to another buckboard and the body buried beneath it in a deep pool in the Yanube. Neither had been discovered, but one day something might yet surface. Dark deeds had a way of coming into focus at awkward and unexpected times.

Later in the day, a clutch of mounted riders passed well to the east as if on the way to Trickling Water. Militia, most likely. When I retreated to the house as darkness stole in on silent moccasins, my ears remained alert for noises. Somewhere inside me, I believe I hoped Lance would seek asylum with me while the army and the militia searched for him. To give him haven would be impossible, of course, but I might be cajoled into joining him in his flight.

Neither the sorrel nor the black was trained in the use of the plow, making me wish for someone to lead them until one or the other was accustomed to the drag of the heavy implement. The first furrows took on the undulations of the Comanche snake sign, filling me with equal measures of disgust and shame. It wasn't until the third day I achieved a straight row, but the black finally seemed to have the knack of the thing and obeyed the reins. I turned the sod again on the entire plot, straightening things out to my satisfaction.

Some likened prairie sod to the mortar used on buildings because of its stubborn hardness and tendency to clot. By the end of each day, both the mare and I were exhausted. The horse could be dried and curried and put away to feed, but my workday was not yet finished. I had to clean up, prepare food for myself, and plan the next day's work before taking to bed.

My reading and studying suffered. There were nights when I did not so much as crack the covers of a book. I chafed at the regimen, but there was no respite because of the late arrival of the plow. The seeds should have been sown by now with tiny green shoots already thrusting through the broken earth. Nonetheless, I was grateful the pace of my life prevented me from doting on thoughts of Dull Lance. Those phantoms were reserved for the dark of night when I was alone and desperate for sleep.

I planted the first forty acres before breaking ground on the second. I would be lucky to get the new plot ready in time to plant a short crop, the best I could do this season. The yield would be meager. Still, the harvest would sustain us for at least a portion of the year. I put in corn and beans and potatoes and a host of other things needed to make our larder healthy and palatable.

I was hoeing weeds in the first field when a line of riders caught my attention. I watched a patrol of blue coats, probably a squad in size, approach. James was not at the head of the column. Lt. Simmons led the detail. He dismounted his men on the south side of the crick and put them at ease before clopping across the bridge on horseback.

"Good morning, Mr. Otter."

I hid a smile. This one had some brains. He'd already figured out I wasn't just a hired hand, although it was unlikely he understood my actual relationship with his commandant. "Morning, Lt. Simmons."

"The Major asked me to stop by to give you the latest news. "On the ninth of this month, General Lee surrendered to General Grant at a place called Appomattox Court House in Virginia."

"So the war is over."

"There'll likely be some more fighting. It'll take time for word to filter down to all the commanders, but I believe this effectively brings the war to an end."

"Now what?"

"That depends on President Lincoln — and Congress, of course. The Major also asked me to let you know he's had word of his family. His brother, Col. Henry Morrow, was killed at Petersburg. The Major may have to go back to Virginia to see to his plantation, but he will contact you with instructions should that prove necessary."

"By my calculation, this is the fourteenth of April, is that correct?"

The lieutenant nodded.

"News of the surrender reached you rapidly."

"As you must be aware, the telegraph stopped at Ft. Ramson some 150 miles to the east. Just this past week, it was extended to Ft. Yanube. We are now in direct contact. If you'll excuse me, I must mount my men and continue the patrol. The Major has decided to show the colors more prominently now."

My breath almost caught in my throat as I asked the question foremost on my mind. "Tell me, what is the news regarding the pursuit of Brown's and Pauley's killer?"

"I was on that chase. We followed the villain for over a hundred miles. But he was a wily skunk. Our Crow scouts found and lost his trail a dozen times. Then he came across ground torn up by a passing herd of buffalo, and his tracks disappeared into theirs. He could have come out anywhere along the line and beat it west, but we never found where that was. We sent word to Ft. Laramie, but so far they haven't located him."

The lieutenant gave a brim-of-the-hat salute and returned to his men. Within minutes, the column was out of sight around the end of the hill. His news left me with a splintered heart. The war was over, or soon would be, but that likely meant the army would have more time and men to search for Dull Lance.

I forced my attention to another part of the Lieutenant's news. The loss of his brother would hit James hard. Even though they were not close, they were blood. That had been the brother who ran the plantation for all those years. Was there an estate left to manage? I shuddered at the thought of James returning to Virginia to live on his land back there. There would be no place for me in his life. I returned to my hoeing, putting my back but not my heart into the chore.

# # # # #

The next evening, I was cleaning up after another long day when I heard the sound of hooves on the bridge. Bare-chested, I opened the door and was surprised to see James. My lover had a wild look in his eyes. He abandoned his mount in the yard.

"They've killed the president!" he shouted.

I stepped onto the porch to meet him. He clasped me to his breast there on the open veranda and told me how Lincoln had been shot while attending a play at Ford's Theater in Washington.

"They tried to get Secretary of State Seward, too, but only managed to wound him. The president hung on overnight and died this morning."

"Who?"

"The actor John Wilkes Booth shot Lincoln. A man named Lewis Powell went after Seward and managed to stab him. I understand he wasn't seriously injured."

"What happens now?"

"Vice President Johnson became the new president upon Lincoln's death. But I fear pandemonium will break out. This may revitalize the rebels and cause the war to flare up all over again. If not, it plays into the hands of Thaddeus Stevens and his Radicals."

James had often complained about the Radicals, a group of Republicans in the United States House of Representatives who demanded a harsher Reconstruction Policy for the fractured nation. Lincoln had administered lenient treatment as the southern states fell into Union hands. With his death, no one knew the eventual outcome of that fierce internal struggle.

"I must find some way of returning to Virginia to visit my home back there. I don't even know if there is any family left to oversee it."

"Or if it's been confiscated."

"No, I've kept an eye on that. An old acquaintance of mine from the Point has watched over the matter for me. Headquarters has denied me leave thus far, so I shall have to call upon my Point contact to intercede for me again. He's on Sheridan's staff, and Phil Sheridan carries weight with Grant."

"I was sorry to hear of the loss of your brother."

"He was a good man. A good man caught in a hopeless cause." He paused. "As I would have been but for the counsel of Billy Strobaw. I'll retire from the army as a major while my classmates — those who survived — wear eagles and stars. But that bothers me not a whit. I should not have liked killing my friends and relatives in useless bloodshed."

"Will you remain the night?"

He looked suddenly exhausted. "Yes, I want you, Otter. Terribly."

James needed fucking, not loving that night. So I gave him what he required, saving the loving for the half hour before dawn when we rose to begin the new day.

CHAPTER 17

As much as I had read and studied history, it was still difficult for me to comprehend the convulsions seizing the country upon the death of one man. I traveled to Yanube City a week after the assassination and found the townspeople's anger and fear had been refocused from savage, murdering redskins onto savage, murdering Confederates. John Wilkes Booth and another of the conspirators had been cornered in a barn on a Virginia farm and shot to death. A whole host of others had been rounded up and faced trial. The death cry was on everyone's lips. Why couldn't they let this man — this Lincoln — walk the Western Road in peace? Because even in death he could be used to accomplish the goals of some people.

James still had not been able to obtain leave to visit his Virginia property, and as more troops began arriving at Ft. Yanube, it looked less likely that would happen. Most were veterans of the terrible battles that had raged across the country, and some were damaged souls.

As I feared, the militia did not stand down. If anything, it was more active than ever. A man by the hated name of Smith took Abel Brown's place. Captain Sam they called him. I assumed he wasn't as big a killer as Hardcastle and Brown because they didn't put an oak leaf on his shoulder.

Since there were few tribesmen nearby, Smith's gang found little opportunity to pillage and plunder. While I mourned the absence of others of my blood and culture around me, I was pleased when James brought news the coach line had placed Yanube City on one of its runs and established a way station at Teacher's Mead. That should leave Cuthan's position more secure, save for falling to an assassin's bullet — as had already been attempted once. Since none of his children were old enough to assume the load he carried, that remained a possible method of forcing the Strobaws off their property.

The farm's hounds, the consummation of the agreement with the stage company, and Mary's family, with three big, strapping men living nearby, defended against that possibility somewhat. At one time, the Jacobsen's proximity would have made me uneasy. Greed often infected families and set them one against the other. But over the years I had come to know Hans Jacobsen and understand the man's innate honesty and decency. Mary's father had been able to see beyond what he considered sinful deviancy and comprehend Billy's value to the family. Similarly, I had earned the farmer's respect, but prejudice still stood in the way of comradeship. Sad. He would have made a sturdy friend.

# # # # #

James came thundering across the bridge late one afternoon a week later, yelling jubilantly as he leapt from his charger. "I've got it, Otter! I've got leave to return home. Well, at least, I have orders to report to Washington."

"How did you manage that?" I eased out of his enthusiastic bear hug and tied his charger's reins to a porch corner post before following him inside.

"Grant wants someone to deliver a personal briefing on the situation out here. Ordinarily, Col. Wallston at Ft. Ramson would be tasked, but my friend in Sheridan's headquarters arranged it for me. My successful relief of Ramson from McComber's siege helped in the matter. There's even talk of a medal of some sort. I will be able to deliver my report and then steal a few days to travel downriver to my home. I shudder to think what I'll find."

"You will deal with whatever you find." My heart shared his joy; my mind fixed on his pending absence.

James clasped me about the shoulders. "I wish you could accompany me. The trip will take a good three months, and I shall miss you greatly."

"You will deal with that, as well. As will I."

"You're so damnably placid. Few would ever guess what a volcano of emotions rages in your breast."

"If you're suggesting guile on my part, I do not admit to it. I am simply Otter."

"Not Joseph Strobaw Otter?"

"Right now I am River Otter, and I have found the fish I wish to catch."

"And the fish is begging to be caught." James laughed and took me in his arms.

He was so charged up by the news of his trip he dragged me inside and immediately assumed control of things. He claimed he could only remain a few hours, but he fair wore me out with his demands. He was probably trying to store up enough loving to last during his absence. I was tempted to remind him it didn't work that way. Ah well, might as well enjoy it while I could.

Apparently, he decided he hadn't sufficiently reduced me to a shell of the man I once had been, because he changed his mind and remained until morning. Despite the fact he faced a long journey two days hence, we got little rest that night. We made love with an uncommon amount of energy before finally resting.

At first light, while sitting at the table nursing mugs of hot coffee, he went over things of practical detail, making certain I had sufficient supplies to last during his absence and informing me his temporary replacement, a Captain Andrew Hickum, was aware that a request from me was the same as an order from him — a slight exaggeration, I'm certain.

All too soon, I was watching my love's broad shoulders retreat south toward the fort and experiencing a feeling of loss. Why? James would be back within three moons. I sighed and then went to work. The first field was beginning to look like a farm. The second had not yet decided to participate in the exercise.

# # # # #

James had been gone a *senight*, or about two weeks, when I heard someone outside as I was reading by lamplight. There had been no clop of hooves across the bridge, so whoever it was came into the farmyard by another direction. Odd, because the crick was still swollen and dangerous to cross in the dark. My pulse quickened. Could Dull Lance have returned?

After taking up my rifle and turning the lamp wick low, I opened the door slightly. Someone was at the barn, but the moon hid her face behind a cloud, so I could not make out who was there.

"Otter?" The voice was shrill. A child's voice.

"Matthew? Is that you?"

"Can I come in?"

"*Hahn*, but first, let's see to Whisper."

I went out into the cool night to unlock the barn door. Matthew unsaddled the mustang and led him to the water troughs inside the barn for a drink. I handed him a curry brush and rag before standing aside so the youngster could care for his mount. When he was satisfied the *shuen-kah-wah-kahn* was dry and comfortable in his stall, we went into the house.

"What are you doing here?" I asked. I fought to hold a stricture from my tone. Although I was delighted to see the boy, the timing of his arrival suggested flight.

"I wanted to see you."

"Now you have seen me, so you'd best get back on your horse and return home."

His face fell. "You ... you don't want me here?"

"Not unless you tell me that's going on."

His head drooped. "I don't like it there."

"Why not? Does Cuthan mistreat you? Or Mary?"

"No." The reply was resentful but forthright. "But they don't even know they're Indians, Otter. Well, Cuthan does, but the rest of them don't. If they start acting like it, Mary calls them down."

I helped him out of coat and boots soaked from crossing the rushing crick somewhere downstream. "How would a good Indian mother treat a son — even a son not of her blood?"

"Like a tribesman."

"Isn't that what Mary is doing? She's a good white mother, so she treats her charges like an American mother would. Is she unkind to you?"

Matthew shook his head. "She treats me like all the others. She yells at me when she gets mad and swats me on the rump when she figures I need it. But she hugs me and tells me she loves me, too." He paused and turned haunted eyes on me. "I get lonely sometimes. Not lonely because there's nobody around, but ..." He dropped onto a kitchen chair and rubbed a dark arm over the bare tabletop. "Lonely for my mother and my brother."

"I get lonely for those who are gone from my youth, too. Then I have to pick myself up and acknowledge they have traveled where I cannot follow until my time arrives. Is that why you did not come across the bridge? You went to visit them?"

He nodded. "I didn't know there was a bridge, but I wouldn't have used it, anyway."

"Why not? It was dangerous crossing the water."

"I know, it almost knocked Whisper off his feet, but he made it. I didn't want you to know I was here until after I went to see them. I wanted to see if I could feel them."

"Did you?"

He shook his head, his crown of black hair fluffing like down feathers in a breeze. "No. Maybe I oughta go sleep there. Maybe they'll come to me in my dreams."

"If they wish to come to you in your dreams, they will do it wherever you sleep."

"Otter, do you believe in this Jesus? Mary's always talking about Jesus and getting saved, and that bad things will happen if you die before you're saved. Did bad things happen to them?"

"I do not believe so. He was never revealed to them, so the fault cannot lie with your loved ones. Do I believe in Jesus? I do not disbelieve. Of this I am sure: there is an All Mighty. And if He is All Powerful, there can be only one of Him. That means He is their All Mighty, as well as ours. We may perceive Him differently, but that is natural. Surely, He appears to us as He made us and to them as He made them. That seems right to me."

"So you don't think he's a white God?"

"I see him as God, neither white nor red. And it would be nice to believe He sent a part of Himself in the form of Jesus to dwell among us and teach us how to live in peace."

"What peace? Men still do bad things."

"Yes, and it will always be so. Man is man. The value of Jesus, as I understand Him, is He is willing to accept our sins and wash us clear of them so we can cross the Great Divide and walk the Western Road with a clear conscience. All He asks in return is that we believe."

"So you do believe."

"I accept. And as the days of my life grow longer, I come closer to belief." Even as I spoke the words, thoughts of a craven crow leapt into my mind. Strange that a man like the Reverend Jeremiah Berglund, an ordained preacher, could so pollute the image of Christianity's Savior. Somehow, the one did not fit into the picture of the other.

My answer seemed to satisfy the boy. He gave a jaw-cracking yawn.

"*Ee-yuen-kahn.* I told him to go to bed in Lakota. "You've had a long journey. Did you tell anyone before you left?"

"Just John. You know, so Cuthan wouldn't worry."

"I should send you back tomorrow to tell him of your intent to his face. You have told it to his back in a sneaky way." At Matthew's stricken look, I added, "You can tell him when you return home after helping me break a new field."

Matthew gave a tired smile. "I'll do that. Where's my bed?"

"You can throw down your blankets by the stove or join me in the bed."

"Bed's softer," Matthew rose and slipped his suspenders over his shoulders. He stumbled across the room. "Where does the Major sleep when he's here?"

139

River Otter

I did not answer, but it didn't matter. The boy's head had barely hit the pillow before sleep rendered him unconscious.

CHAPTER 18

The next morning, Matthew transformed himself into Little Bear once again by donning a loincloth and moccasins and refusing to speak English. Understanding his yearning for his roots determined me upon my course. As long as he was on this farm, he could be Sioux — Teton — without interference. I would indulge his immersion into his culture for a while, perhaps into the summer. As we worked the fields together, the late spring air raised gooseflesh, but Bear showed no inclination to don leggings or a shirt.

I decided to make use of this extra pair of hands to plow a third forty-acre tract. The initial turn-under of prairie sod was always difficult, but it was immeasurably easier with the boy guiding the trace horse from the front while I lent my weight to the plow at the rear. We accomplished the task in half the time it would have taken me alone. As young as he was, only seven, Bear was a good worker. Cuthan's training had taken root in his mind. He put in a man's day without complaint. Of course, he wasn't much for conversation in the evenings, nodding off over his lessons until I sent him to bed.

By the end of the week, we had finished turning the new acreage, and I decided to sow it even if it turned out to be a waste of good seed. When the weather warmed a bit, we risked the cold, clear waters of Turtle Crick to bathe. As we sat in the pool one afternoon, I was suddenly aware I was taking a great deal of pleasure in the child's physique, his developing *dahn-chahn*. Shocked, I took stock of myself. Was I becoming a pederast?

Nay, my interest was not prurient. I was not aroused, merely admiring the intriguing form of the human body and discerning how it developed in stages. I took pleasure in measuring young Bear against the remembered frame of his older brother — for whom I had nursed a list. There was a great deal of the older boy in the younger, but what I saw reinforced my earlier conclusion: Matthew Brandt would mature into a dangerously handsome man.

"Shouldn't you be back at the Mead helping Cuthan with his crops?" I asked at length.

"He has Alexander and John and Rachel Ann to help him. You don't have anybody."

"Yes, but he has many more acres under cultivation than I do. That takes more hands."

The boy turned to me with a frown. A drop of water rolled down his nose and off the end. "Haven't I helped?"

"That you have. I would still be struggling to break the sod on the new field without you to lead the horse. Now I have turned and seeded it, increasing my fields by half. But don't you miss your family?"

The frown deepened. Bear took an uncommon interest in a leaf drifting by on the current. "You mean Cuthan's family."

"No, I mean *your* family at Teacher's Mead."

He transferred his gaze to an insect seeking to find purchase on his belly. It failed, and was swept away. "I miss playing with the others. Even Rachel Ann sometimes." His face cleared and his head came up. "They are, aren't they? They're all the family I've got. Except for you." He drooped a little. "And I don't share blood with any of you."

"Not true. We share a bloodline far broader than families or clans or bands. That means we have to take care of one another."

"I guess. I'm going to get out. I'm cold."

"Let's both go inside. We quit a little early, so maybe you won't fall asleep over your lessons tonight."

As Bear stood, his small penis — stiff from the cold — reminded me of the times Lucas had risen from the water with an erection — albeit one brought about by different circumstances. The boy quickly turned away, demonstrating the influence Mary had exerted on him. Why did whites find shame in their bodies?

Covered with blankets for drying, we walked into the house to dress and warm ourselves before the fireplace. I had discontinued using the greedy stove as soon as spring broke, utilizing the fireplace for both warmth and cooking. I preferred the open dancing flames to the box of glowing hot iron.

We ate the evening meal and settled down for Bear's lesson. He was a bright lad, quick to pick up on things, but if the subject under discussion had little to do with daily life, he did not retain the knowledge, at least not as thoroughly as John. War Eagle was a mental sponge, hearing, learning, and storing knowledge away for later use.

# # # # #

Early the next afternoon, we were weeding in the near field when a horseman drew the boy's attention. I followed his gaze. Even from a quarter of a mile away, I recognized the rider.

"It's John," Bear said. "What's he doing here?"

"Come to see if you made it to the farm or froze to death somewhere along the way, I'd guess."

Bear made a noise through his lips. Despite his attempt to hide it, joy stole over his features.

"Go on. Make him welcome." As Bear scampered for the bridge, John waved and kicked Arrow into a trot.

The two youngsters laughed and chattered like squirrels as they met. I must be getting old. I could understand only every third word or so. Children had a language of their own these days, one expressed in half-spoken sentences. Yet, they followed one another's meaning effortlessly. As soon as they came near, John sobered.

"The militia stopped me on the way here."

"Did they cause you problems?"

He shook his strange gold-flecked head. "No. They just asked me questions. You know, who was I and where did I come from and where was I going? That kind of question."

"Where?"

"About a mile east of here."

"Which way were they heading?"

"North. They said they were on the trail of some renegades. Claimed there's some raiding going on."

"A war party? Where?"

John pulled a face. "They didn't say."

"Maybe it's not Indians." Bear must have recognized he'd been speaking the white man's tongue in the excitement of seeing John because he switched to dialect. "Maybe it's some bad white people."

"That could be." I scanned the horizon but saw no evidence of the patrol. "And what brings you here?"

John, quick lad that he was, scanned Bear's apparel and spoke in Lakota. "Pa said to come see if Matthew got here okay."

"He spared you from the fields for something like that?"

"We're in good shape. Got everything in. He and Alex can take care of things until I get back. Ma was worried about Matthew."

"About me?" Bear asked. "Why?"

"Because mothers worry about their young," I said. "It is the nature of things."

"Then how come she didn't seem to be worried about me?" John asked.

"Because she knows you'll come home."

Bear turned to John. "How long you gonna stay?"

"Tomorrow morning. Pa said he'd come after me if I poked along too slow. You coming?"

143

Bear glanced at me. "I don't know."

"You can go if you want."

"I'll make up my mind tomorrow." He nodded his head as if he'd made a momentous declaration.

After John rubbed down Arrow, the boys went up on the hill to see if they could spot the militia patrol but came down to report no sign of riders. I had only two hoes, so I surrendered mine and went inside to begin roasting antelope steaks for a feast. There were beans and corn and onions in the cooling room to boost the meal. I also had some rice to make pudding, one of John's favorites.

I called a halt to the day's labor early so they could soak in the crick before tackling the victuals I'd prepared. The boys' noses were already twitching. I stood on the bank and asked after Cuthan and his family as John and Bear sat in the water.

"I suppose Hannah's getting big by now."

"Turned three last March," John said. "She doesn't bawl as much now."

"Let's see, that makes Rachel Ann about five."

"And I'm six," John put in.

"I'm the oldest. I'm seven," Bear said.

"Uh-uh. Alex is eight. Got you beat by a year."

Bear shook his head. "He doesn't seem like it. He seems more like Cuthan's age."

John blew through his lips. "Pa's age? He's a kid like us."

"I know, but somehow he seems like he's in a different place."

"Yeah, like stuck up. Too good to play with us."

I wagged a finger at them. "Alexander has a different nature. He's the oldest, and he's always taken that seriously. He's been your Pa's second right arm almost from the beginning."

"He's different, all right," John agreed. "So what have you decided, Matthew?"

"I'm Little Bear. I'm always Little Bear when I'm here."

"Okay, Bear. What have you decided?"

"I guess I'll go back with you if Otter doesn't need me. Better, or you'll get lost on the way, and we'll never hear from you again."

"An owl will change to asking 'why' before that happens."

"I heard one say that just the other day."

"Bird shit!" John snorted through his nose.

"Mary'll cut your tongue out."

"Only if you tell on me."

I got up and went to check on dinner, leaving them wrestling in the crick. After a while, they came in with towels wrapped around their waists, dripping water on everything. John had mud on his legs from falling down, so I whipped off his towel and sent him back to the crick again.

A moment later, I heard him call and stepped outside to see riders approaching. I shoved John in the direction of the house. He should not be standing naked in front of these men — not these American men. They'd seen him, of course, but there was nothing I could do about that.

CHAPTER 19

The wooden bridge groaned like it was about to come apart as six horses thundered across it and pulled to a noisy halt. Churning hooves chopped up grass trying to take root in my yard. Some honeysuckle I'd been coddling was tromped beyond salvation. The leader of the group was a stranger, a thin man in a mixture of military and common dress. A sparse, dark beard over sunken cheeks gave him a rough look, even though there seemed to be something fragile about him. He motioned to the left and the right, sending two of his riders circling around the house.

"Thought this was Major Morrow's farm." The man's rolled-brim, black felt hat was fastened down with apron strings tied beneath his chin.

Out of the corner of my eye, I saw Bear come out of the house in loincloth and moccasins. "It is the Morrow farm."

"Looks more like a Injun camp." The man speared the boy with his right eye. The left one looked off into space. Wall-eyed.

The speaker was likely Brown's successor as head of the militia. My back muscles tightened. "I'm Joseph Otter. The Major is not here, but is there something I can do for you?"

"I'm Smith. Captain Sam Smith. I'm trail boss around here now."

I struggled with my hide-behind-face at the sound of that hated name. *Control yourself, Otter.* The Smith who murdered my people was dead. Stay focused.

The militia leader squinted through his strange, cold eyes. I wondered if he saw equally as well out of one as the other. The irises had almost no color. I'd seen what Americans called an albino before, but this man had little of that look except for those eerie, washed out eyes.

"Major Morrow know you keep nekked boys here while he's off in Washington?"

"What? Oh, you mean the boy who was coming from his bath in the crick. That's my grandchild, John."

"And that 'un?" the man pointed to the porch. "He's near nekked, and he ain't taking no bath."

"He's John's cousin. The boys came to give me a hand putting in a new field."

Another man edged his horse forward, a man in black riding a blue roan with a white stocking. "Sinful creature. Go inside, boy, and cover yourself. Are you a heathen fornicator to show yourself like that?"

My eyes blazed. "He is a child, Reverend. One of the innocents, remember? And don't use words like that around him."

Berglund rounded on me, but Smith interrupted. "You seen sign of any other Injuns around?"

"No, but I haven't been off the farm since I started plowing and planting. There aren't many bloods left in these parts."

"Looks like we got some new ones. They stole some horses from a couple of farms and butchered a cow. You got any beef in your cold room?"

"No, just antelope and venison. Have a look if you want." Bile rose in my throat at bending my neck to these hooligans.

The two men who had ridden the perimeter of the farm returned to muster behind Smith. He looked at each, received a shake of the head, and turned back to me. "You see anything of them renegades, you send word to the magistrate, you hear? I find out you seen them and didn't report nothing, it'll go hard on you."

He wheeled his horse, a nice-looking appaloosa, and led the patrol back across the bridge. I watched them out of sight to the south. The horse with the stocking trailed the rest. The tails of his rider's black frock coat flapped in the wind.

"Tomorrow, I will go with you to Teacher's Mead," I announced.

"What did they want?" John asked from the porch.

"To stick their noses where they have no business."

"They were looking for hostiles," Bear said. His cheeks were ablaze. "But *they're* the hostiles. I don't like them."

"When we go, you will become Matthew Brandt once more." I caught the stubborn set of his handsome jaw, but chose to ignore it and went back into the house. "Now, I have to warm up the *dahn-dohn-kah-lah* again so we can eat." I liked my antelope steaks warm.

# # # # #

I ignored the fields the next morning, opting to set off before dawn for the Mead. The sorrel and the black, my plow horse, trailed along behind us since I didn't know how long the trip would take. The boys grumbled at being awakened so early — although in truth it was only half an hour or so before their usual waking time.

When they grew quiet, I suspected they had fallen asleep in the saddle. I advantaged the pleasing silence to consider the man I met yesterday afternoon. Did the Americans consciously seek out barbarians as their leaders? First Hardcastle. Then Brown. And now Smith. They were as different as three men could be, yet of a similar stripe.

I had understood Hardcastle's nature. A vain man rendered a failure by frail lungs, he overpowered his weakness by using cruelty in the stead of true strength. Brown's ruthlessness was born of personal cowardice and pure greed. For him, money was power, and power was protection. He grubbed for it everywhere — from old Caleb's prosperous enterprise to the Mead's strategic placement.

Smith was another individual altogether. It would be easy to assign his hostility to mere arrogance and pride — something the Americans seemed to have in abundance — but I needed to look deeper than that. Then there was the man he worked for. Whatever the reason, be it bigotry or fear or a grab for land, Gadsby seemed determined to root out the natives. He would not have picked a peacemaker to head his private army.

As the sun broke over the horizon, Matthew began complaining about wearing white man's clothes, and that roused John, which put an end to my ruminations. I broke out pemmican to break our fast, but we ate in the saddle. Before long, the boys reverted to type and set up a chatter that was pleasing to the ears, although numbing to the mind.

The gently rolling expanse of the plains with scarce, scattered groves of small trees lining the banks of an occasional rill was the Great Mystery's present to us this morning. Perhaps He gifted us with a little too much sun, which was bright enough to dry the tongue in a man's head, but on balance, His largesse had been lavish. Broad-brimmed hats helped, but not as adequately as the elaborate umbrellas the Yanube once used. Those had disappeared from the plains along with the tribesmen. The American womenfolk still used them, but they were dainty little things called parasols, devices eschewed by men, both red and white.

My eyes were constantly on the alert for signs of the militia, but nothing rose on the horizon to alarm me. The day was well past its zenith when the hills sheltering the Mead came into view. We had crosscut the countryside, avoiding the road between Cuthan's place and Yanube City, so we approached from the northwest. As we drew closer, I caught movement on the top of the hollow hill, the tallest of the three guarding the rear of the house. One of the children was on lookout. A moment later, the hounds set up a clamor with their baying.

Cuthan and his family stood in the yard to greet us as we rode into view. There had been some changes since I was here last. A broad, sturdy bridge spanned the Yanube, an edifice much longer, heavier, and sturdier than my affair at the farm. Later, Cuthan told me the stage company had built it so their concords could reach the Mead from the road paralleling the south bank of the river.

A new building of wood planking stood opposite the main house to serve as a way station for the stage. Another structure stood alongside it. From the chimney and the broad, open doors, I surmised it was a forge of some sort to aid in shoeing the trace animals.

After warm greetings all around, a little moue appeared on Mary's lips as she hugged the errant Matthew to her breast. "Young man, you are in trouble. The next time you want to go gad-flying, you let me know before you leave."

"I told John." The boy's voice was muffled. His face was still buried in Mary's chest.

"That's not telling me. Or Cuthan."

"All right. I won't do it again. But can I go see Otter sometime?"

"You like it there because he lets you run around like a wild Indian, no doubt."

Matthew freed himself and looked up at her. "I *am* a wild Indian."

"No, you're a civilized one. Now go rub down all of the mounts as your penance."

Matthew smiled as he gathered the reins of our animals and started for the outhouse. John tagged along. Rachel Ann wasn't far behind. Alex mumbled something about going back to work and headed for the fields. Hannah clutched her mother's leg, a thumb stuck firmly into her little mouth. The ferocious-looking hounds raced around whimpering piteously for someone to play with them. Perhaps I should get such a beast for our farm.

We adults settled on the porch to exchange news. Things were well with Cuthan and his family. The stagecoach's way station had proved both boon and bane, as was the case with much in this life. It provided a good income to augment what the farm earned, but it also exposed the children to some unpleasantness. The travelers, most of them new to this country, were often taken aback when they found their hosts were Indians. Some were frightened or hostile, others downright rude — even to Mary, whom they obviously considered nothing better than a white squaw. More prejudices arrived with each new settler.

Cuthan dealt with such discourtesy in his customary manner, simply by being himself and performing his duties respectfully and courteously, his neck unbowed. Mary's cooking helped. She served simple but delicious fare. Little Hannah usually broke the ice first, Cuthan claimed. She was a pretty child and had no idea everyone in the world wasn't clamoring to be her friend.

John's strange hair aroused comment, but it was the family's ordinariness — from the whites' standpoint — that triumphed in the end. Both Cuthan and Mary were capable of carrying on literate conversations, and the Strobaw children were better read than many of the youngsters traveling through.

I wasn't certain I could have put up with the aggravation. It wasn't as if Cuthan and Mary needed the extra money. The farm was one of the most successful in the territory, and Cuthan had been reimbursed — no matter how poorly — by the court for the thousands of acres stripped away upon the settlement of Billy's estate. That didn't take into consideration the gold and silver coins he had hidden beside mine in the hollow hill, specie Billy had left us. This family was wealthier than the merchants in Yanube City, yet dared not reveal it.

When I told of our encounter with the militia, Cuthan said he had heard of some marauders in the vicinity. The stage last week had been fired upon without damage. The driver was unable to identify the shooters, although he laid it at the door of roving Indians.

I remained overnight, sleeping in the little cabin west of the house I had occupied before leaving to live with James. The next morning I packed eggs and a jug of milk Mary pressed on me, even though I suspected they'd go bad before I reached home. I'd given up the idea of getting a cow and chickens, as they would tie me too closely to the farm. A cow had to be milked every day, and a chicken needed to be protected from predators.

My three horses and I took the stage road south of the river to Yanube City. I drank the milk Mary had given me and scrambled her eggs on a heated flat rock when I stopped to rest the animals. Without salt or condiments, it did not make a very satisfactory meal, but I'd had worse.

I raised the town by early afternoon and endured unfriendly stares long enough to buy supplies and stow them in the packs on the other two horses before mounting Patch to resume my trip home. I no longer felt welcome in Yanube City.

"You got any nekked boys with you today, Injun?"

I turned to meet the small, vacant-looking eyes of Captain Smith. Well, one of them anyway. The other inspected something off to his left. Was every man named Smith twisted? "Took my grandson and his cousin home, Captain. I was just supplying up before stopping by the fort to see if the Major's got any instructions for me."

"Last I heard he was off in the east."

"He still is, but sometimes he sends a message."

The preacher, Berglund, appeared from nowhere. "Are you a pederast, Joseph Otter?" His gravelly voice grated against my eardrums. "Cavorting with naked boys. Are you an unnatural fornicator? Repent and be saved."

"Don't guess I'm worth saving, Reverend. At least in the eyes of some in this town. As to cavorting with naked boys, I guess I do that about as much as any other man here who has sons and nephews and grandchildren. They clean up better when you wash them without clothes."

"Take your sassy mouth and get out of here, Injun," Smith said. "Go get your orders at the army post." He grabbed Patch's reins before I could depart. A small crowd was beginning to gather. "You seen them renegades I asked you about?"

I willed my muscles not to spasm. My throat tightened. This man had no right to grab Patch's tack gear. "Haven't seen a sign of them."

"You'd tell me now if you did, wouldn't you?"

"Of course."

Smith slapped Patch's flank, startling the pinto into a gallop and almost jerking the lead reins of the two trailing horses from my hand. I brought the animals under control and rode straight to the post where I asked for Lt. Simmons. I was told to wait.

Half an hour later, the lanky officer rushed across the green and gave me his customary fingers-to-the-brim salute. There had been some messages from the Major, but they were all military in nature. He had no idea when James would return.

"I keep hearing about some renegades, Lieutenant. You know anything about them?"

"Captain Hickum has a patrol out right now. They hit a farm south of town near the Little Islands yesterday. Shot up the place and stole some horses. Mr. Lang — that's the man who owns the place — was in the field and saw them coming. He got everybody inside before they arrived. Have you had any trouble?"

Mark Wildyr

"I've been at Teacher's Mead for the last two days. I'd better get out to the farm to make sure everything is fine."

"You let us know if anybody's done any damage to the Major's place."

I thanked him and headed for the wagon trail leading to the farm. The raid on the Lang place almost sounded like harassment rather than a serious attempt to drive the farmer off his land. Non-lethal attacks on isolated farms pointed to tribesmen engaged in the time-honored custom of stealing horses.

As I headed north, I was nervous. Perhaps it was Smith's public attempt to humiliate me or the lieutenant's confirmation of Indian troubles — or a combination of the two. Whatever it was, something had me on the nettle. I pulled to a halt when I spotted a column of smoke far to the northwest.

The plume was too concentrated for a prairie fire. What could be burning to account for a gray column visible for fifteen miles? There wasn't anything there except a farm up Turtle Crick owned by some settlers from back east. I kicked Patch's flanks and began moving.

The moment I reached the bridge spanning the crick I knew something was amiss. The pinto knew it, too. He turned skittish. The two trace animals trailing him started acting up. I drew my rifle from its scabbard and gentled the ponies with whispered words.

153

CHAPTER 20

I dismounted and ground-hitched Patch, knowing he wouldn't move until I lifted his reins unless he was startled by something. The other two horses weren't so well trained, so I looped their leads around the pinto's saddle horn before kneeling to examine the tracks in the dusty farmyard. Hoof and moccasin prints. The renegades had been here. The lock had been forced on the outhouse door. I glanced around anxiously. Were they still here?

"I see you, River Otter." Dull Lance stepped into view from the corner of the barn.

"I see you, too. Is it you causing all the trouble around here?"

"Me and my men." Lance wore a loincloth and calf-high moccasins. His hair was braided. Painted lightning bolts coursed down his cheeks and across his bare chest in alternating colors of red and black. He was striking in a way that clawed at my vitals.

"And now you come to do me harm?"

Lance looked offended. "Nay, I come to see a man who helped me when I needed it. Why would I do him harm?"

I rose from my squat to face him. "Then why is the latch on my barn forced? Is that your smoke I see to the west?"

"It is a white man's house that did not belong there. We chased him into his hole in the ground." Lance indicated my cool room. "What you call your cellar. We left him there with his wife and fry — still breathing. At least, I didn't kill them like they do us."

"Why? What does that accomplish?"

"It lets them know there is a cost to taking our land. Perhaps it will make another farmer change his mind about settling here."

I shook my head. "You do not understand the nature of greed. The white man's lust for land overwhelms his deepest fears. All you will accomplish is the deaths of you, your men, and any bloods in the area. I can see the future you bring. I know what will happen. Burning them out and stealing their horses will not be enough for you. Soon, you will start killing. Already, the people of Yanube City look at me through different eyes. It will be the same for Dog Fox and his family at Teacher's Mead. And for any other tribesmen who remain in this area. You will destroy us."

"*Wee-choh ee-yea*. A lot of words to say nothing. Have you become a white man or merely his slave?" *

155

"I am slave to no one. Neither white nor renegade."

"Is that what you call us? Renegades? We are Sioux warriors living the life we choose on our own lands. The life you should be living with me."

The invisible fist in my guts twisted. "That battle was fought twenty years ago. The Sioux and the Pipe Stem Draw People and all of the other bands withdrew to the northwest, abandoning this land to the settlers."

"That was the doing of old men. We are young men come to reclaim what is ours."

"With what? Half a dozen men claiming to be warriors?"

Lance's eyes blazed. "We *are* warriors. Keep your tongue in your mouth, or you will see for yourself."

"You have already done me in, Dull Lance. The soldiers and the militia will see the smoke and come running. They may already be on their way. They will stop by here to see if I am unharmed or to determine if I participated in the attack on the farm. Either way, you have harmed me."

"Then perhaps you should do what your nature cries out for. Join me. Be a warrior and torch this place. Ride with me."

Desperate for something to say, I glanced at the tracks littering my yard. "Don't talk nonsense. Are your men still here?"

"No, but they are not far. Safe in a draw close by."

"How many are you?"

"I have six warriors with me. You will make seven."

My heart returned to normal as I recognized the future I would pursue. "Nay, I'll not join you, Dull Lance. Perhaps there is some truth in what you see within me, but I am on a committed course. One I cannot abandon." I paused to give him an opportunity to speak. He drew to his full height and his eyes hardened, but he said nothing.

"Go to your men, Dull Lance, and ride. I'm going to tell whoever comes you traveled north. Ride straight through my fields and then turn in that direction, but try not to do too much damage. Join your men and get out of here. There's already an army patrol out, but I think they're south of the Yanube trying to track you from the farm you attacked yesterday. You'd better lay a false trail a distance to the north. Go to Trickling Water and wade downstream to throw them off. Then go home. Go back to the Laramie country."

"They are looking for me there. That is why I left. They're hunting me for murder."

"Then go to Canada."

"What will you do?"

"I'm going to fire my outhouse and claim I came upon you before you could torch the house."

Lance grunted and went for his pony hidden at the side of the barn. A moment later, he pounded off to the northwest, riding through my plowed fields.

I fought with my emotions as I lighted a brand of twisted hay. The lumber was not yet aged, so I had trouble getting the fire to catch, but eventually, the flames were eating away at the timber. The adobe fill between the inside and outside walls would inhibit the flames, but I would likely lose the roof. I ran for the horses before they could bolt and vaulted onto Patch to lead them across the bridge. I halted and emptied my rifle in the direction of the burning barn. For good measure, I put a couple of rounds through the windows of the house. Then I raced toward the fort, trailing the trace horses behind me.

Three miles south of the farm, I ran into a column of troopers. Lt. Simmons heard my rushed story and ordered his platoon into a gallop. The fire had a good start, but was not yet raging when we arrived at the farm. The troopers quickly doused the flames that had eaten through two of the outer walls and had been consuming the roof. After scouting the other side of the crick for sparks that might start a prairie fire, the officer collected his men and headed off after the Sioux.

In the wake of their departure, I wondered if I had done the right thing. Perhaps I overreacted, but the sacrifice of a barn seemed a small price to pay for making myself a victim instead of a renegade. The fire and the obvious signs of a body of men in my front yard and fields might be enough to take me out of the gun sights of the militia. Even though it was late summer, I should be able to repair the barn before weather set in.

Lt. Simmons returned to the fort by way of the farm to acknowledge he had not caught up with the raiders. I took advantage of his services to send a note to the new lumberyard in town to order supplies required to rebuild the outhouse. When the time came, Timo Bowers could find some trustworthy help for the construction work.

After clearing away the debris left from the fire, which had, indeed, consumed the roof without doing much damage to the interior, I decided the walls were sound, although some of the timbers would need replacing. That simplified matters considerably. When all the charred material had been cleared away, I was left with enough firewood to see me part way through next winter. Satisfied I'd made a good start, I cared for the horses before going to weed the fields. Lance's pony had cut a swath through two of them, but fortunately hadn't done much damage to the green crops.

# # # # #

A week later, I looked up from working the fields to see a wagon making its way toward the farm. The lumber had arrived. The wood dealer, a Dutchman named Erik Maartens, seemed friendly as we unloaded the wagon, so I asked if he knew of anyone who could help rebuild the barn. Maartens, a recent arrival from Philadelphia, suggested his two sons. After we agreed on a wage and settled the bill for the lumber, the man rumbled over the bridge on his way back to town.

I was dipping deeply into my hoard of silver coins, but the decision to torch the barn had been mine, so it was only right I paid for its restoration. Satisfied with my logic, I finished the afternoon working in the fields.

The next morning, Maartens's sons showed up to lend a hand with the barn. Both were strapping young men who spoke to one another in their father's native language and to me in slightly mangled English. Abner, whom I judged the elder by five or six years, was a man of outgoing personality and plain looks. Jonah, about twenty-one, was reserved but handsome. So much so, I often found myself studying him as we worked. At times, a certain part of his anatomy seemed so full a codpiece would not have called more attention to it. I could develop a yen for this one. I mentally shook my head and wished James would get home soon.

The work went well. The two brothers were so adept at carpentry I soon withdrew and went about tending the fields, allowing them to do the work. That put me beyond the reach of temptation from the fetching Jonah.

During afternoon meals, we fell into the habit of sitting and talking about events in town. It became clear the renegades had neither raided nor been spotted in the territory the last few days. Perhaps Dull Lance had taken my words to heart.

By the third morning when nothing remained to be done except a little roofing, the brothers arrived with a note from Lt. Simmons informing me Major Morrow was on his way back to the fort. James intended to reverse his route and return by train to the nearest railroad depot and then take a stage to Ft. Ramson to report to Col. Wallston.

There, he would recover his horse for the remainder of the trip. He was expected back within a fortnight.

Later that afternoon, the Maartens boys were atop the barn putting the finishing touches to the roofing; and I was inside making certain the stalls were the way I wanted them when hoof beats drew me outside.

The militia had approached from the north where they were shielded from our view until they swarmed around the eastern end of the hill. They rode into the yard, stirring up a dust storm.

Smith leaned over his saddle horn and glanced up at my two helpers, who were working without shirts. "Nekked. Half-nekked. You like 'em that way, don't you?"

What was this man's obsession with naked flesh? Could he harbor a deviancy, recognized or unrecognized? Whichever the way, it represented a danger. He would be suspicious of relationships and anxious to reveal them to cover his own longings. I suspected I had found the key to the man's belligerency — fear.

"I don't tell the Major's hired hands how to dress, Captain Smith."

"How come you building another outhouse?"

I indicated the charred timbers I'd salvaged for firewood. "I figured you'd heard about the raid. The renegades burned the barn."

"Injun renegades?"

"When I returned to the farm the day I saw you in town, I found them on the property. I fired some warning rounds, but that just stirred them up. By the time I got here, they'd torched the barn and shot out a couple of windows in the house. If I hadn't come up just then, they'd probably have burned the whole place down."

"How come you're still walking around breathing?"

"So far as I know they aren't killers. I stood up to them, and they left, riding through the Major's fields and tearing up his crops on the way."

Smith squinted at me with his good eye. He held the look of a man who figured he was dodging cow pies. "I told you to report it if you seen any renegades."

I spread my hands. "I did report it. I reported it to the army. In fact, I met a patrol led by Lt. Simmons just south of the farm. He was going to investigate the smoke up Turtle Crick."

The militia commander glanced up at the Maartens, who had come to the edge of the roof to watch and listen. They were impressive men, but I couldn't tell whether Smith was drawn by musculature or suspicion. He shifted his attention back to me.

"I told you to report it to the magistrate's office, and that ain't what you done."

"I reported to the nearest legal authority and came back to try to save the major's homestead. I acted responsibly."

"Responsibly, huh? You talk like some red belly schoolteacher. How come?"

"Because I was taught by an educated man."

Smith sneered. "Yeah, by that old sodomite. What did they call him? The Red Win-tay? The one you serviced for better'n twenty years."

"Billy Strobaw was a respected man. I was lucky to have him educate me."

"Probably more'n you bargained for." His men, four hard-bitten characters, laughed aloud. "Next time, you do like you're told. You come see me or the magistrate, you hear me?" With another glance at the two men on the barn roof, he tugged his reins and came about. The five militiamen clattered over the bridge and circled off to the west.

Abner squatted down and shook his head. "Smith a nasty fella."

"Nasty and odd," Jonah said. "When I see him in town, he make me nervous. He watch me alla time. Sometimes he stare hard. Give me bad feeling."

Suspicion firmed into conviction. A man battling desires he denied or didn't understand would be on the lookout for deviancy in others, finding it sometimes whether it was there or not.

CHAPTER 21

James looked tired and drawn when he clattered across the bridge and dismounted in the farmyard. I stepped forward and gave him an American handshake, resisting the urge to pull him into an embrace. He frowned and gave me a questioning look.

"Come inside where I can greet you properly." I stepped onto the porch and moved aside as a good servant should do, allowing the master to enter first.

James paused on the doorstep to glance at the outhouse. "The barn looks good. Simmons told me about it."

I said nothing as I followed him inside to watch him strip away his woolen uniform. When he started to don more comfortable cotton clothing, I reminded him he'd just have to remove it again.

James laughed and threw aside the trousers he'd been holding. "My God, I've missed you." He moved forward and engulfed me in a bear hug that soon became an embrace. His kiss was almost smothering.

He came up for air and laughed as he groped my genitals. "You'd better get out of those britches or you'll split a seam."

For a moment, it was as if this were our first time. The wonder was the same, the anticipation as great, as was his nervousness. I stepped away to bar the door and then stripped, taking pleasure in the intense shine in his eyes as he watched.

James fell to his knees and nuzzled my bare belly. His morning shave had given way to an afternoon shadow even though the hair on his face was light. He kissed the end of my pulsing rod and mumbled something before taking it into his mouth.

I thought I would come at once, but I willed the rush away, glorying in the feel of his soft lips, damp tongue, and the wet recesses of his mouth and throat. James took me standing in the middle of the room while I clasped his handsome head in my hands. Finally, I could hold back no longer. My groin tightened and I erupted, sending semen stored for weeks into my lover's willing mouth. I would have collapsed had not his strong hands steadied my thighs. He stayed with me until my ejaculation shuddered to a halt.

He got to his feet and smiled at me. "Oh, how I have missed that wonderful experience. I never want to leave you for so long a time again."

161

I was surprised at how much I was gasping for breath. "Let me recover, and we'll see what I can do for you."

"Don't tarry too long, or I might not wait for your efforts. I'm damned close, I can tell you. Just taking you in my mouth almost did it for me."

I led him to the bed. "Give me the news from back east while we rest."

He moved across the bed to make a spot for me. "It's over now. The war, I mean. It ended on June 23 with the surrender of the last Confederate general at a place called Ft. Towson in the Choctaw Nation down in Indian Territory. Ironically enough, that was Brigadier General Stand Watie of the Indian Cavalry."

"Imagine that, a Cherokee general officer."

"We had one of our own, you know. A Seneca who went by the name of Ely S. Parker."

"What of your estate?"

"It's gone, I'm afraid. There was a battle waged right on the front lawn. The house was in ruins. Some Yankee carpetbagger was trying to steal the land out from under me. You should have seen the look on his face when a Union officer showed up to forestall him." James sighed heavily. "Nonetheless, I sold him the land. At a pitiful price, mind you. But it would have required all of my efforts for years to restore things."

He stroked my chest. "I reserved only enough land to allow my sister-in-law and her family a place to live, and I shared the proceeds from the sale equally with her. After all, my brother had run the plantation for years."

"That is only fair. Are they well?"

"As well as can be. I suggested they emigrate out here, but they are rooted in the Virginia soil. Else they're too traumatized to make that sort of decision. It's horrible, Otter. The devastation is enormous. The North is almost untouched, but Virginia — the south — is devastated. People will starve and freeze this winter. We're apt to see a flood of southerners flock to this territory. In fact, it's already started."

James turned into me and threw a leg over mine. "It's not all bad news. The War Department's accepted my papers."

"Good! Are you separated now?"

He laughed. "No, those old dinosaurs don't act that fast. They'll send out a new commander, and I'll have to give him some time to settle in. After that, my resignation will be effective. Just think, three years after we thought I'd be free, it is finally going to happen."

Then he sobered. "They hanged the Lincoln conspirators, you know. One of them was a woman, Mary Surratt. They strung her up right alongside the men."

"They hung a woman?"

"Nobody can remember such a thing happening before." James looked thoughtful. "The President's death is going to make things harder for the Confederacy. The hardliners are in ascendancy, and carpetbaggers are flooding the South to plunder and steal anything that's not already destroyed. There are hard times ahead, I fear, and not just for Dixie."

"What do you mean?"

"The Union financed this war with millions of printed paper money not backed by gold. Greenbacks they call them. No one knows what they're worth from one day to the next. And we borrowed heavily in Europe. The bill's coming due, and everyone will pay the piper. There's already talk of another financial depression. We're in for it, I'm afraid."

I touched his cheek. "We are fortunate to be where we are. We can raise much of what we need to subsist. We have money to buy what we can't. I have most of what Billy left for me."

"I have my share of the proceeds of the sale of the plantation. I left some in a sound banking house back east, although I brought a good portion with me. I'll put most in the local bank, but we need to find a hiding place for the rest. I'm not certain how the banks will come though the turmoil headed their way."

"There's always the hollow hill at the Mead. That's where most of my silver and gold is stored. I have some here in a hidey-hole beneath the kitchen stove."

"That will do for now. And speaking of now, are you up to giving me one of your fantastic flankings?"

"I will not only flank you, I'll fuck you."

I rose and crawled between his long, pale legs. I wanted to watch my lover's face as I performed for him. James moistened the tip of my hardening cock. Then I lifted his knees to my shoulders and moved forward until I made contact. The head of my shaft met slight resistance, and then pushed through into the dark, warm, moistness of his most private place. The look of adoration on James's features was a wonder to behold.

"Give it all to me," he breathed.

For a long time, there was only the sound of sighs and grunts and the slap of naked skin against bare flesh.

# # # # #

That evening, as we sat at the kitchen table after our meal, James discussed the rest of his trip before asking about the raid on our farm.

"It was not a raid."

"What?" His eyebrows shot up.

"Nay. A lot has happened since you've been gone. I have to be careful about going to Yanube City these days. Not everyone is friendly."

"It was already turning that direction."

"Yes, but it's worse than ever now. There's a new preacher in town named Jeremiah Berglund, and he's on the hunt for sinners. He and Smith have started making comments about naked boys and men. They accosted me on the street in Yanube City and deliberately set out to humiliate me." I explained the boys' visit and the two Maartens brothers working shirtless on the barn roof.

"I think Smith's a sodomist who hasn't faced up to the fact. At any rate, he's twice made comments about me having naked boys and men around the place. So he's sensitive to the matter. He'll be suspicious of any close relationships."

"That's why you barred the door."

"Yes. I didn't want him barging in on us."

"We'll have to watch our step. He's a bad seed. That's probably what got him selected to fill Abel Brown's shoes. I'll ask around and see what I can find out about him. But what of this raid that wasn't a raid?"

"Dull Lance showed up again. He stopped here with the intent of sheltering his men in the barn for the night. When I informed him I would have to report his presence, he left. I torched the barn myself, James. I did what I thought I had to do to make it appear I was a victim. But I don't think it worked. Smith showed disbelief when he rode in a few days later."

James made a noise in his throat. "He's as bad as Hardcastle and Brown."

"Perhaps worse.

"Did you know Dull Lance intended to kill Brown and Pauley when he left the farm?"

I shook my head. "He took his leave after the cellar was finished, claiming he was heading back to the Laramie country. Of course, he didn't go, not without stirring things up first.

"Despite all of this, it's good to be home."

# # # # #

Summer passed into autumn, and I was busy with gathering the crops. We got a proper yield of corn and potatoes and peas from the first field. The second was not as bad as I had feared, but the third — the one Matthew had helped me plow — had had been planted too late and yielded little. As I finished the harvest, I was pleased, yet discomfited in some manner. It would have meant so much more had James been here to work alongside me. At the least, it would have banished my occasional lustful yen for Dull Lance.

I chopped the burnt timbers into firewood and stored them in a shed attached to the eastern side of the cabin. I had cut a door directly into the house so we had access to dry firewood without going outside. In addition to all of this, I bagged a deer and an antelope and made a portion of the green meat into pemmican and jerky. The rest, I hung in the cellar.

Winter arrived without James's expected release from the army. The officer selected to replace him had died of complications from a war wound. The second man chosen was on a long period of personal leave. In the meantime, the country was wracked by what would later become known as the Recession of 1865-67.

The expected tide of new settlers, many of them former rebels, took place as James had predicted, and I found myself with new neighbors, one a mile to the west and a second some distance beyond that. Both new homesteads were settled too late to put in crops, so I did not expect either to last the winter.

A new flurry of renegade attacks set the territory on edge, but I did not believe it was Dull Lance because they involved killing. Of course, he had killed Brown and the stable owner, but that had been an act of personal revenge for the death of his wife and men. On occasion, I suspected I was being watched, and once or twice, I found signs to confirm this. But the tracks were blurred, so I could not tell if it was tribesmen or militia with eyes on me.

Then James came home with news the army had negotiated what was being called the Little Arkansas Treaty. Chiefs of all the major Southern Plains tribes — Comanche, Kiowa, Cheyenne, Arapaho, and Kiowa-Apache — had agreed to give up great swaths of lands and move to reservations in Indian Territory south of the Arkansas River.

"Mayhap that will take some of the sand out of the likes of Captain Sam Smith," James noted.

"Nay, none of our tribes are included. The Sioux and Northern Cheyenne made no such agreement. The treaty will little affect us in this part of the country. If anything, Smith and his kind will simply agitate for like treatment of the Council of the Seven Fires — even though they are far removed from here. But they will apply the term to any of the bloods in this area. I fear there is more trouble ahead."

# # # # #

As the first blue northers whistled down and laid a chill on the land, James managed only infrequent visits to satisfy our mutual needs. When the real snows came, I settled in to endure the long, gray months alone. As one day followed another, Billy and Cut Hand and Lone Eagle and Lucas intruded on my thoughts and dreams so often I puzzled over whether they were recollections from the past or ghosts crowding the cabin. What did it matter? I took a measure of comfort from their presence — real or imagined. A yearning for Dull Lance vied with my hunger for James, a fact that both shook and depressed me.

I fought my way to the barn every day on snowshoes to commune with the horses and see to their care. I pounded down the snowdrifts in front of the entrance so I could take the ponies out and exercise them a bit each day.

The wolves made their appearance, putting an end to that practice. They kept their distance at first, howling from somewhere beyond my sight, gradually growing closer until at night I heard them clawing at the outhouse door, seeking to get at the horses. The next morning, I would find paw prints in the snow and scratches on the door. I calculated there were six animals in the pack.

One morning after the turn of the year, I went outside to find the beasts standing in the farmyard right in front of the porch. They were thin and haggard. It had been a hard winter, snow drifted so steeply against the western edge of the house I could almost walk right up onto my roof. The beasts were ravenous, and one, a big male, advanced on me threateningly.

"Calm now, brother," I muttered. "I intend you no harm. Respect me as I do you. Go away, and we will be wary neighbors."

The wolf was starving and beyond rational action. As I had no wish to slay the creature, I stepped back into the house and closed the door when the big animal bunched for a leap. The brute slammed against the thick planking, shaking the latch. Sharp claws scrabbled against the porch as he tried to dig his way inside. The horses would have to fend for themselves this morning.

When I went out later, the pack was howling off to the east like banshees. Wolves were normally silent hunters. What would cause such a commotion? Then I heard gunshots. As curiosity overcame caution, I strapped snowshoes to my boots and slogged across the bridge to head west over the open prairie rather than risk ambush by hungry carnivores from the trees. I had a rifle strapped to my back and a scattergun in my hand.

Everything was quiet now, but still I kept going. Something on the north side of the crick caught my eye. I found a frozen spot to cross over and examine it. From the signs, the wolf pack had caught someone in the open. One of the wolves had been killed, bloody bits and pieces were strewn around the area, but the carcass had been dragged away by the other animals. There were deep red stains in the snow. Someone had likely been injured.

The human footprints I found were made by boots, not rackets. The farmer to my west had probably been out hunting when he was set upon by the pack. I followed the tracks, occasionally splashed with blood, to a small cabin sitting on the north side of Turtle Crick.

I stepped to the front porch. "Hello. Anyone home?"

Muffled noises came from inside.

"My name is Joseph Otter. I'm from the farm to your east. Do you need help."

The door opened a finger-length. The muted winter light was fading, so I could see nothing of the person on the other side.

"Do you need help?" I asked again.

The door opened wider, and a young woman wrapped in blankets stood framed by faint candle glow from inside. "Who are you?"

I introduced myself again and told of hearing shots and finding signs of an encounter with the wolf pack.

"Are ... are you an Indian?"

"Yes, ma'am. I run Major Morrow's farm about a mile down the crick. I followed a blood trail here. Is someone hurt?"

"It's my husband. He's been bitten. The beasts ripped his arm."

"Do you have anything to treat the wound?"

She burst into tears. "We don't have anything. I've tried to stop the bleeding, but I can't help him. He's going to die because I can't help him."

"Let me come inside and see what I can do."

"We don't have anything to steal. We're out of food and firewood and everything else. No one told us about the winters out here. We were fools ..."

I interrupted before she talked herself into hysteria. "Lots of folks aren't prepared for the first winter. Let me help."

She stood aside and allowed me into the house. The cabin was little warmer than my outhouse. A man, also wrapped in blankets, sprawled on a homemade chair before a barely smoldering fireplace.

"Let me see that wound."

A handsome young fellow with a scraggly, days-old beard, stared at me through sunken, wild eyes. "Who ..."

"Someone who can help." I turned to the woman. "You say you're out of food and fuel?" When she nodded, I told her we'd go to my farm where I had plenty of both. "Do you have horses?"

"Wolves got them." The man's voice strengthened with outrage.

"How about rackets ... snowshoes?" The woman shook her head. I sat down on the hearth and removed mine. "Get some clothes and anything else you need. Then we'll strap these on you. Your husband's going to need our help. It's only a mile, but it's a long mile in this snow. Do you have weapons?"

"A rifle and a six-gun." The woman was beginning to recover.

"Get them. They'll be extra weight, but we might need them. Tie all your ammunition in a shawl or something. Make a pack of your spare clothing and blankets and fasten it to my back."

The woman rushed around doing as instructed. When she was ready, she tied a heavy bundle across my shoulders. Then I fastened the snowshoes onto her boots. I glanced to the west as we made our way out of the house with the man propped up between us. We would have to hurry. Night would soon arrive.

The woman floundered around in the rackets for a hundred yards before she got the hang of the shoes, and then she was able to help support her husband. I followed the game trail on the north side of the crick. Walking in the cover of the thin line of trees made the going a mite easier.

The injured man tried to give up twice, but I prodded him along. I half-expected the pack to catch our scent, but beyond a couple of shadows in the trees, I saw nothing. We were within sight of my cabin when the man suddenly went limp and slumped to the ground despite our support.

Then I heard a howl.

CHAPTER 22

I pressed our weapons on the woman and lifted the man into my arms. I managed to stagger to the porch, but my legs, weak from slogging through snow without the aid of rackets, gave out as I reached the steps. She helped me drag him over the threshold as the wolves raced into the yard and bounded up onto the porch. At her scream, I banged the door shut with my shoulder, catching the snout of the big male in the jamb. The beast yelped in pain and retreated into the yard.

I dumped the injured man into a chair and lit the stove, which heated the cabin faster than the fireplace. After his wife changed out of her soaked garments in the bathing room, we stripped the man naked. I held him upright so she could dry his snow-drenched legs. Then I carried his thin, shivering frame to the bed and covered him with blankets, leaving only his head and wounded arm exposed.

I asked her name as I examined the ugly gash on his forearm. The bleeding had almost stopped — because of the cold most likely.

"Bella. He's Andre. Andre Tiller. Can you help him?"

The wolves were mad, but I prayed they were driven to that condition by ravenous hunger, not from the disease that sometimes infected them. No need to add that worry to her cares, but I needed to be honest. "I can repair the wound. It is the infection I'm worried about. There are pots in the pantry. Heat some water from the pump."

While she hurried to obey, I went to a closet and pulled out the Pandora's box of medicines and herbs. I normally husbanded the precious medicines, using natural substances whenever possible, but I would have to sacrifice some of the antiseptics to treat flesh this badly torn. After the water was sufficiently heated, I bathed the wound, causing the bleeding to resume. Bella gasped and reached out to Andre.

"Don't worry, bleeding is a good thing. It will purge any impurities that may have gotten inside his arm. The blood is not pulsing, so no artery has been torn."

"But he's lost so much already," she said.

"I'll apply some yarrow to slow the flow after we've cleaned the bite."

Fortunately, Andre had passed out, so I finished cleaning the injury without causing him undue discomfort. Bella, now recovered from the shock of near disaster, set about boiling a length of thread and a large needle while I powdered the rip in his arm with comfrey and yarrow. For good measure, I added goldenseal as an aid to closing the wound.

When I was finished, she held his arm steady as I sutured the three-inch gash with the sterilized needle and thread. Andre groaned and flinched once or twice, but otherwise he lay like a log as I bound the arm in strips of clean white cloth.

"That's all I can do."

"Thank you. Thank you so much, Mr. Otter."

"Most people call me Otter. When did you eat last?"

"Three days ago. That's when we ran out of food. We weren't prepared. Nobody told us how bad the winters were."

"This is a hard one. The snow is heavier, and the air is colder. Snowmelt will come late, I think. Mrs. Tiller, we're going to be stranded in this cabin for quite a spell. As you can see, it's just one big room except for the bathing room and a storage closet or two, but we'll manage."

She had shown no embarrassment whatsoever in stripping her husband naked in front of me, but now her cheeks reddened at the realization of how closely we would be forced to live.

I gave her no time to contemplate the matter. "Right now, we have to get some food into both of you. There is a stew in the cupboard. Please set it on the stove to heat. It has fat in it, and fat is what you need. You eat first and then we'll feed your husband. He'll have to be spoon-fed. After that, you both need rest. You take the bed."

I settled the sleeping arrangements by laying out a buffalo robe and blankets for a pallet on the other side of the cook stove and assuring her I had slept on such bedding many times. I checked Andre before retiring for the night. He'd had a slight fever earlier, but Bella pressed cool, damp rags to his forehead until he rested more comfortably. I took to my blankets before my usual time in order to allow the woman to slip into bed beside her sleeping husband.

The next morning, Andre was much recovered, yet I insisted he remain abed. I checked the wound and switched to applying honey to the sutures to save the more precious medicines. After I bound the arm again, I urged them to eat small amounts of food often to restore nutrients they had lost. That evening, despite my protests, Andre joined us at the kitchen table for the day's final meal.

He was sufficiently strong to give me his story. Andre Tiller was the product of a French mother and an English father who had farmed in the Shenandoah Valley until the war intruded. His widowed father entered the service of the Confederacy and died in some unnamed skirmish; Andre served as a foot soldier for the Union and escaped unscathed. He finished his military service deep in the south where he met the daughter of a ruined plantation owner.

He had returned home to the valley but could not forget the lass with green eyes and chestnut tresses. When he found most of what he and his father had worked to build was gone, he sold what little remained and ventured back to Georgia to claim Bella Norwood's heart and hand. To escape the wrath of her Yankee-hating father, the young couple had traveled up the Mississippi River and come west in search of a new life.

Andre was a seasoned Shenandoah Valley farmer, but he had not understood how much the plains country altered his trade. His light plow was only capable of scratching the surface of the thick sod of the acreage he'd claimed as a homestead. The Tillers had managed nothing but a modest garden before winter set in.

As the days lengthened, I came to admire this handsome, plucky man and his pretty, aristocratic wife. Andre recovered from both his wound and his near starvation quickly. His wound scabbed over without any evidence of infection. He hardly flinched when I cut out the sutures. I was pleased there was no impairment of the use of his hand or arm. In fact, Andre forgot the injury until he banged it on something.

Bella did not have as far to repair because her husband had pressed most of their available food on her. After observing them for better than a moon, I knew they would make it in this country. The Tillers had the determination needed to survive.

I realized Andre was truly on the mend one night when I heard the stealthy movement of bodies from across the room. A few suppressed grunts and groans and the not-quite-contained sighs brought images that stiffened my rod and gave me a hollow feeling in the gut. I had never lain with a woman, but I raised images of the young couple copulating. Their gasps at the approaching orgasms left me aching before I finally drifted off to sleep again, only to dream of James … and Dull Lance.

# # # # #

As Andre Tiller grew stronger, the enforced activity made him restless. Pleased the young man was not slothful, I allowed him to help with what little work could be accomplished in our confined circumstances. The two could not conceal their astonishment upon learning I could read and write and hold a decent conversation — Andre more than his wife.

"You are an unusual Indian," he said one evening as I was reading the Holy Bible.

"How so?"

"You read and comprehend. You know a lot about many things."

I chuckled. "I know a little about many things."

"There were educated Indians back home," Bella said. "Many of the Cherokee were quite well educated before President Jackson expelled them."

"That was before your birth."

"Not all of them left. Some managed to stay behind. I knew a few."

"I was educated by a friend, a man who was known as a teacher from Fort Ramson to Fort Yanube. His name was Billy Strobaw."

"I've heard of him," Andre said. "I think we halted at the place where he lived on the way to Yanube City."

"You did. He built Teacher's Mead when he first came to this country and lived out his life there. In fact, I spent most of mine there, as well. The stream that feeds the Yanube at the Mead was called Strobaw's Crick by the military. It appears by that name on the official maps of the territory to this day. He was the first white man in the area."

I turned back to my reading, and the conversation lapsed.

# # # # #

The first Chinook blew down on the countryside and lessened the grip of winter, although it would yet be a long time before snowmelt. The warming wind at least made it possible to get outside from time to time. I made a practice of going to the barn or hunting up and down Turtle Crick on rackets, partially for fresh meat but mostly so the young couple could have time alone.

One day, as I forked the dwindling supply of fodder down into the hay bin for the horses, Andre came up into the loft, rubbing his hands together briskly.

"That fire downstairs almost keeps this place warm."

"Warm enough for the horses, anyway."

"It's not bad up here, either." The young man eyed the blankets in a corner. "So this is where you disappear to."

"Sometimes. There is still enough savage in me to yearn for the old ways. In the warm months, I often sleep here or in the woods."

"Woods," Andre said with a snort. "Back home we have woods. Out here, all you have is a scraggly line of stunted trees following a brook

172

or a river. There aren't enough trees to build a proper house. Besides, that's not it at all. You come out here to give us some privacy."

"That is part of it."

"I cannot overstate how much we owe you, Otter."

"You owe me friendship and help when I need it, nothing more."

"I owe you my life, and that of my wife. We wouldn't have made it if you hadn't found us. I would have been dead in days, and she wouldn't have been far behind me."

"You're tougher than you think. You recovered from your wound quickly."

"The wound and the bleeding just weakened me. The hunger and the cold would have killed me. I badly miscalculated our needs. I thought we would be able to subsist on game from the countryside."

"It's been hunted almost to extinction over the past few years." I closed my mouth before I pointed out that the white man always killed off the animals — be they four-legged or two-legged — wherever he settled.

"I was misled by the people who sold us our wagon and supplies. They told me the living was lush out here."

Not wishing to further embarrass the young man because of his gullibility, I asked if they came to the territory by wagon train.

"No, we made the trip on our own. Any way you look at this, we owe you our lives."

"Then repay me by using them well." I walked over to the makeshift bed and began folding the woolen blankets. As I laid them atop the buffalo robes, I sensed Andre behind me.

"I've heard things about Mr. Strobaw. And I figured it out last night."

"Figured what out?"

"That you were together. You know … *together*."

I nodded without turning to face him. "That is true. I am sorry if that disturbs you."

It doesn't disturb me, but ..." His hands came to rest on my shoulders. "I guess it must be lonely for you since he's gone."

"He was a fine man." My voice threatened to catch in my throat.

"What is it they called him? A win-tay?"

"Among the tribes he was known at the Red Win-tay because he wore something red every day. Suspenders. Belt. Hatband. That sort of thing."

"I know you heard us the other night. I think that's why you leave us alone so we'll have time to make love."

I said nothing. His hands shifted to my biceps. "I'd like to help, if you'll let me."

"Andre, that's not necessary."

The slender hands slipped under my arms and closed over my chest, drawing a gasp from me. I should have ended the thing right then, but Andre thought I was alone and needed help. I was on a hook; I could not tell him about James.

His arms slid down to my belly and pressed me to him. The moment I could have rejected his advances passed as his hands caressed my groin. My cock betrayed me, rising swiftly at his touch. Andre moved around in front of me and knelt on the bedding.

"The only thing I know about this is what a friend did for me when I was fifteen." He looked up at me and seemed to be that teenager again. He freed my trousers from their suspenders and tugged them down. Before I mustered the grit to object, Andre took me in his hand. A moment later, he timidly sucked me into his mouth.

Frozen, I watched Andre's brown curls as he moved up and down on my turgid cock. Had I not been so shocked, I would have come instantly, but shocked or not, I was lost. I could no more have stopped his inexpert suckling than I could have climbed to the North Star. I held still and quiet until a delicious feeling rose in my groin and spread throughout my body. I managed to groan a warning before my juices shot from me in an exquisite explosion. Lost in an intense orgasm, I was barely aware of Andre gagging and coming off of my rod to finish me with his hand.

Eventually, I worked through the force of the explosion and returned to the present. Now that he had committed such an act, Andre had no idea what to do next. He stumbled to his feet and swiped his mouth. He grabbed wisps of hay to clean his fingers. His eyes skittered everywhere except to me.

I restored my clothing and clasped Andre by the arms to prevent him from fleeing. "Look at me."

His gray eyes focused briefly before straying away. Andre's groin was not inflamed; he had done what he did for my sake, not for the wanting of the thing.

"Look at me," I repeated.

He finally met my gaze and tried to muster a smile.

"Andre, you have just gone against your own nature to do something in payment of a debt. It was a debt not owed, but you did it nonetheless. By doing this thing, you revealed how much of a man you are. You delivered what you thought I needed no matter the cost to yourself. That is what a man does. Thank you. You need not to be ashamed. We will not speak of this again."

Andre's spine stiffened. "Yes, we will. We'll speak of it the next time we do it. The debt is not yet paid in full."

"Aye, it is. Overpaid. I did nothing against my strictures to help you, but you acted contrary to yours for me. The burden has shifted. I am in your debt."

"Otter, a minute of sucking your member does not weigh against two lives. I will do this again whenever you wish. Even after we go back to our place. I'll come over from time to time. It ..." he stumbled again. "It wasn't all that unpleasant. And I'll get better at it. You'll see."

At a loss for words, I watched as Andre flashed a smile and climbed down the ladder. I heard him speaking to the horses and the crunch of his boots on the snow as he returned to the house — and his wife. I sank down on the bedding and relived the moment. Then I did something totally out of character. I covered myself with blankets and slept away the morning.

# # # # #

I had feared what happened in the hayloft would change things, but Andre and Bella treated me as usual. A friendship grew that had nothing to do with my rescue of the couple. Normally, I am drawn to friendships with men, but Bella was an intriguing woman. It was easy to see the charming debutante hiding beneath the plain broadcloth dress. She held her head straight and looked everyone in the eye. She was courteous and teasing and could usually talk Andre ... or me, for that matter ... into doing precisely what she wanted.

She made our cabin more of a home than it had been before, making curtains for the bare windows and covering the eating table with a white cloth. Even so, the Tillers went out onto the porch each day and anxiously scanned the snow-covered landscape. They longed to return to their own place.

A week later, I took the horses on a short ride to give them exercise. Patch was anxious to be off; the black mare beneath Andre was less eager. Nonetheless, we crossed the bridge and tackled the snowy plain with the sorrel gelding on a lead trailing along behind us. We made it less than a quarter of the distance to the Tillers' cabin before we turned back. The animals did not labor so hard on the return trip because they followed their own broken trail. Still, both man and beast were blowing hard by the time we entered the barn again.

As we rubbed down the wet, sweaty animals, Andre spoke in a low voice. "We can go up to the loft when we're finished here."

I swallowed hard. My rod stirred at the sound of his vibrant voice. "Thank you, Andre, but that won't be necessary."

"I guess I didn't do a very good job for you last time."

I would have been lost had I turned to meet his gaze. "You did a fine job. A good job." My voice sounded tight.

"I've been thinking about it. I can do better."

"Andre ..." My voice died as a hand snaked around me and pressed against my groin. My treacherous staff betrayed me once again, growing hard and eager.

Without saying a word, he walked to the ladder and climbed up into the loft. I fought a silent, losing battle with myself for a few minutes and then followed.

He lay shirtless on the bedding, his white flesh glowing, his muscled torso a stark contrast to the thin, emaciated chest of two months ago. Andre smiled uncertainly as I came forward and fell on him.

The encounter went far beyond the first. Within moments, we were both naked beneath the blankets. We explored one another, and this time, Andre's interest was not feigned.

"What is a win-tay?" he asked when we paused a moment. His eyes were round and expectant.

"I will show you." I turned on my stomach.

After a moment, he understood and mounted me.

CHAPTER 23

The second encounter with Andre had been much more intense than the first. I had very much enjoyed the young man's stellar athletic performance. He was a champion fornicator who beat the seed out of me with his energetic lunges. Despite the gratification derived from the coupling, I was thrown into unfamiliar turmoil. Nay, it was a veritable storm of emotions, something well beyond the niggling of a pricked conscience.

By the laws of my *tiospaye*, I had committed no great sin. Dictated by the oft-short lifespan of warriors, a man commonly took multiple mates, a practical way to ensure the propagation of his line and to increase the size of the band. Therefore, the shadow hovering over those exciting, exhilarating minutes with Andre was cast by another source.

I am not normally an obtuse man, but until then I had not understood how my life-long association with Billy Strobaw had so totally molded me. I had always believed I adopted what seemed right and useful from the white man's ways and discarded all else. Yet, Billy's unwillingness — inability — to share romantic love with more than one partner at a time had infected me right down to the bone. Otherwise, why I had denied myself of the pleasure of Dull Lance's hard body and was curdled with guilt over my affair with Andre?

At first, I blindly railed against these foreign constrictions having soured a simple, joyful act. In my selfishness, I rationalized that my childhood had been a better and simpler time. Had not Cut Hand and Lone Eagle taken other wives to fulfill their practical needs?

My mouth went dry as I realized the true cause of my disquiet. Yes, they had taken other wives, but at what price? Not only to themselves, but also to their hearts' love. Billy had been crushed and despondent when he lost each of them because of it. I shuddered at the recollection of how much it had cost him. This is what I had done to James. As Andre had to Bella.

My revelation moved me to deep depression. I could never reveal my betrayal to James. Never encumber him with that knowledge. It was a burden I would have to bear alone. My breath caught in my throat. Could I continue to live in his home, bask in his love with this massive black secret feeding on my entrails? Surely, James would see straight into my troubled soul.

I already detected a difference in Andre's attitude. He was more outgoing and confident in my presence. He had gained parity with the man who had rescued him from disaster, yet he did not pretend ascendancy. In fact, he demonstrated a sort of affection. It was nothing beyond what a genuine friendship might engender, but had Bella noticed the difference? I was certain James would.

Neither Andre nor I mentioned the incident as winter retreated, although we undertook rides farther from the house almost daily. We made it halfway to the Tiller cabin, and then three-quarters of the distance. Finally, two weeks later, we made it to the front stoop of his small cabin. Andre seemed hesitant as he dismounted and walked up the steps to the porch. He went inside with me close on his heels. The place was as we had left it, including bloody linens lying on the floor. He sagged against a wall and shook his head.

"Not much of a cabin, is it?"

"It seems sturdily built. And you'll make improvements over time."

He thought a moment before standing straighter. "Yes. Yes, I will."

"What needs to be done first?"

"We need better heat."

"The fireplace should be bigger, but I have another suggestion. What you really need is a stove. It will keep you warm and make cooking easier for Bella. Timo Bowers, the blacksmith in Yanube City, can build you one."

"My plow's not heavy enough."

"That's an easy one. You and I will work together to plow our fields. You need some horses to replace the ones that died this winter. Do you have any money?"

"We brought a little with us. It's in the bank at Yanube City. It's not much, but at least we have enough to restock the larder."

We moved outside. It was chillier in the closed cabin than in the outdoor sun. I looked over the place critically. "How much land do you have?"

"Our homestead — 160 acres."

As we walked over the property, Andre decided where to break his first forty acres. We calculated how high the crick would flood during the height of snowmelt and planned a dozen other details. When he completed his mental survey, we rode back through the trail we had broken on the way here.

Once at the farm, Andre went inside to tell Bella about the state of their abode while I remained behind to brush down the horses. A few minutes later, he joined me again.

"Bella feels better now," he said. "I think my disposition was showing, and that scared her. She's more confident now."

"Good. She needs to be as sure of herself as you are."

"We can go up to the loft when we finish with the horses."

I looked over Patch's back at the wiry, attractive man. Muscles played in his shoulders as he rubbed down the sorrel, setting off a desire that almost staggered me. A sudden image of James steadied my resolve. Even so, the words I had to speak were hard to squeeze through my throat. "Nay. We cannot do that again."

Andre turned to face me, eyes wide. "I thought you liked it."

"I did. A tremor still runs up and down my back when I remember you inside me. But there are others to be considered." I sighed at the inadequacy of my words. "If we still lived in the world I grew up in, things might be different." The reasoning was flawed, but I had to end this thing without revealing too much.

Andre's frown wrinkled his freckled nose. "What would that matter?"

"Your culture sees the genders as a man and a woman and nothing else, save for deviants. In your world, sodomites must be hated and extinguished."

"And how was it considered then? You know, in your world?"

"My people understood we live on a wheel. The Circle of Life, we call it. There is no all-man or an all-woman because such humans do not exist. We all have other traits that form us and dictate our actions."

"Are you saying we have some woman in us?"

"That is one way to say it. There are men who are mostly men, but there are also men who are mostly women. They have a man's equipment, but not a man's nature. The point is that each has different wants and needs. In my day, a warrior sometimes had a wife and a win-tay. A man/man would not lie with another man/man, but it was perfectly acceptable for him to lie with a man/woman."

Andre swiped his face with a broad hand. "I don't know. You seem all man to me."

"If that is so, why did you come to me? I understand the first time was an effort to repay me. But the second time? That was different."

Andre blushed and ducked his head.

"And it is eating at you."

179

He nodded. "Some. One minute I felt I was taking something away from Bella. The next, I wondered when we'd do it again."

"Do you love her?"

"Yes! With all my heart."

"Then we cannot lie together again, no matter how much I desire it — we desire it."

I read disappointment in his eyes, but his words were accepting. "Can we remain friends?"

"Good friends and boon companions."

# # # # #

The thaw came very late in '66, but the time to undertake the seven-mile trip to Yanube City eventually arrived. I put Bella on Patch and rode the black mare because she wasn't a very good riding horse. Andre mounted the sorrel. Even this late in the spring, the going was tough. We had to stop often to allow the horses to rest before reaching the road north of the Yanube. After that, the way was muddy but more easily traveled.

I headed directly for the fort, both eager to see James and apprehensive of the meeting. I feared my nervousness was apparent, but he must not have noticed. His greeting was ebullient, although decorous, because of the presence of the Tillers. I introduced them and told of their near disaster. James readily approved of the couple wintering at the farm and rejected Andre's offer of repayment. He also agreed that providing mutual help to one another was a good idea.

"As a matter of fact, I may be able to lend a hand," he said. "My replacement, Major Bettington, is arriving at the first of the month. I'll need some time to orient him, and then a date will be set for my separation. I'll be coming home, Otter."

My heart leapt and then fell. His open, honest face instantly unraveled my plans. I knew with certainty that he merited honesty from me. Even though withholding a confession would spare him pain, our relationship would not survive so momentous a deception. Of course, to reveal it carried a similar risk. Nonetheless, I felt I had no option.

On the pretext of remaining behind to speak on some business matters with the Major, I ushered the Tillers out after receiving a promise to meet me outside the bank later. After they were gone, I closed the door and stood before the desk. James's broad smile faded as he looked into my eyes.

"What is it? What's wrong?"

"I am ashamed. I have betrayed you, James."

CHAPTER 24

James went ashen and then flushed in anger as I revealed the details of my perfidy. "He fucked you?" His voice was hoarse. "You don't even let me do that."

I dropped my chin. "It was what he needed. I perceived your need differently."

"That's hardly the point. How could you do it? I've always been true to you. I've never even looked at another man since we made our pledge beside Billy's grave at Teacher's Mead almost four years ago." He fell into a chair as if his legs would no longer bear his weight.

His despair almost rent me in two. My voice was a mere echo of itself. "I can only say I was weak and beg your forgiveness. I will work hard to regain your trust."

"Easily said." The tone was bitter.

"True. But that is all I can offer. That and my love."

"Love? You speak of love after you've let that man put his cock up your ass?"

"I always speak of love and with love to you. It happened as I described it, and I wouldn't allow it to repeat itself after that time. I denied him for you, not for myself."

"So you admit you'd like to fornicate with him again?"

"I admit the experience was pleasureful. Now I know it was too costly. I will leave, James. All I ask is that you permit me to plant the fields and assist the Tillers in sowing theirs. Then I will leave."

James sat ramrod straight, looking every inch the military officer. His lips barely moved as he spoke. "Granted. You can help your new lover salvage his life. Has he confessed to his wife as you have to me?"

Stung, I shook my head. "Nay, I do not believe so. That decision is his. But I could not play false with you." I paused before turning to leave. The weight of my actions weighed heavily upon my shoulders. "I trust you will say nothing to her."

As I reached the door, he spoke. "You have about two months before I am separated from the service."

"That will be adequate."

"I'll not visit until then."

"I'll leave the black mare and the sorrel gelding. You'll need them for the farm."

"I'll reimburse you for their cost."

I turned to look at him. "Nay. They are my parting gift."

"Where will you go?"

"Back to the Mead, I suppose. I have given it no thought."

James's features tightened. His eyes were unnaturally bright. "Then give it some now."

I walked out of the headquarters building with my life in shambles. I had sought to redeem my dishonorable actions by being honest with James. All I had accomplished was to bring him pain. I would pay whatever price was extracted, but unfortunately he would share the cost of my mistake.

I met the Tillers outside the Yanube City Bank. The handsome young man was talking and laughing with his equally handsome wife, no doubt bolstered by the prospect of repairing a life that had looked hopeless only months before. It seemed we had exchanged prospects. Mine now looked dismal. My heart empty, I approached them with a forced smile upon my lips. I felt like some green actor taking his first steps across a stage — giddy and disoriented.

"Are you ready to purchase some supplies?" The words seemed natural enough to my ears.

Andre's joy slipped a little. "To the extent our funds will allow."

As we made the rounds of the town, the Tillers were greeted politely wherever we went; I was met with reservation. There was an anxious moment when I saw the Black Crow on the boardwalk across the street, but either the preacher did not see me or chose to ignore my presence. I yearned for the years past when I was free to roam the settlement at will. Was remembrance of things that were a sign of advancing age? A better question: Was the remembrance of things past even accurate? How would I recall this moment in the years yet to come?

I ignored Andre's protests and purchased everything they would need to renew their lives, paying with my own silver pieces when theirs ran short. What need had I of these disks of metal the whites set such store by?

I bought lumber to build a barn and improve the house, ordered one of Mr. Deere's heavy iron plows, and paid for a couple of good horses. The Tillers had arrived in this country by wagon, so harness and a new vehicle were not needed. I bought foodstuffs and ordered a cooking stove from Timo Bowers.

On the way back to the farm, I rode with a happy but confused couple trailing horses after them. Their joy rubbed hard against the hollow misery I nursed. It seemed as if my heart had been ripped from my chest and left bleeding on the floor of James's office. A mile into the journey, Andre cleared his throat.

"Did Major Morrow give you leave to spend his money on us? I know he's a fine man and all, but he doesn't even know us."

I fixed my eyes on the trail ahead. "It was not his silver I spent."

"It was yours?"

From the corner of my eye, I saw him flush, no doubt chagrined he had discounted the idea an Indian could have funds of his own. "Billy died a wealthy man, and he saw to my future."

Andre was quiet for a moment, apparently digesting this information. "So it is you we are indebted to. We will repay you, Otter, I swear."

"Every penny," Bella said emphatically. "I don't know what we would have done without you."

"No need. You can name the child you carry Joseph if you want. If it is a boy, that is."

"What?" Andre reined in. Bella and I proceeded down the trail, leaving him behind. "Child? You're pregnant?"

She said nothing, but a smile curled her lips.

"And you told Otter before you told me?"

"She told me nothing," I said over my shoulder. "But I have eyes to see."

"Is it true? Are you carrying, Bella?"

"It's true."

We made the remainder of the journey with Andre bringing up the rear, alternately muttering and laughing to himself. I took little notice of his burgeoning delight. It seemed as if I rode beside myself and critically examined a selfish, unthinking stranger aboard a familiar pinto.

# # # # #

Because my time on the farm was limited, I gave Andre little leave to reflect on his coming fatherhood. I loaded my buckboard with tools and the lumber left over from rebuilding our barn, double teamed the small wagon, and headed for the Tiller farm, breaking a new trail north of Turtle Crick alongside the line of cottonwoods and sycamores. Andre rode one of the horses he had purchased; Bella stayed behind to fix an evening meal for our return.

Andre was puzzled when I began building another frame around the cabin, but I remained locked up inside myself and felt no compunction to explain. When I set him to mixing mud with hay he seemed to understand what we were about. Wolves had taken both of the Tiller's horses early in the winter, so there was adequate straw for the tabby to be used between the inner and outer walls. We labored hard the first day and accomplished more than I had anticipated.

Two weeks after the lumber arrived from town, we had expanded the size of the original house by the addition of a sleeping room. Then we enclosed the water pump already set beside the house to make a bathing room. We also erected a shed adjoining the house on the other side to accommodate and protect firewood they would need for cooking and heating.

I drove both of us hard during the day and labored long over my own chores after dark. Much of it was simply make-work since Bella kept the house spotless. Had I not done so, I would have thought too much —*remembered* too much. Even so, when I first lay my head upon the blankets each night after the Tillers settled into the bed on the other side of the room, darkness pressed in upon me, and I wondered if they could hear the whispered accusations that seemed to drift from the shadowy corners.

Was I grieving for myself or for James? Was he also lying sleepless in an army bunk at the fort, or had he already cast me from his mind? Where was Dull Lance? Should I try to find him?

The ground finally thawed to the point Andre and I could begin plowing. When that was finished, we turned our attention to laying a thicker, sturdier roof on the cabin. Once that was completed, the house was ready. It lacked only the stove Timo had promised to deliver to make it complete.

Andre drove the last nail in the new roof, straightened his back, and shook his head. "I can't believe that raging river is our little Turtle Crick."

I glanced at the churning water, which was now well beyond the stream's banks. "The crick bed is less constrained here than at the Morrow farm, so you will have a hard time building a bridge with enough span to give you access to the property during spring runoff. I suggest you make a deal with the Major and use his bridge for the time being."

He gave me a strange look, but I ignored it. We worked in silence until we left for home. Bella had a meal prepared, but I had to force myself to eat and make appropriate remarks about her cooking.

#

The next day, we finished sowing the fields on our — that is, James's farm — and then went to take care of a few minor chores on Andre's

186

cabin. Those done, I was unwilling to call a halt to the work, so we went for the horse and plow and started to work his forty acres. Andre was as meticulous about the straightness of his rows as I was. He was a good farmer. Absent some disaster, he and Bella would prosper. By distracting my mind from thoughts of James, I had come round the other way with a stinging reminder they would do so without me in their lives.

Although there was a nip to the air by the end of the day, we had worked up a good sweat. Andre laid a fire in the fireplace, and pumped water in his available pots and kettles so we could christen the new bathing room. As we filled the tub, Andre stopped me with a hand on my arm.

"What's the matter, Otter? You've been driving us like a madman."

"There is a lot of work to be done."

"True, but you're really whipping the mule. Besides, you've not been yourself lately. Is something else in the wind?"

I went silent for a full minute. "I'm leaving Major Morrow's farm."

"What? When?"

"When we get the fields sowed. His and yours."

"Why?"

"He's not happy with me."

"Oh, Lord, not because of us, I pray. If he resents your helping us, I'll speak to him."

"No. He approves of how I helped you. He will be a good neighbor."

"Then I don't understand. You're a good worker. You're loyal and ..."

His gray eyes went round. He turned ashen. "He knows. You told him, didn't you? And he wants nothing to do with deviants." He dropped his head and licked dry lips.

"Yes, I told him. I am always honest with Ja ... the Major. I withhold nothing from him."

Andre's head came up. His jaw dropped. "You ... and him? He doesn't resent sodomists; he is one. He's throwing you out because of what we did."

I laid a hand on his shoulder. "Don't judge him harshly. He has been true to me, and I let him down."

"Because I tempted you."

I tried a smile. "You tempted me from the first moment I saw you, even if you did look like a starved scarecrow. Nay, the fault is not yours. It is mine."

"But I've cost you your home."

"You had no knowledge of our relationship. I chose to keep it from you, so the blame is not yours." I saw Andre's brow crease and guessed the cause of his distress. "Do not worry. James will not reveal our actions."

He didn't look entirely convinced but let it pass. He fell quiet and seemed to be going over things in his head. I regretted revealing the cause of my distress. He didn't need more problems at the moment.

"Where will you go?"

"Back to Teacher's Mead. I have a little cabin there. Or perhaps I'll explore the Laramie country. Maybe I'll pursue a warrior's life."

He went quiet then. As the Tillers had only one washing tub, I insisted Andre bathe first. I sat in the other room and wrestled with my misery until I heard him call. Andre stood with a towel around his middle. His white flesh gleamed in the dim light. The sun bronzed arms and head almost looked to be clay appendages tacked onto the marble skin of his torso. With a constricted heart, I remembered James looking like that when he first arrived in this country.

I helped dump the dirty bath water from the porch, and noticed the chill air raising goose bumps on Andre's bare skin. Then we filled the tub again for my bath.

Andre tarried, wrapping himself in a blanket and claiming a seat on a stool. I stripped and lowered myself into the water, almost groaning in pleasure at its warm embrace.

"Otter, I've been thinking. Since you are leaving the farm, you no longer have a commitment to Major Morrow. Does that mean you feel different about what we did? About me?"

My skin puckered. How did I feel about it? James had released me from my obligations. I was undesiring of it, but it was a fact. I glanced at the handsome man in front of me, and the dark fist clutching my heart loosened its grip as I imagined his lean, wiry form naked beneath the blanket. For some reason the pale freckles across his nose stirred me. My rod moved.

"I don't know how I feel." My words *were* true. My mortal flesh leaned in one direction; my heart in another.

"I've thought about what you told me. About living on a wheel, I mean. I can see some sense to it."

"You are going to be a father now. Doesn't that change your thinking?"

"Some. But I'll be a good husband and father. I'll love them both. But you need ..."

"Do not deceive yourself. What you are asking is not for my benefit. If we are to do this thing again, it must be because you wish it — without reservation. When you arrive at that conclusion, then perhaps."

Andre fell silent while I finished my bath. When I rose from the tub, he moved up behind me, draped a towel around my shoulders, and began drying my back. The rubbing turned into a caress; the caress, into an embrace. I felt his breath in my ear.

"Without reservation," he whispered.

There was a pain in my chest as I responded to him. "Are you certain?"

He did not answer. He simply knelt at my feet with his glance centered on my manhood. Then he moved forward to take my rising rod into his mouth. He was not so awkward this time. He did not rush and try too much at once. He took his time, moving his tongue around my glans and then sliding my cock into the back of his throat. I shivered. Andre's hands shifted to my buttocks, pulling me deeper into him. I began to move my hips, all thoughts of resistance gone, blown away in the intensity of the moment.

Watching the brown, curly head working on me took me back to the days when Billy had done this for me. I could almost recapture the wonder of those youthful moments, but this was an acceptable substitute. My thoughts turned to James taking me in this same fashion, and I was suddenly contrite. My affection for Andre was growing by the day — by the minute — but it was love I held for James, not affection.

Such thoughts fell away as my body began its journey toward orgasm. My stones tingled; the hands clasping my buttocks seared my flesh. I strained forward, offering myself totally, unmindful of anything else at the moment. And then I blew. Andre gagged for a moment but continued to work with his lips and his tongue until my juices ceased flowing. Then he slowly came out to the end and held my erect cock in his hand, peering at it before looking up at me impishly.

"Did I do it right?"

"You did fine. Now stand up."

Andre stood, his hard cock jutting out hungrily. I pushed him over on the blanket he had dropped and lay atop him. I lowered my head and kissed those intriguing freckles on the bridge of his nose, and then touched my lips to his. He gasped slightly as I slowly worked my way down his long, wiry form. I sucked and nibbled the large brown aureoles, washed his muscled, hairless chest, and thrust my tongue into his deep belly button. A fine line of pale brown hair trailed from his navel to the thick bush surrounding his eager rod. I licked the underside of his cock and then came up to take the end into my mouth. I swabbed the thick glans with my tongue, causing Andre to start.

When his manhood was moist, I rose up and impaled myself on the pulsing column of flesh. Andre grunted aloud. His eyes closed. He bit his bottom lip.

"Oh, Otter."

He rolled over until he was on top of me and promptly lost control. He fucked. Aggressively. Violently. Making noises deep in his throat with each thrust. I finally figured out they were words of love.

Astounded, I lost a little of the rush, but Andre was enmeshed in the moment and continued his assault ruthlessly. Before long, his cries grew louder, meaningless now except as expressions of joy. Then he gave a grunt and clasped my body to him. Our lips brushed as Andre spasmed and poured semen into me. Finally spent, he rolled off and lay gasping on the blanket.

"That was … that was better than the last time."

I smiled. "Do you know you look very earnest and businesslike while you ply your tool?"

Andre laughed. "Do I?" He turned serious again. "Did I do it good? You know, as good as … well, you know?"

"You lay with me as you do most things, very well, indeed. You are quite a man, Andre Tiller."

"And so are you Joseph Otter. So are you. Can we do this again?"

I sobered as an image of a stricken James absorbing my confession leapt to mind. "We shall see. Perhaps the opportunity will present itself again. Now it is time to go home to your wife and the child she carries."

Andre flinched. "Right. We need to get home."

Without further words, we cleaned ourselves in the bath water, dressed, and tossed out the contents of the tub. Then making certain the fireplace was properly banked, we mounted up and started for the Morrow farm. I saw from his expression Andre was thinking of his wife. My mood deepened as my thoughts turned once again to James.

James … who was lost to me now.

CHAPTER 25

My tryst with Andre turned truly sour when I came face to face with Bella upon our return. Pleasure lit her eyes when we entered the cabin to find her standing at the cook stove. I do not believe she saw the quick tightening of the mouth that signaled her husband's inner turmoil. And then James was once again prowling the recesses of my mind. His image was so clear I feared he had died, and his shade had come to call.

Not since the slaughter of my people had such distaste for this guilt-ridden white culture seized me so tightly. It was a strange guilt. One that dictated a man's coupling should be shameful and secret, yet left him free to murder any native he pleased without culpability or conscience. And now, I was infected by their guilt with neither Billy nor James to ease me back into the reality of the world in which I was forced to live.

Andre broke the spell. "We can move back home, honey. The stove's not installed yet, but we can use the fireplace until it's delivered."

Her big eyes shone, filling her with so much beauty I no longer noticed the sweat on her lip or the tangled tresses of her lush hair. She laid a hand to her breast and breathed a single word. "When?"

"Anytime. Now, if you want."

"Can we? I don't want to seem ungrateful, but it will be so nice to be back in our home."

"I understand. I cannot truly relax until I am home." The word almost caused me to choke.

"Wait until you see the cabin, Bella." Andre grinned broadly. "You won't even recognize it."

After we ate, I helped them stow their belongings on horses and pack them to the farm. Bella was so excited at the first sight of her rebuilt home, she planted a big kiss on my cheek. Andre and I lugged their things inside while she poked into every nook and corner as if she were examining the grand plantation house where she grew up.

I left them alone to wear out the excitement of the homecoming to go rig up a rope corral for their two horses. As soon as Andre got settled in, we would begin work on the outhouse for the animals. He needed something more substantial than this poor corral before the winter drove the wolves in search of horseflesh. There was sufficient lumber remaining to erect a barn a bit more modest than ours ... that is, James's.

# # # # #

My cabin seemed a bleak place with the departure of the young couple. I claim to be a solitary man, but as the years wear on, I am no longer certain that is the case. While I took some satisfaction in my newfound privacy, I caught myself listening for the absent pair on my bed in the darkness. In fact, I continued to sleep on blankets by the stove for the next few nights. Why? I have no rational explanation, but does everything in this life require one?

The following day, wolves of another sort made an appearance. I stood on the porch while Captain Sam Smith and four of his henchmen rode into the yard. I chose that vantage point so I did not have to look up at him. Not for the first time, I wondered which was his lazy eye.

"What can I do for you, Captain?"

"You can tell me where them renegades is hiding out."

"What renegades?"

"The ones skulking around the countryside like the coyotes they are."

"I don't know anything about them. Hadn't even heard there were any in the area."

He lifted his chin and looked sideways, fixing me with his right eye. "You wouldn't lie to the law, would you, red belly?"

"I don't lie, Captain."

He studied me for thirty long seconds. "I hear the Major's retiring from the army." With that, he spurred his horse and led his men back across the crick.

I watched them disappear and considered his implied threat. What did it matter? I wouldn't be here much longer, anyway.

# # # # #

Andre and I spent the next few weeks working feverishly to construct his barn, get the last of the planting done, and our equipment cleaned and in good repair. By lamplight, I labored in the evening to make certain everything in our cabin was patched and mended. A heavy spring rain exposed leaks in the bathing room and in one corner of the outhouse. I repaired those and searched for something else to keep my mind busy and body exhausted.

As we worked together daily, I caught myself waiting for Andre to look at me or touch me in a certain way. He did not, and I understood. Just as thoughts of James put a halter on my wants, so, too, Bella intruded on his.

The one time I perceived he came close to initiating an intimacy, my relief was so intense my hands shook when he backed away. I regularly grew hard for him but always came near to panicking lest he should see.

Once our major projects were behind us, there was not enough work to distract me. I was tired near to exhaustion because I had lost the ability to rest properly. During still times, my nerves twitched causing my hands to start. My mind flashed with sudden mental images: James, Billy, Cut Hand, Lucas, and the others. Was I ghost infected? If so, there was no one to perform the cleansing ceremonies, so I would die a haunted man.

# # # # #

A fortnight later, I watched from the porch as a horseman appeared from the south. Something moved in my chest as the figure drew near. It was James. Had my time already run? I thought of a dozen small, piddling tasks that remained to be done on the Tiller's place. If James had come to evict me, I would temporarily set up my tipi in the glen where Helen and Lucas rested until they were completed.

I stood without moving until his cavalry horse clomped over the bridge. The worst of the spring runoff was past, and the torrent beneath the structure was less turbulent.

"Hello, Otter." James drew to a halt and sat his mount. He was dressed in his military uniform.

"I am sorry if I miscalculated. I had not thought my time had elapsed." Such stiff words when I yearned to speak of more tender matters.

"It hasn't. I came to see you."

The flesh on my back rippled. My heart slowed. "What about?"

"Am I welcome?"

I spread my hands. "This is your farm. Of course, you are welcome."

He shook his head. "I have only a passing acquaintance with the place. By rights, it is yours, not mine."

"The land was purchased with your funds."

"And the improvements and the cost of running it are yours. I'd say there was a standoff in the matter. But I've not come to discuss ownership."

Nay, that was not his mission, but we had both seized on the subject to delay what was coming. Now it was time to face the thing squarely. I sighed. "Then come inside and tell me why you are here."

"I'll see to my mount first."

193

I watched him disappear into the outhouse before turning inside to fix the coffee he put so much store by. I preferred the teas that Caleb Brown's Mercantile Company stocked.

A few minutes later, James entered the house, shed the coat he wore as protection against the wind, and sat at the table. I filled our mugs and took a seat opposite him. The man's open stare seared my soul, but I could not say why. Yes, I could. My renewed liaison with Andre Tiller lay exposed beneath it.

"I have treated you badly," James started and then paused to clear his throat. I made no comment. "When you came to me and forthrightly revealed what had happened, I was angry. I felt betrayed right down to my bones. I don't recall being so hurt since the day Billy left me to return to the *tiospaye.*"

"You had a right. You were betrayed." I pushed aside my mug of tea, no longer interested in it.

"You are human. *We* are human. We all make errors. Mine was reacting in mindless anger. I regret my decision and have come to ask you to stay. I have been happy — truly happy — only twice in my life. With Billy and with you. So I have come to beg you to forgive me, as I have forgiven you."

My heart leapt in happiness even as my vitals curdled. "James, when you released me — when we agreed to go our separate ways, I ..."

He held up his hand. "I know. You coupled with that young man again. That is not important in the scheme of things. The core of the matter lies in whether or not you love him."

"I am fond of the boy. And my feelings for him have grown, but it is you I love. You hold my heart hostage whether I go or stay."

James expelled a gust of air through his mouth. His hand crept forward and rested atop mine. "Then all else can be repaired."

"In truth, this thing with Andre was coming to an end. His wife is carrying his child. He loves her and will be a good father, but he is not strong enough to divide his loyalties and make it work. Don't misunderstand. He's a good man and a loyal friend. He will make us a strong neighbor willing to help when needed and accept help when it is required."

"Us. You said 'us.' Does that mean you'll stay."

"Aye, I'll stay and be glad for it. I will even welcome you in the role Andre has played if you wish."

"No. I am happy with the way we conduct our lives. I see no reason to change. I want nothing but to be the receptacle for your seed."

I rose and slipped my shirt over my head. "So be it."

Highly receptive to my companion's moods, I made gentle love to James. The thing I learned for myself was that when the flesh beneath your caress is precious to your heart, then the physical expression of love is even more intense. The youth and vigor and novelty of Andre's touch were heady, but this man was the true fruit of my vineyard. When we finished, we rose, dressed, and walked the fields, speaking not of the past but of the future.

# # # # #

James was an amazing man. After he departed for the fort the following day, I re-examined the previous night and considered what it meant to me. He had seemingly put the whole incident behind him, although I knew that was not the case. He had been loving and kind and forgiving, yet I would have to work hard to regain his trust — no, to *earn* his trust again. I would begin by informing Andre my relationship with James had been mended. How would he view the news? Likely he would not take it hard.

I toiled in the fields all morning and decided to test the crick water for my bath. The stream was still cold, but despite the pucker it put on my skin, I stripped and plunged in. I soaped quickly and submerged for the rinse. Upon rising from the water, I found a laughing Andre standing on the bank.

"If you're not careful, you'll start a legend about the Indian who bathed in a winter stream, froze into a block of ice, and floated all the way to the Mississippi."

I climbed out and began toweling off with the tattered blanket I used for that purpose. "Does he ever thaw out?"

"Yes, when he reaches New Orleans. But by then, the fishes have nibbled off all his nether parts, and everyone thinks he's a manatee."

"A good tale to tell around the winter fires. That's when you relate myths, you know." I turned solemn. "I'm glad you came by. I must talk to you."

"Sounds serious." Judging from his frown, he thought I was about to tell him the time for my departure had arrived.

"Let's go inside and warm up."

Andre glanced at the sun. "I'm not cold."

"You haven't been bathing in melted snow."

Andre trailed me inside the house, most likely so he could eye my naked body. I was gratified it was deserving of his admiration. No shame in that.

After dressing, I heated mugs of tea, while I told him Major Morrow had stopped by yesterday. His gray eyes flickered. "He asked me to stay on. He would like to restore our relationship."

"What did you say?" We took seats at the kitchen table.

"I said yes."

"So we can't be together any longer?"

I shook my head. "No, but I suspect this comes as a relief to you. What we were doing was riding your conscience too hard."

He paused momentarily. "Perhaps, although I truly enjoyed our time under the blanket. How did you feeling about it?"

"In truth, it bothered me, as well. Even though I looked at this thing through another set of eyes, I came to realize how deeply I had hurt James."

Andre met my gaze. "I understand. But I want you to know I'm not ashamed of fucking you. I got over that."

"And I felt no shame in taking you, but that was not the real problem for either of us."

Andre reddened. "No. The problem was Bella. You know, knowing how she'd feel about it if she found out. So I guess I understand what you're saying about the Major." He dropped his gaze a moment before regarding me soberly. "I will miss you ... that way. I have never said this aloud — or even permitted myself to think it — but I love you, Otter."

"No, you have grown fond of me, as I have you. If I left the farm, as was expected, nothing would have remained between us. We would be parted in every way; separated by a great distance. Now, you will have me as a neighbor and a friend. We can preserve the most valuable part of our relationship."

"I'm not sure how good a neighbor I can be. I don't think I can face the Major."

"Why not?"

Andre looked confused. "Because I took something that belonged to him."

"When you meet, James will greet you knowing you have lain with me, and you will hail him knowing he is my mate. That is insignificant when put beside considerations of fields and crops and family and friendships. You and Bella will always hold a place in my heart few others share. So will your child when he arrives."

He broke into a smile. "Joseph. We've decided to name him Joseph after you. If it's a girl, she'll be Josephine."

# # # # #

James came home two weeks later, wearing his uniform for the last time. There had been a ceremony upon the transfer of command and his separation from the service. I had considered attending, but we agreed that might not be wise. A number of the leading townspeople were expected to attend, and Captain Sam Smith might well be among them.

In preparation for the event, I raised my tipi on the windward side of the house and moved many of my possessions into it. That arrangement would appear more natural to visitors — both invited and uninvited. A hired hand should live in his own quarters. During the warm months, I intended to sleep there often. With James at my side, of course. The winter months would be spent in splendid isolation, and we could sleep wherever we pleased.

I had worried the sudden lifting of military discipline, combined with intimate living with another man on a daily basis, might be unsettling to James, but he handled the transition well. He displayed friendship and affection to the Tillers, looking Andre straight in the eye, as whites were wont to do, and taking an interest in the young man's development.

Andre did not handle things so adroitly. It required several meetings before he could hesitantly meet my beloved's gaze. Yet, I was encouraged enough to hope a friendship would grow between the two men, given time.

Despite the fact his first sixteen years had been spent on a Virginia cotton plantation, James knew little about farming. He acquired a number of books on agriculture and studied them avidly anytime he was not working the fields with me. He was smart and learned quickly. We spent many an amiable evening arguing the advantage of one method of planting over another. On one thing we agreed, totally: We would change crops often and always leave one field fallow. The soil was thin and needed time to recover. I suspect all of this excessive discussion and deliberative decision-making were nothing more than our clumsy efforts to restore our damaged relationship.

# # # # #

The summer passed pleasantly. The militia did not put in an appearance again, leading me to believe there had been no renegades. Smith's last visit had been nothing more than harassment.

From time to time, people from town came to seek the Major's advice on civic matters, and he made occasional jaunts to attend meetings. He initially resented the intrusion but soon looked forward to such diversions.

At first, I was loath to see him go, fearing he was no longer closely bound to me. Fretful he might decide not to come back. I would always be restless until he returned.

During one of his absences, I was drawn out of the house by a sound from my past. Either my ears were ringing or I had heard the shriek of an eagle wing whistle. I mounted the hill behind the cabin and found signs someone had been keeping the house under watch. As I squatted and examined the scuffmark of a moccasin, the hair on my neck rose.

I threw tack gear on Patch and rode over the hill behind the house, making for the grove of trees where Helen and Lucas had died. When I broke into the grove, a figure in buckskin britches and fringed shirt waited precisely where the tipi had stood.

"*Hah-ue*, River Otter, I see you have rebuilt your barn."

I was astonished at how my heart soared at the sight of Dull Lance. He seemed leaner and cagier than when we last met, but as handsome as ever. At the sound of his voice, three men stepped from behind trees and waited at the edges of the glen. Two were blood. One had the look of a breed. All looked to be rough men.

I kept my voice steady. "*Hah-ue*. What brings you here?"

"My men and I have been riding with Inkpaduta. Most of the Santee surrendered to the blue coats at Ft. Wadsworth, but he and his people didn't go with them."

"Why do you run with this man? He is little more than a bandit."

"Chief Inkpaduta is an honorable man," Lance said in a calm voice as his men muttered angrily.

"That is not his reputation."

"Who painted this reputation upon him? You speak the words of the Americans."

"That is true. But did he not murder women and children at Spirit Lake in the Iowa country in '57?"

"Yes, he led those raids. Why? I do not know, but he had cause. Unspeakable things were done to him and his people before that. They killed his father and his brother and many of his kin while he rode under the peace sign. You tell me why they did that, and perhaps I can tell you why he did what he did."

"Where is he headed?"

"For the Hunkpapa country. He will shelter with them. My men and I are going home for a visit before joining him there."

198

"And why have you waited for me?"

"I yearned to see an old friend." His eyes were hooded, yet I sensed warmth in his words. "But we waited longer than I wanted. Life among the whites has dulled your senses. I expected you yesterday."

"I needed to see my companion safely away. It is good for me to see a friend, as well, but if you have come to spread mischief, I have some strictures for you. You will not harm the Major. He allowed me to give you sanctuary. You ate his food and sheltered in his house."

"And he set me to work in payment."

"Little work for momentous largesse."

"All right. He is safe from us." Lance turned his head and spoke to the others in Dakota. "Is this agreed?"

All muttered "Hah," a word that sometimes meant yes and sometimes no, and sometimes was merely an acknowledgment.

"You must leave the farms along Turtle Crick alone. No harm must come to them."

"Then how are we to find provisions and replace our spent horses?"

"Go elsewhere. No one here is to be bothered."

"Since we burned out the farm west of here last year, you must be speaking of the family yonder." Lance pointed with his chin toward the Tiller farm. "The one with the woman in childbirth."

"What?"

"She was laboring when we passed not long ago."

"She's giving birth now? Then I must go."

"What are they to you?"

"Neighbors. Friends. Leave them alone, Dull Lance."

He glowered for a moment and then smiled. "We will leave them alone … for now."

I rode out of the glen and made straight for the Tiller cabin. Bella's struggle was apparent even before I mounted the steps to the front porch. My knock silenced her cries. The door opened abruptly. Andre's face cleared when he saw me.

"Bella's in trouble."

"Nay. She's just in the distress of birthing." I brushed by him and saw the expectant mother lying on the bed writhing in the grip of pain. "Do you have hot water and clean toweling?"

"It's heating now. And I have a clean cloth and a blanket to wrap the baby in."

"Put Bella's sewing scissors in a pan of boiling water until we need them."

As Andre left, I dropped to my knees beside the bed and clasped one of Bella's sweaty hands. She focused on me, recognition lighting her exhausted features.

"Otter! Glad to see ..." She gasped and let out a grunt of pain.

"May I take a look?"

Beyond the point of modesty, she spread her legs and raised her knees. I lifted her nightdress.

"Everything looks as it should be." The words were merely to ease her anxiety. In truth, I was woefully ignorant about how such things should look. "Try to relax now. When the pains come again, bear down and put some pressure on your belly. Help the child along. He's anxious to be out of there and meet his mother and father."

She smiled weakly and nodded.

I considered riding to town and fetching the doctor, but that would take too long. In my old village, there would have been midwives to help in the matter, but alas, none were left. Andre and I would have to handle the situation.

Another two hours passed as Bella's waves of pain came increasingly close together. Finally, her body began expelling the child. I positioned myself at the end of the bed with clean linen and warm water.

Andre clutched his wife's hands and murmured words of encouragement. Bella, in the grip of her pain began babbling, surprising us with a torrent of crude curses that sounded strange coming from such thin, aristocratic lips.

The gist of it seemed to be that Andre would never again place his horse's appendage between her white legs. Horse's appendage — she had not exaggerated by much.

The Tiller heir made his grand entrance into the world thirty minutes later. He was long and lanky like his father and had rusty hair like his pain-filled mother. He screeched as lustily as a distressed peacock while his father cut and tied the umbilical cord before washing him free of blood and afterbirth. Andre wrapped him in a soft blanket and placed him on his exhausted mother's breast before opening the door a modicum to allow the odor of human effort to dispel.

As Bella rested her cheek on the tiny brow, Andre hesitantly touched his son's tiny pug nose with a work-callused hand. Then he opened the blanket to once again examine the boy from head to toe. Satisfied, he rewrapped the child and smiled.

"Welcome, Joseph Norwood Tiller," he murmured with a glance at me.

"I am honored. Joseph is a good name. That is why Billy chose it for me from one of his own names."

We cleaned up the mess while the child slept atop his mother's chest. As I prepared to leave, Andre ran his hand through his mussed hair. "I'm grateful for your help."

"Keep him clean, let him suckle when he's hungry, and allow nature to take her course. What you do not know, Bella will. Come for me if there are problems. As soon as they are strong enough, we'll take her and the baby to town so the medical man can check them."

"Bella ... you heard what she said."

I chuckled. "Do not worry. When she has recovered, she'll want that handsome cock as much as she ever did."

With that pronouncement, I left before confessing I occasionally nursed a hunger for it, as well. James often benefited from that unfulfilled lust. Did he know my efforts were sometimes fueled by images of this curly-headed Shenandoah Valley farmer?

As I neared my cabin, I caught a flicker of movement in the trees. Slipping from Patch's back, I cautiously approached the spot. For a moment, I could not believe my eyes. The creature lying in the grass was a fawn, still tiny even though the dropping season was well behind us. It had been born much later than usual. Beyond that abnormality, the fawn was *sah-pah*. Totally black. I had heard of such deer but had never seen one. Surely, it was a medicine animal, an omen.

Heralding what?

CHAPTER 26

When James returned, he wouldn't hear of waiting until Bella was up for a trip to town. The next morning, he rode into Yanube City to fetch the doctor, a Swede named Helgren. The medic gave me a nod as his black buggy followed James's horse through our yard on the way to Andre's place. I fetched Patch and trailed along behind them.

James and I waited on the porch with the new father while Dr. Helgren examined mother and child. James had brought a flask, so we drank a belated toast to the arrival of the Tiller heir. I wasn't much for liquor, but he had a military man's thirst, and Andre, one befitting a veteran of the ranks. I watched in amusement as the two grew half pie-eyed.

The doctor joined us on the steps where we were taking turns making up toasts — some of them nonsensical — and declared Bella fit to bear other sons and little Joseph healthy. Somewhere along the way, the flask had turned into a bottle pulled from James's saddlebags. Helgren was friendly enough to join in a celebratory round but prudently left after one drink. The matter of a fee was never raised, so James had likely paid for the professional visit before they left town.

On our way home, I watched for the mysterious black fawn but saw no sign of the spirit animal. A white buffalo was an omen of good fortune. Did that mean a black fawn heralded bad times? Were Dull Lance and his band in the area? What was the militia up to? Was the Rev. Jeremiah Berglund plotting mischief? These wild thoughts rattled my head as I recalled another disturbing sign. Back in the month called February by the whites, one complete lunar phase had turned without a full moon, and this occurred during one of the longest, harshest winters I could remember.

# # # # #

A dry summer followed the wet winter. James and I labored long hours to cajole a decent harvest out of the earth. Bella recovered enough to help Andre, but because she had the additional responsibility of the child, I often went over to lend a hand after finishing work on our farm. Occasionally, James would accompany me, but most of his time was spent playing with the infant. Once the child wrapped his tiny fist around my lover's finger, he was lost. He clearly yearned to be a grandfather.

When Bella's breasts dried up, Andre bought a cow and kept us in sweet milk and butter in partial payment of his debt. James purchased a few steers to raise on corn and prairie grass, so we made certain the Tillers had adequate red meat for their diet. I was pleased with the developing friendship between our families. I always drew a denial when I accused James of being uncommonly aroused after trips to the neighboring farm, but I could tell he considered Andre a powerful physical presence. Fatherhood seemed to enhance his manly attributes.

# # # # #

Congress approved the minting of a new five-cent coin called a nickel to replace the old halfpenny, of which I had a number in my secret cache of coins. I held my metal specie close because the recession that gripped the country following the end of the war still raged. This, of course, gave hard chink extra value. James, on the other hand, constantly complained his pension from the army was less certain in its value.

Toward the end of the summer, he returned from a visit to the fort with word that Tennessee had been readmitted to the Union, the first confederate state to achieve that distinction. Then we learned something called the Atlantic Cable, an underwater telegraph, had been laid, putting the United States in almost instantaneous contact with Europe — a feat that strained credulity.

As the days grew shorter and chillier, we gathered our crops and declared it had been a decent season despite the lack of rain. Even though we had visited the Tillers weekly since the baby had been born last March, James fretted over whether they were adequately prepared for the coming winter. We loaded a supply of pemmican and beef into the buckboard late one afternoon and set out to relieve his concerns.

Andre and Bella were glad to see us. As usual, James immediately headed inside to play with Joseph while Andre showed me his harvest. His reap had been adequate, but not as hardy as ours since this was the first planting on his acreage. Thus he was glad to have the extra supplies we'd brought. I helped him store the goods in the cool room of his newly dug cellar.

Andre had acquired some traps he intended to set in Turtle Crick. This was not beaver country, although a few lived in the rivers and cricks. The fur trade had passed its zenith, but even so, good pelts always came in handy. A coat of well-sewn beaver skins would keep its wearer warm, especially a tiny child.

Andre detoured to the barn and threw open the door. "Let me show you something amazing. Have you ever seen anything like this?"

My heart lurched as I saw the hide tacked to the door.

"I've never seen a black fawn before," he said. "Are they common around here?"

"Nay, this is the first one I've seen." An unbelievably deep sadness tinged with anxiety swept me as I eyed the pelt.

Andre noticed my reaction. "What's wrong?"

"Better that you hadn't killed it."

"I know it was beautiful as a living thing, but it will serve a useful purpose. Can't you see Bella or little Joseph in clothing made from that hide? It is truly unusual."

"Yes, Bella would look pretty in such a cape."

Should I tell him this creature had been special? A medicine animal. Andre wouldn't understand. As amiable and affable as he was, he thought like a white man. Why not? He was a white man. Besides, the deed was done. Now it only remained to see the consequences. I silently breathed a prayer to Grandfather Deer asking forgiveness for this unknowing American.

Two days later, I noticed smoke rising over the trees to the west. James watched for a moment before asking if it was a prairie fire.

"Nay, it's too concentrated." I thought it more likely Dull Lance had broken his word and attacked the Tiller Farm.

James must have been struck by the same thought. "The Tillers!" he exclaimed. "Oh, God. The baby!"

We raced for the horses. Without waiting to harness Patch, I leapt on his back and headed down the track on the north side of the crick, guiding the pinto with pressure from my knees. Within minutes, I broke out of the scraggly forest to see Andre stagger out of the burning barn leading a dancing, nervous horse. He frantically motioned back inside.

I threw myself to the ground and ran into the blazing building. I could see little through the thick pall of smoke, but I heard a horse neigh. After locating the animal more by sound than sight, I ripped off my shirt and threw it over the frightened pony's head. With a firm grip on its mane, I half-led, half-cajoled the panicked animal to safety. Once outside, I bent over to cough smoke from my lungs.

James rushed to me and lent a steadying arm. "Are you all right?"

My eyes smarting, I nodded and called to Andre, "How about the cow? Is she safe?"

"I got her out. All of the animals are safe."

"What happened? Where are Bella and the baby?" James asked.

"We're here," she called from the porch. Bella had her son under one arm and a pail of water in her other hand.

"It's no use," James said. "We'll not be able to contain the blaze. The barn is lost."

He was right. If the flames had taken root on the outside, the barn would have been salvageable, but the interior was well ablaze.

"Aye, but we'd better water the roof of the cabin," I said. "Bella, will you call us if the fire spreads? We can't do anything about flying embers, but the blaze doesn't seem to be sparking much."

That changed when the flames reached the loft and the roof collapsed. Although the cabin was now protected, fiery fragments floated into the air on a cushion of smoke. We walked a broad area of the prairie, dousing smoldering embers that threatened to re-ignite. Those that traveled farther were merely pieces of dead ash by the time they came to earth. Others drifting into the cottonwoods and sycamores were of more immediate concern. Despite the dryness of the past summer, they failed to catch. That was fortunate because burning trees would have led the fire directly to our farm. After the blaze had lost its ferocity, we leaned against the cabin porch while Bella brought tea and coffee.

"It's my fault," Andre said. "It's getting bitter at night, so I was carrying some smoldering peat to the fireplace in the corner of the barn." He had adopted my practice of seeing to the comfort of his animals. "On the way, I set the hot pail down when I stopped to check why Apollonia was acting up. She's been nervous lately.

"The cow shied when I walked up beside her," he explained. "I didn't notice she'd kicked over the bucket until the hay in her crib caught fire. I ran to the crick for water, but by the time I got back, it was out of control. I gave up trying to contain it and started saving the animals."

Andre rubbed his face, leaving a smear of soot on one cheek. "The cow was so balky, the place was almost falling down around my ears by the time I got her out and returned for the horses." He stared at the smoldering ruins. "I'll have to raise another barn before winter sets in, or I'll lose my livestock again."

"I'll ride for the fort," James said. "I daresay I can find enough men willing to help with the building in exchange for getting out of a little detail work. I'll order lumber while I'm there. You and Bella won't have to worry about your animals."

"But I can't pay you, Major."

"We'll worry about that when you're secure for the winter. If I leave now, I'll be able to turn back the patrol that's likely heading here to check on the cause of the smoke."

I watched James ride out of the yard. His concern and generosity were clear evidence he had forgiven my lapse of judgment and did not hold Andre at fault. My heart swelled under an onslaught of emotion.

When he was out of sight, I turned to Andre. "We'd better start cutting grass across the crick for the tabby." I indicated the hay pile covered with a tarp west of the burned barn. "You lost the hay in the loft, so you're going to be short on fodder for the animals. We'll use as little of that as possible for the tabby."

Andre's face cleared as he picked up a stiff piece of hide and called to his wife. "Look, Bella, I salvaged this for you."

It was the black fawn.

Without a word, I took it from his hands and threw it into the flickering embers of the destroyed barn. Then I waded across the cold crick and began hacking tufts of prairie grass with my knife and stacking them into small piles.

CHAPTER 27

"You are a strange man, Joseph Otter," James said upon his return to the Tiller farm from Yanube City. "You're as well educated as anyone in the territory, yet you toss a deerskin into the fire because of superstition."

Andre, who had mentioned the incident to him, observed our interplay with a grin.

"Have you not avoided walking under ladders or chosen another path because of black cats?"

"Hmm, well, that's simply in keeping with custom."

"Custom based on superstition. Is avoiding offending Grandfather Deer any different?"

James tut-tutted as we headed home. "And you claim to be a Christian."

"I have a passing acquaintance with the faith and find things to admire in it. In truth, I don't see much difference between the Christian God and the All-Powerful of my culture."

"Well, if burning a black pelt avoids more trouble for Bella and Andre, I'm all for it. Damned curious, don't you think? A black fawn. Never seen one."

"Nor I, until a few days ago."

"The important thing is to get a sturdy barn erected before the first norther. The lumber's due on the morrow, and some men from the fort looking to pick up a few extra dollars will be here, as well. We'll get it done within three days, I'll warrant. I suppose you're going to insist on those double walls you like."

"Of course. Otherwise the animals will freeze despite the roof over their heads."

"Then we'd best add a day or two to that estimate."

#

The following morning, the lumber wagon and ten men in uniforms, or parts of uniforms, clattered over the bridge and pulled to a halt in the farmyard. James strode onto the porch and addressed them as if they were still under his command. Shortly thereafter, they all trooped down the trail toward the Tiller Farm. I followed in the buckboard with a load of hay, which I hoped was sufficient to replenish Andre's winter feed.

James was right. The barn stood tall and sturdy by the third day, after which we began the erection of the outer skin and the packing of the insulating tabby between the two. By the end of the week, the Tiller's animals had a warm dry shelter for the winter. Andre broke out what little coinage he had left and asked the men to divide it among themselves. Back at our place, James supplemented the amount so the off-duty soldiers earned a decent wage for the week.

"Don't let on to Andre," James cautioned as we watched the men ride across the prairie to the south. "Leave him his pride. The Tillers break their backs trying to pay their debts, and I don't want this added to the sum."

"Generous of you, James."

"Nonsense, I'll die with more money than I can spend."

He'd sacrificed the 10,000-acre Virginia plantation at $4.00 an acre, a scandalous sum for rich bottomland downriver from General Washington's Mt. Vernon home. Yet, even after halving the amount with his dead brother's family, he was one of the richest men on these plains — even without the penurious military pension he was always complaining about.

Andre, Bella, and the baby arrived a few minutes later with a pot of thick stew she had cooked in the southern manner. Loaves of hard-crusted bread, fresh sweet onions, and newly churned and salted cow's butter put the finishing touches to the meal.

"Why did you burn the fawn skin, Otter?" Andre asked as we sat at the table amid the ruins of the meal.

"Bad luck."

He let it go at that and surprised us with a bottle of wine he'd been hoarding. We toasted the close of the season and the restoration of the Tillers' fortunes.

After Andre and his family left for home with a tired, fussy baby, James turned to me. "I know it has been a long day, but I would like you to fuck me to sleep."

James wasn't actually asleep when I finally finished, but he was certainly relaxed enough to achieve that state in record time. I cleaned up and then stood gazing fondly at his slumbering form. For at least a portion of the previous half hour, James had doubtless pictured the athletic form of Andre Tiller plowing his channel. That was all right. So had I.

# # # # #

Something called the Medicine Lodge Treaty, actually a series of three agreements signed with the Southern Plains tribes, came only two years after the Little Arkansas Treaty. Although the terms of the first pact were never implemented, Medicine Lodge reduced the size of the non-existent reservations by ninety per cent, and banned the tribes from crossing to the north side of the Arkansas under penalty of being declared hostile, which meant they were fair game for the army. Not many settlers in the vicinity of Yanube City took comfort in the news.

Winter arrived in the form of a sudden snow squall that swept down from Canada and left the earth as white as bleached buffalo bones. The weather relented a bit after the initial onslaught but soon clasped the prairie in a grip that would not ease until the spring thaw. We were well prepared and kept a clear trail broken between the house and the barn. Early in the season, we used racks to traipse the mile to the Tiller farm by foot. James professed to be anxious to see they were snug in their homestead and the new barn was sound. That was nonsense, of course. He wanted to play with the baby.

It pained me that Andre was still a bit reserved with James. At first, I was convinced this was occasioned by his guilt over our intimacies, but in time, I came to understand it was more likely generated by a sense of servility to power, an inability by this former foot soldier to treat a senior officer with familiarity. He unfailingly addressed him as "Major," despite James's encouragement of the use of his Christian name. Bella had no such problem. He was James to her from the start. We are all bent in a certain direction by our upbringing, I suppose.

Despite Andre's reserve, he and Bella were good company. Whether indulging in one of her crystalline laughs or crooning to her infant son, she was always a joy to be around. Andre was more sober-sided, but pleasant and likeable. On one visit, he proudly displayed the pelts of three beaver he had caught along the banks of the crick and jokingly asked if I was going to burn them before Bella could make a fur coat for the baby.

After each of these forays, James would lead me to bed and demand a good flanking. Soon enough, the weather grew more severe, and the wolves made their appearance, driven south by the northern winds. We often heard them howling in the distance, and at night the beasts occasionally snuffled around the barn.

When cold weather had struck, we abandoned the artifice that I lived in the tipi beside the house. Both of us had saved a number of jobs to be attended during these months of confinement. We repaired torn or worn clothing, and I even fashioned new garments from cloth James had bought in town. We read a great deal, pouring over new tomes, also brought from Yanube City, and rereading old ones. Kerosene lanterns were a vast improvement over the milder, flickering light of candles.

Having a companion throughout the snowbound months proved helpful on another front. Due to our frequent couplings, neither of us was as water shy as he would have been if alone. I worked hard to keep my person clean for him, as he did for me. He shaved almost daily, although I required a razor — or the tweezers I preferred — less frequently.

We talked a great deal. James made a good conversationalist, as he was willing to venture forth on almost any subject, even those about which he knew very little or naught at all. We spent many hours discussing how life on the prairie had changed since he first came to this country. The adoption of the white conqueror's way had left something lacking in my life and overthrown much of what was good about the Old Way. The honorable and sometimes privileged position of win-tays had disappeared, washed away by the fear and loathing of the Europeans for berdaches.

I had given such prejudices little import, but now I came to fully appreciate the burden they had placed on James for his entire life. He had lived a harsh military existence in close proximity to men who hated and feared his kind, yet managed to conceal his proclivities and command the respect and obedience of those same men.

The winter of '86-'87 was not as harsh as the prior one. For one thing, it was made far easier for me by James's company. His companionship was exceptionally agreeable, if not as idyllic — if that is the proper word — as my first summer with Billy. That both puzzled and disturbed me until I understood those initial months with Billy had been an affirmation of the kind of life I wished to live. Then it had been the discovery of youth; now it was the reward of comfortable, yet exciting fellowship.

Shortly prior to the arrival of the actual snowmelt, the weather eased enough so we were able to check on the Tillers. Andre and his family had wintered well. Little Joseph had grown beyond our expectations, and would soon reach his first birthday. James was already puzzling over what to get the baby as a proper present. Although he was doing little more than sitting up unaided, my lover saw immense potential in the child. As for me, I was merely pleased my namesake was a happy infant.

From the flush of Bella's complexion, I suspected there would be a new addition to the family, although Andre's attitude indicated he did not yet suspect.

# # # # #

On our first trip to town after the early spring thaw took a firm grip on the land, we stopped at the fort where Major Bettington, the new commander, received us promptly. The respect between the two officers was obvious. They were soon immersed in gossip about military events and political news from back east.

I heard enough to understand the Suez Canal in Africa was nearing completion, which revived talk of a canal across the Isthmus of Panama. That caught my attention because Billy had always considered the canal a fool's venture.

Nebraska was about to be admitted as the 38th state, and rumors abounded that the Union was negotiating for the purchase of the frigid Alaska territory from the Russians. Good. Maybe the flood of settlers would go there instead of inundating us.

There was also talk of the army trying to force the plains tribes into a new treaty, although no one knew much about it except a number of the tribes would be relocated to western Oklahoma if the negotiations were successful. Of course, they would be. The army had more men and guns.

When we left the fort, we gave Caleb Brown's establishment our custom. I noted the sign had been changed from Brown's Mercantile to Brown's Emporium. I pondered the import of that as we entered and was immediately provided with an answer. One of the clerks informed us Caleb had passed away on Christmas Day. Another nephew was on his way from Philadelphia to assume control of the business. The name change was likely an effort to place his stamp on the enterprise. One more tie to the past had been severed.

# # # # #

We were able to get our sowing done early and decided to add another field, which would give us 160 acres under cultivation. With James's assistance, the task went faster and smoother. Once we finished planting, we helped Andre put in another forty acres of potatoes, and beans. Bella had either confessed her condition, or Andre had awakened to it himself. He was bursting with pride and loudly prophesying it would be a girl.

During the next week, we tended to the cleaning and repair of our tools and equipment between weeding the stubborn native grasses that constantly sprouted in the midst of the farm fields. One day, the clop of hooves on the bridge drew me from the barn just as Lt. Simmons and a squad of riders entered the yard. James came out of the cabin and returned the officer's crisp salute.

"Greetings, sir. Major Bettington sends his regards."

"Return mine to him, if you please. What draws you out, Lieutenant?"

"Marauders, I'm sorry to report. Two farms along the Yanube have been burned. Five dead, one of them a child."

James glanced at me. "Along the Yanube, you say? Was one of them the Strobaw place at Teacher's Mead?"

"No, sir. Both places were on the south side of the river between the Mead and the town."

"Survivors?"

"Two adults and three children. The raiders were Indians, sir. Sioux, most likely. They've eluded us, thus far. The militia is in pursuit, and we're checking the farms in this area. The Major has two more patrols raising the alarm south toward the Little Islands and to the west. I respectfully suggest you keep a sharp eye out."

"Were you able to identify the raiders?" I hoped my question did not reveal too much. James gave me a quick look. He had certainly caught the import of my query.

"Beyond them being tribesmen, no. They didn't seem to be as intent on pillaging as on murdering. This was a killing spree."

"They weren't stealing horses?"

"Some were taken, but most were killed. Stealing horses did not seem to be the point of the attacks."

James returned the Lieutenant's salute. "Thank you for your warning. We'll be on watch. The Tiller place is directly west of us, and someone is now occupying the old burned-out farm upstream of there about five miles."

"Yes, sir. Thank you, sir."

As the patrol disappeared down the trail north of the crick, James joined me in the yard. "Dull Lance, do you think?"

"If they are not stealing horses, then I think not. It's someone seeking vengeance."

"Surely you don't think Lance has forgiven the murder of his wife and men?"

I rubbed the back of my hand where a nettle had raised an itch. "If it is Lance, nothing would suit him better than to have the militia on his trail. He would have no qualms about ambushing them along the way."

"You stay here. I'm going to go after the patrol and tell them our ... my suspicions."

I appreciated the way he deftly relieved me of the duty of informing on the Sioux. While I still harbored doubts it was Dull Lance and his group, I preferred to stand mute on the subject so far as the law was concerned.

I frowned, unsettled by my lenient attitude toward Lance. Was he not responsible for Bent Nose's slaughter? Not only that, but if he had gone from harassment to murder, that was as bad as what the militia had been doing.

The Lieutenant was right about one thing. Those committing these raids were bent on killing. They would take enough horses to provide alternate mounts in case of hard pursuit, but would not want a large herd to slow them down. They would kill the beasts they did not need to deny them to the whites.

I grew uneasy. Was there some darkness in Dull Lance I had not seen when he wintered at the farm to recover from his wound?

CHAPTER 28

My partner had no sooner disappeared down the trail than I became aware of another presence. A man stepped out from around the rear of the cabin.

"I see you, River Otter."

"I see you, too, Dull Lance."

For a moment I feared my thoughts had conjured an image of the man, but he was real enough. James would soon return from running down Lt. Simmons's patrol, and Lance could not be here when he returned. James was unarmed — as was I. Dull Lance held a repeating rifle in his arms and had a handgun strapped around his waist. Streaks of red dye lined his brow and cheeks. Red. The color of war.

"The Major will be back soon. You cannot tarry."

"I saw him go after the Silver Bar Chief and his soldiers. No doubt he's telling them the warrior, Dull Lance, is in the area."

"He does his duty and speaks only the truth."

"I am glad you did not go with him. I would feel betrayed."

"I wonder if Bent Nose had time to feel betrayed before he died."

"You think I betrayed him?"

"Did he know you intended to kill those two men?" When Lance did not reply, my heart sank. "Why are you here?"

"I need some of your pain-killing medicine."

"Laudanum? Is someone injured?"

"One of my men has a cut." He elaborated no further, and I did not ask for more information.

"Medication to ease someone's pain I will give you, but do not ask for anything else. I will not aid your raids on the settlers."

"Why not? These are the people who slaughtered your *tiospaye.*"

"Nay, they are not. The man responsible for that was dishonored by his own people and is dead. Those farmers had done you no harm."

"At least one of them was with the men who murdered my wife and companions." His lips twisted in a grim smile. "I killed him and burned his farmhouse and barn to the ground."

"Then he has paid. You have restored your honor. Now it is time to go back home."

"I have no home. They search for me in the Laramie country."

"A condition you brought upon yourself. I am not insensitive to the wrongs we've suffered at the hands of the Americans, Dull Lance, but your way is not the road to take."

"It is the good Red Road."

I shook my head. "No, it is the Black Road. You have lost your Seventh Direction."

"What does a Yanube know of a Sioux's Seventh Direction?"

There was no time to engage him in a discussion. James would return shortly. I went into the cabin and returned with the Laudanum. "This is all I have. Take it and go before the patrol returns. And do not hold it against the Major because he reported you."

"Nay, I thank him. I want the whites to know Dull Lance is causing fear among them."

"This aid I have rendered renews your promise. Leave the farms at Teacher's Mead and those along Turtle Crick alone."

Lance leveled a dark-eyed look that almost pulled my heart from my chest. "Agreed. And I won't harm your win-tay wife either. Unless he gets in my way." He took his leave with an arrogant swagger.

So he knew of my relationship with James. Or suspected it. That would not have bothered me in the old days. For some reason, it did now. Was this a change in me or merely a reflection of the mood of the times? After Dull Lance disappeared behind the house, I walked in his moccasin tracks to hide them from other eyes.

# # # # #

Days passed without further word of hostiles. James visited the fort and town at least twice a week. Once, he returned with news the American House of Representatives had voted a Bill of Impeachment against Andrew Johnson, the Democratic Vice President who had succeeded to Lincoln's chair. The new president had incurred the wrath of the Republicans with his leniency toward the former rebels. They seized upon his attempt to dismiss Edwin M. Stanton as Secretary of War to press their persecution of the man.

"What happens now?" I asked.

"There will be a trial by the Senate. If convicted, he will be removed from office. If not, he will limp through his remaining term and pass into history."

"It strikes me this rapid succession of men claiming the chieftaincy is nothing short of madness. One president no sooner sets his course than another replaces him with a different destination in mind. Yet, perhaps that is your salvation, as well. It means the poor ones pass through the system and are expelled just as quickly."

"You make them sound like human excrement." James paused a moment. "Perhaps that is an apt description for some of them."

Another time, he brought confirmation that Alaska had, indeed, been purchased from the Russian Tsar for about two copper pennies an acre. When he mused aloud about what Washington would do with all that frozen land, I responded with the truth: "They will send settlers to kill off or crowd out the native tribes."

"Um, possibly." He changed the subject. "There's a rumor someone's hiding out in the badlands on the upper reaches of Trickling Water."

My chest tightened. "That is a natural hiding place. But it is not big enough to conceal many people."

"Big enough to hide Dull Lance's gang."

"Are you so certain it is him?"

I saw something in his eyes I did not like. "Aren't you? From all the reports, I don't figure there's more than five or six of them. At any rate, Captain Smith and some of his militia are going up to root them out. I mention it because they are apt to ride past here on their way."

I grunted.

"Have you seen him? Dull Lance, I mean."

A stone face would not fool James for long. "Why do you ask?"

"Because Major Bettington's heard talk around town that you're protecting them. Giving them aid and information. Possibly even directing their movements."

"They say this of the man who fought off an attack that burned our barn?"

His eyes narrowed. "By your own admission there was no such attack."

"I was speaking of what they believe, not what you know. Yes, I have seen him. I did everything I could to encourage him to leave the territory."

"He is as full of hate as Smith. Perhaps it would be a good thing if they met on the Trickling Water."

That uncharacteristic pronouncement made me wonder if James had not looked deeper into my soul than I knew possible. I studied a small cut on my right thumb.

"If they do, Smith won't find anything he shouldn't, will he?" he persisted.

"Nay. They'll find nothing of mine … of ours." There was naught about the bottle of laudanum to reflect on me.

We heard nothing more about renegades, nor did we see any militia in the vicinity.

After a trip to town in May, James brought news President Johnson had been acquitted in his impeachment trial by one vote.

Shortly after that, we were working in the fields when some of the militia finally made an appearance. They approached from the south and drummed over the bridge into the barnyard.

"You there," Captain Smith called. "Injun, come here."

"What do you want, Smith?" James stepped in front of me.

"I want a Injun tracker. He'll do."

"He's my hired hand. He'll remain where he is and work for his pay."

Smith's pale, walleyed gaze flicked to the tipi beside the barn where I was purported to live. His short beard bristled. "He'll do his duty to the civil authorities."

"He's not a citizen under the law and owes you nothing."

"You ain't big dog at the fort nowadays, Morrow. You ain't got no authority over me or mine. Don't you want to see them murdering Injuns caught and dealt with?"

"I put my trust in the military, not the militia. Otter stays here where he belongs."

"What about you?" Smith looked past James. "Ain't you got nothing to say about it?"

"I do as my employer tells me. But if I were free to go, I would not."

Smith's face went red. Some of the men behind him muttered angrily. "How come?"

"I do not hunt men. Not your kind or my kind. I do not kill unless under threat. Not your kind or my kind."

"Some in town say you're the trail boss of these hostiles."

"Then they are wrong."

Smith wheeled his horse. "Come on, boys, we's as good trackers as he is."

We watched the horses out of sight around the east end of the house.

James slapped his pant leg in agitation. "That was deliberate. He challenged you in public in town, and now he's done it again in front of his men."

"It appears to me he challenged both of us."

Apparently the militia found no one in the badlands lying five miles upstream from the cave where I had buried the dead Sioux. At least, no word of an encounter reached our ears. Everything turned peaceful for the summer months. Peaceful or not, anytime I ventured into Yanube City, I was treated rudely and denied entrance to some places of business where I had traded for years. Smith's influence had poisoned the town.

# # # # #

Midsummer, I ventured a visit to Teacher's Mead, leaving James to do the light fieldwork required this time of year. I encountered no one on the way but paused to watch a stagecoach across the river making its way to Yanube City. The man riding shotgun almost broke his neck watching me over his shoulder until they were out of sight.

A lone Indian on a pinto had excited his great interest. Dull Lance's occasional raids had soured the atmosphere and made life more difficult for those of us remaining in this part of the country.

The Mead was a changed place. Not only was there a way station for the stage with a forge sitting beside it, there was also another small house westing of the cabin I had claimed as my own after Billy's death. A stable and a large corral containing several horses fronted the old deer trail, now become a genuine road. A stranger worked the fields with Cuthan and Alexander. Even the stone main house had been expanded to meet the needs of the growing family.

Cuthan came forward to greet me with a huge grin. "Unexpected pleasure."

"I felt the need for friendly faces. Why was I not announced by the hounds?"

"You'll find plenty of friendly faces here. Get down and come in. Mary will be happy to see you. Unfortunately, the children have tamed the hounds, and all the traffic in and out of the place has so accustomed them to strangers, they've retired from guarding."

"There have been other changes, I see."

"More than I like. I almost wish I hadn't accepted the way station offer. Life is no longer simple."

The children swarmed from all directions, bringing with them the errant dogs: Alexander from the fields; Rachel Ann from behind the house; John, with a leather bib apron wrapped around his slender waist, from the forge; Matthew from inside the stable. Mary stepped out of the house with Hannah trailing along behind.

I felt disoriented. My childhood home had changed dramatically. It was a miniature town, and it did not stretch the imagination to envision it as a real community with its own stores and citizens.

Cuthan had hired a young man named Curtis Appleton in aid of the farming, assigning ten-year-old Alexander to his supervision. Appleton's wife, Jane, helped Mary prepare meals and see to the comfort of the stage passengers. Rachel Ann, now seven, helped as much as she could. She was as industrious and responsible as any true Yanube child.

Cuthan had also engaged an Absaroka to man the forge and care for the stage's relief horses. He went by the name of Crow Johnson and looked more like a warrior than a smith. Eight-year-old John worked in the forge, and Matthew, who bested him by a year, helped care for the horse teams. Hannah was five but thought she was as big as anyone, doggedly poking her little nose into the cooking and serving. John assured me she was more trouble than help. Nonetheless, her mother put up with her "assistance," as Mary was unwilling to rein in the child's urge to do her share.

The rest of the day was spent getting reacquainted and catching up on events. Cuthan, privy to the news the stage carried once a week, confirmed that while the recession gripping the country seemed to be easing, its effects were not yet spent. Money was tight. Most of the Mead's crops had been traded for goods rather than cash, so the stage company's hard chink came in handy.

Later, as we walked alone in the fields, Cuthan told me the cavern in the hollow hill was no longer a secret. The cave was the Mead's cold house, so others frequently went in and out to supply the makings of meals for the travelers.

"And it's not just the stage any longer," he said. "Wagons and even wagon trains often stop for a hot meal. Mary's cooking is becoming famous from Ft. Ramson to Yanube City."

"If the cavern is known, does it remain a secure place for the storing of our other goods?"

This had been a far safer place to hide my gold and silver than our farm on Turtle Crick, although I kept a small portion of it there. I had hoped to let the bulk of the money remain here at the Mead.

"Our coin is safe. No one knows of the boxes buried in a dim recess of the cavern. I feel easy about it."

"Then so do I."

After we returned to the house, the other denizens of the Mead soon appeared, opening the door and stepping into the fronting room without knocking. This was apparently an informal group on friendly terms with one another. That was typical of Cuthan and Mary. The

Appletons were an English couple who looked to be barely out of their teens, likely the reason there were no children trailing after them.

Both were apple-cheeked, as was appropriate to their name, and shy. Curtis was a fair man burning brown beneath the prairie sun. His wife was quite pretty when compared to his ordinariness. An uncle already established in New York City had paid their passage from London, but in the hard times following the war, their presence had been a burden, so they immigrated west.

Crow was a man not yet thirty whose dark Absaroka features arranged themselves in a pleasing way. He was fit and finely muscled, again reminding me of a warrior rather than a farrier and horse tender. His father had been a scout for Col. Wallston at Ft. Ramson until he retired and returned to his native hills. Crow remained behind because he had never known the old country. He spoke some Lakota, and Matthew regularly addressed him in that tongue until Mary called him down for the practice. It wasn't polite to exclude others from the conversation, she claimed, which was not the real reason for her objection, of course.

That was unfair. Mary knew that to remain Indian was to remain outside. She was merely trying to avoid that eventuality for her charges.

The others returned to their lodges after a pleasant meal. Before Crow left, I made arrangements to spend the night in his cabin.

John objected. "You can sleep with me. Or Matthew and me can ..."

"Matthew and I," his mother admonished.

"Uh ... or we can double up and you can have my bed."

"Thank you, but I suspect no one would get any sleep with the two of you chattering all night. No, I will sleep in my old cabin."

When I went there later, Crow laid out his blankets on the floor and insisted I take the bed. He wasn't talkative, and I put it down to the Absaroka's dislike of the Sioux. To their minds, there wasn't a copper penny's worth of difference between the Yanube and the Council of the Seven Fires. That made no sense. The man worked for a Yanube. Of course, Crow and the rest of the world thought Cuthan was a breed, but that shouldn't have made any difference.

After we silently slipped into our separate beds, Crow spoke in a deep, husky voice, "You seen Dull Lance lately?"

I came up on my elbow. "You know Dull Lance?"

"I rode with him for a time before he went wild. Didn't mind stealing horses, but he got to liking the killing too much."

His words fell hard on my ears. "I haven't seen him since last spring. Have you?"

"Four suns past. He stood up on the hollow hill and caught my eye."

"The hounds didn't hear him or catch his scent?"

"He's too cagey for that? Besides, them dogs is so spoiled they're no good."

"What did he want?"

"Food and ammunition. I give him what I had put away for my own eating and the cartridges from my rifle. None of Cuthan's stuff."

"Did he want you to join him again?"

"Mentioned it. Told him I liked it where I was. Cuthan's a good man. And Mary's not too bad. She's married to a breed and has a bunch of kids by him, but she can't face up to a blood."

I chuckled. "She tries to turn all of us into white men."

That brought a grunt. "Don't think she means nothing by it, though."

"It means she's determined her family's going to survive, nothing more. Did Dull Lance say where he'd been?"

"With Inkpaduta and the Hunkpapa."

"What's he doing back here?"

"Didn't say, but I figure it's because when there ain't no raids for a spell, everybody lets his hair down. You know, gets careless. He's got a sticker in his foot about the militia down here. He can't get it out, and it pesters him so much he can't forget about it, neither."

I lay back on my blankets. News of Dull Lance's return roiled my insides. It doubtless meant more killing. It also meant Cuthan had been one of those who'd gotten careless. When Rachel Ann came from the back of the house this afternoon, I'd assumed she'd been up on the hollow hill watching for strangers. I must be going slow in the head. If that had been the case, she'd have raced down and let everybody know I was coming.

I had trouble going to sleep.

CHAPTER 29

The next morning, I asked Cuthan why he no longer posted a lookout on the hill, especially since the hounds were not reliable guard dogs. When he said he felt it was unnecessary because of the increased public traffic and the growth of the Mead's population, I felt compelled to repeat the conversation I'd had with Crow last night.

"I have Dull Lance's pledge that Teacher's Mead won't be attacked, but the fact he came to Crow for aid bothers me. If Crow knows about the hollow hill, then he knows of the food and ammunition stored there."

Cuthan shook his head. "Apparently, he didn't betray that knowledge. It sounds to me as if he's estranged from the man because of his bloodlust. Stealing horses is one thing, but killing is another matter."

"That is true, but you'd best keep a close eye on him."

"He seems trustworthy, but I'll do as you suggest."

We strolled the fields and viewed the ripening crops. It looked as if the Mead's yield would be heavy this year, certainly more bountiful than our reap. The soil was better along the Yanube. Still, our farm would take care of our needs with a little surplus to share or sell.

I left Cuthan conferring with Curtis, his field hand, waved at Alexander, who was applying a hoe some distance away, and walked across the farmyard to the forge. Crow was industriously pounding an anvil, fashioning what appeared to be a sizeable pot, while John manned the bellows. Both worked shirtless beneath leather aprons, and I admired the Absaroka's muscles as they bunched and relaxed with each swing of his heavy hammer. Enough of his dusky chest was visible to expose a web of puckered flesh near his left shoulder and an angry, slashing scar protruding from beneath the apron bib.

"Otter," John greeted me with a dazzling smile.

He was a handsome lad, putting me in mind of Cut Hand. Had his father shared the family secret with him and the other children? They probably continued to think they were quarter breeds, with Grandpa Billy's and Mary's European blood diluting their strain, although that was hard to believe with their grandfather's proud features so clearly stamped on their eager young faces.

I greeted both of them. "You were up before I stirred this morning, Crow."

"I go running down by the Yanube in the early morning. Puts me in a mind to face the day." He wiped his brow with a forearm.

"I see you've lived an adventuresome life." I nodded at the scars on his torso.

"He's been shot with a gun and slashed with a saber, but they couldn't kill him." Excitement danced in John's gold-flecked black eyes.

The Absaroka darkened, leaving me to wonder what tales he'd told the child. Crow motioned to his shoulder with a thumb. "Six-shooter bullet fired from a spell away. It was near spent, so I dug it out with the tip of my knife."

I didn't ask after the manner of the assault.

"The other one's what give me trouble."

"He fought with Red Cap back in Minnesota," John said.

A Crow riding with the Sioux? It happened sometimes "Then you saw some hard times."

"Aye, but they coulda been worse. Inkpaduta's a great chief. They say bad things about him, but he went through a lot before he took to the warpath."

"I hope you didn't receive those at Spirit Lake."

"Nay, I was but a teenager then. I joined him later, and never saw the murderer they claimed he was at Spirit Lake. I was with him at Big Mound and Dead Buffalo Lake. I earned these scars at White Stone Hill."

"And then rode west with Dull Lance?"

He nodded. "And rode with him some after that, like I told you. But when he turned from the Red Road, I wanted no part of him."

I switched to Lakota, which I knew he understood. "Do you have certain knowledge he has taken the Black Road?"

Crow wiped the sweat from his brow with a brawny forearm. "Aye. And that was the day I left him and his companions."

His words rocked me. "How far does your loyalty to him go?"

"I will not betray him. Nor will I aid him."

"No matter the temptation? If he raided this farm, would you raise a rifle against him?"

"He will not. He told me of his pledge to you."

"Even so, the food stored in the hollow hill will be a temptation when the cold months come."

"I can talk the lingo, you know," John said.

"And can be relied upon to hold your tongue," I snapped. The boy ducked his head, seeming to send sparks flying from those golden hairs amid the black.

"He don't know of those stores or the hollow hill. Nor will he learn of them from me," Crow said. "Cuthan is more my people than Dull Lance ever will be. He took me in and give me work worthy of a man. I do not have to plow fields or run errands to eat. He sent me to a man named Bowers to learn blacksmithing and give me this forge. It's hard, honorable work. Then he give me the horses to care for. That is warrior's work."

"Well said, Crow. But be prepared. Dull Lance seems less stable now than when I first met him. You have sharp eyes. Use them."

"I hear you, River Otter."

Crow gave John leave to accompany me next door to inspect the stage company's relief team. Matthew was pitching fodder into a trough for the horses when we arrived. He, too, was shirtless, and I saw so much of his slain brother in his slender frame that my breath caught in my throat.

"Morning, Otter." He moved forward and offered a handshake, Indian style, his eager smile belying his reserved manner.

"The horses look in fine condition. You care for them well."

"Crow does most of it. Well, the heavy stuff, anyway. You know, keeping them shod. But I guess I do the rest. Mucking out the stable ..."

"I have to help with that sometimes," John interrupted him.

"Keeping a man's horses fit and ready for action is warrior's work," I said.

"Even if they belong to someone else?" Matthew asked.

"Even if they belong to someone else."

# # # # #

During my three days at the Mead, I noticed the growing divide between the youngsters of the family. Alexander was quiet and reserved and obsessed with earning his father's approval at every turn. Although only two years older than John, he almost seemed an only child. I saw little of the playful exchanges that passed between John and Matthew and Rachel Ann. I put it down to a difference in Alexander's solemn nature.

When a stage arrived on its way to Yanube City, Mary and Jane immediately took charge of the two ladies in the coach, showing them facilities for relieving their physical discomfort and a washroom in the building that served as a dining hall. Cuthan and Curtis showed

227

similar courtesies to the three male passengers. I was amused to see separate necessaries had been provided for men and women nearby. Crow and Matthew saw to the changing of the team horses.

The driver brought unsettling news. Bands of Southern and Northern Cheyenne, Kiowa, Comanche, and Pawnee had undertaken a series of raids on white settlers in Kansas and Colorado and Texas. The fact that some Sioux, mostly Oglala and Brule Lakota bands, had joined in the raids would doubtless put our militia on the prod again, even though these events took place far from Ft. Yanube.

The following morning, I departed for home despite a blustery day with *Wakinyan* nourishing the plains well to the west of us. Sheets of rain pouring from roiling iron-gray clouds obscured the far horizon. I hoped James was receiving his share.

I decided to take the wagon trail on the north side of the Yanube rather than crosscut the countryside, because the going would be easier on Patch if things got nasty. Before I was halfway to Yanube City the wind whipped sand and pebbles against my face with a force that stung. Through a haze of driving dust, I heard thunder, although the rain had not yet reached me. I lowered my head against the wind and plodded onward. After another hard ten miles, I caught sight of a wagon on the main road across the river, and even though it was partially obscured by a howling curtain of dust, I perceived it was in some distress.

When I reached a decent walk-across, I forded the broad, shallow river and turned back to render aid. Some of the settlers were ill equipped to deal with the elements out here, as Andre and Bella had learned when they first arrived.

The wagon stood motionless a distance down the way, its canvas covers whipping and billowing in the gale. One of the animals seemed to be down. As I drew near, it was obvious the travelers were not yet aware of my presence. I hailed the wagon to keep from startling them.

The group instantly grew agitated, and moments later I heard a sharp report. They were shooting at me! I whirled and gave the pinto a kick in the flanks. The pony caught my sense of urgency and bolted. Another report sounded, and then another. Patch grunted and stumbled. He recovered and raced across the grassy plain almost out of control. The gusting wind, now at my front, nearly swept me from the saddle.

Once out of sight of the wagon, I fought my mount to a walk and found another ford. Although the water flow at this time of year was diminished, the current was already rising ahead of the heavy rains west of us, making this crossing more difficult than the earlier one. As soon as we were safely on the north bank, I dismounted and examined Patch. Blood streamed down his left hindquarters. The wound appeared to be a furrow rather than a penetration. Nonetheless, I didn't want to ride him until I knew how bad the injury was.

I ignored the bolts of lightning playing among the roiling rain clouds and took shelter in the tree line to treat the injury. Shielding the wound from the whistling wind as much as possible, I bathed the gash and applied an astringent. Patch danced and nipped harmlessly at me. I gentled him with some Yanube words and smeared honey on the torn flesh to seal the rip and hopefully prevent infection from setting in.

Once the pony was calmed a bit, we left the shelter of the thrashing trees and braved the banshee winds to cut across the prairie. I had no interest in running into the militia, although it was unlikely any of that lot was braving the elements at the moment. I leaned into the wind, leading Patch by the reins.

Something or someone had spooked the immigrants. A horse down because of an accident or illness would have occasioned grateful acceptance of aid. Yet, when I called out, the people in the wagon had panicked. Had someone attacked the wagon or were the settlers merely nervous about strangers? Especially red strangers.

Although I sported no feathers or beadwork, I was wearing fringed trousers and a buckskin shirt. They had probably mistaken me for a hostile. I picked up my pace. I wanted to be home before the militia got news of the incident and spread its net.

After an hour, a heavy rainsquall moved in from the west, causing me to pull my slicker from the saddlebags. The garment was awkward. I did not like the oily feel of the material, but it kept me from a thorough soaking. Patch fought his way through the fading light over the rough prairie, stumbling occasionally as torrents of driving water made his footing uncertain. We walked most of the night before clattering over the bridge and into the farmyard. A lantern came on in the house.

James's delight turned into concern when I told him what had happened. We lit a lamp in the barn and took a look at Patch. The rain had opened up the bullet wound; the animal was bleeding again. James heated an iron and cauterized the gash while I held the pony's neck and spoke gently into his ear. Patch squealed and kicked as the hot metal singed hair and flesh. I was surprised when James laid the iron again, and yet another time. I understood when I stepped away from the disgruntled pony and took a look. The gelding now wore a triangle brand.

James inspected his handiwork. "He'll recover. A close inspection may reveal the deeper furrow where the bullet grazed him, but it's the best I can do to camouflage the wound. We need to put a similar brand on the other animals. Except my horse. He's obviously a retired military animal, and I have papers to support that claim."

"How do we explain why we are we doing this now, and why a triangle?"

He thought for a moment. "Because I have been urging you to do this ever since the raids last year. You never got around to it, but now that I've retired to the farm, I laid the brand myself. As for the triangle, we have no proper branding iron, so it is an easy mark."

We branded the black and the sorrel, to the distress of both. When the job was completed, James eyed the animals critically.

"Crude, but perhaps it will be effective. This is a dangerous situation. If Smith finds the wound he will declare you one of the raiders. If there were any raiders. Do you think the people in the wagon realized the pinto was hit?"

I shrugged. "Patch grunted and stumbled momentarily, but even I did not know he had been shot until I reached safety and stopped to allow him to blow. There may be a blood trail part of the way, although the rain likely washed it away."

There was nothing more we could do other than rub Patch down and lock the horses in the barn to wait out the danger. Our lovemaking in the early morning hours held an air of desperation.

CHAPTER 30

Two days passed before James and I stood on the porch and spotted a line of riders in the distance. He shaded his eyes with a palm. "Not military. Militia, I'd guess. Go saddle the horses while I get the rifles and a few other things."

"You're expecting a battle?"

"No, but when they get here, they'll find us leaving to take some stores to the Tillers. I want White Patch right there in front of them. Sometimes that's the best way to hide something."

I had the tack gear on my mount and was just heaving the heavy military saddle on his roan when James joined me and took over the job.

"They're still too far away. I want them almost here when we come out of the barn. We'll leave it unlocked so they can snoop like old Aunt Jenny — which is to say, as much as they want."

When the first hoof struck the wooden bridge, we led our horses out of the barn. Sam Smith rode into the yard at the head of seven heavily armed men.

"Captain, to what do we owe the courtesy of this call?" James's voice was cordial, holding no note of irony.

"Been another raid. Wagon was ambushed on the road twixt Teacher's Mead and Yanube City." As he spoke, the group behind him broke apart and headed in different directions.

James paid no attention to them. "Casualties?" He sounded like a superior officer taking a report from a subordinate.

"No, but a horse was shot down, stranding the party in the middle of a storm." His eyes slid to me. "It was Injuns, or course. You know anything about it, boy?"

James spoke before I could respond. "My man knows nothing about it. How big was the raiding party?"

"Dunno. It was raining like the Flood, so they ain't sure."

"Raining? So it occurred two days back. I'd like to question the immigrants. Where are they?"

"Bought a horse to replace the one that was down and headed for Oregon this morning."

"This is a little off the Oregon Trail."

"Ain't my business what trail they take."

James gave Smith a look that said the story was hogwash, but he didn't directly challenge the man's word. "We have been working here this past week. Right now, we're off to the farm up the crick. Mrs. Tiller's expecting, and we want to see how she's faring."

"We're heading over there, too," Smith said. "We're hitting all the farms in the area to warn of hostiles."

The militiamen re-assembled behind Smith, who spurred his mount. His gaze fell on Patch's hindquarters as he rode past. He squinted his walleyes but said nothing. We watched the riders out of sight before mounting and following along behind.

"He saw the brand," James said in a quiet voice.

"He saw it, but I'm not certain of his reaction. If I had to guess, I'd say there will be eyes on the farm for a few days. Probably from the hill behind the house. I'd better move back into my tipi for the time being."

"I expect," he agreed sourly.

Smith did not tarry at the Tillers. The group was already splashing across Turtle Crick by the time we rode up. Andre gave us a worried look.

"That's bad news. I don't need a hostile raid with Bella getting so near her time."

"I don't think there's much reason to worry," James said. "Attacking a lone wagon on the open road is one thing. Taking on an established farm with buildings for protection is another. I'd keep a wary eye out, but that's about all."

"Won't this ever stop? What have we done to them?"

I tried to put a halter on my tongue but failed. "Would it surprise you to know two Indian families once lived right here? Or that a little over a mile to the northeast, a Yanube woman and her son were shot to death and their tipi burned by that same group of men who just rode through here? Or another like it," I added to be fair.

Andre's jaw fell. "I had no idea. Please, don't tell Bella. It would distress her too much."

"I spoke only so you can see the tribesmen have grievances, too."

"What did Smith say to you?" James asked.

"He told us about the attack on the immigrant's wagon."

"Anything else?"

"He wanted to know if I'd seen Otter around the farm this past week. I told him we hadn't seen anyone. We're getting ready for harvest." Andre's face clouded. "And Bella's about due. Hope I can get the crops

232

in before she delivers, but I've got to let the field dry out from the storm before I start."

"If there's any problem, James and I will help you gather the harvest."

"Absolutely," he agreed with a nod. "You give Bella whatever attention she needs."

Andre smiled and thanked us for the offer. His work on the farm had laid a deep tan on his once fair features, but those fetching freckles still marched across the bridge of his nose. I felt myself stir.

"Why did Smith want to know if I'd seen you?" he asked.

"Because he's bound I am with the renegades."

Andre took a step backwards; his eyebrows shot up. "What? That's rubbish! Why would he think that?"

"Because Otter is one of the few Indians remaining in this area. Smith hates all bloods and is dedicated to running them off. Or killing them," James said.

Andre shook his head. "I'll set him straight on that. I'll tell ..."

I interrupted him. "You will say nothing. He's a low man full of hate and prejudice. Give him nothing. Answer his questions but volunteer nothing."

"That's good advice, Andre."

"Then that is what I'll do. But I'm going to warn Bella so he can't whipsaw us."

I could find no fault with that. "Where is she, by the way?"

"She's in the washing room." Andre took off his hat and rubbed his thick mop brown hair with a broad palm. "The weather's turning. There's a nip to the air. Are you ready to start your harvest?"

We spoke of farming and business matters for a few minutes before Andre went inside to let his wife know they had visitors. When she appeared, I marveled she had not yet delivered. She caught my look.

"Yes, I know. And it can't be too soon for me." She plopped in a chair on the porch and stuck her feet out in front of her; a public posture I suspect would have caused her acute embarrassment back on her father's plantation.

James dropped the bag he'd brought on the porch and went inside, returning moments later with the chubby baby in his arms. He indicated the supplies. "A few things you might have run short of." He turned to Andre and laughed as Joseph poked a stubby finger in his ear. He was a beautiful baby with pouty little bow lips and a spray of golden angel's hair already fading to a sand color.

"If you need aid, stand outside and fire three rifle shots in the air." James said. "If you don't hear a like reply, do it again. If we don't answer, ride for us. At least one of us is usually on the farm, but it's possible we could be inside and not hear your alarm." He buzzed the baby's belly, and laughed as the child squirmed and giggled.

After assuring ourselves Bella was all right, we took our leave. James rode with the air of a man deprived. He always hated taking leave of the Tiller child.

A week later, we began to harvest the fields. Both of us kept an eye on the horizon, watching for smoke or riders. I often climbed the gentle hill behind the house and examined the ground for signs of intruders. I found none but nonetheless continued to sleep nights in my tipi beside the house.

# # # # #

We worked hard and managed to complete our harvest ahead of a second threatening storm. We had just walked out of the barn after caring for the trace horses when Andre's signal came. James acknowledged the call with three rifle shots while I hurried to saddle our mounts. Andre met us on his porch a few minutes later.

"It's Bella. Her time's come, but she's having problems."

"Do we need a medic?"

Andre's handsome face tightened. "She's in terrible pain. It's not like the last time. Something's wrong."

"I'll ride for the doctor." James turned to me. "See if you can help here." Without waiting for a reply, he splashed across Turtle Crick and headed cross country for Yanube City.

I cast a wary eye on the glowering clouds off to the west for any sign of angry black tails reaching for the ground. It was late in the season for tornadoes, but the whirling monsters did not move in accordance with man's calendar.

Andre and I went inside to render what aid and comfort we could. Bella lay aback on the bed, pain etched deeply into her face. She sponged the sweat from her lip with a soggy rag and turned her eyes on us. I was flattered to see a spark of pleasure at the sight of me.

I moved to her side and clasped her pale, cold hand. "James has ridden for the doctor. Andre and I will do what we can until they return.

In the time the Tillers had been in this country, Bella had turned from a genteel southern belle — albeit one who had suffered through a terrible war — into a hardy frontier woman. Even now, wracked with

234

pain, she retained her beauty, but it had gone from ethereal to earthy. To me, it was a far more winning loveliness.

"J ... Joseph?" she gasped.

Andre scooped the curly-headed child from a blanket on the floor and put him on the bed beside her. "He's fine."

Her pain-filled face softened. There was little else we could do besides tend the baby and lend encouragement to Bella while the seemingly interminable hours ticked away.

At last, James returned with Dr. Helgren and a woman I assumed to be his wife and nurse. They banished us to the porch and went inside to examine Bella.

"I don't like the looks of that sky," James said as we stood shifting from one foot to the other.

Andre cast an apprehensive look to the west. "I haven't finished the harvest. If that storm breaks, I'll lose the rest of the crop."

I stepped from the porch. "I don't know any better way of waiting than working."

The others apparently agreed; they joined me as I went to the barn for the wagon. Labor provided another boon: it was harder to hear Bella's screams from the far end of the field. We worked hard and fast, although Andre stopped often to glance back at the cabin. When no one appeared on the porch after an hour, he trotted back to the house to check on the situation and returned with a worried look.

"Breech birth. They're trying to turn the baby into position." With that, he clamped his mouth shut and took up his scythe with a vengeance.

We finished the harvest before nightfall. The storm, a gully-washer holding ice pellets amongst the drumming raindrops, struck shortly thereafter. The day disappeared before its allotted time, snuffed out by thick, black clouds eclipsing the sun. This was the world James Andre Tiller greeted with a lusty bellow on October 5, 1868.

A few days later, word reached us that Lt. Col. George Armstrong Custer had attacked Black Kettle's Southern Cheyenne winter camp on the Wichita River in Indian Territory as a part of General Phil Sheridan's Winter Offensive. Black Kettle had survived Chivington's murderous assault at Sand Crick, but he, his wife, Medicine Woman, and a large number of Cheyenne women, children, and warriors fell to Custer's attack.

The assault on a peaceful village raised a considerable controversy, but General William Tecumseh Sherman, the commander of the Military Division of the Missouri, had approved the invasion of peaceful reservations in pursuit of hostiles as a legitimate military tactic. To me, it was simply murder.

CHAPTER 31

Winter was not so onerous that year, and a spring rain came hard on the heels of planting, boosting our hopes for a decent harvest at the end of the growing season. Once the heavy work was done, James began to spend more time in town, usually remaining overnight and occasionally longer because of a rising civic interest. Talk of statehood had begun to make the rounds, and James felt a responsibility to represent a moderate political faction. I wholeheartedly approved.

One day, when he was away at the territorial capital, laughter echoing across the plains drew my attention. I straightened up from hoeing and watched a horse with double riders approach from the east. They looked to be children. Alex and John? I scoured the landscape but saw none of the rest of Cuthan's family. The boys weren't riding hard, so it was unlikely they carried urgent news.

The youngster sitting in front spotted me and waved. In greeting, not alarm. If they had ridden from the Mead, they had started early. It was not yet five in the afternoon as the white man called the hour. I moved out of the field and into the yard to check the water jug in the shade of the porch. It was cool to the touch. Good, they would need refreshment.

When the riders drew within hailing distance, the boys shouted a hello. The other voice was not Alex's; it sounded more like Matthew's. Indeed, it was Helen's son.

As soon as the pony, another pinto like Patch, clomped across the bridge, both lads wiggled off and ran forward. Ten-year-old John clasped me around the chest. Matthew, a year older, was more reserved.

"Otter, we've come for a visit," John said.

"Is that all right with you, Grandfather?"

I smiled at Matthew's proper Dakota address. "Of course. Come up on the porch and have a drink of water."

"Sounds good, but I'll bet the crick water's colder," John said.

Nonetheless, the boys slurped two dippers from my jug. I rested in a homemade chair as they settled on the porch, allowing their long legs to hang over the edge. They had grown since I saw them last.

"Where's Whispering Wind, Matthew?"

"He has a stone bruise. Crow says he may be lamed up for good."

"Shame. He was a good mount."

"And he was my brother's." The boy's face closed up.

I sought to send his thoughts in other directions. "What brings you rascals to my door?"

"Been too long since we've seen you."

"That's true," Matthew said in Dakota. "But it's not the reason. We've been banished."

"Banished? For what?"

"John's been covering chicken do-do with dirt and daring his sisters to stomp on it."

John giggled. "They fall for it every time."

"Yeah, and then they go crying to Mary."

"That's not as bad as what you did." John poked him with an elbow.

"What did you do, Matthew?"

"Can I be Little Bear again? At least while I'm here?"

John laughed. "He's just trying to change the subject. Go on, ask him what he did to get banished." Too impatient to wait out Bear, John provided the answer. "He told Rachel Ann and Hannah that snakes like to hide out in the hole in the toilet. Then he put some gravel in a hollow reed and sealed up the ends. Every time one of the girls had to go, he snuck around behind the necessary and shook the reed. He can make it sound just like a rattlesnake."

Little Bear snickered. "They tear out of there with a scream."

"It got so bad, Rachel Ann started packing Grandpa Billy's shotgun in there with her."

"That gun must be as big as she is."

"Bigger," John said through his mirth. "Then last week, when Matthew made the snake noise, she stuck the barrel down the hole and pulled the trigger."

The boys howled and pounded the planking in glee. "Took ... took Ma three days to get her clean," John chortled.

"Yeah, and it would have been worse if the recoil hadn't blown her out the door."

"With her bloomers down around her ankles."

They rolled on the floor laughing and hiccupping while I struggled to keep a straight face. "I hope she wasn't injured."

"Bruised shoulder," her brother said when he could draw a breath.

Little Bear sobered. "Anyway, that was what did it. Cuthan made us tear down the necessary and build a new one. The stage came before we finished, and the ladies had to use the gent's toilet. So Cuthan sent us over here for you to work us to death. Oh yes, and you're supposed to teach us some reading and arithmetic in between the working and the sleeping."

To honor Cuthan's request, I set them to work after they tended John's pony. The boy had named him Arrow Wind, which had been the name of one of Billy's horses. The original Arrow Wind had been the mount Cut Hand brought down out of the Little Island Mountains when he led Billy into our lives.

I had only two hoes, so they weeded while I gave the cellar a much needed cleaning and straightening. Something always wanted doing around a farm.

The next day, we rode into Yanube City to have the blacksmith make more tools. Dressed in loincloth and moccasins, Little Bear rode the sorrel gelding he now called Red Wind.

Timo Bowers agreed to fashion two additional hoes, one to use as a spare. He appropriated John to operate the bellows while Bear and I went to buy supplies, a ticklish thing that had to be done since James wasn't here to do it for me.

I immediately noticed a number of strange people speaking in different dialects, including a black man. I hadn't seen a Negro since a runaway Mississippi slave spent a night in the barn at the Mead, lo those many years ago. None of the Buffalo Soldiers we'd heard so much about during the war had ever served at Ft. Yanube.

Southerners escaping the rubble of the defeated Confederacy were in search of a new life in the western lands. Some of them would stay, others would move on toward the setting sun. Once again, I saw curious looks as Bear and I passed through town. Here were two of the fierce Indians they had heard so much about, had been warned against, had been taught to fear. No matter that one was a child of eleven. I kept a wary eye out for the Rev. Berglund. I wanted no unfounded accusations from that quarter.

No one tried to stop us as we entered the Brown Emporium, but our sudden appearance caused such an unrest that I wished old Caleb were here to personally welcome us. And then, to my astonishment, he appeared. Or at least a younger version did. A man tripped down the staircase and approached with his hand out.

"Welcome. You must be Otter." The mirage grasped my palm in an American handshake. "I'm Caleb Brown." He laughed pleasantly. "Not the original, of course, but the nephew. Also named Caleb."

"Mr. Brown, how are you doing?"

"Caleb. Please call me Caleb. My uncle left written instructions that you are to be treated as one of the stores oldest and most valued customers. I personally assure you his wishes will be followed to the letter."

"I was sorry to learn of his death. He was a steady friend and an asset to this town. I was also sorry to hear of his other nephew's death. He was your brother?"

"No, a cousin. Thank you for the sentiment. As far as my cousin is concerned, I understand he became mixed up in the militia, and Uncle Caleb didn't approve of some of their actions. It caused an estrangement between them. Nonetheless, Abel did not merit a death such as he met."

As I could not fully agree, I said nothing. If Brown noticed, he didn't let on. I turned to the boy standing at my side. "This is Matthew Brandt. Today he is holding to his birth name of Little Bear. He is the ward of Cuthan Strobaw and is visiting us from his home at Teacher's Mead."

"I have seen this young man before, although in somewhat different attire. How do you do, Matthew … uh, Little Bear. You helped tend the horses when the stage my wife and I were on paused to change teams at the Mead last year.

"Yes, sir. I remember." Bear accepted the man's handshake.

Caleb turned back to me. "How can I help you today?"

"Matthew and Cuthan's younger son, John, are visiting the farm, and that puts a strain on my eating tins and cutlery."

"I believe we can take care of that."

A few minutes later, we left the store with sacks that rattled with tin plates and tin cups and knives and forks and spoons. We created an obvious racket as we made our way back to the blacksmith shop to retrieve John and our horses.

Timo had fashioned two iron hoes and was fitting them into stout handles. He talked a blue streak to John as the lad assisted in the labor. My heart skipped a beat when I saw the adoration in the smith's eyes. It was the same fondness Timo had lavished upon Cut Hand now transferred to the boy, a smaller replica of his grandfather.

# # # # #

Despite their youth, both John and Little Bear were accustomed to hard work and did not need my supervision. A small spring feeding Turtle Crick lay close by, so I dug trenches and developed a series of

240

channels I could dam or open as needed in order to water the fields. After a good soaking, the plants took on new life.

A week or so into their visit, I eased off on the hard labor and devoted more time to the boys' studies. This suited John perfectly, but Bear clearly preferred to be outside. I moved the classroom to the porch, hoping to strike a balance.

John was quick and bright and effortlessly soaked up facts and figures from the pages of books. Bear's intelligence shone in a different manner. His eyes tended to glaze when reciting from a tome, but when I plucked a problem from the pages and applied it to daily life, he picked it up quickly. He was hopeless at calculating the velocity of an object, but instinctively used that same lore to grasp how long it would take a man to reach the Trickling Water afoot or by horseback.

James returned from Yanube City and was pleased to find the boys here, even though it occasioned some awkwardness at bedtime until Bear decided he wanted to sleep in the tipi. Thereafter, the boys spent the nights there, leaving the cabin to James and me. The day after he arrived back home, James liberated them from the fields and took them hunting.

After they helped dress a buck Bear had brought down, I released them from both labor and lessons for the rest of the day. They promptly disappeared. I aired out our bedding and hauled it back into the house. When I went to the barn to tend the animals later, I found John listlessly currying Arrow.

"Where's Little Bear?"

"He went over to where his mother and his brother are buried. He's gone tribal on us. Hasn't hardly said anything in English since we've been here. He always puts on his loincloth. I don't even *have* one."

"Not even at home?"

John shook his head. "I've got moccasins and a fringe shirt, but that's all. Ma says it's indecent wearing a little scrap of cloth to hide your privates. Says savages are the only people who run around in that getup. Matthew wears britches at the Mead."

"Your mother has the white man's way of thinking. Such clothing served us well for a long time before they arrived."

James had come into the barn and heard our conversation. "Why don't you make the lad one?"

"Would you like a breechclout?"

John turned big, black, gold-starred eyes on me. "Could I?"

241

"I have buckskin around here somewhere. It wouldn't take long to fashion a simple apron."

I rooted around in a trunk and came up with some soft, tanned deerskin. After laying it out on the kitchen table, I cut out the garment with my knife. John eagerly stripped and tied it into place.

"When we have the time, I will make you one decorated with beadwork and dyed porcupine quills. Then you'll have the proper regalia for dancing."

John sobered. "We don't dance. I mean, Ma makes us learn reels and waltzes and stuff, but we don't powwow dance."

James watched us from a chair at the table. "Perhaps Otter and Matthew can teach you."

"Perhaps," I said.

"I've got my moccasins with me." John retrieved them from his pack and slipped them over his feet. "Now I'm War Eagle. That is who I'll be while I'm here. But I guess you can just call me Eagle."

"Eagle, you are," James said.

"I'm going to go find Little Bear. He might like company."

"Yes, he might find the company of his friend, Eagle, especially comforting right now." I clasped his shoulder.

"But not John Strobaw?"

"Probably not."

"Okay, then I'll be Eagle for him."

James and I stood at the edge of the porch and watched the lithe, nearly naked form climb the hill behind the house. The boy's slender frame held the promise of good shoulders and sturdy legs, provoking a sudden image of Cut Hand as a young man. That brought thoughts of Billy. My mind saw him as he was the first time he had appeared with Cut in the village. Blond and wiry and already speaking the Yanube tongue, he had stolen my ten-year-old heart instantly.

My staff rose and demanded attention. James laid a comforting hand to my shoulder, but we both knew we would have to wait until we had more privacy. No telling when the boys would show up at the cabin. I walked back to the barn to tend the animals while he went into the field.

#

I knew Little Bear had stored up his grief and not dealt with it properly when he was dumped into the middle of a family of four other children. Swept up in learning a whole new lifestyle, he had suppressed the loss of his family. Now, removed from the frenzy of the

Mead and placed in the vicinity of where his loss had taken place, he immersed himself in sorrow — and likely guilt for not confronting it earlier.

I cautioned John — who was now playing War Eagle to the hilt — to remain close but not to stand in the way of his friend's suffering. Roughly what the whites called a month elapsed before the older boy faced me with his thoughts.

"What happened to the men who killed my family?" The three of us were sitting on the porch watching *Han* — darkness — steal over the earth. James had gone to the Tillers for a short visit.

"The man who led them died as they did. Violently."

"How do you know?"

"Because I killed him."

Bear did what no Dakota child would have done in years past; he stared directly into my eyes. "When?"

"When the militia attacked Teacher's Mead. The time the Major and his troops came to help us. I shot him from the saddle when he tried to flee."

"I was there. Why didn't I know about it?"

"Because Mary sheltered you and the other children from the sight of the bodies that day."

"So he's dead? Good. Now let's kill the rest of them."

Staring into the face of mindless hatred, I tried to deal with it before it got out of hand. I had seen the consequences of such blind stupidity. Indeed, it had slain this boy's family and destroyed most of what was dear to me. I ignored the moment of weakness the flood of memories brought and grappled for this youngster's soul.

"If you saw one of the raiders who slew your family standing with some other Americans, what would you want to do?"

"Kill them all."

"Why?"

"He killed my mother and brother."

"Why slay the others?"

"Because they're just like him."

"You would be right, and you would be wrong. Some of them probably would think as he did. Hate as he hated. But there would be others who harbored no such thoughts, no such hate. Yet you put them together in your mind. That is what they do when they see us. They make us over into the image of the Indian they hate and fear the most. They do not see us as individual men. They see us as a clan, a tribe, an enemy, just as you are doing. You must look and discern the friend from the foe."

"Yes," Eagle interjected, "and try to keep from getting shot full of holes while you're figuring it out."

"You need to be just as cautious when approaching people of the blood who are foreign to you. There is a long history of warfare between the tribes. Remember the Cherokee who came with the gray coats to fight us five years ago, Eagle? What I am trying to say, Little Bear, is that even some of the men who rode with Hardcastle that day might not have been haters. But they were under his authority and influence. There is a reason you cut off the head of a snake and not the tail. The head holds the poison."

"Hah." The child uttered the ambiguous expression countless generations had used before him.

"How many men have you killed?" Eagle asked.

"More than I want to remember. But those times are passing, and I hope neither of you ever has to kill. It is a serious thing."

"It's what warriors do," Bear said.

"Nay! Warriors count coup and show bravery in other ways. They kill only when they must."

Even as I spoke, I feared the words were meaningless. News of conflicts between tribes and settlers rolled across the prairie with every wagon train and army patrol. Just this past week, Major Bettington had told James of a massacre of a farm family just west of Ft. Ramson by a mixed gang of breeds and low whites. I prayed this area would be spared whatever was to come.

Taking in Eagle's thoughtful look and Bear's rebellious one, I struck the arm of my chair. "Now, it is time for lessons or for bed. Which will it be?"

"Bed," said Bear.

"Arithmetic," Eagle declared.

I smiled. Such was the nature of each child.

# # # # #

I kept the boys for another moon while I labored long into the night after they slept exhausted from the day's labor and their lessons. I knew what I intended to give Bear in payment for his work; Eagle's wage took some thought and considerable labor in secret. First, I chewed pieces of buckskin until they were as soft as cotton and rubbed oils into the material before washing and bleaching it. Then I began cutting and sewing.

244

When the fields were well weeded and growing nicely, I told the boys to pack up. Eagle showed some eagerness at the prospect of going home, but Bear drooped at the idea. I wished Mary would permit them to feel their red blood more freely, but I understood her reasoning. The world in which they were growing up was a white one, not a red one. Still, the youngsters needed to understand that side of their nature, as well.

Even so, they were more fortunate than many of our children. Most throughout the territory had been scooped up by the government and forcibly removed to distant schools where they were shorn of their hair, forbidden to speak any tongue save English, and encouraged to forget their culture. Thankfully, there had been so few blood children left in this part of the territory that our fry had been overlooked.

The preparations for the trip done, I arranged with James to watch the farm while I was away. The afternoon before our departure, I gifted Bear with the sorrel he had named Red Wind and took pleasure in his pride of ownership. Then I turned to Eagle.

"You already have a healthy pony, so I had to work to come up with your gift."

"What is it?" He eyed the parfleche I was holding.

"Something to remind you of your roots." I handed over the bag and watched the boy tear it open.

"Otter, they're great!" He held up a soft buckskin fringed shirt decorated with beads and dyed porcupine quills. He pulled out a breechclout festooned in the same manner and an equally fine pair of leggings with tiny silver bells from Brown's Emporium attached at intervals down the outside seams. "Look, Bear, aren't they great? Major?" He displayed the gifts to James.

"Great indeed. You'll look like a proper Yanube dressed in those."

"I made them a little bigger than the shirts and pants I measured them by because you are growing so fast."

"Thanks, Otter. Can I wear them home?"

"They're a little fancy for that. They're more for dancing or for courting. You know what that is?"

"It has to do with girls."

"You dress up in regalia like that and take your flute to sing and pipe songs to pretty girls."

"Yuk."

"I miss that," I said.

"What? Singing to girls?" James smiled as he asked the question.

245

"No. The sound of the flute. We used to hear them all the time at the *tiospaye*. The flutes and the drums."

"I remember them," Bear said. "I remember my father and the other men dancing around the fire to drums and flutes and rattles."

"I've never even seen anybody dance," Eagle's voice held a complaint.

"If I hear of a powwow, I'll take you to it."

"There's nobody left to dance." Bear eyed me a moment. "You know how to dance, don't you?"

"Of course. I have done so often."

"You promised to show me," Eagle said.

I stared at the two upturned faces for a moment and then went to the cellar where I stored things not often used. I located a small cottonwood round with buffalo hide stretched tightly across it and an old flute made out of a marsh reed and carried them to the yard. Both were plain, without ornamentation. I began to beat the rhythm of the big booming drums of my youth. Dressed in my white man's pants and shirt and my black felt hat, I fell into the steps of the grass dance. Bear took his place beside me and pranced with a coltish grace. Eagle played around with the flute and managed to produce some high, discordant notes.

As the dances returned to my feet from where they had been stored in my memory, I shifted into a war dance, increasing the pace of my steps and chanting a song about stalking the Pipe Stem Draw People, the enemy. Bear kept up with me. Eagle continued to contribute noise — if not melody — on the flute. Then the younger boy abandoned the instrument to join the dance.

In my mind, I heard other noises: the sounds of a peaceful village going about its daily routine, women laughing, children playing, dogs barking, men chanting to the thunder of drums, and the piping of feathered flutes. Almost overcome by nostalgia, I came to an abrupt halt.

James wore a look of understanding when I glanced to where he watched from the porch.

# # # # #

As there had been word of two more recent raids in the vicinity of Ft. Ramson, the next morning I decided to forego the road and cross-cut the countryside on our way to the Mead. I deliberately delayed an early beginning to the trip to ensure we remained on the plains overnight. I wanted to star-camp with the two youngsters.

We began our journey in high spirits, but it was not long before an uneasiness settled over me. Within a mile, the skin on my back was puckering. I pulled to a halt and scanned the horizon in all directions while the boys continued down the path. After seeing nothing of concern, I decided I was turning into a worrisome old woman and urged Patch forward to catch up with the chattering boys. How did they find so much to talk about?

The lads' excitement had not run its course by the time we hobbled the horses in the shelter of a lonely tree halfway to the Mead. Pleased at my decision to overnight, I went about setting up our camp, doing more than was necessary in order to instruct the youngsters.

We supped on pemmican, just as I had done countless times when I was no older than John or Matthew. It was good and comfortable. After scouring the eating tins with sand and rinsing them with water from a canteen, we settled down around a small fire. Too restless to go to their blankets, the boys demanded a story. Both were still in loincloths; they had put off becoming John and Matthew until the morrow.

After weakly protesting the old stories should be recited around a winter campfire, I surrendered and told them of *Inyan*, the creator of the universe. I spoke of *Maka*, Mother Earth, whose blood is molten stone, and of *Skan*, the sky, made of steam and clouds from Earth's cooling blood when it erupted into open wounds upon her breast. Together, they created the water cycle.

I described *Tate*, *Skan's* companion brother, the Wind. I told of *Wi*, the Sun, who was created from bits of *Inyan* and *Maka* and *Skan* to shine and give heat and make shadows and provide comfort to the earth. And of *Han*, the darkness that obscures Sun so the night creatures can have their time while the day beings rest. *Hanwi*, the Moon took her name from both the sun and the darkness, but is married to *Wi*.

Together we prayed that *Ksa*, the formless son of *Inyan* and *Unk*, Contention, who was known for his wisdom, would sprinkle some of it on us all. As the boys quieted and their lids grew heavy, I finished with the tale of how the Lakota and their kinsmen were descended from Eagle.

It had happened when the great flood killed everyone except a beautiful young woman whom Eagle saved by carrying her to his aerie on a tall cliff, the only place on Turtle Island not flooded by water. Because People and Animals were close together back in that time, they married and lived on the bluff until the waters receded. Then Eagle carried the woman and their two children down the cliff and told them to go found a great nation. The children, a boy and a girl, grew up and married and created the Lakota.

When the boys finally slept, I lay in my blankets and listened to the night sounds. My disquiet returned, although I could not say why. I drowsed fitfully until a sound — real or dreamt — brought me awake. Something vaguely like a shod hoof striking stone rang in my ears ... or was it merely in my mind? I pulled my Henry close and did not close my eyes the remainder of the night, fearful I had put the boys in danger by a silly whim to recapture a tiny piece of my youth.

# # # # #

John and Matthew were apparently forgiven by the time we arrived at the Mead properly attired in shirts and pants and battered hats. My fears of the night before had proved unfounded. Everyone came in from the fields and the house and the forge to welcome us. The dogs danced around our feet, slobbering slavishly and baying loudly, now that it served no useful purpose.

I caught the eye of Crow Johnson and gave him a nod before becoming engulfed in Cuthan's bear hug. Our greetings over, I walked the farm with him at my side. I considered sharing last night's worry with him, but chose not to raise the issue.

Teacher's Mead was growing. With the help of Curtis Appleton, Cuthan and Alex had put in more acreage this year. They had added an irrigation system, using a pump to divert Strobaw's Crick to water the fields. The farm I had a hand in starting those many years ago was now an enterprise that would have stirred Billy's pride.

Neither Appleton, nor his wife, Jane, quite knew how to treat me. I laughed on the inside of my mouth that this young couple drew their wages from Cuthan, who was as Indian as I was, yet were helpless to assign a station to me. From all the books I had read, the English were a class-conscious lot.

Crow Johnson made me welcome in the forge in his own stolid, undemonstrative way. He already had John pumping the bellows and Matthew in the loft forking hay.

"Have you seen any sign of the one we spoke of on my last visit?" I asked in Lakota when we managed a moment alone. I was surprised at how eagerly I put the question and at the flicker of disappointment when he had not, although he'd had word of Lance from a blood family from Laramie passing through last week on their way to the pipestone quarry on the big lake.

"The old man said he knew our friend and claimed he'd gone crazy. Says he kills his own now, as well as the whites."

"I cannot believe this. That is not the Dull Lance I know. Did this traveling man say where he was?"

"Thought maybe he was still with Inkpaduta up in the Hunkpapa country. With Sitting Bull. If Dull Lance gets too crazy, the medicine man will throw him out."

"Then why does Sitting Bull tolerate Inkpaduta?"

Crow plied his hammer to a piece of glowing metal that looked as if it would turn out to be a spike. "The old man ain't so bad. His people ain't treaty Indians, and he don't get paid by the Indian agent. So he goes out sometimes to take care of his people, but he don't kill just to be killing. I'll allow that Inkpaduta used to do that after they murdered his family and cut off his brother's head. But he got that sticker out of his moccasin a while back."

"You tell Cuthan if you see Dull Lance again. You hear me?"

"I hear you."

Troubled by my thoughts, I wandered out to the horse pasture to say hello to Whisper. The animal limped over to the fence, likely in hopes of an apple. All I had was a sugar lump, which he accepted as a substitute. I climbed through the fence and lifted the pony's right front foot. From the look of the frog, Whisper might never recover enough to be a good riding horse again. I patted the beast's long neck and stroked his nose for a few minutes before noticing the red print on his flank. Matthew had kept his brother's hand alive with fresh coats of paint.

I returned to the house where Mary was waiting to carry on over me. I always left the Mead with my waistline padded. It was pleasant being among family again, but already an itch for James was growing in me. We'd not had a proper tumble before I left because of the children.

Crow tended to take to his bed early, so I threw down my blankets beside the fireplace and turned in before my usual time. A guest in a man's home should observe his host's habits. On my third night at the Mead, a tap on the window sometime after the rise of the moon roused me. In the darkness, I sensed rather than saw Crow sit up in bed. The Absaroka slept in a loincloth, so I caught a flash of flesh as he rose and went to the window.

"Who's there?"

I hear a muttered reply.

"It's Dull Lance," Crow whispered.

"See what he wants." Vaguely excited, I got up and drew on my pants.

Faint moonlight broke the darkness of the cabin when the door was cracked. I heard a few mumbled words, and then Crow stepped aside to admit the Sioux.

Lance's senses were sharp. "I see you, River Otter."

"Then you have owl's eyes, Dull Lance."

A Lucifer flared, and the soft light of a candle eased the darkness a bit.

Lance nodded to Crow. "I come to visit my old companion, and find a friend here, as well."

"You come to visit in the dead of night?"

"At any other time, someone would likely die."

My heart stuttered at the truth of his statement.

Lance turned to Crow. "Is he your win-tay now?"

Crow's face turned angry. "I don't hold with win-tays. What do you want?"

"We need some supplies."

Stung by the casual cruelness of his remark to the Absaroka, I asked, "We? How many are with you?"

"Enough."

"I've got nothing besides some hardtack and a little pemmican," Crow said. "You're welcome to that, but it won't feed you beyond a meager meal."

"There's more around here. Lots more. And some ammunition."

"That ain't mine to give away. I'll give you my pemmican and hardtack, but what I've got in my rifle is all the cartridges I have. I need them for my protection."

"There is no help for you here," I said with a heavy heart. A man should be able to enjoy the company of friends, but Lance brought only a sense of danger. "Go away, and we'll say nothing. Go back to Sitting Bull and Inkpaduta."

"That is no way to talk to a friend."

Still smarting, I looked at him like a white man, full in the eyes. "I will speak even plainer. Beyond what Crow has offered, you will take nothing from the Mead. And I will hold you to your pledge."

"That was a long ago promise. Some pledges die a natural death."

The hair on the nape of my neck rose. "The time for an attack on the Mead is long past. There are too many rifles here now."

250

"Then I'll look for easier pickings. There are a couple of farms over on Turtle Crick without so many rifles."

"The Dull Lance I know is not a man to break his word. You do that, and I'll hunt you down."

Lance hissed through his teeth. "The army hasn't been able to do it. Or the militia, either. You talk big, but you're not even a warrior. You are just an Earth-Scratcher. A woman."

His words were like arrows. "Why are we talking like children daring one another to stick hands in a beehive? I have your vow, and I'll hold you to it. So go away and let us sleep."

"Did you know there are other eyes on the Mead?"

"What? Who?"

"They are white eyes. One of the militia likely."

"And yet you came here?"

"He didn't see me come, and he won't see me leave."

"Crow, give him what food you have." I got my Henry and levered the cartridges out of it. "Take these with you. There is nothing else for you here. Now go."

Lance's face hardened as he caught the bullets, but he said nothing. Then unexpectedly, he smiled. A moment later, Crow snuffed the candle, and Dull Lance eased out the door.

My heart thudded in my ribcage as I rolled up my blankets. Would Lance heed my counsel? Would this contentious meeting be the last time I would see him?

"I do not like this," Crow said. "There was something different about him. He's got a hunted look."

"He's worn out his welcome most places. Even at the Hunkpapa fires, most likely. I have to leave. Dull Lance knows Major Morrow is at the farm alone."

"Do you want me to go with you?"

"No, you're needed here. You saddle Patch while I go talk to Cuthan."

"What about the watcher Dull Lance told us about?"

We decided he would be on the hill behind the house. When the moon hid her face behind a cloud, we left the cabin one at a time. Crow crossed Strobaw's Crick to go around the east hill.

I gave him a decent lead and then slipped around the building and passed between it and the Appleton's cabin. From there, I eased across the old game trail into the trees and walked a distance upriver. When I judged I was out of the line of sight of a watcher on the hollow hill, I circled around behind the western hummock and searched in vain for the spy's mount. What if I was wrong and the watcher was not where I thought?

Putting doubt aside, I ascended the mound as quietly as I could. I knew the terrain from playing on these hills as a child, so I had no difficulty finding my way in the darkness. After searching the summit for five minutes, I virtually stumbled over the man. I went into a crouch, amazed my carelessness had not alerted him. He lay prone, stretched out so that his head was right at the peak of the hill. He was absolutely motionless.

I put down my empty rifle and dropped to all fours, creeping so close I could have put out my hand and touched the man's shoulder. Had he fallen asleep? Perhaps, but I picked up a suspicious odor. I leapt astride his back, prepared to hold him until Crow arrived. But there was no need for his help. The man made no resistance. The smell sharpened into that of blood and urine and feces. A moment later, Crow appeared at my side.

"He's dead," I said quietly. "Dull Lance failed to tell us he slit the man's throat. He's left us with a big problem."

"Aye, a dead white man."

"Did you find his mount?" I saw the shake of his head in the darkness. "Dull Lance must have taken it. Let's get him off the hill without waking the whole place. Do you have some canvas you can wrap him in?"

"I got some in the barn."

"When we get him down, I'll fetch Cuthan while you weigh him with stones and tie him in the canvas. I'll take him with me and dispose of him."

"They'll hang you if they catch you with his corpse."

"Anyone at the Mead risks the same fate if they find him here."

"I'll truss him up. Ain't nothing on the canvas to tie it to the Mead."

We managed to get the body down without waking anyone. After reminding Crow to climb the hill at first light to erase any signs of what had happened there, I went to rouse Cuthan.

"How did a dead man get up on the hollow hill?" he whispered as we made our way quietly to the barn. I was forced to tell him about Dull Lance's visit. Even by moonlight, I saw anger tighten his features and guessed the source of his distress.

"It was not Crow's doing, Cuthan. When Lance has needs, he seeks aid from any quarter. Crow gave him nothing beyond what was his to give."

"If the man's presence draws renegades, then he is dangerous."

"There may be some truth to that, but given Dull Lance's temper, I'd say you need Crow near. I have the Sioux's promise to leave the Mead alone, but he's growing unpredictable. And I believe you can rely on Crow."

The Absaroka had almost finished binding the dead man in canvas. As we loaded the body aboard Whisper, Cuthan promised to tell Matthew I had taken the horse to see if I could heal his foot. The pony's limp would slow me down, but to take a different animal might arouse the Appletons' suspicions.

The night still had hours to run when I was ready to go. Cuthan stayed me by pressing a box of cartridges for my empty rifle on me. "Why would a man be watching the Mead?"

"I fear I brought him. I had a feeling someone might be following us, but as I could see no one, I dismissed the notion. Now, I think Captain Smith put eyes on me."

"What bone does he have with you?"

I explained our history and finished with my belief Smith had figured out the relationship James and I enjoyed. "I believe he's an unadmitted sodomist and hates and fears the thing he battles in secret."

"Such men are dangerous."

"Aye. Deadly dangerous."

I made my way out of the Mead much more slowly than I would have liked. At this pace it would be light before I reached the deep part of the river where another body and a buckboard already rested. I needed to change my plans.

When the rose of dawn began to touch the night sky, I spooked four antelope that had come down to the river for a drink. Advantaging the situation, I turned off the trail and followed their tracks through the thin line of trees and out onto the plains. I ground tethered Patch and left Whisper and his grisly load tied to the pinto's saddle horn. Then I eased back the way I had come and carefully blurred the two ponies' tracks.

After a quarter of an hour, I was satisfied no one could locate where I had left the road. Thereafter, I made for the Trickling Water. It was late afternoon by the time I located the cave where I had left the bodies of Lance's wife and men. I unwrapped the bloating corpse of the militiaman and pushed it as deeply into the shallow cave as possible. The spy had no weapons or other possessions. Lance must have stolen them after he killed the man.

The grisly task done, I boarded Patch and paused to regard the place. Here was where Dull Lance's hatred had been born. Here, too, was the genesis of our friendship, a friendship I had steadfastly refused to betray. Yet, he had put everyone at the Mead at risk with this latest killing. This man I had once so admired — indeed, had grown close to — had become callous ... or worse.

I brought the horses around and guided Patch straight to the farm, relying on the wind to erase my tracks. As if granting a silent prayer, the morning breeze freshened.

Tired and hungry by the time I arrived home, I went straight to the barn to take care of the horses and to light a fire in the stove in order to burn the canvas and rope used to bind the dead militiaman.

James came into the barn, rifle in hand, as I was inspecting Whisper's sore hoof. My partner was none too happy when he heard the events of the past twenty-four hours.

"If you are right, and that was Smith's man, you know what it means, don't you?"

"Yes, he will come for me now."

CHAPTER 32

By the time the first blue norther swept down from Canada to encase our world in a white cocoon, there had been no reaction from Smith or his militia. Under the circumstances, we welcomed this forced isolation. I did not mind spending the cold winter months bound to the house with James. I enjoyed his ready mind and quick wit. His turn of phrase was not as biting as Billy's had been, but it was sharp enough to keep me on my toes.

The winter of '68-'69 might not have been as severe as the one in 1865, but it clung to the land beyond the normal thaw and reversed my earlier contentment, making me impatient for snowmelt and its season of renewal. This despite the fact I would soon have to move back into my tipi.

Both James and I were men of action and chafed at the bit to begin work on the farm. Although we had taken to the rackets two or three times during the winter months to check on our neighbors, we were anxious to make certain the Tillers had weathered the winter well. If the past foretold the future, we expected to find Bella pregnant with another child.

"It's likely," James said with a knowing smile. "The cold winter months seem made for fornicating. I wonder how many offspring we'd have were I able to bear children?"

"Do you regret having no fry of your own to carry forward your name?"

He shook his head. "I'd have been a no-account father. My career in the army demanded too much." He smiled. "Besides, I take great pleasure in spoiling Joseph. And little James, too, of course. Then there are Cuthan's offspring, although we see far too little of them."

"We will have to arrange a visit after spring planting."

When snowmelt eventually arrived, releasing us to travel about, we discovered much of what we had imagined had come to pass. Bella had been expecting, but lost the child early in the pregnancy. By the time of our visit, she seemed to have recovered, but Andre was still fretting over the miscarriage.

As usual, Joseph, a bubbly two-year-old with soft hair like raw, sand-colored cotton balls, demanded James's attention as soon as we came through the door. The child had Andre's looks and Bella's bright personality. He delighted in planting sloppy kisses on any cheek presented to him. Before the visit was out, he would have my mate on all fours playing horsey.

Little James, now coming up on six months, divided his time between laughing and fussing. But when his self-proclaimed grandpa picked him up, he was all giggles. His hair remained blond. In time, it would probably pick up some of his mother's chestnut highlights. Both boys would most likely grow up to be popular with the ladies.

Bella struggled to keep from showing favoritism, but I suspected that in her secret heart, the child who had threatened them both from the womb would forever hold the edge. Andre wavered between being a stern, disciplined father and an indulgent one. James was untroubled by any such restraints. He delighted equally in the presence of both children.

# # # # #

My mate ventured into Yanube City for supplies a day or so later and returned with news that Captain Smith was agitating for the removal of the few remaining bloods in the Upper Yanube Military District, claiming he wanted no new raids with the coming of the warm months. The man had become so virulent on the idea of tribesmen the local magistrate, Gadsby, had to tamp down a growing revolt against his command. The Rev. Jeremiah Berglund supported Smith with ringing sermons decrying the "red savages" and calling for their segregation from honest, Christian citizens.

James also brought less worrisome news. Ulysses S. Grant had been inaugurated as President of the United States. The man to whom Lincoln had turned to save the Union had now succeeded the Great Man after the troubled interregnum of Andrew Johnson. The question was, would he match his benefactor in statesmanship?

After planting was completed, I made a quick trip to the Mead. James begged off, claiming someone needed to keep a watch on the farm. I stayed only long enough to ascertain Cuthan and his family had wintered well. The children had sprouted like buffalo grass since my visit last summer. The only significant new development was that Jane Appleton, the young English wife of the farmhand, was expecting their first child. Matthew peppered me with questions about Whisper. I assured him the pony was making slow but steady progress.

# # # # #

The summer passed quickly and without violence, a fact that mystified both James and me. We had expected a confrontation over the missing militiaman by now. It was possible the man murdered on the hollow hill had not been part of Smith's unit but rather a passing ruffian intent on stealing what he could from the Strowbaws before moving on. That did not square with the uneasy feeling I'd had while escorting John and Matthew back to the Mead, but what other explanation could there be? Smith and his gang put in only occasional appearances, usually skirting the farm at a distance.

Our days were filled with endless work and constant vigilance. Late one afternoon in early autumn while James was over-nighting in Yanube City to buy supplies and conduct some banking business, I stood on the porch, rifle in hand, listening to someone approach. Noises carried over the flat prairie like echoes across an expanse of water.

At length, five horses emerged from the thin line of trees hovering hard against the north bank of Turtle Crick easting of the house. I took stock of the approaching riders. A man on a palomino rode with his arm raised in the open handed salute. I returned the gesture.

The rider was a heavy, dignified round belly of advanced years. Sioux, by the look of his dress. He wore fringed buckskins in deference to the autumn chill. His shirt was decorated with beads and quills. Twin eagle feathers stood erect at the back of his scalp. The man was old enough to have earned them on the battlefield, counting coup and taking the life of an enemy. A younger man, similarly dressed, followed close behind on a pinto. Two females on horses pulling pony drags trailed him. A youth brought up the rear on a black.

"*Hah-ue*, Am I speaking to River Otter?" The dialect was Dakota.

"I am River Otter, although the white eyes call me Joseph Otter."

"All the people speak of the Last Yanube as a man who has learned to live among the whites without forgetting his blood. These are good things, so I determined upon looking him up when we passed through this country. I am called Grass Dancer. This is my son, Spotted Panther, his wife and daughter, Bright Eyes and Blue Butterfly. The youth is my grandson, New Star."

"Welcome. I have no meal prepared, but there is pemmican and jerky, fruits and vegetables."

"Aye, some food would be appreciated."

"Then dismount and we will eat together, although I suggest we move the horses into the barn and perhaps join them there."

The old man took my meaning. He climbed out of the saddle and instructed his son and grandson to go back down the crick and blur their trail. Panther's wife was a tall, dark woman whose uncommon grace made it easy to forgive her plain looks. She took charge of the horses with the help of her pleasant-looking daughter, a youngster who moved in fits and starts like a young colt.

I went into the house to fetch parfleches of food and a keg of water. Upon my return, I suggested someone should eat up on the hill behind the house to keep a wary eye out. The old Dakota nodded approval of my caution and sent his daughter-in-law and granddaughter up the slope with an ample supply of food and water.

Then we sat on a blanket in the dirt of the barn and smoked a ritual pipe. I lamented there was nothing but a hollowed corncob for the occasion, but the Sioux noted the result was the same no matter the shape or makeup of the pipe. Spotted Panther and New Star returned from erasing their trail in time to participate in our small ritual.

As we ate, Grass Dancer told his story. The effects of the Dakota War in the old man's traditional home in Minnesota had never died away. The hanging of the Sioux "conspirators" by President Lincoln's soldiers on December 26, 1862 had stirred fear and resentment among the tribesmen. Big Mound and Dead Buffalo Lake and White Stone Hill, battles Dull Lance and Crow had told me about, followed the expulsion of the tribes.

The Battle of Killdeer Mountain in the summer of 1864 had broken the back of the Sioux resistance, according to Grass Dancer. Since that time, life had been hard and hazardous for the red man in that part of the country. Tribes and clans were rendered apart. Families had left, heading westward where they hoped to find peace from the relentless pressure of the Americans. Everywhere they had gone, the reception had been the same.

Finally, he decided to seek the safety of the reservations in Indian Territory. Because Grass Dancer had acquaintances among the Cheyenne and Kiowa, he decided to winter in one of the string of camps along the Washita River. He had been at a nearby Kiowa camp when Custer made his attack on Black Kettle.

The massacre proved to the old man the reservations were no safer than anywhere else, so he decided to leave when the Moon of Tender Grass arrived. More trouble was coming to that country; he could feel it in his bones. They had traveled at an easy pace, detouring around towns and farms and shying clear of any Americans they came across.

"I fear you'll find no respite here," I said when he finished his tale.

"Aye, we saw the blue coats patrolling earlier today." The speaker was Spotted Panther, an impressive man of about thirty-five. He had his father's strong, aquiline nose, but carried none of the older man's girth. "Although I do not believe they spotted us."

"It is not the army you need worry about so much as the militia. They are Indian haters of the worst stripe. At least their leaders are. Doubtless many in their ranks are decent men, but they are driven before their headmen's prejudices."

"As is true of all men," Grass Dancer said.

New Star, an immature version of his father, kept his silence as befitted one no more than fifteen or sixteen snows, but he nodded in emphasis occasionally.

"I was born and grew up in this country," I said. "In my youth, I visited the town seven miles south of here before it *was* a proper town and found welcome. I visited the fort when it was nothing but a rude stockade and walked among the dragoons without harm. Now, I am no longer welcome in town and am uncomfortable in the fort."

"How is it that they tolerate you at all?"

"This farm is owned by a man named Major James Morrow. He was the commandant of Ft. Yanube until last year. I work here on his farm under his protection. But the local militia commander, a man named Captain Smith, makes it clear he wishes me gone. Given provocation, he will take action."

The old man nodded. "Our presence here will give him such provocation. Forgive us for putting you in danger."

"Were I not willing to accept the risk, I would not have made you welcome."

"This Major Morrow, where is he?"

"He is in Yanube City on business. But I tell you truly, if he were here, he would have handed you supplies of food and water himself. He is loyal to his kind, but he is no Indian hater. He does not judge a man by the color of his skin."

"That is good to know. Still, we should leave."

"Is the militia on your trail?"

"I think not. Panther and Star have dropped back occasionally to check our rear and found nothing."

"Then I suggest you and your family get some rest while I keep watch on the hill. Major Morrow is remaining in town tonight. Tomorrow, you should leave before the sun rises. I will follow along later and confuse your trail." I paused, not wishing to give offence with unwanted advice. "You might want to distribute your belongings among the horses and avoid leaving drag marks in the grass. A distance to the north is a stream called Trickling Water. West of there are some badlands that will provide cover. Beyond that, the country is flat, but there are occasional coulees and gullies for shelter."

"We will do as you say, but we will spell you on the hill throughout the night and be gone before the sun comes up."

"I will pack food and provisions for your trip."

"Panther will give you our empty parfleches to hold them. You have our thanks, Otter."

When the moon was high in the sky, New Star came to relieve me on the hill behind the house. I tarried awhile, pleased to be in the company of youth. Although I was not one who hungered for childish flesh, I took pleasure in young people's energy and curiosity. I spoke to the lad a few minutes before slipping back to the house and catching some rest.

The sound of the others stirring woke me while it was still dark. I went outside, carrying extra rations and ammunition for hunting. The old man clasped my forearm in the native fashion before wordlessly moving away. Spotted Panther took his place and nodded into darkness barely broken by a dim moon. Then New Star was there.

"Thank you, Grandfather," he whispered.

"Be well. Take care of your family."

I watched the party out of the yard as they made their way west to circle the hillock before turning north. I mounted the hill and sat in the cool earth, my ears listening for what my eyes could not yet see. When I could make out the shape of the grass at my feet, I rose and erased all sign of the visitors with a limb from a bush.

Then I followed their trail, confusing their tracks as best I could. Grass Dancer and his party had prudently traveled in single file, making it easier for me to do so. I followed until they took a westward turn, and then led the pinto back to the farm. I had done all I could for the Dakota.

Uneasy the rest of the morning, I made a run over to the Tillers to return some empty milk jugs and pick up a full one. Andre greeted me while holding his younger son. The child's golden hair was already picking up traces of amber. Soon it would match Bella's rich locks. I wondered if he would have freckles across his nose, as did his father.

Within minutes, I knew the Tillers had neither seen nor heard Grass Dancer's party. I returned home, put the milk in the cool room, and tried to set about cleaning and repairing my tools and implements. I was too agitated to accomplish much, so I climbed the hill with James's army binoculars in hand to scan the distant horizon. At first, I saw nothing out of the ordinary. Then to my east, I spotted movement in the tree line on the high side of the crick. Someone was on Grass Dancer's trail. His tracks would not lead to the farm, but they would come close enough to bring the militia to me.

I quickly obliterated a moccasin track I'd missed earlier and went back down the hill to the barn. Grabbing a scraper, I set to work scouring the blade of the plow in preparation for storing it away for use next spring. As soon as the riders entered the yard, I stepped outside to meet them. There was no weapon on my person, but my Henry was just inside the doorway.

There were six of them. Smith, as usual, led the group. I looked for the Rev. Berglund but did not find him among them. Smith hauled up on his reins.

"You seen any renegades, Injun?"

"My name is Joseph Otter, as you know. I have seen no renegades. Everything is peaceful around here. I was just over at the Tiller place, and they didn't mention seeing anyone, either."

"What was you doing over there?"

"Picking up milk. We buy milk from the Tillers."

"Where's the Major?"

"He went into town yesterday for supplies. He was going to visit the mayor and the new fort commandant. He'll be back sometime today or tomorrow."

My posture was straight, and I took care to look the militia chieftain directly in his colorless eyes — well, one of them anyway — the one that focused where it was supposed to look. There was no harm in being rude to this one. He was too ignorant to know it was unseemly to stare at people. The idiot took it as a sign of forthrightness.

"We trailed a band of hostiles along the north bank of the crick. That woulda led them right to your front door."

"No doubt they turned north or south when they saw the house. Look around if you wish."

"Then how come the trail just ended?"

I pursed my lips for a moment. "If it had been me, I'd hide my trail while I went around a farm. How big was the party?"

"Five mounted warriors."

I kept my face straight despite the outrageous lie. Smith would have brought twice as many men with him if he thought he was on the trail of five Sioux warriors. Grass Dancer and his family had likely been spotted somewhere along the way, and a message was sent to the militia.

Smith leaned forward in the saddle. "I know you been helping the renegades. I don't care if the Major is your boss. One day, I'll find you out and hang you by the neck to the nearest tree."

"Then you will hang an innocent man." Despite my resolve, my tongue kept wagging. "But I suspect that would not bother you a whit."

"You talk in that high-hat way, but you ain't nothing but a red belly. You better believe that, *Joseph* Otter." Smith tugged on his reins. "Spread out, boys. Search the whole place inside and out. If they's something to find, I want it found, hear?"

The militiamen dismounted and scattered around the farm. They tromped over rows of crops, barged into the house, and into my tipi. They went through the barn, the cellar, the necessary, and even pulled up the flooring in the cabin's bathing room to check down the well. The found my hidey-hole packed with spare buffalo skins. Yet they failed to uncover the false wall leading to another space beneath the stove where some of our gold and silver coins were hidden.

The house was a wreck by the time they finished, but they found nothing. That merely enraged Smith further. His face was almost black by the time he led his men down the trace toward the Tiller place.

Worried, I retrieved my rifle and trailed them by foot, keeping far enough to the rear to remain out of sight. I watched from hiding and observed they treated the Tillers with a modicum of respect. I could not hear their words but saw Andre shake his head.

I slipped back to my own place as they trailed out of Andre's yard and headed north. Grass Dancer and his family had had ample time to reach the badlands by now. They could have already negotiated the breaks and moved on west. Nonetheless, worry played with my mind and put a chill on my back. Before saddling Patch, I left a note in case James returned to find the place in a state of high disorder.

I crossed the Trickling Water and worked my way west along the far shore of the stream where a network of small hills and gullies provided more cover. There I found what I had feared. A campsite. I read the signs and saw where Grass Dancer had halted his party. Tracks, most likely the youth's, went down into the streambed. My mind's eye could see him handing for fresh fish. He had caught some, too. I found bones in the still warm cook fire.

They had paused after eating to rest and then affix a travois to each of the women's horses and reload their provisions. I muttered a prayer they had not dallied too long. Smith and his men had angled in a more westerly direction, which would put the militia right on their tail.

When the sound of gunfire reached me, I knew my prayer had not been answered. I mounted and resisted the urge to race forward. Instead, I urged Patch halfway up the slope of the crick bank so only my head showed, making me harder to spot, yet giving me a view of the flat plain ahead. A short distance later, I spotted a horse lying on its side with an overturned travois behind it. Spotted Panther's pretty daughter lay sprawled in the dirt nearby. I did not need to check to see that she was dead.

Trying to ignore my rising blood, I plodded ahead carefully. A few minutes later, movement in the streambed caught my attention. The palomino Grass Dancer had been riding was grazing calmly. Another still form lay at the top of the small ravine. Drawing closer, I saw the old man. His dead eyes seemed to beg for help as I drew abreast of the corpse. He had almost reached the relative safety of the badlands when the killers caught up with him.

Gunfire continued to rage, which meant Spotted Panther and the remainder of his family must be holding the militia at bay. I urged Patch forward at a faster pace. Within half a mile, I reached a spot where I could see what was going on. One militiaman held the group's mounts behind a small rise. The remainder of the gang was somewhere ahead seeking to drive out the Indians.

I turned around and cautiously approached the palomino, trying not to frighten the animal. When I had his reins firmly in hand, I rode back to where the round belly lay on the lip of the ravine. I dismounted and worried the heavy body across Patch's rump. He turned skittish, but I calmed him with a hand to his muzzle. I draped the old man's blanket around my shoulders and worked the eagle feathers from his gray hair into my black locks.

Mounted on the palomino, I rode to a spot where the militia's horses shielded me from the guard. Patch followed along some distance behind. Dismounting, I began a cautious approach afoot, seeking to sneak up on the guard without spooking the animals. I was moving among the beasts before they began to shy and snort.

I had intended to club the guard senseless with my rifle butt, but the horses' nervousness had likely put him on alert. I dropped my Henry in the dirt and drew my knife. Creeping along in the midst of the six horses, I put a gentle hand on each one as I passed. Even so, the guard's legs shifting nervously on the other side of the last horse alerted me the man was alarmed. I pushed hard against the roan's side. She sidestepped, forcing the man back.

I slipped beneath her belly and thrust the knife into the panicked man's gut. I withdrew the blade and sent it into his kidneys, paralyzing him before could alert his comrades. I saw recognition in the frightened brown eyes before they went out. The man was young, hardly more than twenty-and-one years. Did he have a wife and family back in town waiting for him?

I gathered the dead man's weapons and my Henry, clutched the reins of the six ponies, and led them to the ravine where I had left the palomino. As I guided the horses over the edge, Patch came up the floor of the crick bed, the old Sioux's body still across his broad back.

The gunfire continued unabated while I lashed the six militia horses together before remounting the palomino. Leading the horses up out of the gully, I emerged into the open, easily within view of Smith and his men. I was out of range of a handgun, but a rifle still posed a risk. Nonetheless, I pointed my Henry into the air and fired. It took three shots to claim their attention. The startled militiamen grew careless. One stepped into the open, rifle to his shoulder and toppled over, shot dead by Panther or Star. The militiamen scrambled for cover and began firing at me. I turned my back and led the horses down into the gully again.

Half a mile later, I emerged from the ravine so I could once more be seen. Then I rode hard to the north, putting distance between the enraged killers and myself. The gunfire had ceased, so I assumed Panther and his family had taken the opportunity to slip away from the stranded militiamen.

Some distance farther, I paused to consider whether or not to shoot the animals. When released, most would eventually find their way home, which didn't serve my purpose. Although six mounts represented wealth to an Indian family, the horses also presented a danger. Yet perhaps not if they were removed from this general area. My decision made, I turned back and approached the badlands by the route Panther and his family would likely take. Before long, I ran into them.

Spotted Panther drew up sharply. Hope flared and then died as he recognized me wrapped in a familiar blanket.

"I am sorry, but I had to make them think it was someone else stealing their horses. Otherwise, they would come for me."

The warrior's eyes strayed to the corpse across Patch's back. "He would be proud he had a hand in saving the rest of his family, even though it was a dead hand."

"I could not retrieve the other one, but when things calm down, I will see to her care."

Sudden pain filled his eyes. "Thank you."

"Are the rest of you all right?"

"Aye. We're not injured."

"The killers' horses and weapons are yours if you wish them. You cannot trade a single item until you are far removed from this territory. If the horses pose too much of a risk, slaughter them."

"I understand. Thank you, River Otter. Not for my life, but for theirs." He gestured to his wife and son.

"I must hurry now. I need to be back at the farm before any alarm is raised. Goodbye and good fortune."

Panther and his son removed the body from my pinto and bound it to the palomino. Then they moved off. After a hundred yards, the boy looked back and raised a hand in farewell. Even at this distance, the anguish of his look cut like a bone blade.

I headed straight south until reaching Turtle Crick. Then I turned Patch into the stream. The water was shallow enough so the pony had no trouble maneuvering the crick bed. I passed an anxious moment as we neared the Tiller farm, but the house was set back from the bank enough for me to elude scrutiny. Just short of the pool where Lucas and I had once bathed, I came out of the water and headed straight for the barn. James's cavalry horse was not in the stall.

I rubbed down Patch, curried his coat, and forked fodder into his crib before rushing into the house to repair the disorder Smith and his men had left. I was halfway finished when I heard the clop of hooves across the bridge. I met James on the porch.

Usually, I was totally honest with my lover, as when I had confessed my liaison with Andre, but I was unwilling to place James squarely on the horns of a moral dilemma by confessing the killing of a white man. There was no benefit to either of us in that. While relating the visit by the Sioux and his family, I was forced to call out the old man's true name lest I alert James to knowledge of his fate. I was surprised at the ripple of superstitious fear that played down my back as I did so.

I told of the subsequent invasion by the militia; however, I carried the tale no further than watching them ride off to the northwest after visiting the Tiller place. James looked askance but held his tongue in the face of such an abrupt ending.

The dying sun was piling vivid colors high into the late afternoon sky when the Tillers' wagon approached the farm. James and I had finished restoring the house and my tipi to order and were taking our ease on the porch when the wagon appeared on the trace. Andre sat glumly on the bench with a surly Captain Smith beside him. Three other men rode in the bed. All were silent with heads bowed and faces hidden by wide-brimmed hats.

Andre pulled to a halt before the porch and peered over at us. "Otter, will you go stay with Bella and the children while I take these men to Yanube City? She's panicked at news of a war party in the vicinity."

"Aye. I'll stay with her until you return."

"What happened, Smith?" James asked.

The man's head whipped around like a snake. His jay-wonky eyes seemed to stare directly at each one of us. "We was ambushed by hostiles, that's what happened. Bushwhacked us without no warning. Kilt two of us before we could fight them off."

"Where are your mounts?"

Smith's broad mouth pulled down at the corners, emphasizing his gaunt cheeks. "One of them slithered in among us like the scaly serpent he was and knifed the guard. Then he run off with the horses when the others opened up on us. Let's get on outta here, Tiller. Need to get back to organize a search party. Pick up our dead."

"I'll ride along and keep Andre company on the way back. In case of another attack," James added dryly.

After James clattered across the bridge in pursuit of the wagon, I rode straight to the Trickling Water. It was dangerous riding at speed across a darkening prairie pocked with gopher holes and unexpected washes, but I had no choice. I made it to the crick and followed the north bank, locating the pitiful remains of the little girl. She had been a pretty child of about thirteen, and I was glad the rising darkness shrouded her features. The vultures had been at work. I could see the gleam of bone.

I carried her into the badlands and found a place with an abundance of stones. After reciting prayers for her safe journey down the Western Road, I piled rocks atop the frail form. Then I made for the Tiller farm, judging I should arrive well before James and Andre returned from Yanube City.

Bella was in the cabin stoically waiting with the children. I excused my tardiness, but she was so fixed upon renegade warriors that she paid my words little attention. I noted a rifle leaning against the near wall within easy reach. No doubt, she would have fought like a mama grizzly to protect her brood from harm. Her conversion from southern belle to pioneer woman was now complete. Nonetheless, she took obvious comfort in my presence. I uttered a few words of reassurance, and we settled down to wait for James and Andre to show up. The Moon of Colored Leaves was high in the sky before they arrived.

James was in an agitated state. "Smith was utterly disgraced. He lost two men and all their horses. Can you imagine how humiliating it was for him to be hauled back to town in a wagon by a farmer? I do not intend offense, Andre."

"I take your meaning."

"If we're lucky, he'll die of that humiliation," I ventured.

"Nay, he'll not die of it, but whatever rational reason was left him has been dealt a death blow. He'll be healthy as a horse and prickly as a porcupine and deadly as a rattlesnake. He will be looking for vengeance without caring where he takes it."

James turned to me. "I am relieved you had no hand in his misfortune, else my protection would be meaningless."

CHAPTER 33

Winter came early in '69, so Smith's mortification remained unavenged as far as we knew. Despite the early onset, the weather had not been overly harsh, allowing us to take to the rackets for nearby hunting and a little ice fishing in the crick beside the bridge.

Snowmelt arrived on time, and when we were finally free to travel, we headed west to find the Tillers had survived the freezing months in good form. Bella was in the midst of another pregnancy, making me wonder if a new child would overfill the small cabin.

Shortly thereafter, James visited the town and returned with a winter's worth of news. Events had moved on apace while we hunkered down by our fireplace with snow swirling about the house. That was all right. At least the world had left us alone for those few months.

Smith's activities — or more properly, lack of activities — puzzled us near to distraction. The nature of the man should have dictated a blustering, public search for redemption after his humiliation last year.

James had no gossip of the militia commander, although he'd heard of thunderous sermons from the City on the Hill denouncing fornicators and pederasts and heathen Indians. It would almost have been a relief had Smith showed up on our doorstep to level accusations against me. This was contrary to my perception of the captain. I grew nervous with expectation. My hackles rose whenever I heard something unexpected, even if it was only the chatter of an angry squirrel or the squawk of a curious jay.

James and I both worked with an anxious eye out for trouble. One summer day, Andre came thundering into the yard to announce Bella had delivered her baby. We trailed him back to his place to find mother and child doing well. Andre was nearly as proud of attending the birth alone as he was of his new daughter. He took the tiny infant from her crib and held her protectively during our stay. It was almost as if he and James were vying for the attention of the child. In this, they had competition from Joseph and little James, who were enchanted by their tiny sister. The boys pawed and petted the child, driving everyone to distraction.

They had named the girl Liberty because she made her appearance on July 4, the nation's birthday. Neither of her brothers could pronounce her name, so she immediately became Libby.

#

A week later, I came across a careless — or deliberate — moccasin track on the hill behind the cabin. That, alone, did not mean much. Some of the white settlers had adopted the comfortable footwear of the tribesmen, yet it was enough to send me scouting on Patch's broad back.

I found what I was looking for along Trickling Water. Six ... no, seven ponies had drawn abreast to drink from the clear rill. Some were shod; others were not A sign of the times. I turned the pinto and rode to the lip of the badlands where the forces of wind and water had chopped the undulating hills of the plains country into gullies and coulees — miniature canyons, really — that ran for perhaps two leagues to the west.

Holding to the south shore of the crick, I entered the badlands, making no effort to conceal my movements. Pony tracks led into one of the deep draws, but I continued to follow the stream. There would be eyes on me, and when Dull Lance was ready to talk, he would appear.

My scalp prickled when I reached the western edge of the badlands without seeing or hearing a soul. The baked clay walls seemed to echo with nothing but deep silence. I retraced my steps and met no one, but I came across a short lance decorated with hawk feathers stuck upright in the trail. It had not been there when I rode in. Dull Lance was letting me know he was back but had no wish to palaver. Then why leave a message? It was pointless, unless it was a warning.

With my head full of troubling thoughts, I left the lance where it was and negotiated the rest of the breaks without further sign and rode back to the farm. Was the Sioux angry because I had withheld aid that night at the Mead? Could his joking reference to me as Crow's win-tay have deeper meaning? More likely, his veiled threats to the farms along Turtle Crick had taken root in his mind. Dull Lance had grown prickly and was quick to take offense. The fact I had saved his life and shielded him from the militia was fading from his consciousness. It was almost as though another man stood in his moccasins. I dry-washed my face with a palm, trying to wipe away the sudden, deep sadness that descended upon me.

When I arrived home, James was working in the fields, which promised a good harvest in the fall. He met me in the yard before the barn, curious over where I had been.

"Dull Lance is back." I explained what I had found in the badlands.

"I heard of raids south of the Little Islands the last time I was in town," James said. "That seemed remote from us at the time, but it might have been Dull Lance's work."

"I fear his debt to me — to us — is weakening. There is no reason for him to be in this country where he is wanted for murder. I need to talk to him before he commits mischief."

James gave me a sharp look. "There is no reasoning with a man who is obviously unhinged."

"The man who wintered here with a wound in his side was not irrational." My words sounded hollow. Had I not nursed James's very thought on the way home?

He eyed me closely. "Why do you defend him?" His voice had taken on an edge. "What is he to you?"

He was thinking of my betrayal with Andre, yet I dared not issue a denial. To do so would be to put a name to it. "A friend and a tribesman."

He rubbed his chin and backed away from the precipice. "It seems strange he haunts Trickling Water when the Little Island range is so near. The mountains would provide better cover."

"Trickling Water is closer to us. To this farm. And that gives me cause for concern."

# # # # #

Within the week, the farm five miles to the west, which had once before suffered Dull Lance's attack, was raided and burned again. A little later, we watched a column of cavalry pass to the south on their return to the fort from the site of the attack. Edmund Simmons, now sporting the double bars of a captain, detached himself to inform his former commander that the farmer and his entire family had been slain in the raid. Simmons had dispatched riders to all the farms in the area to warn of the rising.

Sam Smith and the militia thundered down upon us soon thereafter. While the venomous man wasted time and breath mouthing imprecations at me, another place went up in flames. A distant towering black plume on the other side of the Yanube immediately drew the captain and his men south. The smoke had seemed to be in the general vicinity of Smith's own farm.

Although it distressed me another family had been attacked, I breathed a bit easier. By all the laws of logic, Dull Lance should have ridden for the sanctuary of the nearby Little Islands after this latest raid. As James had noted, the mountains were a much larger haven than the Trickling Water Badlands.

The following morning, Major Bettington arrived at the farm, alone and unattended. He had come to visit James, but his message was for me. Captain Smith's place had, indeed, been the renegades' target. The man had lost his home and a teenage son — who'd been scalped — although the rest of his family escaped with their lives. The militia chieftain, beside himself with grief and rage, had openly accused me of directing the renegades to his farm out of personal spite. The captain so vehemently spouted vows of personal vengeance, Magistrate Gadsby had felt compelled to step in and put an end to his ranting. The verbal torrent may have abated, Major Bettington allowed, but the hatred had not.

"How can an act of compassion lead to such a state of affairs?" I asked after the officer took his leave. "I cannot believe it would have been right to abandon Dull Lance to his fate after he was shot. But if what everyone believes is true, how many people will die because I saved him?"

James's face softened. "This started when the militia murdered his wife and companions, which led to Dull Lance killing Abel Brown. The after-clap is still resounding to this day. You hold no guilt, Otter."

"Then why do I feel as if I do?"

"Because you nurse a false sense of responsibility. The fault lies with Dull Lance and Sam Smith."

If only I could talk to Lance ... reason with him.

# # # # #

Two weeks later, I was in the corral inspecting Whisper's nearly healed frog when the sound of gunfire reached my ears.

"The Tillers!" James yelled, running in from the field where he had been working. "It's coming from their place. Get the horses. I'll get weapons."

Moments later, I paused beside the steps for James to toss me a rifle and mount his horse from the porch. It sounded like a war as we pounded down the wagon trail toward Andre's farm.

We burst out of the trees to confront mounted men racing around the yard and firing into the barn loft. I threw up my Henry and squeezed the trigger. The man holding a knife over a fallen figure in the yard dropped. James shot one of the riders from his saddle. Another renegade tore out of the house holding a screeching, blanket-swathed infant in his hands. Without thinking, I shot him in the head and watched in horror as he fell atop the bundle.

A bullet knocked the hat from James's head. Dull Lance went into a crouch and cocked his long gun for another shot. I fired on him without thinking or taking aim. He staggered backwards. Clutching his right shoulder, he reeled around the corner of the barn and disappeared into a cloud of smoke rising from flames eating at the building. Lance had held onto his rifle, so I was forced to move carefully. Although unable to believe he would deliberately harm me, I feared my defense of James may have freed him from any lingering traces of restraint.

As I moved to rescue the infant from beneath the fallen renegade, another man rode for me with raised hatchet. James blew him away. Then everything grew suddenly quiet. A moment later, Andre raced from the barn and dropped beside Bella, who lay in the yard. Cradling her still form in his arms, he begged her to wake up. But she would never rouse from that sleep.

I ran to the porch and rolled the body of the dead raider off Libby. I feared she might have been smothered, but the instant she could draw breath the baby let out a yell. After scooping her into my arms, I turned to survey the scene.

My heart constricted as I spied two small forms lying on the west side of the porch. Joseph's brown, cotton boll curls fluttered in a gentle breeze. His eyes were closed, as though he were asleep, a look belied by his shredded torso. One hand lay against his cheek, the other lay open at his side.

Little James's lids were half closed over vacant blue eyes. His rusty locks were matted with darker, bloody stains. His tiny fist lay nestled in his big brother's palm. They had been trying to flee the horror of the brutal attack together when they were cut down by the murderers' bullets.

I carried Libby to where James stood helplessly watching Andre grieve for his dead wife. I handed the baby to my companion and motioned toward the end of the porch.

For a moment, I thought James would collapse, but he cradled Libby in his arms and straightened his shoulders. My lover was a steady man in a crisis. He would do his grieving in private. I whirled and went for Patch.

"I'm coming, too," James called in a steely voice.

"You take care of them."

"Don't be foolish, man. You don't know how many got away."

"Aye, I do. There were seven horses on the Trickling Water. We killed four of them, and there's another one over near the barn Andre must have shot. Dull Lance is alone or has one man with him. And Lance is wounded."

"That's when a bear is most dangerous. Let me come with you, Otter."

I motioned around the yard. "I'm responsible for this. But I'm going to take care of the problem now. Dull Lance broke his vow to me." I glanced over my shoulder. "The barn's trying to burn. It doesn't have much of a start, so you can handle it without my aid."

"Let it burn. It will draw troops from the fort."

I kicked Patch into a run and followed the plainly laid trail. Halfway to the badlands the tracks showed where a second horseman had joined the first. Shortly thereafter, the two men had pulled up. Perhaps Lance needed help with his wound. Or maybe they argued about which way to go. That made no sense. There was only one place that was even remotely safe — the badlands.

My suspicions aroused, I slid off the pinto and examined the ground. Ten yards off to the left of the trail, I found moccasin tracks. The man with Lance had abandoned his mount to slip away. Likely to find an ambush site. Dull Lance had gone on down the trail with both ponies to deceive any pursuer.

How far would the bushwhacker go? Was I in his gun sights right now? Possibly. But just ahead the scanty forest jutted out to the east. Those scrubby trees would be a perfect place to wait for me.

I mounted and paused, fighting the temptation to run down the potential assassin and allow Lance time to gain the sanctuary of the badlands. Maybe he would keep on going and leave this territory behind. Maybe ...

Thoughts of the murdered Tiller family made my decision for me. I reined Patch east and put him into a dead run, making a wide circle around the tree line. I soon raised two horses ahead of me. One was riderless. My detour had been too costly. I would never catch Dull Lance before he reached sanctuary.

Even so, I kept after him at speed, even when he glanced back and paused to raise his rifle. His shoulder wound apparently made it difficult. His shot went wild. Lance dropped the long gun and rode for the badlands. I kicked Patch into a faster pace, but I still had to be cautious. Lance had a six-gun strapped to his waist.

I was gaining ground, but it would be a near thing. The mouth of the badlands loomed ahead. Drawing my rifle from its sheath, I pulled Patch to a skidding halt. I steadied my aim, but at the last moment, shifted the barrel from Lance's broad back to bring down his mount — the very mare I had gifted him with after nurturing him back to health.

He scrambled to his feet and staggered for the other horse. The skittish animal danced out of his grip. As I bore down upon him, Dull Lance made a hunched, uncertain run for the badlands. He turned at the last minute and tried to claw his pistol from its holster. Before he could clear leather, I sent the pinto barreling into him. He tumbled in the dirt. With one eye on him, I dismounted with cocked rifle in hand.

"So you turn on your own kind?" He gasped in obvious pain.

"No. My kind would not murder a woman and two children. You pledged your word, Dull Lance. And today, you broke it."

Speaking to Lance was to invite irresolution, to seek alternatives to what I knew I must do. He made it easy for me. A snarl twisted his broad features. They were familiar features, features I had seen in Stone Knife, this killer's honorable father, and in hundreds of other fine men and women.

Spittle sprayed from his mouth. "A warrior's word to a stinking white-lover means nothing. You aren't even man enough to fuck a woman. You fuck a white man's ass."

My heart sank. Suddenly, I was bone tired; too exhausted to take offense at his words. "I'm man enough to take you down when the army and the militia couldn't. A man's word is a man's word, whoever he gives it to. You are going to pay for this."

"You will not take me back for the white men to hang me."

I had been dreading the moment he made a move. When it came, Dull Lance fooled me. He made no attempt to gain his feet. Given the wound in his shoulder, he didn't even try to draw his pistol; he merely cleared the trigger guard and lifted the barrel, firing through the end of the holster. Even as impaired as he was, the shot plucked a piece of meat from my left arm. I didn't even flinch; I squeezed off a round into his chest. Lance grunted aloud, and I watched the life go out of his eyes. How could dead eyes hold so much hate?

I checked my wound. Blood was flowing freely, but it was merely a scratch, like the gouge laid to Patch's rump a while back. Ignoring it, I gently talked my way to the horse Dull Lance had been trailing behind him and led the animal to where he lay.

The Sioux was a big man, but I managed to get him aboard the nervous pony and bind his hands and feet together. Pausing to look into his dead face, I was struck with the feeling my bullet had brought him a modicum of peace after all these years. At least, it was a release from his bone-deep fury.

My bullet. A wave of sorrow nearly brought me to my knees. I should have been able to put a halt to him with words ... not an ounce of lead.

I pulled myself together and retrieved the rifle he had thrown away before mounting Patch. I took a long detour to the east on the way back to the farm in order to avoid the other renegade, who was now stranded and in desperate need of a mount.

By the time I reached the Tiller farm, two platoons of cavalry under Captain Simmons and a fresh-faced lieutenant I didn't know had arrived and doused the flames on the barely scorched barn. They had also carefully wrapped and loaded the bodies of Andre's family in our buckboard. The slain raiders were already gone, doubtless on the way to the fort to be identified. Simmons accepted the reins of the pony I led.

We were interrupted by the thunder of hooves before I had a chance to explain what had happened. A group of militia splashed through Turtle Crick and pounded into the yard. A wild-eyed Sam Smith glanced at the body lying across the pony.

"Is that the murdering bastard?"

"Yes, that is Dull Lance." James stood on the porch with little Libby in his arms. Andre sat with vacant eyes in a chair beside him. "Otter went after him and brought him down. To his own harm, as you can see." He gestured at my blood-encrusted arm.

Smith turned on me, madness written on his face, and a deep loathing gripped my heart. I had only felt hatred — true gut-wrenching hatred — once before in my life. Ironic that it had been for another captain named Smith. That foul creature had earned my hatred by killing my kinsmen, my entire band. This one had earned it for his love of killing the few of us who remained.

Smith fixed me with his good eye. "You stinking red belly. You shoulda brought him to me alive. I wanted him hanged! Hell, I will hang him. Bring a rope, boys. We'll drag him by the neck all the way back to town. With any luck his mangy head will come off."

Simmons stepped forward. "Captain Smith, the military is in possession of this body and will see to its transfer back to the fort. Do you have any problem with this?"

Mark Wildyr

Smith almost strangled on his fury, but outnumbered by the soldiers, he backed down. "We'll see what happens when we get back to town. What about the rest of them?"

"All dead except one," I said. "He's stranded out near the badlands without a horse."

Smith immediately transferred his wrath. "Come on, let's go find the yellow killer." He led his men out of the yard, riding recklessly for the Trickling Water.

I hoped the renegade died quickly.

CHAPTER 34

James had been rocked to the core by the death of Bella and the boys. He wept from his soul for two days before repairing to tend Andre and me — Andre through his overwhelming grief and me through my rage.

"It makes no sense, Otter," he said to me the third day after the tragedy. It was Amos Brown who sent the militia to Trickling Water. If you must assign blame, he was responsible for killing Dull Lance's wife and companions."

I stared at him. "Brown ... Smith. Hardcastle, even. They are the same snake in different a different skin. Brown started it, but Smith pressed the issue. If they had eased off and allowed me to reason with Lance, maybe ..."

"I'm no defender of the likes of Sam Smith, but it's you I am concerned with. You are a logical man, but this is not logical. Dull Lance killed Brown and Pawley. Ambushed them. Of course, the militia had to go after him. So did the military, as you recall. While I was still in command."

"Aye, but Smith is the worst of them. He is a hater. A hater of people of the blood, and a hater of people like us. He represents all that is wrong with the white man."

I spun and walked from the cabin into the fields. My arm was mending but still tender, although it did not hinder my activities unduly. After a bit, James took his place beside me and worked without speaking. The tension soon leaked out of our systems.

It was Andre who troubled me most. He still moved as if in a fog since his family's funeral. Sensitive to the mood of the times, I had hung back at the fringes of the crowd during the service and murmured a prayer of thanks the Methodist minister conducted it, not Jeremiah Berglund.

After the heart-wrenching laying away of the murdered Tillers, James lavished his attention on the only child left — little Libby. Because Andre was barely able to take care of himself, let alone an infant, James arranged for Dr. Helgren's wife to care for her for the time being.

Although Andre tended his fields daily, his work was desultory. James and I were forced to lend a generous hand. I argued to brace the young man with the hard facts of his family obligations, but James counseled patience. A week passed with no improvement in our neighbor's condition.

I was in little better shape. Killing a man I could easily have loved was a harsh thing to deal with; nearly as difficult as witnessing a man's degradation into mindless insanity without being able to stop it.

James made numerous forays into town, claiming the need to check on Libby, so we were aware the militia had not caught the last member of Dull Lance's gang. Some argued the man had escaped, but there were occasional signs he still haunted the Trickling Water Badlands. In time, however, most of the militiamen had had enough and finally rebelled against Smith's relentless pursuit of the fugitive. Even Magistrate Gadsby was losing patience with his henchman. Nevertheless, Smith rode daily to the badlands, first with three or four men, then with one or two, and finally, alone. He was known to overnight in the small box canyons and gullies there.

These days I rode Whisper more often than Patch. I had despaired of the pony ever recovering from the hoof infection, but my patience was paying off. The mustang had mended to the point I could return the animal to Matthew on my next trip to the Mead. That meant the boy would own two horses. In the old days, that would have represented wealth for one so young.

I was exercising the pony on the plains within sight of the farmhouse one day when I heard a rifle shot. I pulled up and cocked an ear. Another report followed, and then another. Out of the corner of my eye, I saw James step out onto the porch, rifle in hand. I waved and kicked Whisper into a dead run, heading straight for the Tiller farm.

I had no weapon other than my knife, but I would render what aid I could if Andre was in trouble. As I splashed across the crick, there was another shot. A bullet burned the air near my head. I quickly dismounted and tied the pony to a bush behind a bank of earth.

"Andre!" I shouted. "Are you all right?"

"Come on, you bastards! Come on. I'll kill you all!" His shrill voice was almost unrecognizable, but it was our neighbor.

"Hold your fire! It's me, Otter." I cautiously raised my head, ducking down beneath the crick bank when Andre raised his rifle. A bullet gouged earth from above my head.

"Andre! Stop firing, dammit. You're shooting at Otter," James shouted.

I slipped to the right and saw him dismount and walk into the yard. My heart froze when Andre whirled and loosed another shot. James jumped behind a tree bole and loosed a string of curses.

280

Andre stood hatless in clear view at the corner of the barn with tears streaming down his cheeks, firing blindly when either of us moved. Despairing of talking him out of his madness, I waded up the crick to a point behind the barn where I couldn't be seen. I left the stream and cautiously made my way around the west end of the building. The next time James called out, I eased toward the far corner. Andre still stood just out of my view, so I inched forward, darting inside the building as he took a step backwards and came into my line of sight.

"Dammit, Andre! Put down that rifle. We're here to help you, man!" James's had abandoned his military mode and was begging.

I risked another look. Andre was out of sight again. I edged through the door. Flattening myself against the building, I sidestepped toward the corner. James began talking again. He'd seen me and was trying to distract the crazed man.

I reached the corner. Andre's stood with his back to me. I lunged and grabbed him in a bear hug. He twisted in my arms. His rifle barrel crashed against my head. I lost my hold on him. Dazed, I was virtually helpless as he whirled and brought his weapon to bear. James crashed into him, slamming him into the wall of the barn. His rifle went off. The projectile plowed harmlessly into the ground.

I snatched Andre's legs from under him and rolled atop his chest. James sat astride his feet. Suddenly, all resistance went out of Andre. He went limp. James pulled the rifle from his hands and laid it out of reach.

When Andre opened his eyes, he looked puzzled. "What happened?"

I cautiously lifted my weight from him. James rose and offered a hand. When we got Andre to his feet, he shook his head and rubbed his face. Then a wild look came into his eyes. He looked around frantically.

"They're back. The renegades! They're back. I caught one of them trying to steal a horse. Then two others came at me." He spun and peered at the crick. "One was in the stream bed. The other was in the trees. Did you see them?"

"Did you hit the man trying to steal the horse?" James asked in a calm voice.

"N ... no. He got away." Andre put a hand to his forehead. "What happened to me?"

"You struck you head on the barn," I said. We could explain things later. Right now we needed to know more about the horse thief. "How was the man dressed? The one who tried to take the horse?"

"Buckskins."

"Was he armed?"

"Don't know. Why? Why are you here?"

"We heard the shooting and came running."

"Thank God! Or else they might have finished the job. He glanced at the house, fear etched on his face. "Bella! The children!" He started for the cabin, but James held him back.

"They're not in the house, Andre. Libby's with the doctor's wife in town."

He blanched; his eyes went round. "The doctor's wife? Is she sick? Is she hurt? Is Bella with her? I've got to go to them."

"Libby's fine. You weren't able to take care of her, so Mrs. Helgren is tending her for the moment," James explained.

"What do you mean I couldn't take care of her? Bella takes care of her. Of all the children."

"What day is this?" I asked.

"Must be Thursday."

"No, it's Wednesday. The raid on your farm was almost two weeks ago. You've already buried Bella and the boys."

For a moment, I feared shock had sent Andre back to wherever he had been. He sagged but caught himself. He closed his gaping mouth and swallowed hard. "Buried them? I ... I don't understand."

"They're gone, Andre. They died in the raid. Bella and the boys are in the cemetery in Yanube City. We'll take you to see them when you're better." James laid a hand on his shoulder.

"All of them? Dead? Oh, God, why wasn't I able to save them?"

"You did all you could. It was a surprise raid, and you were outnumbered."

A dull look returned to his gray eyes. "I should have died with them."

"No, you were spared to take care of your daughter. Your Libby."

That brought no reaction. "Was I there? At the funeral?"

"Yes. You saw they were taken care of properly. They're at peace," James said. "And now you have to get better so you can take care of Libby."

I turned to James when Andre seemed calmer. "Can you handle him?"

"You figure it was the renegade. The last of Dull Lance's bunch?"

"Likely."

"I had hoped he'd be in Wyoming or somewhere by now."

"Not without a mount. He wouldn't get far with the militia looking for him. He'd hide out and try to snatch a horse from one of them. Guess he couldn't manage that, so he thought he'd steal one from the farm they shot up."

"You're going after him?"

"I'm responsible for him."

"That's tripe, and you know it. Leave him to the militia."

"They haven't caught him yet. And if I leave him, he'll try again — here or somewhere else. Next time he'll kill first and then take a horse."

James insisted on coming with me, but when Andre tried to tag along, I convinced them it would be safer to do this alone. It was a little less than four leagues to the badlands. I squinted at the sky and calculated that if the renegade was in decent physical shape, he would reach the badlands before I caught up with him. Especially since I would need to take it slow to avoid an ambush and provide him what he needed most — a mount.

I borrowed Andre's rifle and set out on the fugitive's trail. He was making good time, not running but going at a steady lope. There was no sign of him on the horizon, but there were enough small hills and vales to give cover.

Two miles before reaching the badlands, the man's gait changed. It was more uncertain, less steady. Any warrior worth the name could run the day through if he paced himself. This man was weak. He'd been out here for a fortnight. There was plenty to drink, the Tricking Water ran through the badlands, but game was likely scarce. The fugitive was hungry, on foot, and being hunted by men who wanted to kill him.

I made it to the mouth of the badlands without incident. There, I found a careless moccasin print. The runner had made it this far. There were also pony tracks, but they were indistinct, either old or blurred by the wind. How was he armed? Could I talk him out of hiding? Maybe the promise of a pony would lure him out into the open. I kicked Whisper into a walk and entered the badlands, calling out loudly in Lakota.

"Brother! You do not have to die. I bear you no ill will." I almost choked on my words as I pictured Bella and the boys lying in the grave, but I managed to convince myself that was Dull Lance's doing. Dull Lance's and Smith's. "Come out, and we will talk like men."

The mustang was beginning to limp a little, but I walked him the length of the canyon country, periodically calling out to the fugitive.

When I reached the end, I could find no sign the man had exited the badlands, so I turned back, this time riding silently. I had reached the point midway into the breaks where the Trickling Water pooled almost to pond size before seeping out to meander eastward when a gunshot echoed off the walls of the coulees and draws, making its source hard to pinpoint. Up ahead somewhere. How far? Who?

I pulled up, and the world went silent except for the faint cry of an eagle soaring high overhead. Suddenly, a loud report sounded, and a passing bullet stung my ear. I jerked on Whisper's reins as the concussion almost knocked me loose from my senses. The terrified horse went over, dumping me onto the bank of the crick. I tried to hold onto his leads, but he jerked free and climbed to his feet. Immediately, another shot rang out. The mustang screamed and flopped over onto his side.

Then everything went quiet again. Who had shot at me? The nameless Sioux I'd been trying to coax from his hiding place? No, he would not have shot a horse he needed so desperately. Someone else shared the breaks with me.

A loud laugh, half full of madness, floated across the distance. "I got you Otter. What kinda Injun are you. You passed right by me and never seen me. How bad you hurt? Dying maybe?"

Smith! Mad Sam Smith. My heart pounded so hard, I thought it would burst.

"I knowed you was with them renegades. Now I got proof. You rode through here calling out in that devil's tongue. Thank ya for that. Took your friend's mind offa me long enough to slip up on him. Now you're the last one. When you're dead, all the filthy redskins who killed my boy done gone to hell."

Whisper lay on his right side with Andre's rifle pinned beneath him. I swore to start carrying a handgun if I lived through this. I was stranded here, armed only with a knife while a mad man stalked me with a rifle.

Making as little noise as possible, I slithered over to the pony and dipped my hands in the animal's blood. Then I crawled backward, dabbing the blood intermittently along my obvious trail. I slid down the stream bank, making certain the blood was obvious. Then I smeared some over my face and neck. After slipping my knife from its sheath, I leaned noiselessly back into the water, allowing my body to float downstream until the crick became too shallow to carry me farther. Hiding the hand clutching the knife behind my right pant leg, I froze, eyes open but unfocused.

As time passed, I began to fear Smith might have simply ridden off and left me to die. No, that wouldn't satisfy the insanity gripping him. Finally, I heard the clink of a horseshoe on rock. A shadow moved at the top of the bank. Smith's drawn, bushy face appeared. I willed my eyes not to move.

"Gottcha, you murdering bastard. Took me awhile, but I got every last one of you killers."

For a moment, I thought he was simply going to shoot me to make sure he finished the job, but his head disappeared from view. Minutes later, I heard him ranting as he came down the bank.

"Lotsa blood. Yes sir, a good blood trail. But if there's any justice in this world, you ain't dead yet. When I take your crown, I want you to feel me ripping your scalp off. Just like my mama and papa when you took their crowns. I want you to scream just like they done."

His mother and father? Was that the source of his hatred? I caught sight of him in my peripheral vision. He was afoot, carrying his rifle in one hand and a knife in the other. A moment later, he stood over me, his colorless, walled eyes glaring madly in two different directions. One was fixed on me.

"Yep. You ain't dead. So I get the pleasure of watching you die when I slice you up, Joseph Otter. *Joseph.* That's a blasphemy if I ever heard one. Giving a lying, thieving, murdering red belly a Christian name like that is sinful."

I waited until he reached for me before coming up out of the water with all the force I could muster. The knife slashed through Smith's guts and reached for his heart, but he jerked away and put his hand to his stomach.

"You shit, you killed me!"

"Not yet, but I'm going to." I stepped forward and plunged the blade between his ribs. Smith stiffened and stared at me in rage until he toppled over. Again, I wondered at the way hate froze in a dead man's eyes.

I found the renegade farther up the canyon. He'd been shot in the chest. I was surprised at how young he was. He couldn't be much older than Lucas had been when he died. I experienced a pang of sorrow for all of the young men of blood. Their world was a dismal place.

Smith was a tall man, but he was surprisingly scrawny, so I had little trouble dragging him to where the dead raider lay. I removed the warrior's knife from its scabbard and pressed it into the ribcage where my blade had penetrated. I arranged the two corpses as if they'd struggled. A struggle that ended in mutual murder. Considering the young Indian's gunshot wound, the ruse might not hold up, but it was the best I could do.

After scuffing the ground to make it look as if a fight had taken place, I stood looking at the man I had killed. Like a prairie wolf I'd brought down when I was a child, he no longer looked fierce, merely small and pitiful. Then I washed away the blood covering me and went in search of Smith's horse, blurring my tracks as I went.

After talking my way to the pony's side, I returned to my fallen mount and worried the tack gear off of him. Satisfied I'd left nothing to identify me, I rode out of the badlands heading west before circling south to Turtle Crick. When I reached the stream, I dismounted and slapped the horse's flank. After hoisting my saddle and gear over my shoulder, I waded downstream in the direction of the farm. With any luck, the appaloosa would make its way home and set off a search for his rider.

I deeply regretted killing Dull Lance and experienced a pang of sympathy for the young renegade who had died, at least in part, because of my actions. But I felt nothing at knifing Smith ... not even a sense of triumph.

James was sitting on the Tillers' porch talking earnestly to a dazed Andre when I came up out of the brook. My partner said nothing except to call attention to my arrival.

Andre seemed to recover himself at the sight of me. "Otter, did I really try to kill you?"

"I explained what happened," James said.

"No, you were trying to shoot whoever had killed your family." I handed him his rifle. "You didn't harm either of us, so don't worry over it. It is a thing in the past. And you don't have to worry about that thief coming back."

"You found him?"

"Smith found him."

So I began to spin the story I hoped everyone in the territory was ultimately going to hear and accept. People might or might not believe it, but there was one man I knew who wouldn't. Not for a minute.

EPILOGUE

James never asked the questions that lingered in his eyes that day, but I harbored no illusions my companion had not figured out what happened up on the Trickling Water. After all, I had walked home hauling a saddle and tack gear, and there was no sign of Whisper. I regretted the loss of the gallant little mustang.

None of us reported Smith's death, and it took the militia the better part of a week to blunder upon the scene of the "duel," as Magistrate Gadsby called it. He loudly proclaimed the captain a hero who met a violent end pursuing and eliminating the murderous heathens who had terrorized the area for years. Acquaintances told James few of the citizens of Yanube City paid any attention to this puffery.

So far as I knew, no one questioned the story of the captain and the last renegade battling one another to the death — not even when a mustang no one could explain was discovered lying dead nearby. I gave thanks to the Great Mystery I was aboard Whisper that day instead of Patch. The whole countryside would have recognized my pinto.

Although Andre was no longer semi-catatonic, he had little interest in much of anything except working the farm. Rejecting our offer to accompany him, a week later, he hitched up his wagon and brought Libby home. He tended the child dutifully, but affection somehow seemed to be lacking. It seemed at times he felt guilty that they had survived.

One night, James looked up from the Bible where he'd been seeking solace in the Book of Psalms. "I'm worried, Otter. Things are not right in that household."

I glanced up. "You don't think he'll do the child harm?"

"No, not physical harm. From what I've observed on our visits, he's taking care of her physical needs. But he seems so cold to her. Who knows what injury he's doing her psyche."

"He's not a cold man. At least, I've not seen it in him before. He loved Bella and his children. All of them, little Libby included."

He closed the book in his lap. "I'm going to town tomorrow for a civic meeting. I think I'll stop by Helgren's office and talk to him. He may have some ideas. Maybe I'll try to arrange for a nanny. Libby needs a woman's touch."

"Perhaps you're right."

"Then it's settled. I'll likely overnight at the Rainbow House. Why don't you go see Andre and prepare the ground?"

"You mean ask about bringing a nanny ... a woman ... into his house?"

"Hmmm. Maybe not. Just try to make him see what he's doing to the baby. He was so proud of attending her birth alone. He's bound to respond to the girl."

# # # # #

The next afternoon — during the Moon of Falling Leaves — I found Andre in the field chopping weeds. As he greeted me, I noticed he was unkempt. Nay, filthy. I coaxed him into the house and found Libby asleep in her crib. The child was far cleaner than her father. In fact, she seemed plump and well cared for. Perhaps James's concerns were unmerited.

Those doubts fell away as I studied Andre. Both he and Bella had been resolute about personal hygiene. Cleanliness had been almost an obsession. Yet here he stood with shaggy hair and a streaked, greasy beard. I doubted he had cleaned up beyond dipping his head in a bucket of water once or twice since the raid. The clothing he was wearing looked like the shirt and pants he'd worn the day before and the day before that. There was a pile of dirty shirts, trousers, and underclothing thrown in the corner of the front room.

Without a word, I took down tubs hanging in the washing room and began heating water on the stove. I laid a fire in the washing chamber's small fireplace to take the chill off the air. The dirty clothing went into another pot for boiling.

He took my meaning and sheepishly admitted he'd gotten sloppy. Andre shaved his scraggly beard and agreed to take a bath if I would stay with him. I poured his bath water and checked on Libby while he stripped and crawled into the tub. Returning to the warm and humid room, I claimed a three-legged stool, expecting that he wanted conversation. But he scrubbed away in silence, startling me when he finally spoke.

"I can't feel anything, Otter."

"You mean your mind is numb?"

"Yes, my mind. But the rest of me, too." He held his hands in front of him. "I can't feel my hands. Sometimes I have to put a thumb to my wrist for a pulse to see if my heart's still beating. My guts are empty. It's like my skin covers nothing but dry bones." He stared at his hands as if he'd never seen them before.

"Bring back your mind, Andre. And the rest will follow."

He fixed me with a gray-eyed gaze. "I'm afraid to."

"Why?"

"Afraid of how much it'll hurt. What am I going to do without Bella? And my boys?"

"You're going to live for your daughter."

"My daughter. Libby. That's a crazy name. Like Liberty Belle's a crazy name. But that's what her mother wanted. Liberty for her birth date and Belle for — you know, for Bella. I'm afraid of her, too. Everybody else I ever loved is dead. Well, except you."

The words hung there in the semi darkness as yellow flames danced in the corner fireplace. Suddenly, Andre rose and stepped out of the tub.

I tossed him a towel. "Here, dry off."

Still dripping wet, he came to me. "Make me feel again, Otter. Make me feel ... *something*. Hurt me. Love me. It doesn't matter, just make me feel." He placed his lips on mine in a hot, scalding kiss.

I almost recoiled, but I didn't. Instead, I slowly slid down Andre's hard, rangy frame, keeping my lips on the light trail of brown hair leading to his bush. I gently kissed his long, flaccid cock. When I slipped the crown of his rod into my mouth, he groaned as if in pain. He clasped his hands behind my head as his hips twitched. Then he began to feel. I knew he did, because his cock thickened and hardened from the blood pulsing into it.

I came out to the end and tongued the slit; Andre gasped aloud. "Oh, Otter!"

I rode the big cock down to the root, burying my face in the soft pubic hair. Andre came alive slowly, timidly thrusting with his hips, and then with growing animation, he began fucking my face. His explosion came suddenly. He held my head in his hands while he finished his journey with hard thrusts of his pelvis. Then he seemed to lose his newfound strength and slipped down upon the pile of towels we had dropped on the floor, taking me with him.

The room was quiet for a few minutes as his breathing eased. But he wasn't finished. His cock, which had softened, firmed up again.

"I felt that, Otter. I *felt* it. Thank you for understanding." He rolled over and pressed his groin to my hip. He was rampant. "Can I ..."

I turned to stare at him. In the dancing firelight, Andre seemed younger, more his true age than the shell he had been only minutes earlier. I reached up and touched the sprinkle of faded freckles on the bridge of his nose. "Yes. I'd like that, too." I rose to strip my clothes away and made to lie down on my stomach, but he stopped me.

"Can we do it so I can watch you?"

"Of course."

Andre grinned and became handsome once again. Without speaking, he moved between my legs and lifted them to his broad shoulders. He leaned forward, and still slick with cum, entered me easily. A look of utter bliss claimed him as he began to move, slowly at first, and then more energetically.

"You're beautiful," Andre mumbled, his voice full of emotion.

"Nay, but once I was."

"You still are."

Andre's voice died away. His lids slipped over his eyes as he moved rhythmically over me. After a long time, his breath grew labored and his efforts more demanding. He leaned forward, and I experienced the beginning of my own climax. Andre threw his head up and howled like a wild beast as his orgasm seized him. He beat himself against me. I felt the first spurt of warm cum, then another load and another.

My own ejaculation hit. My internal muscles contracted, seizing and massaging the big cock stroking my channel, drawing more and more of Andre's life essence from him.

Finally, he collapsed atop me. Our hearts pounded in unison. The heat of our skin pressing against one another was almost blistering.

Andre whispered into my ear. "I'm sorry, Otter. What about James?"

"Don't be sorry. This is something you needed — we needed. It is past now, and it won't happen again. Don't let what we've done trouble you. James will be all right. You must begin to live your own life again. Be a father ... a loving father to that little girl in there."

His eyes came alive. "You're right. Libby's what's important now. I have to take care of her."

I sighed. Yes, James would be all right ... *we* would be all right. This was one more thing I would not tell him, but which he would know anyway. And we would all survive.

MARK WILDYR

A native Oklahoman, Mark Wildyr has had a lifelong interest in history, Native American cultures, and mythology. After taking an undergraduate degree in history, Mr. Wildyr served in the United States Army before pursuing a career as a businessman. He presently resides in New Mexico, the setting of many of his stories, which explore developing sexual awareness and intercultural relationships.

Over fifty of his short stories and novellas have been acquired by such houses as Alyson Publications, Arsenal Pulp, Bold Strokes Books, Cleis Press, Companion Press, Green Candy Press, Haworth Press, STARbooks Press, and *Freshmen* and *Men's* magazines. His fiction covers many genres, including mystery, adventure, fantasy, sci-fi, military, police, and sports.

The Hawk Takes Flight, a Novella (STARbooks Press) follows the adventures of two Native American trackers on the trail of drug runners along the Arizona-Mexico border.

In *Cut Hand*, his first published novel (STARbooks Press), the author indulges his passion for both history and First Nations in a 19th Century setting.

His second, *The Victor and The Vanquished* (STARbooks Press), examines the delicate path a young Native American gay man must travel in today's world.

Mr. Wildyr welcomes comments on his work through www.markwildyr.com. His philosophy is that he learns from the reactions of readers.

earing any underwear. "Excuse me," I said, having a hard time look

linded by that bulge in his crotch, "but don't I know you?" "Maybe

ind of to   bout a

with Ray   God, y

t loser?   in?" h

iid. "Lik   s stron

ce body   e on G

lly, he l   I ever

i up to t   any ide

staking   ie sam

i, I coul   ery lor

ood raci   ie swe

ng with   e in st

we go   behin

ill see u   in pub

ed?" he   vent to

rivacy.   grabbe

hard. I

k, traci   t, so fi

ed it, ha

with m   bing d

obing, I   n cock

ie sound of unzipping filled the small space. I don't know who's ha

but before I knew it, I had his rod in my hand, and mine was in his

it to do?" he asked, his tone challenging. I knew exactly, and sank t

www.ingramcontent.com/pod-product-compliance
Lightning Source LLC
Chambersburg PA
CBHW051524260626
47170CB00003B/779